First published in the United Kingdom 202_ _,

Copyright © LifeZone Publishing, Parkhurst, Johannesburg, RSA

The right of Simon Paul ridgeway to be identified as the Author of the Work has been answered by her in accordance with the Copyright and Patents Act 1988.

All rights reserved. No part of this publication may be reproduced, stored in a retrieval system, or transmitted, in any form or by any means without prior written permission of the publisher, nor be otherwise circulated in any form of binding or cover other than that in which it is published and without a similar condition being imposed on the subsequent purchaser.

All character in this publication are fictitious and any resemblance
To real persons, living or dead is purely coincidental. Serendipitously, this Work has been constructed from experiences the Author has established in the course of a Life well Lived.

A CIP catalogue record for this title (Boy Soldier) is available from the British, New York Metropolitan and Shanghai Libraries.

"Father Spirit, (Mother Gaia) I pray that we will see the world as a harmonious place of abundance with no one person dominating by their attempts to govern other countries, or their own; dictate financial opportunities for others, or enslave anyone into working for no just reward. We want to see a free world, where politics no longer determines what a human being can do, but assists them to become the person they deserve to be. A world free from the agonies of poverty, determined by the wealth of nations which have resources that belong to them; and not to people from other nations, who have not got those resources, but are willing to plunder, and deprive the owners of that land of those resources, without a fair and equitable return. A world, which respects the integrity of life, but entrenches the dignity of someone, not blessed with the education of other more fortunate countries, which can use their higher learning to deprive others less gifted."

Boy Soldiers

Forward

"The general crisis that has overtaken the modern world everywhere and in almost every sphere of life manifests itself differently in each country, involving different areas and taking on different forms." - Hannh Arendt (The Crisis in Education; 1954)

Despite this crisis, Britain and many 'Western' countries have muddled along, fighting against the prevalent socio-economic factors driving these crises. But underlying the deconstruction of two thousand years of Judea-Christian influences on education, the drive to assimilate multi-cultural, multi-ethnicity and water-down any non-secular influences in schools, the globalists, under the guise of a more caring, transparent, inclusive society, have attempted to erode every facet of Western Civilisation, in their efforts to dominate a 'New World Order'. It was Rudolf Steiner who said; "Think of Christian Prayer… in relation to the Spiritual-Scientific world view…. Another method of elevating the human being - the human soul - to contact with the Divine, Spiritual, cosmic forces. This method is meditation, by which a person experiences the Spiritual content within himself, and receives something of what is given by the great guiding Spirits of humanity or by the Spiritual content of great civilisations in which the human being immerses himself and so identifies himself with The Divine Spiritual currents in the world."

What Steiner is referring to, is The Global Consciousness. That great accumulation of Knowledge, Wisdom and Discernment, that is never lost, but simply transferred from civilisation to civilisation; from nation to nation; from person to person. This is The Wisdom of The Saints. Spiritual Wisdom, which can never be lost; a component of the Great Akashic Record. But ultimately, by accessing this Akashic Record, Mankind can move forward. It is this Great Akashic Formula that the Elite Powers & Principalities attempts to retain control of, by distraction, subversion and intimidation.

But these Powers & Principalities are losing that power, because the more they attempt to control, the more the Great Akashic Record is disseminated among Mankind.

"Letting such a formula really live in the heart and experience, brings a person to union with the Higher Spirituality."

"A Higher Power, in which he Lives, streams through him, and patient perseverance to the point of letting this flow of power strengthen him enough morally and intellectually, brings him to the moment when the content of the meditation can awaken the deeper forces latent in the human soul."

Many great thinkers have declared the education system of the Western World to be in crisis, for over half a century. One notable outspoken spokesperson was Scientology founder L. Ron. Hubbard, who claimed that the Holy Spirit, or that great global consciousness was akin to what he referred to as a 'Thetan', as he explained; "the person himself—not his body or his name, the physical universe, his mind, or anything else; that which is aware of being aware; the identity which is the individual."

With the science of Quantum Mechanics, creating the foundation of what Nikola Tesla described as 'The Unseen World', physicists have subsequently unravelled what is the science of Leptons as discovered in practical experiments at the

C.E.R.N. Large Hadron Collider. The Tau particle and its corresponding Neutrino form a still unfathomable arena of 'Known', 'Unknowns'.

It was this 'Unseen' world Tesla had alluded to in his commentary of science, and to which he had applied his entire life's work. In one decade, science has moved from the identification of the Higgs-Boson Particle, to the ability to weigh its magical structure. Regardless of who supernatural all these elementals appear to mere mortals, it is the study of this science which will ultimately lead mankind full circle; and back to a mysterious world of the 'Unseen'.

Boy Soldiers

A book about soldiers of war, here in West Scowlsdown, East Sussex. Using a correlation of circumstances, in which lads as young as nine, are being co-opted into the drug wars, that flourish, unabated in this town, the story follows Josh, a teenager whose single parent mom, battles alcohol addiction and an abusive ex-husband, who has left them, to become a coordinator of the drug mules in the city of London. Following the 'County-lines' that have taken a vice-like hold on the society of English country life, the reader is asked to suspend their previously ambivalent attitude to drugs, and look further into the swamp that has become the reality for so many young lads.

The reader, sits, as a voyeur might, as they witness first hand, the devious ploys, drug suppliers have sunken to; even for their twisted minds to envision, just to spread this cancer that is the new weapon of choice the 'Deep State' has employed to destroy social order and control the minds of the future generation; of the Z-Generation.

Josh meets a teacher, who is a retired Sociology Professor from Southampton University, now returning to a school in West Scowlsdown, a quaint little town in rural England, where he had retired with his wife of forty years, into what he believed was to be his twilight years. His wife Marge, dies unexpectedly and Merlin is left with a two bedroom bungalow, in a neatly appointed street, and no one to challenge his immense intellect; that is until he runs into Josh on one of his regular deliveries and the enigmatic Oscar!

After witnessing the rampant crime unfolding in the streets of his adopted town, Merlin Drinkwater, vows to challenge the impassive acceptance of this reality, a fight in the new trenches of Europe, one hundred years after that last 'Great War' had been fought. This becomes a battle for the minds, and for the souls of this lost generation of zombified boys, whose hearts have been hardened by social media, cyber bullying and where the acceptance of the previously unchartered murky waters of the drug-trade, has been complicated by the insidious assault of consumerism on young minds.

Merlin threads a path through these murky waters, in order to connect with this generation, as the end of the second decade of the twenty-first century closes, and a pathway to the next generation is enlightened; and the Omega Generation emerges.

"To live as gently as I can;
To be, no matter what, a man;
To take what comes of good or ill
And cling to faith and honour still;
To do my best and let that stand
The record of my brain and hand;
And then, should failure come to me,
Still work and hope for victory."

E. A. Guest

Contents

"I heard my country calling, away across the sea,
Across the waste of waters, she calls and calls to me.
Her sword is girded at her side, her helmet on her head,
And around her feet are lying the dying and the dead;
I hear the noise of battle, the thunder of her guns;
I haste to thee, my mother, a son among thy sons."

Cecil Rice

The Scream

Merlin Drinkwater awoke. His heart was pounding, adrenalin coursing through his sinewy veined body, his ears throbbing. The scream had roused him from a deep slumber. The haunting lament, a merciless expression of near-death. But what was it?

He clambered off the bed, a king-size, for a widower. The night-light had ben activated outside the kitchen and now threw a suggestive light down the passage from the kitchen window of his two-bedroom bungalow in Fairdawn Crescent. There was someone afoot, or at least something!

Following the trace of light, casting an enticing pattern of skewed steps across the carpeted hallway floor, he tread the hopscotch labyrinth to the kitchen door and on into well-appointed kitchenette, with its twenty-first century eating nook. Beyond the kitchen blinds was the source of the invasion, and he peered, almost with trepidation through the slanted slats.

Outside there was nothing to be seen other than the multi-coloured wheelie bins, with their cavernous innards, destined for Malaysia and whichever other third-world shithole was ready to welcome in the trash of a civilized society. The light, which had been activated by a motion sensor, told him there was a lurking beast in the driveway, so the fox must be around. He strained his lanky neck down the exposed pavement, to where the small two-door Korean sports-coupe sat, a testimony to a wasted bucket-list. It had, he recalled sombrely, been intended for those lazy excursions into the South Downs and the reservoir he had grown up fishing from.

That was a lifetime away and seemed to plague him with regrets every time he recalled the last conversation he had shared with his deceased wife. The two, were to spend their twilight years gallivanting through his childhood haunts, on fishing expeditions and clambering over moss-covered hillocks. But Ruth had not shared his passion for the outdoors.

As the thought had entered his conscience, suddenly, so too did another. Out of the side entrance to the neighbour's garage, appeared Josh. He was dressed in his usual sweats, and a rucksack adorned his back, somewhat incongruously, given the time of night, and venue. Fairdawn Crescent was a million miles from Arlington Reservoir, and Josh was not about to embark on a fishing trip. Merlin raked his head and neck further, as the young teenager headed down the drive, stopping for a moment to scrutinize the car in the opposite driveway, then smirking, headed off down the crescent and then out of sight.

This was peculiar, and Merlin stood for a moment, almost losing his footing as the lad disappeared from his sight. The expression on Josh's face gave Merlin a troubling edginess to his gut. This was the makings of his understanding of how the 'Force' as he lately referred to it, would raise his mindfulness regarding an inexplicably disquieting event. It was his gut-instinct yes, but it was more. Lately, Merlin had taken to dreaming of ghosts and unwarranted forces, for who he had no explanation.

These dreams were accompanied by a rational awakening, in which Merlin would recall the exact details. They had become so provocative he had taken to writing them down. So intense were they that he would memorialize each for several paragraphs, in a journal he now kept beside his bed. This event now troubled him all the more. It was déjà vu with a dose of steroids. There was something achingly acute about the lads' almost cynical smile that now caused a real sense of disquiet. Merlin threaded his way back to the bedroom that had its bay windows looking outward, impartially to the street.

Merlin was a creature of habit, so he knew that this ache in his stomach was a clarion-call to arouse his sensitivity. In the journal would be his answer. He flipped on the sidelight, throwing a yellow vale across his bedside table, and slipping back below the covers, he plumped a pillow and stretched his left hand sideways to retrieve the leather-bound journal. This had been Ruth's side of the bed, but lately he had reverted to the left side, so as to accommodate his more frequent night-time expeditions to the bathroom.

The journal was a good-sized A5 with a healthy volume of pages. He flipped to the centre, almost recalling the exact dream, and when it had occurred. The pages were unlined, but Merlin's distinctly cursive writing willed him into a revisit of another lifetime of nocturnal pursuits. The dreams were so real he had taken to explaining to himself that he was living in a multi-dimensional world. There was the reality of number forty-six, then there was the vastness of his expansive world. This was where he pursued his boyhood passions, and embarked on exhaustive expeditions into a world he could only dream of now.

The dream he sought jumped back out of the pages. He had double-underlined the words – "A fleeting flight of fancy" and the name – "Josh", followed by "Driving through the country! Familiar fields – must have been Chalvington? Blue waters and Green pastures! Awoke with Psalm 23 in mind!" Merlin knew the psalmist's mantra, but was no church-goer.

There was a sinister comment below the entry – "What was Josh hiding?"

Merlin recalled the dream, but it had been some months earlier, when the shouting was still in its infancy. Now mom had taken to rebuking Josh openly, in the garage, or outside the neatly appointed conservatory, with only the green hedge to shield her displeasure. Merlin's stomach tightened once more.

There was undoubtedly something afoot. The nocturnal escapades of the lad were not necessarily an indication of nefarious activity, and Merlin wanted to remain impartial; but the evidence was mounting in favour of a troubling series of events leading up to tonight. He looked at the bedside clock, with red digital numerals. It was two-thirty in the morning.

Merlin placed the journal on his lap and began to meditate on what he had just witnessed. The blood-curdling scream, clearly a cat cornered by the fox, or even a rival in pursuit of the contents of an overturned wheelie bin; but that aside, the light had thrown some evidence Merlin's way. He prayed a simple prayer. "Spirit Father, reveal to me your will for Josh and his mom, Mrs Goodenough. Show me what you have in store for this troubled family. Help me to help them.

Merlin placed the journal back on the bedside table, clicked the light switch and rolled over onto his right side, away from the door, and hugged the soft linen pillow.

His mind raced. The image of the infamous Edward Munch depiction of twentieth century paranoia, haunted him for a brief moment. The anxiety that evoked that image, was to Merlin, an expression of life in suburbia.

Sleep would come slowly, as his mind reflected on that smile. Josh was a good-looking mixed race lad, whom he had recalled kicking the ball for hours next door, but of late had withdrawn into the naturally hostile mannerisms of any teenager. No longer did he greet Merlin at the bus stop, as Merlin had walked to get his Saturday paper. No more was there a friendly gesture of neighbourliness as he passed by the front garden, as Merlin tended to the violets and agapanthus.

Merlin recalled how he had become insolent to his mother, no longer carrying her groceries for her, and leaving the flap open on the wheelie bins, attracting the fox, who had previously snuck into Merlin's garden, laid down, and waited for his early evening dog biscuits Merlin had placed on the lawn.

The fox had taken to more salubrious activities such as the event that had clearly awoken Merlin, but now having dragged the contents of the bins across the driveway, was brazenly rummaging on top of Merlin's bins as well.

As he drifted off into neverland, Merlin invoked, "give me this insight......" He would always provoke a conscious thought, before retiring to bed, but this midnight sojourn by Josh seemed particularly edgy.

Morning arose early, as was the northern hemisphere challenge. At these heady latitudes, the summers came achingly slowly, but dimmed far too soon. The sun was up by four in the morning nowadays, but Merlin had cloaked the bay windows with a darkened drape, allowing his late starts, despite what Ruth had always insisted. They had differed on his early morning routines, he wishing to stay asleep for as long as his retirement would allow, and she, insistent that he keep to a regular start, for the sake of his mental awareness. Sadly, Ruth had kept to the routine, but had been unable to fend of an early onset of Parkinson's.

Merlin had tended to her for as long as the illness had allowed, then Josh and his mother had moved in next door, usurping the couple who Merlin had relied on for the occasional cooked meal. They too, had heeded the call of early Alzheimer's and been carted off to a retirement village, in which Mrs Goodenough had been employed. The world was going mad, but Merlin was intent on ensuring he would not fall victim to a similar fate.
This morning, when he awoke, he had a strange feeling following the uneasiness of the early hours traipse to the kitchen. Was Josh up to something which involved his car?

He would have to be doubly sure he was not aiding and abetting some illicit behaviour, and this he knew was highly likely, now that the evidence was mounting against the lad.

But the scream he had heard last evening was more than just a warning of something strange and foreign to his world; it was an awakening of his consciousness. The boy was clearly up to no good, but he was not a bad boy. Merlin had an uneasiness about this event and it sat with him through his morning routines.

If he was to uncover the meaning behind that smile, he would need to delve deeper into this situation.

During the errands he required to run this morning, Merlin was to attend a weekly coffee meeting at the library. This was an opportunity to catch up with all the latest gossip, and to chat to one or two of the locals he had become friendly with. There was a hard core of pensioners in West Scowlsdown, a steady stream of exiles from the city, retiring to East Sussex to escape the mounting surge of foreigners swamping the suburbs in search of housing close to their places of employment.

The failure of multiculturalism in Britain had created ghettos in the inner regions of all major cities and London had become a cesspit of foreign identities, unassimilated into the general populace. Merlin had witnessed this in Southampton and the effect was to send retired couples scurrying to the country. The commonwealth countries after 1945 had sent boatloads of the Windrush Generation, whom the city of London had required, to rebuild the destroyed infrastructure of London and all the major urban areas bombed by the Nazi's.

If nothing else, the Nazi's had succeeded in destroying Britain, after the fact. But today, Merlin knew, it was the insidious forces of consumerism that was destroying the fabric of Britain's society. Multiculturalism aside, the people of Britain now faced the prospect of losing their identity entirely. It was this sense of foreboding that had ignited the Brexit vote, and it was the constant surge of immigrants across the channel from France and the continent, that now forced even more to follow the retired generation to the country.
These were the children of retirees, who having begun their work in the city, now required affordable homes to live in for their burgeoning families. Despite the collapse in birth rates across Britain, West Scowlsdown was on the ascendency. Many young seventies and eighties children, followed their parents to the country, and satellite towns such as the town became popular for many reasons, one of which was the rail link to Victoria and London Bridge.

Merlin had shared his observations with his mate Simon one day when the downstairs library foyer was populated by buggies. The town had become 'Buggy Park' and everywhere single moms and young couples paraded the High Street with toddlers and new-borns in these prams.

The sleepy little town of West Scowlsdown stood out on the map, because of the ample land available for development, not to mention its nodal attraction, connecting it to the larger urban sprawl of Crawley and the proximity to Gatwick airport.

Merlin now met his coffee buddy, Simon in the library, and they shared their anecdotal conversations about the rise of this paradigm and the resultant demand for housing. Old office blocks were being converted at a rate never witnessed, as the old town, a former hub for companies connecting with Gatwick and the thriving airfreight facilities it offered, had gradually gravitated to closer office parks, as traffic became increasingly desperate on roads that had not been widened since the advent of the motorways in the fifties.

"Hiya, how's your morning been?" The library was filled with the aged, the curious, and a smattering of the homeless.

"Good morning Simon," Merlin liked his informality. He was a Zimbabwean, who as Merlin discovered, was a devout bachelor and keen fitness junky, who held no regard for sacred cows and disliked the social hierarchy of a class centric Britain.

"Yes, I have had a slow start to the day. It's all been a little wearisome," Merlin added.

"Oh! Why's that?" The curiosity of a mind, piqued by constant adrenalin!

"Well, it's about that lad next door again." Merlin had confided once or twice before.

"Oh, has he been shouting again?"

"No, this time, I was awoken by a fox scavenging in the bins, but when I got up to see what was going on, I found out that Josh was loitering outside, and then set off on one of his nocturnal deliveries."

"Uhhmm, I see," Simon seemed to have a grasp of these things.

"What concerned me was that he is up to something, and I cannot put my finger on it." The furrow of his brow arched between a balding pate, and those carefully manicured eyebrows, which if given free reign, would have left him looking vaguely Einsteinium.

"You know, I don't have to tell you about the moral decay of our society, especially relating to delinquency. You probably wrote the book on the socialisation challenges of these kids today." Simon smiled.

He had a kind looking face, disarming and quieting. Honed from the years of meditations and early morning prayer vigils. Merlin liked this.

"The truth is I cannot understand why Josh is so resentful of his mother's efforts to provide a decent home and a good education for him!"

"Yes, it does seem odd, given they have a lovely home, and his mother works all hours to keep it neat and tidy. But, the truth is he is no different to the kids we grew up with in the sixties and seventies. Think about the Mods and the Rockers, and the moral outrage they created in the media, when they went on the rampage in Brighton!" There were boatloads of empathy in those crystal clear eyes.

Merlin watched intently for the usual tearing up of his eyes. He had noticed this before when they had spoken about issues pertaining to the youth, and Simon would always display this emotion.

"Your right, but we must remember that the media sold those stories as grossly exaggerated dramas, which were hyped for maximum effect to sell newspapers. The truth is every society deals with rebellious youth and that generation was no different to any other. This has been the way the mainstream media has kept people in fear for so long." Merlin had studied the effects of that social disturbance whilst at university himself, and his interest in sociology had been sparked by the disunity those events in his hometown of Southampton had caused.

"Yes, I suppose you're right. The mass media outlets have been dividing our society for as long as they have been printing their putrid garbage." It was clear Simon was no fan.

"That is so true, but it did not start with the mainstream media." Merlin listened as he sipped his coffee, over a plate of biscuits disgorged by the helpful ladies behind the serving counter.

"If we are honest, this has been the agenda of the Shadows for thousands of years. Ever since the dawn of the written word, the people who controlled discourse controlled the morality of any society. It was the Levites who wrote the Pentateuch, from the oral traditions of the ancient Hebrews. It was those moral guidelines that had seen the Israelites safely across the Jordan River and into the land of Palestine." Simon spoke intently, his knowledge of historical events clearly of interest to him.

"I have a feeling that the mainstream media also orchestrate these events today, to keep people fearful." Merlin continued.

"Yes, but they do so through the power of consumerism and when people are fearful, they purchase insurance, or security devices for their homes. Fear drives consumerism, and advertising on television and in the print media, cement that reality." The glint in Simon's eyes told Merlin he cared.

"I agree," Merlin switched channels every time the adverts appeared.

"In essence, the powers that control the entire consumer market, have managed to achieve more than what all the religions throughout history attempted to do." Simon took a sip from the steaming mug.

"I believe they have succeeded in controlling the hearts and minds of the people through their innate sense of greed. When the mind of the youth can be dictated by social media concerns, then the rationale for freedom of speech and freedom of expression no longer exists as a fundamental premise of integrity. Groupthink has conquered the platforms that were once touted as the answer to mass communication. The idea of social media being the answer to connect the global village has all but eroded any true sense of freedom. I know kids today that are being harassed like school-yard bullies used to rule the quadrangle."

"It has become all-consuming hasn't it?" Merlin jested, taking the edge off their conversation.

"I remember the time we never had to have a mobile phone to keep in contact with our friends. They lived down the road." Simon laughed; his banter was infectious.

"It is all so incredibly invasive. Mrs Goodenough told me the lads at school are on their mobile phones in the classroom. I can't imagine trying to compete against all the rubbish they watch on their phones."

"Oh, yes, that reminds me. You asked me to look out for any positions to tutor and keep yourself busy after the passing of Marge." Simon reached into his shoulder bag. He carried this as the adjutant once carried dispatches for the Royal Corps of Signals.

"Here is an advertisement from the high school looking for study supervisors. They don't pay very well, but the work is quite rewarding." Simon proffered the piece of paper.

"That sounds interesting," Merlin reached over the table to look at the advertisement. "Will certainly keep my mind off the loneliness."

"Yes, and they have a pension scheme you can join, not that you need that." Simon realised money was not the intention.

'It all helps, but yes, Marge left a substantial legacy, which I have placed in various accounts for the kids. Mind, they don't really need it, but it may help with the grandchildren's education one day." He paused.

"By the way Si, did you know you must never place more than eighty thousand quid in any one account? Just in case that is." The question resounded rhetorically given their discussion on the global banking elite and the many conspiracies they discussed.

"Yes, ummhh, I am wondering all the more that this might be a timely intervention opportunity." Simon gazed out the window, then back. "Yes, indeed, you may find that on applying for the job, you will be successful."

Merlin smiled. It was one of those moments when Simon seemed to slip off into another dimension almost. He had voiced his opinion on many ideas of Spiritualism, but Merlin could not grasp those concepts. His world was the world of science, of facts, and of formulated theories, based on evidence. The evidence of the fall of British values, determined by the rise of multiculturalism that constantly reminded him why he had studied all those years to understand human behaviour.

All his knowledge was based on studies of existing social conventions, and he had no discerning recollection of why anyone would rely on a feeling, or an instinct. But Simon it seemed had acquired knowledge of this intuitive perception, and he often recounted fascinating tales of how these quirks of a seemingly subconscious rationale, assisted him to make decisions.

Merlin was suddenly reminded of the feeling of unease he had that very morning, when he awoke with the picture of a gleeful grin on Josh's face. Was this, he wondered, what Simon was relating to?

"But, why would Josh be loitering around my car at midnight?" Merlin had his suspicions.

"Well, if it is any help, I can tell you categorically that the lads who run errands for the gangs, have extremely sophisticated systems for ferrying their wares." Simon had his ear to the ground.

"What do you think he is doing?" Merlin asked.

"I can't be certain, but I know that some of the lads store their drugs in the wooden shroud covering for the pipes in the library toilets. They have found a way to lift the wooden covering, where they deposit their drugs, for their customers to collect." Simon was assured that this was happening.

"What? Downstairs in the bathrooms?" Merlin was incredulous.

"Yes, I have been told by a reliable source at gym, that the lads run any contraband they can including steroids." Simon elaborated.

"If you see any lads using those conveniences, it's because they are storing their drugs for collection." The evidence must surely be in plain sight, thought Merlin.

"What are you saying?" Merlin, who had been concerned, was now alarmed.

"Without the proof, I cannot be sure; but I would imagine Josh may be using your car to transport his product!"

"Bloody hell!" Merlin was not someone prone to swearing.

"Yes, I am afraid we live in a world, it seems, where right and wrong have been blurred." Simon conjectured.

"You know, getting back to the issue of why this behaviour is more prevalent today, I am reminded of what Enoch Powell warned us about over fifty years ago. Yet we have not learned from his wisdom." Merlin was thoughtful. He recalled the speech had been extremely controversial, and yet here they were talking about social disunity in the villages and towns of rural England, and the blood that was flowing was from the stab wounds to young men, barely out of boyhood, but ensconced in a war of neighbourhoods.

It was a war fought in hand-to-hand battle, bayonets if you will, raised to the fore, shadowing the open trench warfare of a bygone era, but nonetheless firmly entrenched in the minds of combatants.

The social disharmony was what the powers relied on. It was evidenced by the plethora of advertisements today selling life insurance, or funeral plans, and those pesky advertisements for mobile phone apps, designed to make one's life simpler, but simply capturing more of the time the young people had, to actually relate to one another. Battle lines were drawn on social media, where so-called celebrities pontificated for hours every day on the most socially ridiculous issues, and were paid handsomely by corporates all vying for their advertising platforms.

The world had finally reached the edge of the flat-earth, and like lemmings the people were ready to jump.

"Be yourself; everyone else is already taken."

Oscar Wilde

The Interview

Merlin had been invited to attend an interview at the local school. The process was miraculous, if not pre-ordained, if that was at all possible. He had submitted his application on the Monday after meeting Simon at the library, and the interview was scheduled for Wednesday. By Wednesday afternoon he had received a confirmation of his job position. Highly qualified as a professor of sociology, it was opportune that his interview had been conducted by the head of department for Beliefs and Values. This was an ideal in that the teacher spoke Merlin's language. They got on famously and before the end of the interview there were smiles aplenty.

The concept of having beliefs and values was an interesting one. Merlin knew what he believed, and his values were mainstream, but he could not help feel the absurdity of a system that skirted the authenticity of thousands of years of knowledge, in favour of the multi-culturalism of inclusivity of muslim, sikh and a myriad of religious and quasi-religious ideas that evoked the founding of ethnicity based freedoms of expression. This had opened the door, in his opinion to a plethora of questionable values.

So, to his mind, beliefs had been turned on their head by access to the internet and a vast array of information that vied for the hearts and minds of the youth, least of which, was the idea that it was acceptable to express an opinion on Satanism!

Well, that would be a minefield he might relish, and given his proclivity for successfully expanding the minds of university students, he welcomed this opportunity to understand the core values of a subject the church had hidden from, amidst symbolism and devout signals of salvation through the Christian cross. None, least of all the catholics had been more erroneous in his opinion, about misconstruing the Biblical references to the original sin.

Not a Christian, Merlin had nonetheless studied the Bible in its entirety, and his final verdict had been that the early Christian leadership had extrapolated many ideas and symbolism from the ancient Judaic religion, and through the writing of the supposed Apostles, had formulated vast reserves of information from the library at Alexandria, not to mention the surrogates of early Christian values in the early church that had adopted 'The Way'.

The history of Christianity was chequered with the untruths of many scriptures from The Torah, which had been an oral tradition passed down through the Hebrews, and then the Israelites returning to Jerusalem after the Babylonian exile. The Torah had not existed as a written document until after the exile, and much of the Pentateuch, which formed the first five books of the Old Testament, was a transcript of the stories of the Jewish people as they had lamented their constant enslavement through centuries of repression under successive armies of occupation. Le Vant, as it later became known, was the focus of access to the Middle Eastern region from the

Mediterranean, and the Israelites had chosen a strip of land, less than fifty miles wide in places and often well below sea level, as their adopted home.

Just how they had survived was in itself a miracle, but their values and more importantly, their keen intellect, had been a source of considerable interest to invading armies. Merlin was mindful of this when he spoke of the Palestinian debacle, yet it was the beliefs of the Jews, which had ensured their continuity.

Merlin believed that they had harnessed the concept of supernatural power, as a mechanism to obviate indefinite persecution, by utilising superstition among lesser-educated people, to drive home their advantage. But he was aware through his study of neuroscience, that the idea of using extra-sensory perception was in fact a distinct advantage to those who would harness it for psychological warfare.

History, he always contended was written by the victors. Thus, the Jews, who had controlled a dominant stranglehold on the financial mechanisms of the twentieth century, and subsequently adopted vast wealth through the Military Industrial Complex, would always succeed before the Palestinians, because they held the purse strings.

Here was a subtle equation that resulted in a systemic eradication of religiosity, in favour of Consumerism based values. Merlin accepted neither as the favourable alternative, but he was keenly aware of the need for society to maintain values that may cement social cohesion. Religion had been that glue for centuries, but now the Mainstream Media touted consumerism, as their weapon of choice to control the proletariat. The only difference between communism and consumerism, was a twist of dextrose verbiage.

When confronted with such a challenge, Merlin would not resist the opportunity to counter those in the MSM who had bought the controlling shares in every major media outlet, including the new social media avenues. This was a struggle for the hearts and the minds of the Zed Generation, and sadly, they had already succumbed to the ravages of its intense pervasiveness.

Taking a quick tour of the school, Merlin was escorted through warrens of fifty-year old classroom corridors, with row after row of classroom desks visible and neatly attired youths succumbing to the daily regiment. Here and there, were signs of spontaneous combustibility, as stern faced teachers raised relentless voices, in a vain effort to compete with secreted mobile phones tuned to a scrimmage of social media sites.

In the staffroom and happily introduced to friendly study supervisors, Merlin sat in comfortable sixties-style armchairs, a mug of brewed tea in hand, and customary glances of acknowledgement. These were the coal-face workers; thrown deep into the caverns of contemptible conflict, as teachers conceded to tireless itineraries and reluctantly gave way to cover supervisors, to carry out hastily drafted cover-work.

Here was a middle-aged grandmother, thirteen years a veteran of the gapping chasm between qualified teacher and cooperative stand-in; affably affirming her calling. There, was a bearded would-be sports coach, amiably mulling over what may have been. But in consensus, all stood shoulder-to-shoulder, a camaraderie of sorts, as veterans of a modern-day battlefield!

Merlin was struck by the magnitude of this vocation. The system was designed by default to catch all who might fall through the cracks, and none were to be left behind. Conversations revolved around who had been 'parked' and why. Names glibly rolled off the tongue, as might fast-food menus with multiple alacrity. The usual suspects, they said, would raise your consciousness of the pitfalls of mainstreaming questionable socially diverse conditions of personality traits.

But Merlin was more than equipped for this. He would ask endless questions and with a mind like an encyclopaedia, he would keep a mental note of all who might fall into his sphere of influence, if only for a fleeting respite from mediocrity.
On his way out the reception, Merlin was met by a charmingly gracious head teacher, and his ably equipped personal assistant, clipboard to hand.

The small talk affable and the acknowledgements bounteous; Merlin would fit right in. He was socially engineered to meet the multiple expectations, and therein provide spontaneity to a chosen class of professionals. Here, they held the future of the world in their meticulously scripted regimes for the day, and the systematic structuring of daily calendars maintained that cohesion. Anything less would be unproductive.

But, if it were of intrigue to Merlin, it was certainly for all intents and purposes, calamitous to one erstwhile teenager, called Josh, who rounding on the clique of teachers in the administrative entrance hall, en-route to an early lunch in the dining hall, looked up in alarm, squarely into the bespectacled face of his mother's next-door neighbour.

With an atypical youthful flurry, Josh went ashen, lost his footing, bumped into the swing-door, crashing with a volatility of momentum, that hastened a reprimanding, "tut-tut', from the head teacher; but social decorum dispensed with, he disappeared with equal energetic impetus.

Merlin smiled inwardly.

Head teacher, a mental note sequestered, ushered Merlin through the reception and gratefully out into the bracing wind.

Merlin gave a good chuckle as he headed for the car park. This was going to be an interesting assignment.

"Science, my lad, is made up of mistakes, but they are mistakes which it is useful to make, because they lead little by little to the truth."

Jules Verne - A Journey to the Centre of the Earth

Simon Says

"Life is a series of choices we make, and there is no doubt I have made some significant choices recently." Merlin suggested. He was sharing his thoughts during his usual Saturday morning meeting with Simon. There was to be an intervening weekend before the start of his new job.

"Yes, and remember, Nelson Mandela, the greatest advocate of freedom, never held his captors responsible for his imprisonment. He saw the inevitability of his release, and with that realization he likely made the decision to let go of all old thoughts and moved forward to meet the new challenges of a free democracy in South Africa." Simon implored. They had been discussing Simon's fallout from the non-profit organisational position he had held in Africa.

"It is interesting to see the new leaders who came after him, resorting to old slander tactics, because they have failed this democracy, and have not delivered on promises made to the electorate." Resignation hung on the timber of his voice.

"It is simply a case of shooting the messenger; and I believe they have never been willing to discover their Spiritual nature as they are too intent on salvaging their own careers, having plundered the state coffers for so long. Twenty-five years after democracy, the ANC have now turned on the safe preserve of name calling, now that they have been found wanting. This is the tactic that has kept Mugabe and the Zimbabwean ZANU party in power for thirty-nine years, and look where they are!"

Merlin turned his eyes upward and to his right. He was searching for something.

"Isn't it fascinating that when we research the effect words have on the psyche of a nation, there is a common consensus of opinion that positive affirmations will lead a country out of poverty, but negative rhetoric by its leadership will always keep them in servitude? It seems to me that those leaders are not leading."

"Yes, it is a sad reflection on the damage that a society will inflict upon itself when greed becomes the all-consuming motivator." Simon understood what was driving these liberation struggle nations, devoid of all positive direction. Inward looking and focused on acquiring materially, instead of Spiritually.

"I can understand why they need to accumulate what they may have lacked in the past, but they still seem to fail themselves when push comes to shove. It is a very short-term mentality."

Simon gazed back at Merlin. His eyes swimming, he touched him on the shoulder. "It is interesting that I once heard a lovely description of what personified a truly Spiritual person. It relates to three people walking along a narrow wall. There was Faith, Love, and Inspiration. When Inspiration stopped walking along the wall, to ask for Love to guide them further, and found that Love was no longer behind him; Faith faltered and fell. This resulted in Inspiration on his own, without Love or Faith, and a soulless Inspiration was likely to fall."

"In other words," he took a breath, "when the ANC, turns its attention to the politics of negative slander, it is because they no longer have the vision of the great leaders like O.R. Tambo and Madiba, or as he is known here, Nelson Mandela. They fail because they lack a credible vision and have lost their way unable to negotiate the narrow path they have created for themselves."

Merlin cocked his ear. The noisy café seemed a distant hum away.

"It is remarkable for the fact that not less than a generation ago, Madiba had written his 'Long Walk to Freedom', but the leaders of today, have either not read it, or have not learned from it. There is also a possibility that for political expediency, they are ignoring it."

Simon took a sip of the steaming coffee.

"Focus is what gets us to the end of that wall. Our thoughts beget our experiences. The trapeze wire walker, does not look down to see where he is; he focuses on the far end of the wire, and continues to walk." Simon looked up. Merlin was still searching.

"Thoughts that we don't want are easily removed. The ANC could choose to focus on getting the country to the end of that wall, or they could choose to look back. Each has a resultant effect, either negative or positive; but looking back will only unsettle and unbalance the country."
Simon was in his element, a receptive audience captured in that foggy corner. The world seems at odds with his rhetoric, but Simon was his own one-man advocacy.

"A leadership that dwells on gutter politics such as they have embarked on recently is a leadership out of synch with its electorate. The blame game of the ANC has been vilified and proven contemptuous in countries such as Zimbabwe, The Congo and other African countries where the politics of the blame game have proven to be ineffective. Those countries are mired in controversy and failure, because there is no credible vision."

Merlin was intrigued that Simon used the old name for the Democratic Republic of the Congo.

"I always get a sense that Mugabe had lost the plot, after he was found with his hands in the cookie jar. Now he blames the devil on his shoulder for making him do it; but he nonetheless still has not removed his hand. He has played that hand since the early eighties, after he expediently removed Joshua Nkomo and the threat of a political rival through Gukuhurundi."

Merlin knew this to be the slaughter of over twenty thousand Ndebele rivals in Matabeleland, in the south of Zimbabwe. Zimbabwe had been known as Rhodesia, and was colloquially referred to as the Bread Basket of Africa; now it was a basket case.

The former liberation struggle veterans had become bitter rivals and Mugabe and Nkomo were vying for political supremacy. Mugabe had been chosen by the powers in London through a haphazardly constructed Lancaster House Agreement, because they knew him to be corrupt and malleable to their devious intentions. It was all about maintaining control of the resources and Merlin was keenly aware of how those in The City manipulated those political puppets, pulling the strings from their cocooned offices in Canary Wharf.

"When Mugabe lost the 2008 election to Tsvangarai, his new political rival twenty years later, and the puppet masters pulled the strings in Harare, and Tsvanagrai and the Movement for Democratic Change were forced into hiding for fear of their lives. Ultimately, they conceded, and Tsvangirai was paid off with a handsome sum of money, so that they did not even contest a particularly pathetic run-off election. Mugabe stayed in power, but it was at this very time in Zimbabwe's history that so much could have changed!" Simon spoke. Merlin noticed how his eyes became translucent and his pupils dilated. Behind those eyes was a soul worthy of engagement.

"That was the year they had found the diamonds at Marange, and then later at Marapi, which were provisionally considered 'Blood Diamonds'. When Mnangagwa and the generals who were in charge of the military found out about these rich fields; I mean literally fields, that the local tribesman were collecting the diamonds off the ground from, they stepped in and used Allouette helicopter gunships to mow down the people."

"Mow down?" Merlin questioned. "Like they did in Vietnam?"

"Yes, it was horrendous, but the generals had complete control over those fields. They sent their troops in on the ground and the diamonds were initially under their control. They killed over 214 people that day, and the irony was, they all belonged to the local church, after which the mine was named!" Simon continued.

"Johanne Marange was a local chieftain from royal descent going back centuries. This did not stop Mnangagwa and his cold-blooded killers; and The City kept quiet, until it was time to benefit from those Blood-Diamonds. Only when they required the capital to begin underground mining operations, which the Chinese with the help of the Israelis, who stepped in." Merlin sat up.

"The Chinese colluded with Mugabe through a company called Anjin, and they in turn colluded the diamond cutting industry. Which set up shop locally to negate The Kimberley Process, where uncut diamonds cannot be sold internationally, if they come from blood-diamonds. Ultimately the centre of trade for diamonds has moved to the east from Antwerp and Amsterdam." Simon smiled, a twitch curled his right upper lip, accentuating a dimple; charming, but knowingly rueful.

"Is that when you were working in Zimbabwe on one of those Missions?" Merlin recalled a conversation.

"Yes. It was at that time I was helping an American charity group linked to the Founders of Zion." He stopped abruptly.

"The Israeli's had sent in a group of Mosad agents to reconnoitre the operations. Ultimately they became Mugabe's 'go-to' intel guys and they set up offices in Harare. They were known for their brutality and helped Mugabe with his next election campaign in 2013. The group was called Nikuv, and they manipulated the voter registration records to include millions of Zimbabwean's who had already died. Mugabe stuffed the ballot boxes and remained in power until it was politically expedient to get rid of him."

"Yes, well I have never trusted the Zionists, they have a One World Order agenda that is troublesome." Merlin quipped.

"Huuhh, you say!" Simon guffawed. His grin now spread across his face, large teeth flashing.

"It seems we will never get rid of them and the insidious greed they represent." Merlin sensed the irony. Simon had been co-opted by an American Christian organisation with ties to the powers and principalities.

"That was when I was stabbed in the chest, after I had uncovered their devious ploy to solicit money from American and U.K. fund raisers." Simon tentatively touched the scar tissue, a keloid that still troubled him. It was like a warning bell. When Simon sensed danger, or spoke about his experiences, the scar seemed to throb in a psychosomatic pulse.

Merlin noticed this unconscious move, and knew this was real.

"I believe that the Zionists are the greatest existential threat of our time. Worse than climate change, or nuclear threat; they want complete power." Merlin conceded.

"They are what we refer to as the 'Powers and Principalities'. The Gospel writers warned us of them. I still have a suspicion that despite the power they have, they will ultimately lose." He was an optimist.

"Do you agree that they have that much power?" Merlin quizzed.

"Oh yes! If you have any understanding of the insidiousness of their grip on power, you might consider what is happening here in West Scowlsdown, no less a part of their plans, as the control of diamonds in Zimbabwe." One or two elderly ladies looked up from their teacups.

"The Zionists have taken complete control then?" Merlin whispered.

"Yes, and I agree that they have control now. But I believe that there are massive changes afoot." Simon whispered back.

"The drugs trade in this town is no less a symptom of their control, and the County Lines element is a testimony to the invasiveness of their planning." Simon continued, his hand shielding his mouth.

"Yes, it is very well organised." Merlin agreed.

"When I was working up at the train station, you know, when they had that line closure between Brighton and Three bridges?" Merlin reminded Simon.

"Well, I used to ask the permanent staff, why these young lads were coming down on the late trains from London, and then cycling off up London Road, only to return minus their ruck-sacks twenty minutes later! They then boarded the last train back up to Croydon." Merlin whispered.

"Oh, and what did the guys on the platform tell you?"

"They laughed, making light of it all. Everyone knows that these lads are being used as couriers and that 'County Lines' is alive and prospering in East Sussex." Merlin shook his head.

"It is an indictment on our society. Sadly, everyone is complicit." Simon agreed.

"The dealers conduct their lethal orchestra of poison from one boy to the other, as the drugs are transported by the fledgling soldiers in this war. The boys are the foot soldiers, if that is what you want to call them, who run the errands." He took a great gulp of air.

"It's the perniciousness of a system that rewards the boys with a small fee, for couriering the drugs on behalf of the dealers, and when the boys get caught, as inevitably they do, they plead ignorance, or worse; they claim they are being used by the dealers in the form of 'Child Labour'!"

"But what can we do about it?" Merlin thought of young Josh, a pawn in the hands of those puppet masters.

"Pray and Meditate!" Simon said.

"Remember, there's always something cleverer than yourself."

Merlin in Excalibur – attributed to Thomas Malory

The First Day

His alarm went at 5.55 and Merlin awoke. His dream had been of a wonderful trip over an island in an azure sea. He had been gliding over the island, and it felt as though he were suspended, almost as though tethered to a balloon. It took him a minute to gather his thoughts. When Merlin was awoken in this deep state of sleep by outside influences, he always made a note of his dreams. He would continue to write them down, and this one was particularly uplifting.

It was, as he knew, a symptom of his positive psyche and a reflection of his positive thinking. Thirty-five years of teaching sociology had taught him that everything came down to the word. The spoken word, uplifting and encouraging; the written word, affirming and cementing thoughts and inspirational ideas. He had never known that of Marge. She had been the opposite of everything he advocated; strange as it was, they were well suited but his was the paradox of her psyche. Marge had been the counter-balance to his enthusiasm, tempering his child-like expectation of good, with adult certitude.

Marge had been his talisman, and a good one at that. She kept his feet on the earth, as he drifted off on clouds of grandiose daydreaming. But it was Marge who had brought on her untimely demise despite his constant reminding to her of all the joys they had of life. Now she was gone, he was like an expectant child. Each morning was a new surprise and this morning he was as a six year old might be, at the anticipation of his first day at school.

Merlin leapt from the bed, ignoring his slippers and charging for the bathroom, and a welcome respite from a full bladder. Next was a visit to the kitchen, where the kettle and prepared cereal bowl was at rest. Thus armed, he slipped into the living room, crouched into a ball and rolled back onto his back, relieving the compressed vertebrae of a long sleep, with a resounding cacophony of clicks. As the kettle began its riotous charge to full steam ahead, Merlin stretched out, performing his daily routine of Pilates and yoga poses.

He would always end this adventure, with what he had dubbed 'the dog', having observed the terriers in the park on his walks with Marge, and having commented on how they smiled in their prostrated positions, performing a series of twists on their backs. At first, he had believed they were indeed scratching an irritant itch, but the more his scientific mind had been indulged, the greater was his respect for nature. Those mutts, although of earthier origins than man, had happened on a vast treasure-trove of instinctive self-preservation tactics. Merlin was certain that the twisting of the spinal chord was somehow related to the release of white-blood platelets in the bone marrow, and that this activity, was invoking that happenstance smile; perceived as Marge had commented.

But to Merlin it was obvious. They were somehow stimulating a smile which, when imitated whilst lying on his back on the Axminster-clad floor, evoked a bellicose rebellion of giggles, which provided Merlin great happiness.

This five-minute routine would lead him back to the kitchen, a mug of tea, and a good dose of fibre and fruit. Merlin missed his time alone, before adopting a more routine trek through to the bedroom to deliver a pot of tea to Marge, whilst she would rouse herself from slumber. His routine had been interrupted by life and the daily monotony of caring for himself. But, this morning he was eager to get to the school as early as possible, and beat the eight twenty-five bell.

Today, he was to meet with the team of study-supervisors and learn the routine for the mornings. At precisely seven-thirty he closed the door, and turned on his heels towards the bus stop and a regimented fifteen-minute ride to the school. He had planned this precisely, with the scheduled arrival to bring him through the doors in time for a search of the Sims program and a quick check of his emails.

School life was thus structured like the boot-camps of an antiquated army, for a reason. Nothing less than total observance of the system could result in a systemic adherence to rules and regulations. Merlin was in his element.

The bus ride up to the school gave him an opportunity to casually observe the commuters. The bus was filled with students, but here and there were some early starters. Merlin made a mental note of the bus stops they disembarked on, and a handful of errant scholars who jumped-ship before their intended destination outside the main entrance of school. These were the rebellious few, whose penchant for extra-curricula activities before school, were to be marked down. Merlin would soon come to learn their intended detours, but today it was the front door and his destiny with the head of his section.

The bus descended on the school with conquest its goal, as time-scheduled stops were to be maintained, and traffic reluctantly observed when approaching a calming-circle from the right. Otherwise this juggernaut would be unimpeded by the monotony of the daily commute and Merlin would begin to recognise the patterns of frustration that would creep into the impatient agenda of the various drivers. Today was to be the turn of the heavy-footed, dour driver from Linksfield. Merlin observed how he would career down London Road, with the precision of a saddle-maker with his foot on the pedal, weaving his way through the traffic, twenty-five years of service unrecognised.

The bus would certainly get him to the front door on time, but he found himself wedging his left foot into the corner of the bulkhead in front, a firm right-hand grip on the railing. The bus slew to a halt, outside the neat hedgerow in front of the school, and disgorged the majority of its occupants. Merlin allowed the students to disembark first, making observations about those who might catch his eye inquisitively.

In the staff-room and pleasantries dispensed, Merlin was given his schedule for the day. He was to be thrown to the lions, and the group of Year Ten science students would be his chewing cud. Shadowing the bearded sports-coach into a class, where neither study-supervisor, nor student was prepared. The students looked up reluctantly from their mobile phones to acknowledge the amiable fellow. Merlin skirted the room, to gather what territory was to be had. The students responded with teenage tenacity to an instruction to put mobile phones and bags aside in favour of workbooks.

First here, then there, a muted resentment passed from murmured lips, then a tangible acquiescence filtered through the science lab. The mobile phones were deposited into bags, and pockets, and sullen faces turned expectantly, one then another.

Merlin was intrigued by the general lack of respect the bearded man wielded. First one, then another fourteen year-old student turned from surly disquiet, to face their accuser, appeasement their goal. The bearded man took centre stage on the dais, with computer screen reflecting through an overhead projector, related the cover-work set. Armed with this instruction, bearded man set to work on a monosyllabic outline of the instructions. It appeared no thought had gone into what was required, for the students to perform the set-work. Merlin made a mental assessment of the bearded man, then, parked his thought, to take a seat to the left of the screen to read the instructions.

Before long, first one, then another casual glance had been levelled in his direction. Assessing this intruder, the students began to grow in confidence, in the knowledge that bearded man would pose no crucial threat to the stalking to come. Merlin could see the intent in their eyes. Malevolent and directed, this was the opening salvo, and Merlin was better prepared for it, than his feigned disinterest alluded to.

"What are you supposed to be here for?" The remark directed by a robust-looking teen, with a supercilious countenance.

Merlin simply smiled, acknowledged the question and left it to hang. The teen, unimpressed and aggressively seeking some attention glared back at Merlin. The lad was clearly the centre of attention in the class.

"Mr Drinkwater is a study supervisor and he is……" the answer was offered by the bearded man, who had looked up from his mobile phone, annoyed by the interruption, but never completed.

The lad descended into howls of laughter, not echoed by anyone in the room.

"Drink what?" He shouted, seeking confirmation. Merlin smiled disarmingly. No one else gave him the affirmation he sought.

"Mr. Drink, water," the bearded man repeated. But Merlin sensed that atypical condescension in his tone, which only spurred on the lad.

The other students seemed distracted by the study sheet on their worktable, but the air in the room seemed to be sucked out the one open window as the lad drained all semblance of energy from the atmosphere. He was combative, aggressive and on the offence.

Merlin knew the symptoms of pathological attention seeking, and he would be able, invariably, to locate the cause with two particularly pointed questions aimed at the lad. But now was not the time, and he knew it would present itself again sometime soon.

"Conan! Get on with your work." Bearded man responded with a lazy drawl, the emphasis on neither the work, nor the subject of his irritation.

"Conan!" Merlin thought. "Uuhhmmm, well, therein lay the immediate transgression." Any parent intent on naming a child after the source of such a mediocre myth, was bound to project their failures upon the lad.

Merlin eyed the lad, his emerald green eyes penetrating the heart of fifteen years worth of failed nurturing. The lad was clearly not as bright as he would like to have thought himself, but deep within that soul, there would be a spark of something worthy of salvaging.

"Where are you from?" Conan was clearly not impressed with his line of attack falling short of its mark.

"Conan that is none of your business." Bearded man sat on the dais and seemed intent on surveying the students with minimal effort.

"That's alright," Merlin responded. "I am local, living here in West Scowlsdown." The question was an open invitation to provoke further lines of enquiry. Merlin knew what would come next.

"Where?"

"Conan! That's enough. Mr Drinkwater does want to be quizzed by you." Bearded man now claimed his authority on behalf of Merlin.
"Actually its okay. It believe it's a natural inquisitiveness of the human psyche to want to put people into little boxes." The answer unsettled the lad.

"What do you mean by boxes?" Conan was now content, as the conversation and the energy in the room flowed back to him.

Merlin looked up at the dais, as bearded man looked menacingly at Conan.

"It is a sociological concept Conan." There was the affirmation.

"What is?" Conan un-cowed by bearded man.

"Well, as humans, we have a natural propensity to want to create groups with whom we can identify, and putting someone in a box allows us to relate to them, or not." Merlin returned his gaze.

"Are you a sociologist?" The lad wanted more.

"Yes, I have a professorship in Sociology from Oxford." The class raised their heads.

"A Professor? So you are a university teacher." The bearded man now put his mobile device away and sat up.

"A Lecturer. Sociology is my main interest." Merlin gave him a smile, holding his gaze until the lad looked to bearded man for his recognition.

"Sir is a boffin." He crowed. The animosity was tangible. It seemed Conan was playing them off, one against the other.

"Well I am retired to be fair, and now I am working here as a study supervisor." Merlin was forgiving.

"Yes, but you're still very clever!" The question was rhetorical, but Merlin knew the barb was aimed at bearded man.

"Well, let us see if we can get you to become a university professor Conan. Then we can say that we achieved something great." Merlin approached the lad, turning the work sheet over, so that the questions were visible.

"Okay, what is the name of the man who first discovered electricity in clouds? Last name begins with an 'F'. His face is still on the American dollar bill!

"But if thought corrupts language, language can also corrupt thought."

George Orwell, 1984

The Zionists

"I followed your advice and when I woke up this morning, I had been dreaming of this weird word, which I could not get out of my mind." Merlin had met Simon for their regular coffee morning.

"What was the word?" Simon chuckled.

"It was 'ish-i', or something ending with an 'I' but I recall specifically thinking it was an 'ish' at the beginning." Merlin was on the computer whilst they chatted.

"When I put the 'ish-I' into google and searched, it came up with several options, but at the top of the list was an organisation called the British-Israel Federation.

"Nooo! I can't believe it." Simon swivelled his chair towards where Merlin was seated. He looked intently at the screen.

"The chances that you would be researching them, when I have been looking into the origins of 'usury' in Britain, which originates from the Zionist movement, is almost uncanny!" Simon's eyes lit up.

"The British-Israel Federation was formed in the early twentieth century. Here is a gazette, I had asked for yesterday. Would you believe that they, and many other pro-Israeli organisations are responsible for the rise of the I.R.A.?" Simon was reading from an article in the library.

"How so!" Merlin turned from the computer console to see what he was quoting.

"Well, according to historians, the Irish were not too enamoured with the rise of a Jewish elite in Ireland during the early twentieth century, so they formed the Republican army to counter the surge of usury by wealthy Jews, intent on profiting from the working classes." Merlin knew of the moneylenders.

"According to this article, the I.R.A. sent their early militia into the places of business in Dublin where the Jews were extorting vast percentages of interest off the poor families of the city, with the intention of destroying their ledgers and any record of the loans made." Simon spoke as he continued reading.

"Was the militia armed, or did they simply use brute force to secure the records from them?" Merlin had no sympathy for the purveyors of usury.

"It seems they were unarmed when they originated, but because the British put so much pressure on the Irish government of the time, the I.R.A. ultimately turned to violence to remove the illegitimate forces that wanted to maintain their financial stranglehold on the Irish people." Simon pointed to the article.

"It seems there were a lot of deceptive forces used to keep the money-lenders in power." Merlin shook his head.

"Well, it is not the first time!" The gazette deposited on the desk, Simon stood up.

"I think it is time for some fresh air."

Merlin ended his session on the library computer, stood and followed Simon out the automatic double doors.

In the basement of the local restaurant, they had discovered some comfortable armchairs and a closeted safe space to speak.

"When I see the lengths these organisations go to, I often wonder how the Brits have allowed themselves to be duped so easily." The cool air in the basement lounge was a relief from the unusually humid conditions.

"I suppose we are all responsible in a way." Merlin conceded.

"Yes, to an extent, but these same powers have bought out the independence of the media networks and control the public narrative." Merlin knew this to be true, having studied the effects of media on sociology.

"They are funded by trans-national corporate actors." Simon spat the words out.

"Yes, the City has been creating this monopoly for centuries." He was the first to recognise that the real enemy of the British, was not any foreign power, but the very hegemonies that profited from the enslavement of the people; "We have become slaves to the consumer glut that has ensnared us."

Merlin could see the passion in his eyes, but the timber of his voice gave away the sense of powerlessness.

"Some of my kids from 7th Year History were asking me if slavery still existed. I told them they were slaves to their mobile phones! I mean, they are barely able to conduct an intelligible conversation anymore, without resorting to their smart phones." Merlin had witnessed this first-hand.

"I'm almost certain that some of them are doing drug deals in the back of my classes!"

"Unbelievable, but not surprising." Simon grinned once more. "Those kids I see on the bus are so adept at using their mobile phones, they have almost grown a third knuckle on their thumbs."

"The intermediate phalangeal bone." Merlin corrected him.

"Oh! Yes, they seem to be able to use the end of their thumbs like a finger. It's almost like the bones have become more articulate."

"Well, that would be the only thing they are articulate at." Merlin quipped, irony spilling out the side of his mouth.

"Yeaah! Good one!" Simon applauded.

"But seriously, these kids are truly the lost generation. I call them the Zed Generation, before the apocalypse." Merlin gestured. The play on words not lost to Simon.

"Well, for what it's worth, my take is that the world of marketing, talks about the Baby-boomers after the Second World War. Then came Generation X, who, were prepared to embrace new technology. This was the generation, which took humankind ten steps forward on the evolutionary ladder. Now we have the Generation Y group, who ask the questions Why? Why do we have Capitalism, versus Socialism? Why do so many people go hungry? What can we do, as individuals to change the way people behave? These are questions we as the Generation Y, have to ask ourselves." Merlin understood the sociological aspects to his argument.

"But soon, this next generation will be adults and the kids of tomorrow, who are born out of wedlock, out of loving, monogamous and conventional relationships, with fifty percent of our population divorcing and a large percentage of our kids growing up in single-family units; they will be asking a different question entirely." His analysis was influenced by socio-economic factors.

"The kids of tomorrow will be born predominantly through Artificial Insemination and the artificial intelligence of technological advancements will play a factor here. Without fathers, or without mothers in some cases! Born to surrogate fertility wombs, and snatched away to be with their biological parents, or parent. These will be the Generation Z kids, and aptly, they will be the last generation of children, as we know them. They will be the Omega and the end generation." Simon indicated his understanding of an Apocryphal teaching.

"After the Alpha, and before the end of times as we have come to know our world. The beginning, and the end! The Z Generation will bring a closure to a world that has lost all sense of compassion and with which the dawning of the end time will beckon." There was an ominous energy, but Merlin recognised Simon was speaking his truth from what he had experienced. Merlin's truth was somewhat more optimistic.

"Well, one great thing about the kids today, is that they have grown up with technology, so they have an innate sense of sophistication in regard to the ways of the world." Merlin conceded.

"Yes, but that does come with a caveat. It is a blessing and a real threat to societal values." Simon knew his nephews used the internet to chat with friends about everything from sex, to drugs and every other subject, but he was keenly aware their parents had brought them up with common-sense values.

"I'm not certain that is detrimental to society." Merlin interceded.

"I mean, it is this age of technology that has lifted the majority of people out of poverty. Education is now at the tips of their fingers, or thumbs!" Smiling at his synchronistic word connection.

"I believe that today's kids are not only smarter than we were, but they will lift themselves out of this self-induced enslavement, once there is a global consensus on morality." This was his ideal of a system of socialization that lead to greater consciousness.

"My understanding is from a Spiritual point of view, in that they are conscientized by a powerful spirit of awareness. Call it God, or whatever you like, but it is a real energy field."

That is interesting, because you and I come from the generation Xer's that grew up during the sixties and seventies. This was during a time of huge shifting societal values like the sexual revolution and the Vietnam War. We grew up with reduced adult supervision as we became divorced from out parents, and they sought greater economic freedom through economic empowerment; especially our mothers!" As teenagers we were dubbed the MTV Generation." Merlin recounted.

"But the truth is the 'Y' Generation became known as the Millennials, because they always asked 'why?' That was the beginning of what then transcended into the Zed Generation."

"Yes, the Zombie Generation." There was a rueful edge to Simon's voice.

"The media won't use the expression, but if we have had the X; the Y; then it makes complete sense we should now have the Z generation!" Simon knew the Mainstream Media did not acknowledge this, because after Z, what was left?"

"Yes, but remember that the Biblical reference to the Alpha and the Omega, would require that after the Z Generation, will be the renewal of societal values and an Alpha Generation!" Merlin pointed out.

"It seems crazy, but these values are espoused as having real value by some in the media. My thinking is that the Zeder's will be the final generation who are not born with some genetic coding introduced by science." Simon prophesied.

"Genetic modification is happening in our food chain. Krill are consuming microscopic plastic beads, broken down from discarded plastics in the Southern Atlantic, and the food chain results in tuna packaged in our stores, being contaminated. The kids of today are eating microscopic levels of carbon toxins and once consumed, ultimately our kids will grow up with plasticized bones." Simon was intent or exploring this cycle.

"Well that will save on hip replacements in later life." Merlin enjoyed the repartee.

"The truth is not too far away from fiction." Simon reiterated.

"Yes, I agree, but I have an innate sense of an intervention; almost as if what we wish for, we can achieve." Merlin was more optimistic.

"You're right to be optimistic, because it is our very thoughts that beget our reality. It would not surprise me to know that the globalists have set us on this path for the express purpose of controlling the minds of the youth, and ultimately virtual slavery." Simon mused.

"You mentioned the generational changes, but it was the Fourth Turning book that laid out the idea that we have for the 'Millennials', and Howe and Strauss suggested the Generation-Z for this new generation of kids." Merlin paused.

"How so?" Simon was keen to learn more.

"I suppose then, the Zeder's will raise their game, because they will have no choice. If the Fourth Turning is to be believed, this generation is the 'Artist' generation, which will cut down social and political complexity in favour of a society of thinkers and dreamers. If the kids in America are any indication and we study the anti-gun lobby, there is an over-arching sense of ethical personal sacrifice. Because they have grown up overprotected by adults preoccupied with the crisis of child-protection, the question is, will they come of age as the socialized and conformist young adults of this iGeneration onslaught from big business?" Merlin conjectured.

"My question would be, is there an Awakening, and a potential age of thoughtful post-Awakening elders amongst them? They may be the only hope we have against this consumer onslaught!

**"Your beliefs become your thoughts,
Your thoughts become your words,
Your words become your actions,
Your actions become your habits,
Your habits become your values,
Your values become your destiny."**

Gandhi

Back in Class

Monday morning and Merlin found himself supervising a class of Beliefs and Values. How the world had changed since his humble upbringing in the quaint hamlet of Summer Rise, in the sleepy county of Herefordshire. He had grown up in the country, with geese and hens to feed every morning, and long summers frolicking in the hay barn with the local lads. Then, a class of religious education was conducted by the parish priest, once a week and the discussions of infidelities were kept as virtuous secrets, lest the adults would put paid to the joys of the forbidden fellatio on offer.

Today, the idea of religiosity was taught like a smorgasbord of facts, in which each child would be free to choose where fiction ended and reality started. As someone who had not suffered the fear-mongering of a Catholic-based religion, Merlin felt no sense of loss where education would be poorer for the eradication of doctrine based on fear; but there was an irony that this morning he was shadowing a young muslim woman in a hijab, with a set task, to instruct thirty or more young minds, to create a leaflet that they might put out into the their community to celebrate Eid.

Merlin carefully negotiated between the computer consoles where thirteen year-olds were busy cutting and pasting a series of comments from their google search and placing them into a make-shift word document. But the morning was about to get so much more interesting as he supervised two young lads who had placed a picture of a dog on the screen.

"This is interesting," Merlin commented.

"Yes, my favourite dog is a bullmastiff," the lad whose name he had not yet learned, and which now escaped him, was editing the jpeg picture into his document.

"Okay, and may I ask you the relevance of incorporating your dog into the leaflet?"

"I think it looks more interesting." The lad had not seen the irony.

"That makes sense to me," Merlin continued along the networked table.

"Who has nearly finished their leaflet?" The lady with the dook announced. Several hands went up around the class. Merlin stepped back to allow the study supervisor to check on the work.

"No, no, that is not going to be acceptable!" Came the provoked lament as she had rounded on the two lads with the dog picture.

"What's wrong with it?" The lad looked confused. He and his mate had spent the better part of thirty minutes laboriously refining their pamphlet.

"You know what I am talking about! You did this on purpose." The female study supervisor looked affronted.

"No I don't," the lad jumped to his feet, defence of his cherished pooch a priority.

"Just remove the picture of the dog, it's an insult to Islam!" The lady stormed off.

"What the hell are you talking about?" The lad's voice was raised a decibel higher.

"Let me see if I can assist," Merlin stepped in, a polite grin enveloped his face, his back between the lady and her student. This was what resulted when you threw cultures, religions and sexes together, he surmised.

Sitting with the two lads, Merlin calmed the boy, then opened a page to a Wikipedia link, where the prophet Mohammed had called dogs out, as dirty.

"You see, unfortunately muslim people have been taught to fear dogs and their culture has not understood the relevance of domesticated dogs in the concept of the urbanisation of humanity." Merlin paused.

"Why do they hate dogs?" The lad was mortified.

"It's not that they hate dogs, but just as an African is taught to fear a snake, and that is why they place their beds on top of bricks covered in a herb, usually consisting of cannabis remedy, the idea of a dog to muslim people is similarly contentious." Merlin explained.
The two lads looked at one another quizzically.

"What do you mean 'contentious'." The lad was at least inquisitive.

"It means," Merlin lowered his voice, as the other students returned to their computer screens, "that the idea of domesticating dogs existed in early Arabic societies, but when Mohammed became influential, he choose to vilify dogs from the urban setting. They were considered unclean, because the purpose in early civilizations of domesticated dogs, was as scavengers in the community, where they were responsible for cleaning up human excrement!"

The two lads looked at him, furrowed eyebrows pointed like chevrons.

"In other words, they ate all the human excrement that they threw out of their huts, or as with the advent of more structured cities, they helped keep diseases at bay."

"So why would they not want dogs?" This was entirely illogical to the lad.

"I don't know, truly, but it may be that their perception of them is one of uncleanliness!" Merlin smiled again. "Perhaps they feel threatened by them."

The lads looked on hopelessly. Merlin leaned in, "If you were an extra-terrestrial, dogs might find you of interest." He stood, keeping the lads gaze, then winked.

"Can you say that?" The second lad was trying to be pc.

"I don't mean any disrespect," Merlin quipped, "after all they believe that Mohammed died, then flew off to the moon on a winged horse."

"He what?" The lads had a churlish grin on their faces.

"Shhssshh!" Merlin indicated with his index finger.

The rest of the class moved along without incident, and as the lads left, the newfound respect for Merlin was evident. "Cheers sir," they chorused, high-fives offered in salute.

Back in the staff room, the conversation flowed, but Merlin sensed the conversation was somewhat insular. The talk was all about which student had raised the greatest ire of that particular study-supervisor, and what points of conjecture throughout their morning had annoyed them greatly. Despite the challenges of having to supervise those students whose teachers were absent, it seemed that there was never a dull day on the job.

But in Merlin's mind, they had already lost the war. The study-supervisors were largely ambivalent soccer-moms, or as the football mad English would say, "foot-ball moms". They were bored housewives, whose husbands were missing-in-action from six in the morning, when they boarded the train to London, working in The City all day, and mainly showing their faces after nightfall. These moms, whose only wish was to participate in the upbringing of their kids, were now embedded in the schools where their tribe were now studying. With no previous teaching experience, and a certain bias to the other students, which was obvious, theirs was a catch-twenty-two existence.

The job entailed ensuring supervised work was completed within the time allotted, but the evidence of their ineptitude was howlingly obvious. De-merits were handed out like candy bars, and the desire to conform to a study-supervisor in attendance was seen as a challenge for every student. Merlin sat listening to the other study-supervisors for the duration of lunch, during which he vowed to sit with the teachers at the next break.

But it was not their fault. He knew this innately. The job was really an excuse to get out of the house during the day, when kids were at school and fathers were in the trenches. The obvious fall-out of boredom, this was an occupation with little merit. But, sadly the vast size of the school and many others like it, guaranteed the vacancy of permanent teachers on a regular basis, with the stress of the work of controlling a riotous rabble, many teachers succumbed to the ills that perverted their greater calling. In the interim, the trenches at home were now being manned by the unconscionable women, as was the case during every Great War.

West Scowlsdown was a once sleepy little village on the mainline to the coast. Now it was at the end of the train line, where commuters ploughed their trades in the financial markets and where parents, who had abandoned the dull-grey terraced homes of London for a happier, healthier existence in the country, found themselves slaves to their mortgages. The irony was palpable, as they had now eked out their living with the insidious enticement of big money, attracting them twenty-five miles northward every day.

It was these absentee fathers and mothers, who were really to blame and it was obvious that Merlin would need to step up and fulfil that place of mentorship, now abandoned. But Merlin was of no illusions that his position was untenable. Every war had sacrificial lambs, and he knew there would be a price to pay for idealism.

But every war had to be fought with the tools at hand, and West Scowlsdown was no exception. Merlin resolved to speak to Simon this weekend and get his take on things.

"We are not born into the world. We are born into something that we make into the world."

— Michael Talbot

Taking Stock

The week had passed largely without incident, and Merlin made his Saturday morning visit to the library. On his way out of the house, he had noticed Josh rummaging around in the garage his mother kept packed with all her family trinkets from Nigeria. But Josh was so focused on his search, he had not noticed Merlin until he was almost standing opposite him on the other side of the wooden post fence. Josh jumped; a reaction that gave Merlin pause for thought.

"Good morning Josh," Merlin nonchalantly ignored his reaction.

Josh was staring at him, almost akin to a deer caught in his flashlight in the Forest Row rambles he had so often embarked on. Josh mumbled something. Dressed in his rugby gear, he was clearly on his way to the rugby club for their weekly game. He was a strapping lad merlin realised. Despite the weeks that had passed since starting at the school, Merlin had always thought him a little under fed and somewhat on the lean side, whilst togged up in his grey flannels and over-sized blazer.

But now standing, as the sunlight peeped over the early morning eastern horizon, Merlin reassessed his previous belief. The lad was lean yes, but what had once been juvenile musculature, had transformed into sinewy quads and hamstring muscles, which gave his once adolescent frame an adult silhouette and transformed Merlin's view of the lad's now obvious physicality. The white rugby shorts, neatly pressed, now bulged over those brown quadriceps, and the nylon jersey seemed to almost pronounce an expanded chest and arms.

Merlin did not embarrass him with any obvious remarks, so had turned and walked down the driveway to his trusty coupe.

When Merlin arrived at the library, Simon was busy making coffee for the ladies at the corner table. It was their regular spot and the morning was just getting busy with the members of the book club settling down for a good natter.

"Morning Si," Merlin offered.

"Good morning Merl," the informality a pleasant refrain, unfamiliar, but refreshing. "What are you having? Tea, or coffee?" Simon was in his element.

"Thank you, a coffee would be great," Merlin smiled, their easy going relationship had been nurtured over the past months in which Merlin had grown a deep respect for Simon's intellect.

"Coffee it is," as he spun around, whipped out the coffee and deposited a healthy spoonful of granulated brew into the mug in hand.

Merlin waited until Simon had poured the steaming hot water from the urn and then took the mug full of coffee, added some milk, and the two moved to a table near the door, with a view through the glass panel, into the computer room beyond.

"So, how has your week been?" Simon waited until they were comfortable. His world was constructed in polite procedure and his unstressed servitude, a welcome change from the frenetic staffroom with its schedules a dire contrast to the reality, which manifested itself in Simon's world.

"Uneventful, in the main," Merlin responded, his mouth now on the lip of the mug. Steam evaporated into the cool air.

"Oh, good. I would take that as a plus, knowing what shenanigans you probably have to face each week." Simon grinned.

"Yes, they are somewhat of a challenge," Merlin agreed, "but I have taken a leaf from your hymn sheet!"

"How's that?" Simon quizzed.

"Well. Simply put, I am not allowing myself to fall into the trap some of these lads set for us." Merlin looked somewhat expectantly through the glass panel." He was not sure why.

"Ha ha, yes! That would be a self-fulfilling prophetic disaster."

"You can say that again." Merlin looked back to where Simon was about to repeat himself. They intuitively laughed.

"I think some of your Spiritual stuff is rubbing off on me," Merlin joked. "You know this week has been a roller-coaster ride of déjà vu moments!" This got Simon's attention.

"Pray do tell." He leaned in, surreptitiously eyeing Merlin.

"Well, each class seems to bring with it a sense of expectation," Merlin confided.

"What do you mean? Like you almost know what is going to happen?"

"Yes, exactly. The kids come into the classroom, and I am left with a sense of what to expect." Merlin's voice trailed off.

"Well yes, I am sure you expect chaos!" Simon jibed. Merlin dropped his eyes, conceding his point, then wistfully returned to the glass panel.

"You do know where the idea of serendipity comes from, don't you?" Simon asked, a matter-of-fact tone sensing Merlin would know the answer.

"Yes, and I understand the idea that déjà vu literally means to see in front of you, or something 'already seen'? But serendipity is far more complex." Merlin looked to Simon for help.

"Well, it is quite simply a happy accident. Or so the ancient Vedic tradition speaks to this idea as a series of coincidental happenings that result in the person, or persons affected, suddenly, and unequivocally realising they have been connected, or placed in a position for which they have no logical explanation, nor do they have any rationalisation for why it has happened." Simon elucidated.

"You know of course, it was George Santayana who said; "Those who cannot learn from history, are doomed to repeat it."

"Oh yes? Why do you say that?" Simon furrowed his brows.

"I am not certain, but I get the sense that these kids have already forgotten the evils of Hitler, and the dangers of communism." Merlin was forthright.
"It's just that when they ask me questions about issues like slavery, or how Britain survived the Second World War, I cannot help feeling that the garbage they listen to on social media, has already informed their moral compasses."

Merlin watched as a light ignited somewhere in the back of Simon's eyes; "If that is the case, it is a travesty of justice that will doom our society to another hundred years of servitude to the powers and principalities."

"Ah, you mean the 'Illuminati'?" Merlin gauged.

"That is a myth, served up by none other than the mainstream media, or as Trump says, 'the Lamestream Media', and those who control discourse in the public domain. What they refer to as the Illuminati was the reference to a cult, of religious scholars, who literally had sought to forge their own path towards Spiritual enlightenment. Made famous by the Dan Brown novel, it has no foundation in fact." Simon offered.

"Okay, I concede there is no historical records of a real group called the Illuminati, but the church has hidden evidence of the foundation of a post-Crusade group of elitist aristocrats, who had returned home to Europe after the Crusades in The Holy Land, a thousand years ago."

"Remember, the church are the precursors to what we call the media today! It was the church who controlled the flow of information in the Western World before the Gutenberg printing press and printing became common place. Once the genie was out the bottle, the priesthood had to change track because accessibility to books allowed the commoners to gain an insight into our history." Simon's eyes remained illumined.

"Yes, I suppose history is always retold by the victors, or those who controlled the financial resources." Merlin knew the truth was always illusive.

"But with the advent of the information age and computers, it has now become doubly important for the powers and principalities to take control of the technology." It appeared to Merlin that Simon must be schooled in Biblical references.

"I suppose the real issue is whether we will revert to a society such as the pre-Gutenberg populace that allowed the church to run rough-shod over their freedom of expression?" This was his bone of contention.

"But you make so many references to the Biblical context, so why do you believe they are to blame?" Merlin was confused.

"I believe one can be a Christian, without having to be constrained by the dogma of the church. If the average church-goer would only realise that the Catholic church is not the church that Jesus ordained the Apostle Peter to form. That would make it so much easier for them to rationalise why the church owns over one million hectares of land, but cannot lift the majority of its people from poverty!" The fire in his eyes was incendiary.

"So, if the church is not the mechanism Jesus wanted his followers to embrace; what is?" Merlin had never been a church-goer.

"The million dollar question I suppose! I would like to think that people have the discernment to worship their God in their hearts. It would make life so much easier if humanity could embrace Christian virtues with a sense of compassion as Jesus did, but that can only happen when we recognise our ability to create our own reality for ourselves." Simon mused.

"Oh! Like a Dale Carnegie sort of manifesting?" Merlin understood psychology enough to be comfortable that sociology had its origins in how people thought.

"Yes, surprisingly, the majority of people can think for themselves and don't need some dogmatic ritual to determine how to interpret their feelings." The conversation flowed.

"But the truth is human behaviour has always required some form of structure to remain integral to a concise functioning society. For example the Biblical Exodus from Egypt required a structure, in order that the people would remain focused on the 'Promised Land'. Over forty years they supposedly wandered through the Sinai looking for a new home." Simon was in his element.

"So when they required a system of rules and regulations to keep the clan together, they opted for a series of edicts, written down by the Levites, who were the scribes, or what we call the modern day 'media'. They were the educated clergy who were able to write, hence the reason they were called 'scribes'." Simon alliterated.

"So you are saying that the Bible was not written by God?"

"By no means! Moses and the leaders determined the laws as they believed they had been told, then the Levites wrote down what they were told, in order for the clan to survive the harsh environment they found themselves in. They needed rules as to how to behave amongst each other, so that they would not dissolve into a hoard of anarchistic hoodlums." Simon smiled.

"Ah! Yes, I can attest to the need for rules and regulations." Merlin quipped. "I recently had to cover 'Lord of The Flies' in class, with a group of year tens. I can't imagine them being left to govern themselves! In this day and age, with mobile phone technology, pornography and drugs! Good Lord, it would be complete mayhem!" Merlin knew all too well the ramifications of self-governance.

"But the truth is, they would make many mistakes along the way, lots of people would be hurt, but they would ultimately work it out for themselves. That's what the Hebrews did under Moses. By the way Moses is called by his Hebrew name, but his Egyptian name was Utmoses. In the history of the Pharaohs, he was a powerful leader, so would have had the support of the people." Simon continued.

"What then happened was that Moses had the scribes write down all the rules they needed to follow, and today we have the Book of Leviticus, written by the Levites, and in that is a bunch of do's and don'ts that the people adhered to."

"But today we have a constitution of legal laws, and we know that society has a degree of understanding through which we can self-govern. It all depends on our maturity and our ability to work together. However, the rules that were written four thousand five hundred years ago, do not need apply today." Simon paused.

"You mean there are laws that have been included in the Bible that no longer have relevance today?" Merlin asked.

"Well, yes. I mean, let's be honest, the Hebrews were a large group of people, some believe numbering in the millions They required to get through the desert and out the other side with as many of the clan as possible. The family unit was integral and to survive, not only the harsh conditions, but also the potential of being attacked, they needed to be strong in numbers."

"Today, the world is over-populated, and there is no requirement for the family unit in order to maintain civil society. Gay and Lesbian couples can live in harmony with society, because there is no demand on them to keep having children. I can tell you, without question, there were Gay and Lesbian Hebrews, but the strict conformity to those rules, ensured they were not allowed to follow their hearts. It had nothing to do with God condemning them, it was strictly conformist thinking that led them to deny their feelings for one another. I can guarantee God had nothing to say about that!" Simon was animated.

"Yes, I understand." Merlin thought back to the young couple he had seen playing 'footsy-footsy' in his geography class earlier in the week. The two boys in Year nine, were obviously smitten with one another, but could not openly hold hands, as some of the boys and girls in class did. He again looked towards the glass window, into the library. Now he realised why.

"You know, I fully accept that the Bible is not the actual word of God, but is the interpretation of what the ancient tribes believed they were being instructed! But how did that work?" Merlin was intrigued.

"With Panpsychism!" Simon explained.

"Panpsychism?" Merlin had heard the term used.

"Yes, Panpsychism is not just a theory, but is founded in actual examples of science. You see, when the human brain was formed, we were endowed with the thinking brain, which is the main frontal lobes, and the inner brain, which is the limbic brain. This is the part of the brain that allows us to create."

"Okay I understand that the second brain is called the limbic brain, or the emotional brain, or chemical brain, but how is that related to Panpsychism?" Merlin enthused.

"Well, what I understand, is the mind is a fundamental feature of the world which exists throughout the universe, and everything is connected. In fact, my thoughts and your thoughts can be connected, even if we are not in the same room!"

"Like extra-sensory perception?" Merlin quizzed.

"Let's take one step back shall we?" Simon proposed.

"We can agree that every time you learn something new, you make new connections in your limbic brain. Studies have shown that one hour of focused concentration on a concept or idea doubles the number of synapses connections in your brain. So it is this knowledge, when applied, or demonstrated to an idea of a Spiritual nature, which allows the body to calm itself, and it is the same technique Buddhists use when meditating. The limbic brain now instructs the main brain chemically, allowing the body to form new genes that allow the body to understand what the mind has already understood."

"In other words, the brain regulates the body's ability to function efficiently, without which the body spirals into melt-down?" Merlin surmised.

"Yes! Think of the brain as the computer chip in your smart phone. The chip allows data to be downloaded into your memory banks, which allow you to recall a number, or email address when you need it. The chip requires software, or instructions to operate, as does your brain. So, when our emotions are triggered by the limbic brain, our memory knows how to react."

"But without clear instructions, uncluttered and forthright, the brain becomes confused and begins to malfunction. This happens when our brains are cluttered with sensory-overload! That is why youngsters today cannot study efficiently with all the mass-media onslaught of social-media and the likes." Simon was laying out his perception like a road-map.

"But, likewise, when the brain is not being used regularly, with clear precise instructions given on a consistent basis, it fails. The neuro-pathways are not being exercised, just as a smart phone becomes slow when there is too much software downloaded and you have to delete files, the brain cannot function clearly when there is too much external noise from television and media." Merlin could see the clarity of Simon's argument.
"That's interesting, because there are many case studies that show dementia and the early onset of Alzheimer's and Parkinson's is correlated with early retirement and the fact that many sufferers have not regularly been subjected to healthy stimuli in the brain, to keep the memory functioning!" Merlin had read the studies.

"So you are saying that men and women who do not regularly focus their minds, have brains that will lose functionality?" The subject was fresh in Merlin's mind. He knew all too well, Margaret had been so dependent on him that she had not thought for herself.

"Yes. I believe there is a direct causal link between early retirement and those who do not follow a healthy daily, intellectual regime of reading and meditating." In Simon's mind, the government had deliberately 'dumbed-down the elderly generation, but mental health issues were the consequence.

"But the truth is they are stimulating their limbic brains through meditation and mindfulness?" Merlin quizzed.

"Just like the ancient Vedic chants and early Mesopotamian tribes, the use of meditation and ritual prayer, had many benefits; and not simply because they were evoking Spiritual help!" Simon elucidated.

"But, what is your understanding of Spirituality?" Merlin was not convinced.

"Many scientists maintain that the development of ideas within the limbic brain, have formulated our technological progress for thousands of years." Simon continued, he was enjoying the discussion.

"When humans encounter a problem that must be resolved in order for humanity to move forward, we use our creative brains to formulate solutions to the puzzle. Those puzzles are deconstructed, then re-constructed in our minds, so that we can formulate practical models for our benefit. This is no different to other mammalian brains, and evidence of this can be seen in a scientific study called the 'One Hundred Monkey Syndrome'. It is really worth looking up!"

"Yes, I have heard of it. So they were communicating with one another on a sub-conscious level?" Merlin could recognize the symptoms.
"Yes, precisely!" Simon was encouraged. The conversation was stimulating.

"That means the ideas for Spirituality are manufactured in your brain?" Merlin frowned.

"No, not exactly. What scientists believe, is strangely not unlike what Spiritual people understand! It is that when our bodies are in a state of serenity, or completely calm, that we begin to generate clear neural pathways for greater learning. There are chemicals in the brain that allow us to concentrate better." Simon knew he was in unchartered waters.

"I know for example that when our actions begin to equal our thoughts, the limbic brain, which is also called the autonomic brain, or automatic brain, begins to create connections in our neural pathways that strengthen our perception. This regulates blood sugar levels and hormone levels, which also allow us to control stress. When neuro-chemical controls are triggered, we continue to learn to change our thoughts, chemically. Hence the reason for prayer and meditation." Merlin was happy to intercede.

"Yes, exactly!" Simon interjected. "It was explained to me that we go from knowledge, to experience, to wisdom, or from mind, to body, to soul."

"Yes," Merlin agreed, "our thoughts, when concentrated on, will become our reality."

"The problem is we don't have the correct frame of reference between the scientific community and the Spiritual. It looks as though with consciousness, that a new kind of reality has been injected into our universal sphere. This is our current dimensional reality. But there are many dimensions and Nikola Tesla alluded to these because he believed that when science began to study non-physical phenomena, it would make greater progress in one decade, than in all its history." The evidence for 'non-physical' phenomenons was everywhere one looked; but one had to look!
"Yes, but how can we 'see' non-physical stuff?" Merlin argued.

"Through Mindfulness." Simon was happy to explain.

"So you are saying that our thoughts have real energy?"

"But the question I have always asked is, how can mere matter originate consciousness?" Merlin looked inspiringly up and to his right, as if attempting to draw the substance of the universe out of thin air.

"Ah! Did you notice what you just did?" Simon quizzed.

"What, I was just thinking."

"No! When you asked that question you averted your eyes towards your right frontal lobe." Simon teased. "That means you were activating your right frontal cortex to search for an answer you know is not tangible, but has Spiritual origins!"

"Really," smiled Merlin. "I was not aware that I had a Spiritual bone in my body!"

"Perhaps there is still hope for you!" Simon jested.

"I do not think you can name many great inventions that have been made by married men." – Nikola Tesla

Raising Consciousness

Monday morning and Merlin was co-opted in to a Business Economics class with a group of Year Tens. Their project was a business-plan, in which they must create a business model for a business they wish to start, and then supply a set of financial statements to back up their business model.

The teams were working well, with the exception of a group of lads, intent on furthering their social media profiles.

Merlin approached the group, asking them first to put away their mobile phones. Two of them did so reluctantly, whilst the other three glibly ignored the request.

"Lads, I have asked you to put those phones away. We are finishing your teacher's business plan, so I expect you to concentrate for the next forty minutes." The request hung like an unanswered call.

"Okay, you two! Show me the business plan." Merlin pursued them.

"We've already finished it," the first lad countered. Merlin knew his name to be Lochlan. He was a good rugby player.

This was a positive start, and Merlin was aware that the travails of rugby training were a great marker of good discipline.

"Okay great! Let's start with your Mission Plan." Merlin proposed.

"What's that?" Lochlan was confused.

"Your Mission Statement is the summary at the beginning of your business plan, which will identify what your business is about. What you want to do, its name and the purpose for the business."

"Oh! Like the summary? Here," Lochlan turned the large A2 pages of white sheet paper over.

"That's good," Merlin read down the page. "Okay, so you are going to open a shop in town, and you are selling apparel."

Lochlan looked up at Merlin. The other boy was reluctantly listening.

"Apparel is clothing, merchandise and shoes. The generic name for a clothing store." Merlin knew enough about clothing to be a reasonably well-dressed gent, but certainly not up to the street-smarts of these lads.

Reading on, he could see that they were, for all intents and purposes, going to be running a pretty successful business. Profits from month one, and by the looks of the profit and loss statement, they would be living life well.

"That is a healthy turnover you have." Merlin praised them. What kind of clothing will you sell?"

"You know, nike and adidas!" The second lad, Tom was now engaged.

'Okay, so sporting apparel?" Merlin asked.

"Yes, but also D&G and tommy Hilfiger and stuff." Tom knew his brands.

"Interesting! Okay, so you are looking at high-end stuff, with I imagine a good profit margin?"

"Yeah, it's gonna be, like in the High Street." They had got their store location sorted, it seemed.

"So, will all of you be working in the store?" Merlin looked hopefully to the lads still glued to their mobile phone screens.

"No, we are gonna have staff. You know ladies selling the stuff, like." Tom seemed to have it all worked out.

"So, you have included their salaries in the Profit and Loss?" Merlin had made a rudimentary assessment.

"Ah! Where does that go?" Tom, was now an active participant.

"Here." Merlin flipped to the profit and loss summary.

There was no allowance for salaries. This oversight would blow them out of the water.

"No worries." Merlin added. "Let's put an allocation in here for two salaries, shall we?" Merlin pointed to the statement.

"How much do we pay them?" Tom could see their profit slipping from their grasp. The other three boys fidgeted.

"This will have to be a living wage; say one thousand five hundred pounds each!" Merlin instructed.

"Okay," Tom seemed to accept that was reasonable. Writing in two amounts of one thousand five hundred pounds, he looked at the others. They continued oblivious of their predicament.

"Okay, don't forget to extrapolate that over a year, so your year end profit margins reflect the true situation." Merlin teased the equation out of them.

"That's one thousand five hundred, times by two… times by twelve…" Tom was working through his calculator on the mobile phone in his left hand, whilst twirling a blue ball-point pen like a magician in his right.

"That's thirty-six thousand pounds!" He seemed dismayed. The three social media proponents were getting distinctly uncomfortable.

"Okay, so now you must exclude that from your yearly profit." Merlin pointed to the statement.

"That makes the profit one hundred and twenty five thousand now." Tom conceded. The three minstrels were not looking happy, despite actively focusing on their screens, they had frowns of concern.

"So what if we worked instead of having ladies," the ice, was broken by Lochlan. Discipline had risen to the fore.

"Yes, that would be one option." Merlin agreed. "The other would be to focus more online, with electronic sales, which would increase your profits, without additional staff."

'Yeah, that way, we can all do the selling." Tom had not made any allowance for internet sales.

"After all, you would be using your mobile phones every day, so you could concentrate on those sales to a younger segment of your customer base!" Merlin offered.

"Doesn't that require a software program to sell," the question came form the outfield. It was Alfie.

"Yes, that means you would have to invest in a software programme and then it's maintenance." Merlin smiled, the effect was hypnotic.

"Yeah, I know a bloke who can write this kinda stuff, and he doesn't charge a million!" Alfie finally looked up from his phone.

"Okay, great!" Merlin stood back a little, making room for Alfie.

"The cost of purchasing the software is a capital expense. So it does not reflect in your profit and loss account. But you will have to pay for it with your start up money." Alfie had procured the ball-point from Tom and was already making adjustments.

Finally, the two other lads entered the circle and slipping the hand held devices into their pockets, began to actively contribute. Merlin made a mental note to engage Alfie more and more, if he was to teach him in any further classes.

"Great lads," keep going, and let's have a look at your statement when you are finished. Merlin walked away.

Twenty minutes into the class, the students were fully engaged, and with several monumental efforts being made, Merlin could see that these students had a grasp of basic economics. What was puzzling, however, was where the students had proposed they would secure their start-up business loans. Some were going to make a loan from a family member; these interestingly tended to be the more continental looking kids. There was a lass from Italy, and a lad from Greece, and each had proposed to their relevant teams, that their father's would lend them the money.

Sadly, to the English youngsters, it quickly became evident from a simple assessment that their loans would come from the banks!

Merlin knew all too well, that the likelihood was little to non-existent. But he was willing to enthuse those involved, that the potential for the success of their business models, had great merit.

As the class progressed, Tom, Lochlan, Alfie and the two unnamed lads actively engaged in resolving their potential financial dilemma. Fictional, or not, Merlin found himself smiling. These lads had a rude awakening, and it was fundamental to the success of the education system, to catch them as gently as possible, and allow a soft landing, that would not decimate their enthusiasm for life, but would provide a greater sense of realism for the time when it would certainly matter.

Merlin caught Lochlan's eye several times, and was aware of the enthusiasm garnered. At the bell, Lochlan lingered.

"Everything okay?" Merlin asked.

"Yes, thank you Sir." He grinned.

Changing track, obviously intent on saving the lad any embarrassment, Merlin quizzed; "You're a rugby player aren't you Lochlan?"

"Oh yes Sir," the pride of being recognised evident.

"Tell me, I know you are in Year ten, so you likely don't have too many friends in the lower forms, but I wanted to find out about my neighbours son, Josh. I believe he is in year eight." Merlin attempted to be as subtle as possible, feigning interest in rugby.

The averted eyes spoke volumes.

"Yeah, I think I know who you are referring to." Lochlan too, feigned anonymity of reputation. "Is he the coloured lad with the afro?"

Merlin smiled. The reference was charmingly refreshing, given the global drive for political correctness.

"Yes, he was playing rugby on Saturday, and I wandered how they had gotten on?"

"He scored a try, and he is being nominated for a county placement in the coming trials." Lochlan enthused.

"Wow, that is wonderful. I don't get to speak to his mom these days, so it is difficult to know how he is doing, without asking him directly." Merlin allowed the point to hang.

"Oh, you mean, like… his rugby and stuff?" Lochlan again averted his eyes.

Merlin was fishing, and Lochlan intuitively knew it. But the lad was no tittle-tattle. "I know his dad is not around, and it is difficult for most kids today to grow up without a father, let alone have to care for oneself, almost every day."

"They say!" The generality of commentary was remarkable. "That he was awarded a bursary to study here, and that the school wanted to strengthen the teams by bringing in ringers!" Lochlan repeated.

"Ah, yes, the age-old conundrum. Teachers and coaches intent on being the best?" Merlin posed the comment with questioning integrity, aware Lochlan already knew the answer. He was a bright lad.

"A lot of the boys think it is unfair." Lochlan had warmed to the level of discussion, like a spaniel finds the hearth.

"Do you think it is unfair?" Merlin was aware the bell had gone a while back, and the tea break meant Lochlan need not rush to his next class, but he was also aware of a certain decorum. They were in the business block, and it was somewhat isolated from the main school.

"Well… yes, it does make it difficult for most lads to get a shoe-in, when they are importing players from London schools." The conversation was sounding like a regurgitation of a dinnertime discussion.

"Let's walk back up to the canteen," Merlin offered, aware they were now the last to leave class.

"Oh, I don't have any credit on my account!" Lochlan had misinterpreted Merlin's suggestion.
"You don't?" Merlin queried. "That's not an issue, I have plenty of credit on my account." The offer was an open invitation, but Merlin knew not to push it to sound like he was currying favour.

"Oh, thank you Sir. I usually just have a toastie, but I forgot to bring my money this morning." Lochlan smiled. It was more of an embarrassed admission of carelessness, than a request for help.

"Consider it my treat, but don't let the teachers know; they love to make unnecessary judgements." Merlin laughed.

"Thank you Sir, I won't, I find Miss to be a little possessive!" Lochlan espoused.

"You mean your Economics teacher?" Merlin drew the link.

"Yes, she is a little too smothering, and that's why the class love to have you teaching." Lochlan was effusive.

"That is very kind of you Lochlan, but you know I cannot be drawn into a discussion about my teaching colleagues?"

"Yes, I understand Sir. But I wanted to ask you if you think she is a socialist?" Lochlan's brevity was alarmingly charming.

"Is that what your father says?" Merlin deflected the question.

"Yes, he says that she is a failed business-type, who has become a teacher because she could not cut it in the business world!"

"Okay! Sheeww! That is interesting, because I don't really know her. I am not at liberty to comment." But Merlin was aware of how condescending she had been towards him during the music event a month before.

Merlin had been helping in the drinks tent, and she was somewhat dismissive and almost rude about his efforts. Merlin knew he had a conspirator, but did not want to push it too far. He also knew that the education system in England had often been high-jacked by liberal-minded socialists, spewing hatred over the system that had often afforded them a descent education, but had continued pushing for socialist agendas.

"I find she talks down to me, like I am stupid." Lochlan elaborated.

"I am sorry you feel that way!" Merlin knew the symptoms.

"My dad says she probably can't get a husband because she is so controlling!" Merlin was now aware the conversation was going south.

"Yes, but don't mention that to anyone else, will you." Merlin grinned.

"Right, here we are! What was it, a toastie?" They had made their way to the canteen.

"Yes, Sir! Thank you."

In the staffroom some minutes later, Merlin found a comfortable chair, with its slowly subsiding cushion of green velour.

The study supervisors had settled in to their daily lament, so Merlin ate his sandwich and mused about his discussion with Lochlan. The lad clearly knew something about Josh that he was not letting him onto. This would have to be a very gradual prying-open of the truth, which Merlin suspected was going to lead down a rabbit warren he surely did not want to go. But if it were to lead into a land of unchartered territory, he would have to put his brave face on and venture down that 'yellow brick road' with a skip in his step, and a sympathetic ear.

There were layer upon layer of unspoken truths that the system hid from public view. But it was evident, that when altruistic teachers and administrators opened the Pandora's Box of inter-ethnicity, there were huge cultural and socio-economic consequences at stake. Whether it was for a greater cause, or a selfish quest for greatness, would only be revealed in time, but the sadness, was that there were always victims. Whenever change was required, and the status quo was challenged, some one, somewhere would be its consequential victim.

Merlin mulled the conversation over, debating the pros and cons. He was a mile away, when the first bell rang, to resume classes.

"It was almost as if LSD provided the human consciousness with access to a kind of infinite subway system, a labyrinth of tunnels and byways that existed in the subterranean reaches of the unconscious, and one that literally connected everything in the universe with everything else."

— Michael Talbot, The Holographic Universe

The Understanding

The week slipped past expeditiously, with Merlin making contributions of significance, or at least to his mind, making a difference for some lost soul. The school was positioned neatly between three major economic sectors of society. These were the children of commuters to London, the local business interests, and then the communities of the South East, built over centuries of localised industries, some of which were entrenched in the folklores of the region.

But there was one arena that really intrigued Merlin. From a sociology perspective, he found the religiosity aspect, an intriguing arena. Not unlike the ancient city of Ephesus, a Mediterranean city, perched between the vast chasms of belief systems, of middle-eastern superstitions and the Roman conquered world of reformist moderation, which was dictated by personalised gods and an open society representation.

That ancient society had been the singularly most diverse accumulation of cultures and beliefs, ever drawn together into one city, numbering in the millions according to archaeological studies and historical records.

Ephesus was a cosmopolitan society of Roman citizens, and the mish-mash of Diasporean businessmen and the intelligentsia of Greek, Jewish, and an accumulation of every culture from the known world of the time. Interestingly, the slave population of Ephesus outnumbered the Roman citizenship by a factor of three. Theirs was a society where work requirements for manual labour and those jobs deemed to be beneath the station of the elite class, were provided by imported slaves. Strangely enough, not unlike West Scowlsdown!

Ephesus had survived centuries because it was governed with an iron fist, but given a free-reign to explore freedom of religion and expression, within reason. West Scowlsdown, originally had been a society of retirees, care homes, and an expanding overflow from the London suburbs. The reality was that as longevity had ensured a vastly aging population in England, carers had to be brought in to help with the exploding number of positions required for a burgeoning Health Care Industry.
West Scowlsdown was no different to Ephesus in many ways. Within the confines of Sussex, it was fundamentally driven by market forces arranged around the modern-day facets of economic dynamism. But, sadly, the imported workers were deemed to be little more than modern day slaves.

However, lurking within the bedrock of the South Downs, was a peculiar Spirituality that had drawn every religious and Spiritual group from around the world, catering for this hodgepodge of humanity, a cornucopia of cultures, ethnicity and convictions, where every religion, to a greater or lesser extent, was represented. Unlike the effectiveness of the Roman occupation of Ephesus, West Scowlsdown had been abandoned by any effective policing authority so it was left to the community to police itself!

From the temples that stood out on the approaches from London, to the vast labyrinth of science-based beliefs arrayed across the estates of the eastern hills, and back to the neatly appointed churches of the old establishment, the town was a plethora of somewhat quirky and often new-age religions.

West Scowlsdown stood as a testament to the willingness of an open society to embrace free speech and beliefs. But to Merlin there was one major area that was not represented, and it troubled him. Despite the town's willingness to embrace an open society, he was aware, almost to a degree of being pained by its absence, that there was no actively open LGBTQ+ community.

Was religion at such grandiose divergence of thought, to the open societies of ancient Ephesus; and if so, who and what were to blame?

Saturday morning could have not come quick enough. Merlin was up and off to the library before he would have to run into Josh, or his mother. There was a disquiet that verged on discomfort every time he had seen Josh in the hallways of the school, and Merlin was determined to get some good advice.

Simon arrived a little later than expected, but nonetheless with the requisite humour and enthusiasm he had endeared himself to Merlin for. He wanted to ask a favour of Merlin, but it could wait until after their coffee.

"Si, I had a long discussion with a youngster at school this week, and I want your opinion on something?" The question imposed no prerequisite for formality.

"Yes, of course, if I can help, I will."

"You know that West Scowlsdown has a reputation amongst the younger folk for drugs, and many nefarious activities?" Merlin brushed away convention.

"Yes, I think I may have mentioned County Lines before." Simon was un-phased.

"Let's say a youngster wanted to get his hands on some drugs, where would he go?" Merlin quizzed.

"What? In this town! Just about anywhere, sadly." Simon said, adding.

"The main places are the park, the clubs, and definitely the area opposite that fast-food restaurant on the main road where all the youngsters hang out." Simon was concise.

"Okay, because I was aware of the park, especially around the pond, because I have seen the lads entering and leaving there when I finish my swim session in the evenings." Merlin agreed.

"Yes, I suppose anywhere today is likely, given the availability of mobile phones and the drug dealers use the system to their advantage. Like I said before, they use 'burner phones' Disposable mobile phones so they cannot be traced." Merlin was glad he had asked, as Simon had his ear to the ground.

"The local nightclub was closed as a result of gang violence and drugs, but by closing it, the authorities have simply driven it underground." Simon added.

"Yes I know about the nightclub, but who would you say are the main suppliers now?" Merlin quizzed further.

It is mostly small time gangs, with the drugs being ferried into West Scowlsdown by train!" Simon reiterated the County Lines issue.

"Okay, so the drugs arrive by train, but who are the local dealers?"

"Any one of those guys in their German sports cars, who literally drive from one park to the next, coordinating the deals with these young lads collecting the contraband from a pre-defined location. They handle the drugs, so that the real culprits cannot be prosecuted." Simon elaborated.

"The lads who are carrying the drugs get paid, often in contraband, therefore ensuring the dealers have a willing work force." Simon knew the evil of the system was perpetuated by addiction, and the dealers knew the young lads were cannon fodder!

"Yes, I have seen those young lads, no more than boys, cycling through the park." Merlin knew this to be true, and this was despite there being cameras all along London Road, and in the park.

"Why? Has Josh been up to his usual antics?" Simon was brief.

"Well, yes, and I have an inkling that he might be involved with something even more nefarious than I originally thought; and he is only fourteen years old!" merlin lamented.

"That's nothing! These scumbags, who run the County Lines, use kids as young a nine to ferret their drugs all over the country." Simon was disdainful of the low-life's who exploit these lads.

"There is a recent example of a dealer called Syed Ahmed, who was caught out by an undercover officer, trying to sell heroin to an underage girl. Because of the fact that he was caught in an illegal sting, he walked free." Simon was all too aware of the need to prevent the peddling and misery that was causing deaths.

"I know how you feel. Isn't amazing that these scumbags use those 'Woke' laws to escape justice, but the victims don't. They end up in Crack Houses in Crawley and what's worse is that a friend of mine, whom I had been mentoring, has disappeared recently!" Simon had tried to counsel Reece, but he was unwilling to listen.

"The problem today, is that the police cannot prosecute these youngsters, because they are protected under a new regulation that is intended to curb slave-labour.

Ironically, a law which was intended to protect the very people who are importing these drugs is being used to protect their supply chain!" Simon was adamant.

"You mean that, when they catch the kids who are carrying the drugs, they cannot be arrested?" Merlin asked.

"Yes. The police have had a ten-fold increase in the number of slave-labour crimes reported, because when they do catch the kids involved in County Lines, they cannot hold them. The kids have been told to claim they are being forced to carry the drugs, by the sleaze balls who are making all the money; whilst the kids are then placed on Anti-social Barring lists." Simon explained.

"The crime gangs lure children into becoming drug mules by telling them they will not be punished if they say they were coerced," Simon lashed out explosively; "That is a legal defence in the Modern Slavery Act, intended for human-trafficking victims! It is unfair, but often these kids are mostly savvy to what is going on." Simon reiterated.

"So these gangs are using the very laws intended to help the innocent victims of slave labour, to profit themselves; how ironic!" Merlin shook his head.

"Look, when you invite strangers into your home, it is usually with an incitement to do good. But this system does not know who they are inviting!" Simon used a basic analogy frowned on by the liberal bleeding hearts.

"Yes, so you are saying the problem is we have been too lenient with our open-minded attitude towards immigration?" Merlin recognised there was a social agenda being played out at government level.

"I also believe it has so much more to do with the speed with which we have attempted to incorporate foreign communities into our society." Simon elaborated.

"Having lived in Johannesburg, I am mostly in favour of diverse societies, but the authorities here are to blame. The institutional powers opened the doors to immigrants in the fifties and sixties, because of the need for manual labour workers, and a workforce requirement to rebuild the infrastructure after the war." Merlin listened intently.

"But, what transpired is that we opened the doors to all sorts of illegal activities, as the vast swathe of Caribbean and Pakistan immigrants, brought with them a legacy of cultural and societal permissiveness in the realm of drugs and polygamy. The muslims have destroyed many inner-city areas of the North, and have brought with them a tide of terror and trafficking. But, don't criticise them, or you'll be labelled a racist." Simon smiled ruefully.

"But despite their religious beliefs, some seem adverse to our more traditional taboos engrained into this society during a century of Victorian prohibitions." Merlin intonated a chasm that was evident in some Northern cities where young girls were targeted.

"I understand those prohibitions, but whenever you bring two opposing cultures together, it may either work; or they will clash!" The evidence showed a significant clashing.

"Yes, but those laws which were a legacy of our historical correctness have no place in our society today. I think the government has gone too far." Merlin was aware of most social ills of multi-culturalism.

"My sense of this dichotomy, is that it is a cultural disaster, waiting to happen. But it has to be said, that if the government had the intention to create fear and division among social classes, the easiest way to control a population is through diversity." Simon was realistically pessimistic, despite being usually sanguine.

"It's a catch-twenty-two situation?" Merlin appraised.

"The average man in the street recognises these sociological paradigms, but naming and shaming has become a British sport. The media have a go at anyone they believe is anti-Semitic, or who maintains a dim view of black neighbourhoods in the cities; but the truth is they are awash with crime and violence." Merlin recognised the need for a balanced approach to the immigration issue. Britain was a cultural synthesis of many European cultures, and with the invasion of Britain over the past two thousand years from every tribe imaginable, the country was incredibly diverse and forward thinking.

"I recognise all the same symptoms South Africa was labelled with, but we must remember, when the Witwatersrand was invaded by every culture imaginable over a hundred years ago, there was an obvious natural apartheid that existed. The English lived in the Northern suburbs, the Portuguese and Italians in the South and East, and the Jews collected the rent!" Simon paused; Merlin grinned.

"Oh! I get it. But South Africa was a largely unpopulated country, with only the tribal areas inhabited. The Dutch farmers could not have cared less who were their neighbours, as long as they were able to continue farming." Merlin had studied the sociological values of apartheid; it worked, purely from a cultural values point of view.

"Yes, and the Zionist bankers and money-men only arrived after the Boers had established the Boer Republics. But the Zionists not only wanted the gold resources, they went after the tax revenues from the mining companies. President Kruger was targeted because he was the fall-guy for the Rothschild's, who with the help of Rhodes had already usurped the Kimberly Diamond fields; so they went after the gold too." Simon reminded.

"That was The Boer War? Yes, I understand that it was the Jewish money that financed the war against the Dutch settlers, and if we remember how the British fought that war; we should hang our heads in shame!" Merlin had no doubts as the machinations of the political class in Britain, then and now.

"Wars are financed and benefit the super-rich only, and remember who controls the purse-strings both here and in America." The tone was accusatory.

"It does not take much research to see that when Henry Kissinger visited China in 1973, it was at the behest of the Zionists." Simon vilified those evil tyrants.

"Ah, yes it was Mao Zedong, who was a Chinese communist revolutionary and who was the founder of the People's Republic of China, who led as the chairman of the Chinese Communist Party in 1976." Merlin gave his assessment.

"Those communists took the Zionists' money and now the Fentanyl is flowing through our streets." Simon spat out the word.

"Afghanistan was awash with Heroin, as it was in the days of the Opium Wars in China. But now the Chinese Triads are entrenched in London, even operating their businesses out of The Shard, and yet the authorities turn a blind eye!" There was a cultural enigma even Simon could not explain.

"But is that not Karmic Justice?" Merlin offered.

"Yes, it is somewhat ironic that the British colonialists pushed the trade of opium in the nineteenth century, which sparked those wars, but the key to what I believe is missing, is the connection between the Zionists and those within the C.C.P. who proliferate the trade of drugs now!" Simon conceded.

"Is it not all about profits?" Merlin asked.

"Yes, it is, and I have always maintained, when one wants to learn about a so-called 'conspiracy' just follow the money."

"But when we say diversity is the essential concrete of a society, there is usually a caveat, and that is where social cohesion exists, it is because those within a community have shared values." Merlin offered.

"But when we purposely exclude the cement of those who want to make it work, then we have social disorder!" Simon used a familiar analogy.

"Why do you believe that the government would purposely create social unrest? Surely that is counter-productive to law and order?" Merlin was candid.

"Okay, when was the last time you saw a 'bobby-on-the-beat'?" The question hung like the proverbial guillotine.

"Not in ten years," Merlin conceded.

"Exactly, and yet despite cameras on every corner, drug-dealers are never brought to justice!"

Simon let the consequence of remote-policing lay suspended as an African mirage, shimmering in full view, but inconceivable to the eye.

"Law enforcement has failed this country, and it is because we have become a liberal society of leftist lunatics. The bleeding-heart liberals have sold this country to the highest bidders, and the youth are the victims!" Simon was uncharacteristically vocal.

"Are you saying that this is a strategy of some sort?" Merlin understood the makings of conspiracies.

"Well, if the statistics are to be believed, we have seen a reduction in the number of drug-related arrests in the past ten years, and the number of deaths due to drug overdoses has doubled in the same period!" Simon fought linguistically with the stats.

"Oh! That does not auger well for a functioning society!" Merlin conceded.

"Most of those deaths, nearly four and a half thousand last year, were a result of Fentanyl being shipped into this country in vast amounts!" Simon was on a mission.

"Fentanyl is a synthetic pain-killer, manufactured in China, in factories, and the Chinese government has invested heavily in port authorities all over the world, and through the investments they are able to control the flow of goods!" Simon just let the detail simmer for a moment.

"Think about that! The Chinese government are completely aware of where those drugs are manufactured, shipped and sold. This is a reverse policy to The Opium Wars of the nineteenth century, when Britain allowed the trade of heroine to flow into China. Its 'tit-for-tat' if you ask me, and they are openly attempting to undermine social structures in the West!"

Merlin gazed in amazement. Surely this was an exaggeration, but knowing how well Simon researched the information he spoke, he suspected not!

"The truth is that the Chinese government has massive control of world trade routes, and now they control other countries and their governments through the purchasing power of their industrial success. But the Chinese did not simply get the funds to begin mass-producing the goods they now sell, by simply snatching it from out of the air; there was massive investment in chine from the early 'seventies' and guess who were the investors?" The question was hung out like a piece of rice-paper to dry.

"The British government has allowed China to become too influential in local politics and economics. Just as Chamberlain tried to appease Hitler in 1939, this government is holding a rabid tiger by the tail, and it is the youth of our society who are getting bitten. This is a war, regardless of political niceties, and our lads have become the boy soldiers!"

"Yes, isn't it interesting how the government has now opted to send the Queen Elizabeth Aircraft Carrier Group to the South-China Sea?" Merlin had seen that great aircraft carrier in dry-docks in Portsmouth on one of his regular trips.

"But, remember, that aircraft carrier was ordered twenty years ago!" There was an air of conspiracy laid bare in his whisper.

"Yes! Strange that we would have needed to invest in aircraft carriers, when we were only fighting terrorists in Iraq and Afghanistan. But remember, without the American F-35 jet fighters, that carrier group would be pointless!" The evidence of a bi-lateral deal between America and the Blair government had been the carrot-on-the-stick to get Britain embroiled in the most nonsensical war of the past century.

"Oh! I wasn't aware of that aspect!" Merlin conceded.

"Yes, the deal with Blair was done at the time Bush junior was raring to bomb the hell out of Iraq!" Simon grinned; it was no laughing matter, but in his mind, there was a huge conspiracy involved.

"Didn't Blair sign a deal with Bush to supply components for that aircraft?" Merlin had read this somewhere.

"The engine and vertical lift systems are Rolls Royce, and the electronics are BAE, both United Kingdom based companies. The deal was for twenty-five thousand jobs to be created in Britain!" The point Simon was making, was to highlight that yet again it was the money-factor that dictated war.

"That makes sense." Merlin could visualise that maggot Blair, sitting with Bush, divvying out the lions-share of the money to be made from the deal. It would not be unlike them to have bought shares in the major arms manufacturing companies!

"Even if you were a complete cynic in regard to conspiracies, the profits Lockheed Martin have made since the First Gulf War are staggering. But, the share price suddenly shot up over thirty-thousand Dollars, as soon as 911 happened!" Simon knew that Blair had been offered shares in those companies at basement-discount prices. Twenty years later and he was a multi-millionaire; but like the larvae laid by the profiteering of those who had sent thousands of men to die in Iraq, Blair's legacy was now so loathsome, his credibility was non-existent; but yet he still believed he had the right to keep harping on about BREXIT!

"Wars are always profitable for those in 'the know'! But I have a sense that the truth is coming out, little-by-little, and regardless of how much the Mainstream Media try to spin it, there will be a reckoning." Simon added.

"Yes", Merlin agreed.

"The latest Raytheon Scram Jet missiles travel at three-thousand five hundred miles per hour and the Americans and British have China firmly in their sights!" Simon elaborated. "The irony is that the Vice-President of Lockheed Martin and the father of the latest scram-jet technology is William Blair, and he is a war-hawk, like his namesake!"

"It is all so incestuous." Merlin agreed.

"The Lockheed Martin Skunkworks, is the brainchild of the Shadows, and in my opinion, the technology we know about, is a fraction of what we are being told about." Simon loved the conspiracy story about alien technology.

"Isn't that always the story?" Merlin was a fan of the Excalibur mythology; that sword had been no less devastating a weapon; adding:

"What do you mean by 'The Shadows'?"

"The Military Industrial Complex. But now we have the Medical Industrial Complex, as well as The Media Industrial Complex!"

"Yes, wasn't it President Kennedy who warned everyone about them?" Merlin had heard his speech when he was a student in college, but had not understood the nuances of that fatal warning.

"Yes, but not just Kennedy, there were many who recognised the rise of those in the shadows of society, pulling the strings in government and the military; President Eisenhower also warned the world about the Military Industrial Complex in his very last speech he made." Simon understood the dangers these men had spoken out about! He was all too aware of the rise of a shadow government which had taken control of the economic transactions in America, and the world.

"And remember on September the Tenth, 2001, the U.S. Defence Secretary Donald Rumsfeld disclosed that his Department was unable to account for roughly two-point-three trillion dollars' worth of transactions."

"One day later, the entire world had changed!" Simon allowed that thought to sink in.

"Do you believe that there could be a war between The West and China?" Merlin broached.

"Absolutely! But what I find of interest, is that the complicities' of Raytheon and Grumman, who manufacturer those missiles, can be traced all the way back to the Gatling Gun manufactured in America in the nineteenth century, after the British bought the rights to manufacture it, the Birmingham Small Arms company was eventually founded; but not before the Brits wiped out thousands of my fellow South Africans with that gun in The Boer War!" Simon lamented.

"Yes, I know that Britain has been a war-mongering nation for centuries." The distaste of British war legacy, a vile flavour in his mouth; but Merlin was pragmatic. If the British had not done so, then it would have been the French, or the Spanish.

"Well, their taste for war is something China had better be very conscious of!" Simon spat out those words.

"If these wars are planned decades, or even more in advance by those in power, then the real conspiracy is when we all keep quiet." The evidence of war looming on the South China Sea was evident to all with any intellect.

"But the war on drugs is another matter entirely!" Simon continued.

"The drugs issue has really only become an epidemic, since the European Union opened its doors to every Tom, Dick and Harry from Eastern Europe and the Middle East." Merlin complained.

"You mean, every Faz, Baz and Shaz?" Simon was merciless.

"Yes, but the trade routes between the East and the West have been around since the time of Jesus, so little has changed, despite those who now profit. Remember the Silk Route has now been superseded by the Chinese Silk-Road Initiative. The only country standing in the way, of that complete globalisation is Iran." Simon spoke his truth.

"But," Simon continued, "The Chinese and Iranians are happily doing business today and they want desperately to build an oil pipeline between the two countries. They call it 'The Belt and Road Initiative', and it is how the drugs like Fentanyl are being shipped. The whole saga is a complex cornucopia of profiteering, with everyone out to benefit themselves. But add to that our ruling class's persuasiveness towards political correctness, and anyone mildly critical of the system is shut down mercilessly. What we have, is a recipe for disaster! My sense is that we are damned if we do, and damned if we don't!"

"You mean, we can't speak out about the failures of our society because someone might get upset?" Merlin conceded.

"Yes! Exactly. The ruling elite have control of the medium of information dissemination through the mainstream media, and now all of social media as well! They own the newspapers and the television networks, so they can spread this multi-cultural time bomb at will, giving no credence to the damage it has on the lower classes, whilst they sit in their ivory towers and orchestrate the damaging effects it has on social cohesion." South Africa had also been the whipping-boy of the powers in The City.

"Just remember who benefitted from the annihilation of the Boer Government in South Africa. The Rothschild's and their ilk couldn't have given a toss about the black mine workers; what they were after was control of the gold and diamonds. Once Rhodes was dead, they had control of De Beers and then they set to work accumulating the gold mines and more strategically, the taxation of those mining companies." Simon explained.

"Do you see a parallel with what is happening in China?" Merlin had gained a sense of where this was leading.

"Likely! But they will be a little more subtle this time round. They know that world opinion would be against the flattening of China, but by de-stabilising the Chinese Communist Party and gaining control of the PLA, the Chinese army, navy and air force, they fundamentally would control the economic wealth of Chinese industry." Simon postulated.

"In the meantime, they create division amongst our populations in the West, and control public discourse by the threatening language of political correctness!" Merlin's voice rose as his emotion intonated that displeasure of social-hegemony.

"There is a wickedness within the evidentiary facts of this social-engineering. But, even so, my sense is they will lose, just as Hitler lost ultimately. Remember, he tried to socially-engineer the German people by force; here, they use vitriol and involuntary subservience to silence dissenters. The one major ally we have on our side, is the evidence of the rottenness of their systematic efforts to manipulate public opinion. The facts are all around us, in the parks and in the general degradation of social values, starting with the war on drugs." Simon believed it all started in the fifties and sixties, but now it was an epidemic; adding.

"Social engineering is everywhere!"

"Yes, it is alarming to see how many adverts on television depict cross-culture and mixed marriages!" Merlin agreed. "It's completely out of synch with the true demographics of our society. When the youngsters get bombarded with these images, it becomes a way of life. But what they neglect is that the more you force-feed a child, the worse will be the obesity!" The analogy made sense.

"Don't get me started on that! The bloody industry is to blame. The liberals have a hand in this slime of society, and casting agencies are happy to employ non-unionised actors, because they will pay them less than the union rates. The scourge is based on pure greed." Something told Merlin, Simon was not a fan. They both laughed, breaking the tension.

"This is all about political correctness. You know, I make a mental note of every company peddling this charade, and I won't purchase anything they are offering because I don't have to!" Simon endorsed.

"It is so sad, but it is incredibly misguided." Merlin understood the damage that anti-social conventions played, when a society felt the need to push-back against authority. It was evident by the rise of the Brexit Party, and the desire to reverse decades of decay in social etiquette that had resulted in the dumbing-down of British society. Heaven forbid, even Merlin's cousin had felt the need to vote for Brexit, and he was a socialist!

"But apart from voting with our wallets, how else can ordinary folk voice their displeasure?" Simon added.

"There is one revelation that occurs to me, and that is possibly, a positive aspect of migration!" Merlin allowed Simon a moment to catch his breath; this was not expected.

"Migration may be a vital aspect of human development, from the point of view that, in order for population groups to survive, and tribes to proliferate, competition is vital. The increasing number of muslims and blacks in the United Kingdom has forced the indigenous Anglophiles to start thinking about bigger families once more. Competition for women has meant that white men have once more become virile and aggressive. With increased prosperity, diets have become more protein oriented, and white men are growing in stature." Merlin laid out his argument with a degree of rationale.
"I see your point!" Simon nodded.

"The reducing populations of Anglo-Saxon and Caucasian populations since the war have had many positive benefits to our longevity and enhanced health, but Britain and many European countries have a paradox to contend with; the well-fare state!" Merlin pronounced his remedy.

"If populations do not increase, the Pension Funds will be bankrupt, and the political class recognise this." Merlin continued.
"Ah! Yes, I read an article about this many years ago, when Italy was considering allowing migration across the Mediterranean." The macro-economic issue was centre-stage.

"Indeed! But the good news is that there is a solution, so to speak!" Merlin smiled.

"What's that?" Simon sensed where he was going.

"In-vitro-insemination." Merlin raised his eyebrows comically.

"Oh! You mean to get the population going again?" The number of women requiring IVF was growing proportionately to the number of working women.

"No! I literally mean 'Sperm-banks'! Merlin wasn't smiling. He was being serious.

"What was the favour you wanted to ask of me?" He remembered.

"Oh! Yes, you know I do not have a car presently? Would you mind if I were to borrow yours next Saturday? I have an errand to run."

"Yes, or course. I will simply need to arrange some insurance."

"Thank you Merl, I am indebted."

"Nonsense, don't think any more of it!" Merlin was assured.

"If you don't believe in something, you'll fall for anything. I believe everything happens for a reason. If you are strong from within, you can will anything. I'm a firm believer that where there's a will, there's a way."

-   **Eric Davis**

Chasing Subjectivity

Another week of challenging classes and Merlin was on a roll. The students we had been teaching regularly, had now developed a rapport with him, and gotten to know what were his trigger points, but had not overstepped their boundaries. Merlin was at pains to ensure they did not make him a victim of the system as the other Study Supervisors had become.

During the course of the week, Merlin had found himself in another Beliefs and Values class, but this time on his own, without the 'little witch' he had come to call his muslim colleague. She had the air of superficiality that often came with her class. Privileged by the rights of her social standing within a community that seemed hell bent on trying to embrace every creed, colour and instance of social interaction with anyone from anywhere in the world, Merlin had recognised a flaw that showed in relief just how vacuous she was.

Every morning for the past three weeks, Saima had bemoaned her fate, which was that of a working-class mom, with three growing lads, one of whom was in school. She was constantly tired, and it was not due to her fervent acknowledgement of Fasting, a month long activity, which had been and gone!

No, what Merlin had observed was the feminine wiles of a woman, bereft of any social standing within her household, who knew how to turn on the sympathy vote, with colleagues whom she was able to manipulate into taking classes she felt emotionally incapable of administering.

So it had been, that Saima, had asked Merlin to cover her B&V class for that morning, and Merlin had agreed, happily knowing that the alternative was a boring class of Year Sevens, in a language lab. Saima was bereft of any values, or so Merlin had come to realise, when he had overheard her talking down to a young lad, who was challenged by a debilitating form of A.D.H.D.

It was to the abject failure of the system, that teachers, albeit Study Supervisors with no teaching qualification were unleashed onto a group of adolescents, themselves suffering every form of emotionally challenged hormonal deprivation known to humankind.

The system was failing the most sensitive to changes, and in refusing the funding required, the Education Department limited by budgetary constraints, forced these schools, which were having to opt for the most cost-efficient tools to fill the vacancies posed by an over-regulated education system.

So, Merlin found himself in a class of Year Eights, whose parents in the main had relinquished all sense of moral servitude to a Higher Source, by revoking their rights, to a government sponsored secular society. It was hugely evident that religion was frowned on in most homes, and being a non-church goer, Merlin could sympathise with them.

However, life and circumstances had taught him, that there was some credence to the value of a higher calling, despite what the consumer driven zealots on television might wish to spin. If, as Merlin suspected, Consumerism had become their new god, then society was likely to be challenged by a moral compass that spun in which ever direction the media would wish to see it spin.

The mere fact that Religious Education had been dumbed down to Beliefs & Values, made it patently clear to all with any semblance of a moral compass, that the system would be able to redirect those Beliefs & Values on a whim. Merlin understood how each generation was challenged with its own moral gravity, through which the state-sponsored 'talking-heads' on television, would manipulate the discourse. This was a subject in sociology, very near and dear to his heart.

"Good morning class." Merlin was waiting for them as they entered.

"Sir, sir! Oh its you!" A cry for help which, Merlin had found welcoming, but concerning of late.

"We like having you teach us," they all cooed. The smiles evidence that he was doing something right.

"That is very rewarding for me to hear." Merlin was flippant. But underlying this assertion, he gauged a more troubling grievance.

"Okay, just because it is me, does not mean you have the right to slack off. Today, we are going to discuss a very interesting subject, and I guarantee you will learn something new!"

"Sir, I'm so glad it's you and not that other lady." It was Jason, a young lad with a penchant for the dramatic.

"Okay, I know you have an issue with Mrs Mohammed, but I have to keep a neutral position. Let's settle down and take out your work books." Merlin surveyed the class.

"But Sir, she called me stupid!" Jason was insistent.

"Jason. If that is so, I suggest you speak with me after class. This is a worrying issue!" Merlin was aware of the possibility of exaggeration, but the school code meant he was service bound to take this further.

"She did Sir, I promise you." Jason pleaded.

"Okay, I will investigate this further and have a word with her." Merlin suspected that if there were grounds for exaggeration, the thought of him speaking with Saima would either call his bluff, or not.

"Thank you Sir!" Jason smiled.

That was the last thing he had expected, and now armed with this affirmation, he made a mental note to speak with her. No wonder she did not wish to teach the class!

"Today we are going to look at the theme, 'The Environment: What have we done to our world.'" Merlin paused, looked up to see who had shown any interest. Great; he had a full house!

"Great! Our task today is to write down ten key words that speak to the real issue of the environment and what humans have been responsible for in terms of the changes we see."

"Sir, Sir," it was Jason. "I was watching a video on YouTube that says it is all a hoax!"

"Thank You Jason. What exactly is it that they are saying is a hoax?"
"Global warming and climate change Sir." Jason had an audience.

"Yes, Sir," it was Oscar. He was a small lad with an extremely vivid imagination. "Sir, are you a 'Time Traveller'?"

"Yes Oscar, I am a time traveller, and I am travelling down the aisle right now to re-focus your attention on page 94 of your book." The class erupted with appropriate humour.

"Yes, Oscar, you're an alien!" Jason led the pack.

"Okay, let's not dissolve into personal attacks." Merlin cautioned.

"Well Sir, if you were a time traveller, you would be able to go back in time and warn everyone about climate change?" He posed it as a clever rhetorical question, rather than a statement.

"Ah! I get your angle." Merlin conceded. "Does anyone else have any other good reasons for me to be a time traveller?"

"Yes, Sir, if you were a time traveller, you would be able to go forward in time to see if it is a hoax!" It was Josh. Merlin had not seen him arrive. He was standing at the door.

Merlin smiled. The ice was finally broken.

"Thank you Josh," He gestured to the lad to find a seat.

"Okay, great answer Josh." He allowed him to find his seat and the two lads in his circle made way for him to sit between them. Merlin noted a reverence of sorts. An unchallenged rites of passage, made all the more evident by his bulk in comparison to the other lads.

"Indeed. The question we must ask ourselves is; 'If we had the technology to travel through time, would we have good reason to question our motives today, or would we simply be reneging on our fundamental responsibility to good governance today?" Merlin asked.

"I think that if we could time travel, we would not have to worry about what we do today." Oscar replied. Merlin could sense the makings of a useful ally.

"Okay Oscar. Let's say you are correct, and that if we could all time travel, we would be able to live our lives today, and treat the environment disrespectfully, and then go back in time and relive it when the whole world is a cesspit." Merlin let the thought sink in.

"Would that make us responsible for whatever happened, if we could not reverse the effects of climate change?" Merlin continued.

"Sir, if we were responsible for causing irreparable damage to our environment today, what would be different if we went back in time to fix it? We would still be the same people, with the same values." Josh spoke up.

"Thank you Josh. Yes! Indeed. If we could time travel Oscar, we would end up in a sort of 'time warp', where we would have to keep going back and resetting the clock, because we would not have learned anything new about ourselves." Merlin was effusive.

"If we cannot take responsibility for our actions today; then we will never learn from our mistakes. The whole purpose of a linear, time constraint in the physical world, is to ensure that we progress as humans in this lifetime."

"So you're saying we have multiple lifetimes?" Oscar inferred.

"Yes. I believe we do not simply have one existence." Merlin found himself in unchartered waters.

"Let's say, I was born for a specific purpose, and that purpose was to teach you all one single piece of evidence for your own lives; what would you wish me to teach you?" Merlin offered.

"I would want to know where we came from." Oscar piped up.

"I want to know what the purpose of life is!" Josh was more introspective. And Merlin heard a myriad of differing questions.

"I would want to know when the lunch bell will ring." The sarcasm was from Jason.

"Well Jason that does not inform me of who you are, other than a hungry lad! But your assertion is wrong, because you are able to define when the bell will toll!" Merlin infused his answer with a level of repartee, he knew would be lost on the class.

The class, nonetheless descended into guffaws of laughter aimed not a Jason, but at an unspoken understanding that Merlin was using his wit and the class was encouraged by that challenge.
"Sir, what does that have to do with multiple lives?" Oscar was unrelenting.

"Good point Oscar! Yes, the purpose of having multiple lives, is that of enlightenment. We are all born with one objective, and that I believe is to awaken our consciousness. So, if we were able to time travel we would not be awakening that consciousness, and subsequently we will have learned nothing." Merlin swung round, picked up a marker pen, and then, drew a line along the entire length of the white board. Placing several points along the length, he demarcated points in time.

"Okay, Oscar, show me on this line where you would want to be, if this line represented an historical period of say, five thousand years."

"Alright," Oscar jumped to his feet, and headed for the front, ever the first to define his place in the pecking order.

"I want to be here," Oscar placed a line on the board, writing his name 'Oskar' with the black marker pen. The point was right at the end of the right side of the board.

"Good. What do you think that says about you?" Merlin quizzed.

"That I want to be a time traveller!" Oscar reiterated.

"Yes, but more importantly, what it tells me is that you want to know what will happen in the future. Yes?" Merlin held his gaze.

"Yes, but that is why I want to be able to time travel, because I want to know what will happen in the future!"

"And that is entirely understandable. But I would challenge you to explore your sense of destiny! I would challenge you all," Merlin turned back to the class. "I would challenge you all to ask yourselves how you can make a difference in this world, because it is that contribution that will make a difference in our future world."

"I get it," Josh spoke up again. "We cannot be expected to change our world for the better, if we don't step up and contribute!"

"Yes, exactly right," Merlin ushered Oscar back to his seat, kindly resting his hand on his shoulder all the way.

"Are you saying that you believe that we all have multiple lives on this earth, and that we keep coming back as different human beings?" Josh was circumspect.

"Yes, I suppose I am!" Merlin smiled, inwardly reflecting on a life well spent. "Imagine yourselves coming back as another person, in the future, then imagine what kind of person you would want to be, and in doing so, you are raising your consciousness to a level, that will fulfil your existing life going forward. You see; I believe that we are all given certain talents, and we can use those for benefiting the world, or just ourselves. When we learn to use those talents to benefit society and the people around us, we have already raised our consciousness level."

"It will be your generation, who will determine what the environment looks like in the next twenty to fifty years. Think about what your contribution could be, then write down ten points that you believe can make a difference."

The class looked enthused, then one by one they opened their workbooks and began to write.

Back in the staffroom the opportunity presented itself for a discussion with Patrick, a short, somewhat diminutive teacher of political science. The subject fascinated Merlin, and with a background in sociology, Patrick was forthcoming in his assessment of the interaction of socialization and politics.

It was clear to Merlin, that politicians were for the most part psychopathic, with a tendency towards prevarication of facts. The road to a political career was paved with many flag stones and it was clear, in speaking to Patrick, the majority were set in somewhat shallow foundations.

It was the first meaningful conversation Merlin had with anyone since joining the school and he felt somewhat redeemed to have had the opportunity. In the background, with his back facing the array of chairs set forth for the Study Supervisors, a makeshift social curtain was drawn.

The staffroom was peculiar in that it was intended to be a retreat for adult conversation, safe from the drudgery of the working day; but the reality was far from the truth!

Having had his conversation with Patrick, and an ensuing discussion inevitably was broached regarding BREXIT, Merlin stayed in his seat when the after-lunch bell rang. Armed with a book on the politics of 21st century European governmental influences, Merlin settled in to have a good read.

Unbeknown to him, four Study Supervisors had also settled down for a break from the rudimentary cover work incumbent on the lesser class. Oblivious to the usual fare of post-congratulatory war stories, Merlin was well into the second chapter of a somewhat beguiling, but frank analysis of the evils of Open Society dogma, foisted on the Hungarian Parliamentary system, when a word crept insidiously into his subconscious antennae.

It was the middle-aged veteran, and she was positioned at the computer, on a table steadfastly allocated to providing resources required for any reputable Study Supervisor. The computer was evidently opened up to the school information management system, on which every detail from age, school records and dietary requirements, for every child in the education system was stored.

"This is the trans-child I was telling you about." Her voice was pitched just loud enough for Merlin to hear the social stigmatisation in her tone.

"What, you're kidding!" It was bearded-man and he had leapt from his chair, to view what was on view.

"She identifies as a boy, and we are not allowed to refer to her as a girl!" The veteran was a master of the social-justice warriors, or as Merlin deemed, social-worriers.

"You mean it?" The question was pointedly aimed lower than the belt.

"I've had her in my class, and she wears boys' clothes!" The hijab-clad lady was saying.

Merlin rose, he headed straight to the door, and without any acknowledgement of having over-heard them, he headed for the sanctuary of the men's toilet.

The staff offices opened, one after the next in the corridor to his right and a windowed balcony view gave him a view of the courtyard to his left. The sun broke through a few lofty clouds, windswept and driven by the approaching fall weather fronts.

Merlin saw the door to the feisty one standing open, and the deputy-head secure behind a computer screen. Making a mental note to himself, he continued down the wide corridor, and at the montage of smiling faces, posted to a glass-covered chipboard collage, he turned to use the men's toilet.

Emerging some minutes later, having splashed some cold water on his face Merlin had his first opportunity to truly look at those faces. Fixed at alternating angles, a series of happy volunteers of varying ages, were pictured during a recent school trip to some lost African cause country. The smiling faces belied some darker travesty of justice, and Merlin had to admit, were in stark contrast to what he knew to be true.

Armed with a realisation that every whistle-blower in the history of African politics had been swept aside by the rising tide of despotism afforded liberation-drunk regimes, Merlin headed back to speak to the feisty one. His nickname fashioned by the Study Supervisors, was a testament to his grit and determination to see no child left behind.

Knocking before entering, Merlin stepped into the open office.

"Hi Mr Feeble," Merlin pronounced the name as diplomatically as could be done.

"Yes, Merlin. Can I help?" The feisty one looked up from the copious reports arrayed on a wooden desk, surrounded by certificates.

"Yes, I was wandering, if you have a moment?" Merlin would not be able to put a subtle slant on this issue, he knew, so jumped in at the deep end.

"Certainly, have a seat." Merlin sat in a comfortable chair to the right of the desk. He had seen this chair used as a place of safety by several students during lunchtime recesses, and felt warmly assured he was now doing the right thing.

"I have just come from the staffroom," Merlin broached the subject, "where I overheard a disturbing conversation regarding a trans-gender student, being discussed by a few of my colleagues."

There was a pregnant pause whilst the words sunk in.

"Oh dear! That is most unfortunate." The words carried with them a sense of betrayal.

"You are aware that you may be required to make this official?"

Merlin recognised the reference to legal-speak, and nodded. "Yes, I have read the school statutory guidance report and summarized the rules and regulations."

"Ah good. I suspect you may want to give this some thought?" The feisty one knew all the pitfalls and had traversed every known summit of intolerance it seemed. Having been born into a family with the unfortunate stigma so attached to name-calling, merlin could only wonder at his ability to endure such adversity.

"No, I have had a moment to consider what the ramifications will be, but I feel confident that this matter broaches every known safe-guarding prerequisite." Merlin countered.

"Yes, I see!" Mr Feeble pronounced, whilst, it seemed he had already visualised the consequences, he appeared reluctant to encourage Merlin.

Merlin realised it would be their word against his. But he had an ace up his sleeve. Computer records. The Microsoft based program could be monitored and every log-in and page visited on each account, was available no doubt.

"Shall I send you an email?" Merlin knew the requirements for the record to be logged.

"Yes, please do," Merlin could already see Mr. Feeble's brain allocating this new file into a series of required allotments. It required work, but it was a part of the system of checks and balances, and Merlin knew in that instant, he could never be envious of such administrators.

"Thank you," he smiled disarmingly at the feisty one, but knew all too well he would have to be locked, and loaded for what was to come.

"Arrogance is only bad when you lose. If you are winning and you are arrogant it is self-belief."

- **Eddie Jones – before the RWC defeat**

Saturday Morning

On Saturday morning Simon arrived early and with his hand-held navigation system, he borrowed Merlin's car and disappeared.

Merlin had a quiet morning, pottering around in the back yard. The October winds had dissipated with a flurry and the basking sunshine of an early autumn bathed the garden in hues of mottled browns and greens. There was a gentleness to the days with the gathering leaves adding a subdued crunch to the pedestrian footfalls on Fairdawn Crescent.

Occasionally a car door could be heard, or the furtive bark of a young pup, in anticipation of walks to come, but otherwise a particularly uninspiring morning. But this was all to change and Merlin was to learn of things he would rather not have known. Secrets shared, that he would now have to carry carefully. Knowledge that would reluctantly require a degree of sophisticated mentorship and application!

Merlin had poured himself a mug of coffee, and with a paper in hand, notwithstanding his revulsion of the mainstream media broad-sheets, he had retired to the garage, where the autumn sun peeked through an open window to the garden, and an almost balmy radiance smothered him with vitamin D3 drenching fortitude.

Relaxing, he collapsed into a deck chair, once reserved for Margaret's sojourns to Eastbourne and the casual weekends they had enjoyed in the south of England, Merlin felt at ease. He had only just settled down when he heard and felt the garage door, on rusty hinges next door.

It was Josh and he was with someone. The door raised to the height to allow entry, was suddenly slammed.

Merlin froze. The voices told him it was Josh and one of his mates from the school. The second voice sounded deeper, almost husky.

"Josh, what the fuck are we doing in here?"

"Relax mate, I don't want anyone to be able to see us from the street." It was the voice of his neighbour's son.

"Fuck, it stinks in here! What the fuck has your mom been hiding in this shithole?" The lad sounded older, almost too old for a classmate. Either way, Merlin could not identify who it was.

"I keep my stash in a cooler in the back." Josh again.

"What the fuck! You're crazy man," the older lad was wiser. Suddenly Merlin felt a discomfort, borne of the need to either make his own presence known, or beat a hasty retreat from his eavesdropping vantage.

"No man," Josh was insistent. "My mom never comes in here, since my dad left." Josh sounded assured.

"Here, it is." The sound of a heavy item being dragged across the concrete floor. Merlin knew now was the time to leave, but he was glued to the canvass bucket seat of the chair, and inert.

"Fuck man, you's weren't kidding!" The older lad was clearly impressed.

"Yeah! I have been storing what I don't use, and every so often someone at the gym will ask me for a dose." Josh was sounding like some seasoned dealer.

"How do you not get bust?" The older lad, clearly this senior was being schooled.

"Cause that fucking Steve is supplying!" Was Josh referring to the gym manager? He swam there every Thursday, but did not know the staff. Merlin knew he was now in too deep. It was that moment when he either extricated himself, at the expense of giving his position away, or waited until they left.

"Holy shit, you kidding right?" The older lad was obviously impressed.

"I've been using for a year now, and coach hasn't got a fucking clue." Josh must have be referring to the rugby coach. But what was he using?

"Listen, if they find out you're on steroids, won't they kick you off the team?"
"Naw, the coach looks the other way! All he wants is a team that can win him some trophies so he can sit in his fucking sweat-infested rat-hole at school, and pretend he is fucking Eddie fucking Jones!" Josh almost spat out the words.

"Are you kidding me? Fuck this is awesome." The older lad was game.

"So, do you want a dose, or not?" Josh was the seasoned dealer.

"Yeah, but I don't have the cash; you know that?" The older lad was insistent.

"Yeah, but like I said," Josh was in control, "You can owe me and maybe do me a favour sometime?" The hint of a question was clandestinely invoked.

"Yeah, of course mate," the older lad was keen to deal.

"Okay, take your sweats down," Josh ordered.

"What the fuck!" The older lad seemed hesitant.

"Well, if you want a dose, I have to inject you in the groin; that way no one will ever find out." Josh was way too seasoned. Merlin was feeling so uncomfortable, he had a knot in his stomach. It was a 'Catch Twenty-two' scenario. Give up his position; or keep mum. But had he another alternative to help!

"Okay, but it won't hurt, right?" The older lad might be older, but he was the novice.

"Just sit on the mattress, and let me show you how to apply the dose." Josh took control.

"This is the vial here," Josh may have been showing him something, Merlin could only surmise.

There was a minute as Merlin heard a plastic packet being ripped and a few less unfamiliar noises and then Josh.

"Okay, just relax," then the slapping of flesh.

"Fuck what's that for?" The older lad remonstrated.

"I have to get the vein visible," Josh, steady and in command.

"Okay, but fuck, I don't like needles!" The lad lamented.

"Okay just look away," Josh persisted.

"Ow, oww, oww," then the sound of a sharp intake of breath.

"There we go! That's it done." Josh sounded almost casual. The silence that followed told Merlin the worst was over. It was time to get the hell out of the garage, and pray Josh and the other lad did not hear him. He attempted to raise his backside out of the chair, but the aluminium legs scrapped against the smooth concrete surface.

"What was that?" The older lad whispered.

"Relax, you're paranoid mate. My neighbour left early this morning, I saw his car leaving like eight or so." Josh had obviously mistaken Simon's exiting with the car, as that of his own departure.

"Ya sure? I thought I heard a noise next door?"

"Yeah mate, he goes to the library every Saturday morning." Josh had obviously worked out Merlin's routine.

"What about his wife?" The older lad was still suspicious.

"Naw, he's widowed. The poor old bloke lost his wife a year ago. Me mom says he's heart broken, but I'm not so sure!"

"Is he a fag then?" The older lad was drawing a peculiarly sociological conclusion. Merlin understood all the symptoms.

"Naw, I know he's not, 'cause he was married for forty years."

"Yeah, but that don't mean he ain't." The older lad obviously knew more that Josh.

"Naw, I don't think so mate. He could be, but I don't think so!" Josh did not sound convinced, even though he repeated himself.

"You gonna give yourself a dose?" The older lad changed the subject.

"Yeah, then we can go to the gym." Josh was back in his element.

"Fuck mate!" There was a stifled laugh from the other side of the garage wall. "Wot you all boned up for?"

"It happens when I am injecting myself." Josh seemed un-phased.

"Wot, like you get turned on or something?" The older lad joked.

"Don't know," Josh was unrepentant. Then there was the sound of a torn plastic sheath.

"Whoa mate you's is hung like a horse." The older lad was clearly impressed.

"Oh! Yeah, I have never had any complaints." Josh seemed at ease with whatever predicament he was observed to be in. Merlin was now squirming to get out of the chair, but could not rise fast enough to overhear what came next.

"Geez mate, I've not seen a dong like that before!" The lad was no longer concerned about any potential eavesdropper. Merlin heard the older lad wince as the needle went in, but Josh was stoic.

"Listen mate. If you're talking about me doing a favour, so's I don't owe you no cash, like!" The older lad's voice trailed off hopefully.

'Yeah," Josh had somehow picked up on his innuendo. "You will get a mouthful though!" Josh guffawed.

"That's okay; my cousin told me once, it is full of protein." Ever the connoisseur.

"Help me drag this cooler box back into the corner, then we can get down to business."

With that, Merlin took his cue, and as the lads next door scrapped the offending box back across the garage floor, he rose in one deft movement, and headed for the kitchen door. Whatever the favour was, Merlin was not inclined to want that knowledge to cloud his opinion all the more.

Having abandoned his coffee mug in the garage, Merlin put the kettle on one more time then made a beeline for the sanctuary of his front room. Masked behind the lace curtains he would be privy to the comings and goings of his neighbour's guest, but would not wish for them to know he had overheard their dealings. Merlin was as conflicted as a sociologist could ever be, but recognising all the needs of human beings, he gauged that Josh was simply of the age, where he had to experiment, and the knowledge of this would not help his attempts to connect with the lad at school.

From this day forward, Merlin would have to maintain an honest secrecy regarding what he had overheard. It was not something he had wanted to be a witness to, but at least now, he knew for certain. He would want to be as diplomatic in his newfound understanding of what made Josh tick; but nonetheless, knowing what he did about the human mind, and what drove the Etheric Mind, when lust was provoked. Lads their age had no rational obstacles to lust, as the works of Shere Hite, a sexologist who had interviewed tens of thousands of men in the past forty years, only to discover that fellatio between adolescent males was far more predictable than many educators were willing to admit.

It was evident from what he knew to be true, that this was often deemed to be a Rite of Passage to adulthood, practiced far more among males, than among their less physical female counterparts. Merlin did not need to know why. It was what it was.

This generation was no more an enigma than his generation during the sixties, but the last sexual pandemic of Biblical proportions had somehow driven the truth below the surface of the social scabs of that post-hedonistic sexual revolution. Like those visceral wounds, the social paranoia of the class-system had won their moral victory and the stringent decrees of a totalitarian European experiment had cowed those educators who understood the truth, into submission.

But as with the famous line from 1984, Merlin knew that the Shadows, like that 'High Group', had sunken its claws into the very fabric of society, creating a generation that was subservient to its every pervasive bidding. It was unsurprising that these youngsters today would want to rebel against the tyranny of this Surveillance State!

Merlin would want to ask Simon his opinion as to the 'why', but would be circumspect with the 'what and how'!

"Synchronicity is an ever present reality for those who have eyes to see."

- **Carl Jung**

An Unsurprising Awakening

Browsing the SIMS system Monday morning, Merlin was able to organise for a meeting with Josh. The system allowed teachers to check what classes were planned for the week and to see which students were in those classes. Unsurprisingly, the very first class of the week was an arts class in the Arts Block, and it was the group of Year Eights Merlin had won over and was able to teach constructively. Amongst this group was Josh.

Having arrived early for the day, Merlin printed out the cover requirements for each of his classes, then armed with a series of printouts from Google, he headed for class.

The students were late getting to class, but Monday morning aside, they had been delayed in registration with their class mistress demanding everyone stay until the last of the late arrivals had been checked off on the system. This was how far education had descended. Where every child was a number, and computers kept check of who was, and who wasn't in class. No longer was a teacher able to scan a class and immediately see who was absent, they had to rely on a registration system that with Artificial Intelligence, would one day predict who would be late or absent from Monday morning first class!

Merlin had never had to rely on such a system in his forty years with the university, but then he was also aware that with the advent of this technology, humans had abdicated their sworn duty to protect every child, by allowing machines to do it for them. Teachers were no different. They had become lazy, inefficient and obsolete, as they allowed the Machine to take over. But there was a fight-back coming and Merlin knew exactly how.

With all the students in, and Josh for all intents and purposes nonchalantly unaware of Merlin's Saturday morning eavesdrop, the class began.

The set work, according to SIMS, was to provide each student with a series of pictograms, arrayed before them on a worktable, with the help of the art room supervisor, and allow them to draw freehand, the image before them. This was a task Josh was reluctant to begin, given his rugby prowess and a reputation for being a man's man. Merlin observed how he dragged his feet to the front, to secure a laminated pictogram, having allowed the class to go before him, and then hung around longer then usual flipping through the leftovers.

Circling the class, Merlin made certain that each student was equipped with art resources, and that they were setting to work, all the while keeping Josh in his peripheral vision. The lad sifted through the pictograms, but could not choose an option worthy of his attention. Merlin knew all the symptoms, and given it was Monday morning, decided on a different approach.

"Right! Josh, what have you decided on?" He was now standing alongside the rangy looking teenager, with a mess of dark curly hair that gave his stature a surprising advantage.

"There's nothing here." Josh lamented.

"Okay, but you do know that they are all much the same? It's not about the picture, but how you're brain interprets the image." Merlin explained.

"What? Like how you see the picture, instead of what the picture looks like?" Josh was on the money.

"Yes, exactly Josh. Our brains have an incredible ability to register what we are looking at, but by staring at the picture for long enough, we can visualise the smallest details with our intuitive mind." Merlin advanced.

"Is that like, when you are watching a video game, your brain begins to focus on the small things, and not the bigger picture?" This was clearly an area he had knowledge of.

"Yes, that is the gist of it. When we train our brains to concentrate on what our eyes are looking at, we can visualise that image, whenever we feel like!" Merlin elaborated.

"Let me show you an example. Bring any one of those pictograms and come and stand against this blank wall." Merlin suggested.

Josh dutifully picked one of the pictures, which Merlin knew he had already decided on anyway, but had been using his supposed indecision to initiate this discussion, and followed Merlin to the wall.

"Okay, stand facing the wall, and lift the picture to eye level and stare at the image, generally. Not on any specific part of the picture, but an overall view of the whole image." Merlin had Josh facing a white washed wall, with no artwork covering it. Josh lifted the laminated image to head height and stared at the image.

"Keep looking at the picture until you start to get blurry images in your mind. Don't focus so that your eyes become cross-eyed, but just focus enough that you are able to incorporate the entire image in your vision." Merlin continued.

"It's getting a bit fuzzy!" Josh blinked, then dropped the picture below his eye level.

"Good, now let's try again, but try not to blink, and keep the picture there until I say to lower it. When I say lower the picture, I want you to remain looking at the wall. Don't change the direction of your eyes, even by a millimetre." Merlin calmly instructed.

"Okay, now lower the picture!" Merlin had given Josh at least thirty seconds to stare at the picture. Then within five to ten seconds, Josh smiled.

"Oh! Wow! I can see the image on the wall." Josh cooed.

"Yes, great, that's the idea." Merlin was enthused. He knew he had a captive audience of one.

"That's amazing!" Josh kept staring at the wall, enraptured.

"You see the power of the brain to recall." Merlin suggested.

"Yes, it's incredible." Josh blinked, then for good measure he lifted the picture in front of his eyes again, and repeated the exercise.

"Any idea what this is called?" Merlin quizzed. Josh shock his head after completing another exercise.

"I call it 'Intentional Technology' or In.T." Merlin offered.

"What? Like IT?" Josh was remarkably perceptive.

"Yes, but IT for the brain! The concept of In.T. is the Intentional Technology of our Consciousness, which allows the perceived ideas in our minds, to become our reality!" Merlin explained.

"Imagine, if you can, a picture of something very specific that you want to create as your reality." Merlin elaborated. "Let's say it is a picture of your dream car, or a holiday you would want with your mom and dad!" Merlin purposely allowed that faux pas to sink in. He noticed Josh smile inwardly; it was a fleeting recognition of a deeper-seated desire.

"Just as you were able to recall that image, as you had literally burned that picture onto the back of your eyeball retina, by staring at it for long enough, I believe we can visualise our DVD's or dreams, visions and desires, into reality by concentrated applications." Merlin was in his element.

Josh nodded. He was listening intently.

"Each picture we look at is made up of thousands of pixels. Just as a camera captures each of those pixels, so that our brain can register each and form a picture in our brain, so our eyes can also capture those pictures, and by training ourselves to concentrate on what we truly want, we are capable of recalling those visualisations on a whim. That is called 'Intentional Technology'."

"The higher the resolution, the higher the number of pixels. So a High Resolution picture consists of over twenty thousand pixels. A Lower Resolution picture, say only twelve thousand." Josh was mesmerised by the conversation, and by now several of the students seated nearby had abandoned their artwork and were listening. Merlin could see that Josh felt extremely comfortable with the attention he was afforded.

"So the higher the resolution the better. Our eyes, perceive the mega-pixels, as a series of patterns in that image, which are translated into an electronic message to our brain. Our optical nerve translates that pattern as a coherent message, which our brain translates specifically. This message is assimilated into our consciousness as a memorized image, which, like photo-image recognition technology, can be downloaded into our brains."

Several of the class had now taken their pictograms and lined up along the wall.

"Because we see millions of images on a daily basis, some of which we instantly recognize; others which we ignore, or gloss over, our brains can be trained to keep those we see as valuable to our own circumstances, and those we don't we can train our brains to discard." Merlin was now preaching to the converted.

"Is that what they do when they teach gamers to simulate real time battles in cyber-space?" The question from left field was unexpected. It was Oscar.

"It certainly is part of the process." Merlin conceded. "You know when we see an image that our brain has memorized, it is called recall. The image is imprinted in our memory cells, so as to raise our Consciousness. So I would not be surprised that the plan would be to familiarise gamers with certain scenarios in battle, so that when they reach a real-life situation, they will know how to react."

"I knew it, I knew that," Oscar turned to Jason, who was still staring blankly at the wall.

"Give over!" Jason turned, annoyed at having been interrupted. "You and you're stupid conspiracy stories!"

"It's true," bleated Oscar. "I told Jason that when we play those video games, the CIA is watching us through the cameras on our phones to check out our progress!" Merlin could not help but laugh. It all sounded so far fetched! But was it?

"Well, it fits in with what we see in the images in real Life scenarios. If the projection of the real image into our mind, immediately triggers the recall function, then I don't think it is too outlandish to imagine that it could be manipulated for future applications." Merlin was learning too.

"See! I told you guys." Oscar was triumphant. Josh simply smiled, took his pictogram and headed back to his seat. The moment was lost, but Merlin knew that from now on he would be able to connect at will. The lad was reaching out for some paternal influences.

"Well Oscar, if Intentional Technology allows us to store the imagery for later recall, my understanding of this technology is that we can train our minds to achieve what ever we wish. The danger is that through computers, we may also be submitting to a globalised threat of mind control." The lad was fixated on Merlin, gazing intently into his eyes, seeking his soul. What Merlin referred to as an 'old soul' who could recall past life experiences on a subliminal level.

"Yes, sir, it is true. The CIA is training kids to learn how to fight Aliens, because they know that an invasion is planned! I watched a YouTube video about it. I'm telling you it's true!" Oscar was the one child in the class who had a mind of immense intellect. Merlin knew that if he could direct it, this kid had an incredible future ahead of him.

"Well Oscar, to store the In.T. which, as we learn to recognize more information, our recall function becomes more effective. We are training our brain to become a channel for the images we want, and making sure we can close off the images we don't." Merlin was forthright. "There is a reverse function, called Unintentional Technology Unin.T. So the more we focus on our In.T. the more effective we become at closing off our Unit.T influences. If practiced this will lead us to a very effective degree of visualizations for what we desire for our world."

"Are you saying, we can stop an invasion of Aliens, just with our minds?" Oscar was the brightest kid Merlin had ever taught.

"Yes! I am saying that through our visualisations, we have the power to control our future. We will become a Level One society, as has been explained by astrophysicist Nikolai Kardashev. It is interesting that we have known about this since the sixties, yet our society refuses to acknowledge this, and I can only surmise it is because we are being manipulated by a consumer elite, who want to keep selling us things." Merlin smiled. He hoped his explanation had not been lost on Oscar.

"Sir, that is what my dad calls 'The Deep State'. He says that the people who control the money, also control what people can buy and what we are supposed to believe!" Oscar alliterated.

"Oscar, if you continue to study this idea of Intentional Technology, I would like you to record your findings." Merlin proposed.
"Oh yes sir, I will. Can I tell my dad what you said?" Merlin had a co-conspirator.

"Yes of course, and don't forget to explain that I believe that we can change the way we perceive our future and also how our future will manifest." Merlin led him by the elbow back to his seat.

"Right everyone. Let's see what you lot have drawn." He knew intuitively those lads lives would never be the same again. But Merlin was unlikely to share the entire mystery with them yet!

Synchronicity was a term that Simon frequently used to represent the method of capabilities in the mind of formalising some sort of meaning from seemingly random events. Synchronistic incidences were a function of formidable manifesting and thrust human beings forward as a society.

Merlin knew that synchronicities were not just coincidences, as recorded by Vedic traditions of serendipity, that allowed humans to rationalise the mind to contemplate a supernatural power, but instead it was as Simon related, a spiritual synchronization of the mind strategically orchestrated and perfectly aligned to deliver messages, often provide some form of guidance, and reassure the human mind of its' intuitive path.

He knew that synchronicity was actually electrical energy emitted in the brain, and when the vibrational energy was focused on the pictures we formed in our brains, somehow those visualizations became our truths! This, Merlin believed, was because the synapses in the brain were learning to connect the Higher Brain, in the frontal lobes of the brain, with the primitive Limbic Brain that drove desire and tenacity to achieve. Simon had said this was what religion determined as the Duality Syndrome.

Duality was what the Jews called the Yetser Tov and Yetser Ha ra, an ancient form of wisdom that engineered progress throughout society. It was the Yin and the Yang of the ancient Chinese traditions, and modern science was unravelling how these ancient mysteries were formulated in the brain.

But the danger was when these powers were vested in too few hands, and not enough people understood their relevance in modern society. The church had actively destroyed all discussions of the Duality Syndrome, preferring to dumb-down their congregants, so that the power was concentrated in the Vatican.

Merlin knew of the destruction of the Library of Alexandria, and the volumes of wisdom written down and preserved in those archives; the Catholic church had orchestrated that destruction purposely!

But he knew that when we, as humans began to work on the law of attraction, it was then that humans would notice a plethora of synchronicity. Merlin recognised that receiving these signs from the universe to move ahead in a particular direction, was a facet of the human brain's ability to record and store information in compartments of our brains. Whether he believed what Simon had told him about the memory function of our DNA to record past-life experiences, he was not sure; but what he could recognise was that weird things kept happening around him, and it had only begun after Marg had passed away!

There was a chilly air to the staffroom as Merlin arrived back for tea. Seated in his comfortable chair, the group of study supervisors he had reported, perched themselves on the extreme end of the row, avoiding his scrutiny.

This was symptomatic of the system. A whistle-blower was only effective if their identity remained anonymous, but clearly these four had made an assumption based on who had been in the staffroom late last Thursday. So with the requisite email deposited for the record, the Feisty one had clearly had communications with the offending gaggle of study supervisors. Merlin was not one to be undone by perception, so he decided to use reverse psychology.

"Anyone want a cup of tea?" He announced rising from his seat and engaging the group. There was a pregnant silence, in which a metaphorical umbilical chord could have been cut.

"Yes, thank you, I would love one." It was Pauline, but she had not been one of the guilty four.

"How do you take it?" Merlin passed the four conspirators, who glibly hung on to their frosty glares, now directed at each other, attempting to implicate each other by reason of an implied guilt.
"No sugar or milk please." Pauline was clearly not in on the controversy.

Returning some minutes later with his mug filled to the brim and a mug for Pauline, which he attempted to not spill, Merlin regained his seat. Pauline thanked him then with the grace of a spiritual life of regular meditation, she took her cup of tea, and a lunch box filled with healthy tit bits, and came and sat directly opposite him.

"That looks good," Merlin observed.

"Yes, I try to keep as healthy as I can." He had exchanged views with her on a retreat she was running for her brother, a Reiki Master.

"It is invaluable," Merlin agreed, lifting to his mouth another fork-full of vegetables secured from the kitchens below them.

"I have been vegan for twenty years," Pauline was an attractive forty-something, with two spritely looking lads in school. The oldest was an invaluable contributor to his rugby sides winning formula, zipping down the wing at pace, scoring tries, whilst the younger was an extremely gifted middle distance runner. Merlin mused over the potential relationship of mother, father and healthy children.

"I admire you for doing so," Merlin conceded, "but I find myself drawn to the odd steak, or fish dish when available!"

"I believe it is based on our blood types," Pauline offered as commiseration.

"Yes, I believe so." Merlin was thinking of Josh and the success he was having on the field.

"Does your lad in year nine, have any interaction with that rugby player Josh, in year eight?" Merlin inquired, lowering his voice.

"No, not at school, but they do know each other from the rugby club." Pauline piped up; her lads were her pride and joy.

"Oh good. You know that Josh is my neighbour's son?" Merlin confided.

"Yes, I think you told me." Pauline was an effective listener. "Is there something worrying you?"

"Ah! No, not that I am at liberty to discuss, but just that I know he is an incredibly bright lad! But his father is missing in action and he has been a little down recently." Merlin offered no insights that were not obvious to all who taught him.

"Well Brookland knows him and says he is a very powerful number eight for his team." Pauline smiled, enthused to be speaking all things sporting.

"Yes, he certainly is a big lad." Merlin would have to tread carefully. He was not able to disclose what he knew, but, knowing the safe guarding principles of the school, he also knew he was treading a fine line between exposing unsolicited knowledge and being pro-active. The understanding of his own whistle blowing firmly etched in his mind, gave credence to objectivity with regard to divulging what he knew.

The brood of vipers pretended not to be eavesdropping.

"I will ask Brookland what he has heard. You know how the boys talk to each other?" Pauline spoke, but the cryptic element of her suggestion lay subtly below the surface.

"Yes, that would be helpful. As much as I am his neighbour, I cannot be seen to interfere with what his mother tells him; albeit that he does need a father-figure, especially now, at this age." Merlin added.

"Well, all the boys know each others business. If Brookland knows anything I am sure he will tell me." Pauline was clear.

"Yes, I agree, and I know that he needs help, but I do not want my name being used." Merlin whispered, he was adamant anything he had gleaned from that unfortunate Saturday morning discussion, would not be helpful.

"That is not a concern you should have. I will also pray and meditate on this," Pauline offered. "If there is any way we can help, I am sure we will get a positive answer."

Merlin smiled. The answer he knew, lay somewhere between pro-active thinking and an unseen force, he had yet to connect with fully.

"Thank you Pauline."

"Truth will always be truth, regardless of lack of understanding, disbelief or ignorance."

- **W. Clement Stone**

Divulging the Truth

Simon and Merlin were settled in once more at the library. Merlin had taken up his position at the table facing the door.

"I meant to ask you how your trip went last Saturday?" Merlin had not had a chance to speak to Simon when he had returned with the car.

"Yes, thank you for letting me borrow it. Everything went well and I was able to get to see the people at the hotel." Simon had returned with the car, whilst Merlin was out getting his newspaper.

"Yes, I know the place. So did they offer you the job?" Merlin had seen the car keys, popped through the post box when he returned.

"Sadly, no!" Simon pursed his lips in noncommittal annoyance.

"Why not? I can see you as an events manager. You definitely have the personality for the position." Merlin gauged his dejection.

"No! Don't get me wrong. The meeting went just great. When I got there I was met by a lovely young lass, who is the hotel public relations lady. The interview went well, but then as I was sitting with the hotel bookkeeper, and chatting about my salary expectations, a weird thing happened."

Merlin did not respond. He allowed Simon to gather his thoughts. He clearly, had not yet worked through what he was thinking.

"The bookkeeper," he continued, "was very effusive and had a lovely, bubbly personality, but when she asked me how long I had been a Scientologist, I was a bit confused."

Merlin looked on quizzically.

"Yes! She straight out asked me how long I had been a Scientologist." Simon laughed.

"Are you saying that the hotel is a Scientologist hotel?" Merlin had visited the castle.

"No, but I think it may be owned by them."
"So what did you say?" Merlin was intrigued.

"I just said, No! I am not a scientologist, but was introduced for the job by a lady who is!" Simon grinned.

"I was given the referral by a lady called Brenda, and she works in a local business I had been helping out with some volunteer work."

"So, did Brenda think you were a Scientologist?" Merlin was confused.

"No, not at all. In fact I told her I did not know anything about the church when I was helping out. I think she took that as an open door to introduce me to the church!" Simon conceded.

"You mean induct?" Merlin smiled.

"Well, I am not going to be induced into anything frankly; and least of which would be some cult." Simon had a firm grip on his own beliefs.

"Strangely enough, I had read 'Dianetics' as a student whilst living in Johannesburg. I was a strange time for me, and I was searching for answers to the ancient mysteries." His South African accent was still strong.

"You know that Scientology is based on so much of those mysteries?" Merlin knew a great deal about the history of Scientology.

"Yes. I believe they have some understanding of the ancient technologies, and they use them in their rituals!" Simon was an advocate of positive visualisation, and he had conceptualised the idea of Intentional Technology. Merlin recalled their previous conversation.

"You do know that the machines they use to advance their knowledge of the occult, are extremely dangerous?" Merlin inclined his head, as he thought he recognised someone walk past the door. Merlin looked behind him instinctively.

"Yes, I know that the Christian church refers to someone who can predict the future as a Prophet. Someone who can change the future as an Intercessor; but the Scientologists refers to this process as 'Prediction Technology', in which the members pray for Intercession, through a process called postulating!" Simon replied.

"So, someone who uses their machines is capable of seeing the future? I thought that the idea of postulating, is based on using our imagination?" Merlin surmised.

"Well, it is more than that. The Christian church, has warned the faithful about trying to predict the future because they claim it is a dark art. However, if imagining ones future is deemed to be evil, then what's the point of living?" The hypothesis became all the more realistic to Simon. Religion limits mankind. Spirituality frees.

"But the Scriptures also warn them that their future has already been pre-ordained. The Apostle John wrote the book of Revelation when he was isolated and alone, having been exiled to the island of Patmos." Merlin knew the historical records well.

"But Revelation is a good news story for Christians who believe that Jesus will return!" Merlin wanted to explore this more.

"Indeed! But if you read the first eleven chapters, it is all very alarming and that is why they call it an Apocryphal book." Simon had had this debate with his pastor, and the guy had avoided any further discussions about it. He was somehow fearful of that eventuality, but Simon knew that in his heart he was hiding some truth from the faithful.

"Well the Catholic church would want you to believe that we are all going to go to hell because we aren't Catholic!" Merlin grinned.

"That goes without saying," Simon grimaced. There was some element of knowledge he was holding onto, and Merlin was now certain he had been correct in his presumption.

"Do you think the Scientologists have mastered the art of intercession, because if they have, don't you think that we would all be living in a better world?" Merlin redirected the conversation.

"No! The purpose of intercession is a deeply personal and meaningful experience that we can all have with the Spirit. When we meditate and pray for a specific and visualised objective, there is a force that transcends everything we know about the physical world. The machines that Scientologists use to access intercession are like the shock therapy machines the Catholic church has tried to use for centuries to convert homosexual people." Simon raged.

That was Merlin's affirmation. He had prayed, asking Father Spirit to reveal all the hidden truths in his relationships, so as the mysteries would be revealed. This was why he now knew, categorically that the conversation he had overheard last Saturday, was not at all by chance. He had asked his Angels to place him in the right place, at the right time to help Josh. Now, his prayer for Simon was also being revealed.

"The stupidity of it is mind boggling," Simon wanted to be abundantly clear.

"Yes! As sociologists, we are trained to recognise those aspects of behaviour that warrant a global perspective of social patterns. It has always amazed me that the Catholic church believes that homosexuality is a sin that the devil has created. That is patently stupid!" Merlin concurred.

"Yes! Think about it. If the majority of homosexual men, or women live largely within communities where they have no children, and they do not pass on their genes as a result, why do you think it is possible that the 'Gay' Gene that scientists refer to, would still be evident." Simon continued;

"The Catholic's believe that Jesus condemned homosexuality, but there is not one shred of evidence to support their contention." Simon was in his element.

"Uuhmm. I know that Jesus does speak about the Centurion's Servant being healed." Merlin had often wondered why Jesus would have healed a sick young boy, who was clearly the sexual partner of the Centurion in the Gospel story.

"Well, the Centurion, it turns out was not necessarily a Roman Centurion, because no archaeological evidence can be shown to exist of a Roman Garrison in Galilee." Simon agreed. "That does explain why the Centurion would not have wished to take Jesus to his home. He did not feel worthy enough."

"That is the reason why homosexual people have been persecuted by society for thousands of years; it is a Melian issue!" Simon was animated.

"I am not familiar with that concept?" Merlin sat forward in his chair.

"The Melian Dialogue is well worth reading, because it goes to the root cause of so much evil being perpetrated in the 21st Century and for thousands of years before today."

"The Illuminati, or the 'One Percenters' as I call them, attempt to destroy societal cohesion by dividing and conquering." Simon was clearly agitated.

"Ahh! Yes, that is what we were speaking about last time. The 'High Group' as George Orwell said, controls the media, big business and as a result, controls the minds of the young people, by spreading their obnoxious lies." There was an edge to Merlin's voice.

"Yes, and they render our society dependent on their drugs, their incessant consumerism based advertising, and their obsession with controlling the hearts and minds of the world's population through deceptive 'Red Flag' events, like 9/11 and the Iraq War."

Simon paused for a moment. "These evil men and women, who control the world through economic power, will loose the ultimate battle, because they cannot control the Spirit World; that is the preserve of Spirit Father only." Merlin felt they were getting to the meat of the bone.

"I was drawn to a series of extremely interesting and pertinent discussions about 'The Hegelian Principle'," Simon offered.

"The first thing they do is to create a problem or conflict by dis-information and controlling the mass-media to spin their story. In the past they used the Catholic church to spread the lies because they were the only ones allowed to read and write."

"Then they publicize the problem and create opposition to it by relentlessly talking about it and secretly manipulating the minds of the public to a danger they say it represents, to social order. That was what the church did to homosexual people for two thousand years."
"Then when they see that the people are completely incensed by the story they have been spun, they offer a potential solution that has a powerful emotional influence on the public conversation, playing on the fears of the general population, and then, when they see they have divided the people, they provide a theoretical way out of that perceived problem." Simon spoke with clarity, as these words tripped off his tongue.

"Yup! That is exactly what they have done." Merlin acceded.

"The Catholic church is a part of the problem, no doubt. The more they try to drive their antiquated beliefs into the minds of our youth, the fewer there will be in church. I believe that this factor has caused more people to leave the church, than any other single factor in our two thousand year history. But it goes back way beyond that!" Merlin pursued his thoughts.

"That is why anyone who is different is targeted." Simon added.

"Yes, and it is why teachers still have such vitriol about transgender of gay, lesbian or anyone who might have a slightly different viewpoint to theirs!" Merlin had not yet told Simon about his whistle blower letter.

Have you ever noticed in people, when un-forgiveness becomes bitter, and they become angry and slander others; nobody wants to be around them. They tend to lose the people close to them, because they are full of rage and malice, and become sickly as a result. All these attributes become a downward spiral in their Lives, which I believe ensures that they lose their salvation, and as a result their entrance ticket to heaven. When we forgive, God intervenes and deals with our enemies.

"There is a method to their madness." Simon concurred.

"I believe that the education system is designed to subvert any attempt at individual thought, in favour of a Groupthink, because by doing so, they can control the minds of the youth. Thank about the crap they shove down the throats of kids today. All this negativity about global warming, and advocating socialism, when we know these are lies, is intended to keep the kids ignorant of their real intentions."

"What do you think is their ultimate goal?" Merlin raised an eyebrow.

"I think it is a ploy to delay the ultimate time of enlightenment! We are truly Spiritual beings, trapped in a physical form. The longer we allow the pernicious men and women of this new world order to keep lying to us, the longer it will take before we reach out ultimate destiny." There was a wistful conjecture in his voice.

"Whatever has happened in time, is there as a file in our memories. When we as human beings realize we are beyond the scope of time and space, we will be able to decode the Spiritual records deposited deep within our memory. It is available in the language we understand, and in a frequency we can receive for our benefit, to improve our lives, and to reach our ultimate goals and the ultimate goal of humanity, which is Enlightenment."

"This is why we have a sense of history repeating itself, because our stored memory banks have not been accessed by our Consciousness. Somewhere deep in our sub-conscience we require that awakening, like the accessing of a computer file. The feeling of déjà vu is precisely that; some event that has gone before. As we meditate and pray for the opening of that file, to access Higher Consciousness, we become aware that it is within us, rooted deeply in our DNA, and freely accessible as we emerge from the darkness."

"It was Jules Verne who said: "Science, my lad, is made up of mistakes, but they are mistakes which it is useful to make, because they lead little by little to the truth."

"Yes," Merlin offered, "and he also said: "Anything one man can imagine, other men can make real."

"Déjà vu is not a prediction. These events, people, circumstances have happened before, and our coded DNA has stored the information for sharing. That is what they want to stop us from doing. The idea of prophecy or what the Scientologists do, through their machines is counter-productive; all we have to do is awaken the Spirit within us, which has always been within us!" This seemed reasonable to Merlin.

"That is why I agree with you that we can time travel. The past, present and future are recorded, because there is nothing beyond time and space, as creation and destruction happen simultaneously. This is what Christians call 'Duality'. In our physical dimension of time, the past, present and future seem to be defined by intervals, but in the Spirit, or what the ancient Hebrews called 'Rua'h Ha kodesh', there is no past, present or future. That is why what you recall as happened, is what is happening, and what is still to happen, has clearly already been recorded!"

"So what must we do?" Merlin sensed a powerful 'Aha moment'.

"We have to relearn to meditate, inwardly return to a more peaceful time when our lives were not controlled by electronic gadgets. These are simply the distraction that The Shadows have fed to our children, to keep them Spiritually ignorant. The more they are distracted by social media and the invasive information they are being spoon fed; the longer it will take to reach Nirvana."

"The study of Anthroposophy has illuminated my understanding of the true meaning of Spiritual Power. I can recommend an incredibly enlightening explanation of 'The Lord's Prayer' in which Rudolf Steiner speaks to the very nature of the four lower principles of mankind. He uses the basis of Etheric, Astral, Physical and Ego, to determine the real meaning behind the prayer." Simon stopped speaking; Merlin was nodding approvingly.

"Yes it is the basis of all religions, and philosophy engages all four aspects of the human spirit, in order to determine how psychology works through our self-awareness." Merlin agreed.

"Exactly!" Simon was truly engaged. "My understanding of the four lower principles, is that in order for the human to suffer from guilt, there must be an Etheric concept evident. Without the Ethericism, no guilt would exist. Likewise, for the concept of sinfulness to exist, there must be ego. Ego, is the function of human behaviour that creates a desire to rage against society, or to buck the trend! Think about that for one moment; in order for a person to trespass against his fellow man, he must have an ego. But that does not make any sense!" Simon paused.

"When Gay men choose to be Gay, it is not because they have somehow decided to swim against mainstream thinking; it simply happens! One day they wake up and recognise that the feelings they have for another man, is sexual, because they are attracted to them, not because they have chosen to rage against society." He breathed in, a large powerful inward drawn explosion.

"I have no concept of ego when I am attracted to another man! There may come a time when I say 'fuck them, especially the self-righteous Christian types, but I am not doing so because of ego." There was a silence of thought that followed; Merlin had never considered this.

"So, what does being Gay have to do with sin? Nothing. But those in the church who use the Pauline Epistles as a self-congratulatory badge of honour to condemn the LGBT+ community have never gained the Spiritual insight to recognise this." Simon smiled.

"From what I understand it is all about the chemicals in our brains!" Merlin had an understanding of the science.

"Yes, there is an American Neuro-scientist, a Dr Lembke, who advocates that having the ability to withstand addiction, there is a process of allowing our Astral Brain to process stabilising chemicals that balance out the brains production of Dopamine." Simon was aware of the science involved with drug addicts.

"It is the Dopamine produced in our pineal gland which intensifies the brains, pleasure pain threshold. By resisting temptation and allowing the individual to access these Astral Compartments of the mind, we also negate the Brain's Etheric production of the counter-balancing guilt, or indebtedness functioning of our mind." The chemistry was the key.

"The human mind is so powerful, we have the ability to resist temptation, by constantly strengthening the neural pathways connecting the Limbic, or primitive brain, with the conscious brain, or frontal cortex. It is the front part of the brain which is our motivator, or creator brain! The intuitive part of the brain. Do you know that by constantly reaffirming our mind's ability to fight off temptation, as Rudolf Steiner suggests, is a function of that conditioning." Simon was on a roll.

"When that 'Conditioning' is constructive and comes from a place of 'homeostasis' based on positive mantras in our psyche, and not from the 'Etheric', guilt-based function of religiosity, that's when the Mind is capable of taking control of the balancing of a healthy Lifestyle." Merlin listened intently; there was method in what Simon was illustrating.

"Religious prescription is counter-intuitive and only serves to render the Etheric Brain subject to massive swings in the guilt-redemption function of sin and salvation. The Catholics have the moratorium on this dis-ease based symptomatic conditioning. The average Catholic staggers from guilt to peacefulness, because they have not understood the true function of the Lord's Prayer as proposed by Rudolf Steiner." Simon smiled;

"The Jewish people have us beaten hands-down! They have known this for five thousand years."

"So the four lower principles have the answers to balancing the release of Dopamine into our body, and by controlling this functioning, we reach what Dr. Lembke calls homeostasis?" Merlin surmised.

"Yes. It is this which is the same concept Christians and Buddhists refer to as the peaceful rest."

"I Am convinced that my affirmation comes from the Rua'h Ha kodesh, and will be borne out by this understanding of how the Spirit of God, The Rua'h, or Breath of

Life, communicates to us, through our connection to The Global Consciousness. What I refer to as The Torus." The writing was on the wall.

"It's not dissimilar to the 'Force' in the Star Wars movies." Merlin agreed.

"Perhaps that is the job of Prayer Simon." Merlin offered. "To bring them to a point of Spiritual Discernment."

"Yes, I believe you are right. We have to pray for that Discernment, for the church, as a gift of the Spirit, and hope they change their ways. So many young men are lost and seeking help, and the church should be there to help; but they don't. They are searching for something that is physical, but what they cannot recognise is that the answer is Spiritual?" Simon posed the statement as a question.

"That state of Nirvana, is like an ecstasy, but is achievable for every person, regardless of their sexuality. But the message is being distorted by well-meaning, but erroneous thinking." Merlin conceded.

"Yes, it is important to get the church to recognise their error." Simon was reflective.

"And drugs only perpetuate that ultimate state of ecstasy." Merlin made the connection.

"Yes, those kids who feel so hopelessly lost in the system, and resort to recreational drugs, are only exacerbating their pain and suffering. We could easily become a 'Level One Society' if we all shared half an hour every day to connect on the Spiritual." Simon was clear on his mission; he was keen to bring meditation into the school curriculum.

"What would you propose if you were a teacher?" Merlin asked.

"I would ask my students to get together in groups before their classes, and spend five minutes simply meditating. Switch off those phones and spend some quality time together reflecting." Simon was a million miles away already.

"Stress exposes a person's true heart and character, so when those kids come to class stressed, the chances they will learn is zero. There brains are producing cortisol and that deadens the brains ability to think clearly. If our thoughts are unclear, how can we generate meaningful manifesting powers?" Merlin understood the 'Fight or Flight' sequence.

"If they keep themselves in servitude to fear, then fear is the one factor that limits our growth." Simon added.

"My understanding is that since guilt is a low vibration emotion it tends to resonate at the lower levels of our intuitional brain, and once a drug addict, for example, is indulged with the process of taking drugs, that function of the brain gets compartmentalised for convenience, whilst the rush of whatever they are involved in takes over. The primitive brain takes control, and that is when things go wrong!" Merlin could see the connection.

"When they are going through an impossible situation, they must believe that they have the ability to connect on a Spiritual level. This in my opinion is the balancing, or homeostasis solution." Simon added;

"That is when we see the works of miracles."

Merlin knew that when he meditated, Spirit was able to release the power of a supernatural consciousness to connect him with all the people important in his life.

Just then, a shadow passed by the window through the door to the computer section of the library. Merlin grunted triumphantly.

"What?" Simon returned.

"There is a young man I would like to introduce to you." Merlin's gaze past his shoulder told Simon he was intonating their coffee morning was about to get even more interesting.

"Education is what remains after one has forgotten what one has learned in school."

- **Albert Einstein**

Back to the Coal Face

Merlin found himself covering a Science class mid way through the week. Until then, he had not bumped into James so vast was the school with its warrens of classrooms, halls and poorly connected hallways. The school was a hodgepodge of additions to an original Secondary School facility built in the early sixties, as the demand for educating the children of the local town, became a flood of migrant escapees from the city.

No thought was given to the dynamics of how to squeeze one thousand seven hundred school children into rabbit holes the size of a standard hallway, designed for a tenth the number. These county schools, run badly by the local councils, were an indiscriminate second-thought answer to burgeoning populations, and the victims were the scholars; not the over-worked teachers.

Merlin realised why in a school of this size, he was expected to conduct five classes a day, from the early registration, then claw his way to the first class, sometimes on the far side of a facility the size of ten rugby fields. There was no thought given to logistics, as the teachers and mainly study supervisors ran helter-skelter from classroom to laboratory, back to classroom, then drama hall.

The challenges were evident, the morale low and the administrators getting more ill by the day. It was a recipe for failure!

So, to find himself in a laboratory, covering for a sick science teacher was an event in of it self. The Year Nine students were in no mood for an elderly, somewhat quizzical looking, grey haired man, to begin to attempt to inspire them about a subject they had already lost all hope of ever understanding; least of which would empower them to a future as a reality-social media jockey!

If the evidentiary proof was not displayed in a reluctance to put away all mobile phones, and keep them deposited in bags underneath the lab tables, then it would have to depend on the discussion that ensued, regarding the question on most teenage girls minds; the right to free abortions.

Attempting to redirect these social media junkies, from a topical debate was the current challenge, and Merlin deftly deflected dubious questions from fourteen year-old girls, whose nail polish and eyebrow plucks, gave great cause and concern for the future of humanity, least of all the chances of administering any serious supervisory education.

However, endeavour he did, and eventually Merlin was able to motivate several tables to the cover work provided. The real question was as to whether Isabella, a fiery Italian lass with a tempestuous demeanour, would play second fiddle to Amy, the voluptuous blond in the shortest skirt in school.

Merlin understood feminine egos, and regardless of how the 'Me Too' movement wanted to portray their cause, these lasses were not doing them any credit. It was a wander that any red-blooded male teacher would not have a moment to skirt conformity. But for Merlin, the feminine wiles of over-active hormone induced heroines, was not a potential blip on his sixty-five year-old radar screen.

His attention was turned to a happy-go-lucky young soul, quietly getting on with the work provided. It was James from the library. Merlin had recognised all the clues, and with a sociological precision, had been able to identify that behind those surreptitious smiles, was the haunted eyes of a preoccupied soul, dealing with its own demons.

James was a quiet example of what the system produced, regardless of social engineering. This was a lad, whose over-zealous mother dragged James and his two younger brothers off to church on a Sunday, with high ideals for future prospects. It was yet another example of how the town had managed to attract every ambit of religion to within the scope of the naturally occurring Ley Lines.

But, to Merlin, James embodied everything that was wrong with Christianity. Merlin had witnessed James and his mate, play footsie-footsie under the table in the geography class, when given a video to watch. Whilst the class was preparing for a field trip to London, James it seemed was preparing for something other of an undisclosed liaison.

So, when James had turned up at the library on Saturday, Merlin knew that his Transcendental Inspired thoughts, or what he called TI, had worked.

The premise of his scientifically, spiritual inspired experiment was to have inserted thoughts about attending the library in the town centre, by projecting his thoughts into James' mind, over a series of classes in which James had been taught.

The answer was unequivocal. When James had arrived at the library, he had no reason to be there, other than to begin a random search through the science books on hand. Merlin had walked Simon through the array of neatly appointed shelves, arriving at the science section, then introduced James when the lad had looked up from a book on physics, the likes of which, even Merlin had been surprised of.

"What are you studying?" Merlin was impressed.

"Oh! Hello Sir. I have been thinking about the link between science and religion. I want to find out more about Quantum Mechanics and how it works in theory." Simon had smiled broadly.

"Wow that sounds deep!" Merlin added. Then turning to Simon, "Si, this is James, a young man from school."

"Hello James," Simon leaned in and shook the young man's hand, a firm handshake and penetrating gaze had the lad mesmerized.

"Hello Sir," James returned the handshake, with a firmly applied assurance.

"Please, Simon, or Si! I am not your teacher, and it only makes me feel too old!" He winked.

"Oh! Thank you…. Simon." James felt the social pressure application of an adequate amount of decorum, based on their age difference.

"Simon is an avid scholar on all things science and spiritual." Merlin attested.

"Really?" The lads eyes brightened measurably more than even he would have reason to. So young, but searching for so many philosophical answers. Merlin suspected he had gotten there by recognising an element of spirituality, based on past-life intuition.

"Yes, do you have an understanding of what is Mental Causation?" Simon took over.

"No? What is that?" James enthusiastically responded.

"In our physical world there is what we call 'Materialism'. You know, the physical reality of our existence, but in the Spiritual world there is Duality." Simon did not speak down to him, but lifted him up to his level.

"What is Duality?" James was eager to learn.

"The structure of the flow of energy from one polarity to another happens when energy naturally finds its lowest path of resistance. Energy requires that we have two opposing poles. Negative to Positive! So, when we think of our physicality, we want to be able to move from one pole to another, seamlessly and without fear of a blockage in the journey. Duality exists when our minds finally access the Rua'h, what the ancient Hebrews called The Spirit." Simon paused. He searched those eyes to ensure he was being followed.

"Interestingly, Nikola Tesla once said, "My brain is only a receiver, in the Universe there is a core from which we obtain knowledge, strength and inspiration. I have not penetrated into the secrets of this core, but I know that it exists." And we know how powerful a thinker Nikola Tesla was!" The lad gawked. Merlin knew he had done the right thing.

"Simon, James, I am sure you have a lot in common! Would you mind if I excused myself, I have some errands to run?" Merlin broke the invisible chord that spanned the generational gap, for just a moment.

"Thank you Sir," James quipped. "I want to stay to talk, if that is okay with you?" James was somehow broaching an unchartered social dimension he may have once considered the domain of adults.

That had been four days ago, and Merlin was eager to get some feedback.

"Good morning everyone," Merlin repeated, having rounded on the gaggle of girls at the back of the class, seated around a towering presence, that was young James.

"Good morning Sir," they looked up expectantly, work books open and notes being furiously transcribed. James lifted his head momentarily, as a desert fox might, previewing the boundary of his domain.

"How are we getting on?" The class all muttered effusively, but no one broke ranks.

"That is excellent. As you were." Merlin retreated, only too aware of an unspoken rule between student and teacher; 'do not seek that which, is unsolicited!'

The class passed with little more than a few jibes from Amy, only to be met by a torrent of unintelligible retorts in Italian.

The bell rang, and with that a flurry of activity as students headed for tea break. James was the last up, but as he approached the door, rather than exit unapologetically as all the others had done without a word, he turned, all six foot of him, built to be a swimmer, with shoulders to match, and simply smiled.

It was all the thanks Merlin needed and he knew James was in good hands.

The staffroom was a mix of warm sentiments and icy stares. Merlin gravitated to the urn, seeking the comfort of a brew of tea, followed by a raison bun, deposited by one altruistic teacher with time on her hands. Merlin was aware of the enigmatic highs and lows of academia, but as always was generous with his praise. The teacher glowed with pride.

At the allotted chairs meted out for the less salubrious study supervisors, Merlin dismissed the evidentiary glares and sat down to munch on his titbit. The unspoken conversation was like a bottled volcano, and it would only require a single word, or look of contempt to ignite. Merlin mischievously ignored all efforts to return a sullen look; such was the bond of conspirators.

The bell arrived all too soon for Merlin, who was now playing this game with every facet of his brilliance of forty years in sociology reflecting the daggers of hatred, spewed upon his wiry frame. All the walking, swimming and years of activity was a wonderful antidote for simmering deceit. There was such a wonderful expression he had taught his Master's Class, and that was to ensure, that if one were ever to find oneself 'holding anything against another human being, it was an arduous exploit to adhere to, when one had to continue following that person, simply to keep holding whatever the perceived transgression was, against them!'

Merlin recognised all the symptoms of aggrieved disloyalties, but for this sorry world to progress from a Level Three society, the aggressive antics of a hunter-gathering clan would have to be superseded.

The balance of probabilities would be recriminations, and Merlin was aware that the bearded man was due to leave any day soon, to pursue a teacher training course. Merlin was the outsider, he was all too aware of this, when a toxic mix of jealousy and misdirected animosities, fuelled the human brain. Merlin would be meeting Simon, in an unusual setting this Friday, and would seek his opinion such was the level of disdain dividing the team of study supervisors currently.

The week passed without further recriminations, but Merlin was aware that the requisite legalities were being dealt with. The veteran was heard to lament her thirteen years of service, with such veracity claimed in defence of that time, one would have imagined her wishing to claim her gold watch. But her gripe was not so much with Merlin, whom she knew had done what the system expected of him; but with herself, for failing in her motherly duty, to have any compassion on someone in a less fortunate position. Merlin recognised her anger, directed towards a comment about safeguarding, which explained everything. Perhaps there was an opportunity for redemption?

Sadly, Friday evening was to prove otherwise.

"The fool who persists in his folly will become wise."

- William Blake

Friday's Follies

Simon had texted Merlin, saying he was unavailable Saturday morning due to the rugby semi-finals being played.

This was an opportunity for them to cement a growing friendship over a few beers at a local tavern. Simon was a gregarious fellow and Merlin, having foregone any opportunity to have a close circle of friends in East Sussex, jumped at the chance to restore a social life, devoid of any semblance of structure, after Mags had passed on.

She had been the socialite; he the rambler. Mags had organised events with her side of the family, but Merlin, due to his being the only child, had never developed committed relationships. Merlin was the solitary purveyor of social constructs from afar. He had always maintained friendships in his head. This was the consequence of being the only son of a mother and father, who had been academics all their lives. His mother had sacrificed nine months of her precious time to spawn the only child she would deem necessary, in order to solicit the social approval of her peers.

So, Merlin had grown up a lonely child, with imaginary friends. But had he?

His was a world constructed of unseen influences and now that he had the time to deliberate over the past forty years in university life, Merlin was beginning to unravel a multitude of consequential events, that had the hand of some divine inspiration written all over it!

It was to this end, that Merlin would parlé with Simon for the duration of a sociable evening at the Craftsman's Joint. They had chosen the venue due to its central location, and close to the municipal parking area, where timed facilities were not of consequence. But the evening was to throw a wonderful curve ball, which would leave Merlin and Simon recognising otherwise!

"Hi Merlin," Simon greeted him as he stepped in off the High Street and into the cavernous interior.

"Good evening Si," their bond now an affable dimension.

"Do you want to sit down here, or go up onto the deck, with a view over the cemetery?" It sounded eerily like an episode of Dr. Who.

"Upstairs if you like." Merlin would welcome the cooler autumn breeze, after a sweltering week at the coal face of twenty-five classes, rammed one into the next, and little thanks given.

"Great! What's your preference?" Simon pointed to the array of draft beers.

"I'll have a pilsner, if I may?" Merlin smiled. The regular preference of a Friday evening had always been his domain. Mags had all but given up asking.

"Okay, great. I will join you." Simon was a beer man, his South African heritage all too dedicated.

"So you are watching the rugby tomorrow?" Merlin asked, as they found some seats looking out onto the old churchyard.

"Yes, England against our old nemesis; The All Blacks." Simon was smiling.

"Dare I ask who you will be supporting?" Merlin knew that Simon was a recent economic refugee to these parts.

"It will be preferable to meet England in the final!" Simon was assured of the outcome it seemed, of the semi-final to be played on Sunday morning.

"What, you don't think England can beat New Zealand." Merlin grinned.

"No! I believe they could beat them, but if we beat Wales on Sunday, our chances are better, if we play England in the final." Simon knew a thing or two about rugby.

"Ahh! The options are obviously better for South Africa then?" Merlin asked, his knowledge of rugby as a sport limited to what he read in the broadsheets.

"I'm not certain. But I believe that the Springboks have yet to show their best, whilst the All Blacks have been playing really well. One good thing about this is, however, the All Blacks would have to beat us twice to win the world cup. We would only have to beat them once." Merlin understood the odds were stacked on the side of South Africa.

"Yes, it would be amazing to win again!" He looked saddened. "South Africa has been through a deplorable time of late! However, with the demise of Zuma and a potentially weakened China, I believe there are blue skies ahead." Simon had lost his business to a greedy business partner, who had offered a twenty per cent margin on all the sales he made, but reneged once they had a viable business.

"So, South Africa and New Zealand in the final?" Merlin proposed.

"That would be great, but I am not counting my chickens; just praying for Divine intervention." Simon acceded.

"You and all the other millions of rugby fans?" The question rhetorical, but Merlin knew Simon was no fading spirit when it came to his prayer life.

"Huuhhh yes!" Simon laughed. "It's not unlike that great poem written during the Great War, that the allies had used to embolden the troops in the trenches." Simon explained.

"Which one was that?" Merlin knew his poetry.

"I vow to thee my country." Simon offered. "It was a wonderful poem written by Cecil Rice."

"Yes, but Rice was a diplomat to the United States when he wrote the original poem in nineteen o' eight!" Merlin explained.
"Uumhh, indeed!" Simon mused. "But he wrote about the fears of a nation drawn into never-ending wars, and in which the military-industrial complex was subverting peace, in order to finance the armament of nations obsessively fixated on Nationalism."

"It is not dissimilar to what we are witnessing today in the U.S.A."

"You know? It is intriguing and disturbing, but yes, the Trump administration is gearing up for war; but against who?" Simon conceded.
"Well they won't be going to war against the Russians!" Merlin let the subtlety of his comment sink in; it was not necessary.

"Yes, hahhah, Putin and Trump have been happy bedfellows it seems!" Simon joked.

"When you look at the historical evidence of wars, what is the singular factor that the protagonists use to justify war?" Simon continued, "it is trade and the acquisition of wealth."

"Maybe it will be China then?" Merlin surmised.

"Or maybe some other army, or for that matter entity?" Simon quipped.

"What do you mean by that?" Merlin could only guess, given Simon's obsession with all things other-worldly.

"I mean, it could be something other than those countries or enemies, which the media keep alluding to! It could be even more intriguing."

"What? Like extra-terrestrial!" Merlin frowned. The evidence of all wars fought for territory, natural resources, or religion, were always pre-determined by evidentiary circumstances. A war against an extra-terrestrial entity would come out of left field, for the average citizen of the world.

"Well, Trump has just started building a Space Force, to go along with the Army, Navy and Air force. He calls it his Sixth Branch." Simon offered.
"Yes, I have often thought that peculiar. Why now, when the world is a global village, and we are all so much better off than we were a hundred years ago?" The sociological parameters for war were often framed in years of aggressive behaviour of one or more opposing forces, as Merlin understood it.

"That makes sense, if you look at the past hundred years. But as the general population has become better educated, and information is so much more readily accessible, the chances of a Catholic church, or a Colonial government inducing the proletariat to take up arms, is far less likely!"

"Unless you are in control of the information you are distributing." Merlin understood the power of the Mainstream Media to influence the minds of people.

"Wars are always fought by the poor and the lesser educated of a society. They are the canon fodder, as with the Great War, or even the Vietnam War. It is interesting that the number of deaths in the American Army, as a percentage, pro rata, were Negro."

"So, if there were a war today against an Alien Army, who would that canon fodder be?" Merlin was intrigued.

"It would be the young men and women who have grown up playing video games, and who have the technological skills to fight that war." Simon was absolutely correct. Their minds had been warped, by a generation of video games that have immunised them to the effect of death. When they die online, they simply reboot and continue their struggle!

"But why would they fall for such an obvious ruse?" Merlin could understand why young men would wish to join a Space Force, but why would they wish to put themselves in harms way, if they knew the consequences were death?

"It comes back to the nature of mankind. We are ostensibly an aggressive being, with vast stores of memories of the past, as we had to fight against every predator imaginable. Now we must fight against an enemy that is unimaginable, unless we have had our minds warped by technology. A technology that has dumbed down the reality of what war is about." Simon was obviously in his element with this discourse.

"Okay, I concede that a Space Force would be a very attractive adventure for a young man, and I realise that the Atari's and game makers have been preparing our youth for something vastly more consequential than a video game. But in the final analysis, why would a young man be duped into joining the Space Force?"
"Drugs!" Simon let the word simmer.

Merlin looked into those almost reptilian eyes, they were green reflections of something deeper in Spirit. Then it dawned on Merlin; the steady flow of drugs into their society was being orchestrated. Little by little, the government had opened the doors to Nigerian, Bulgarian, Russian and every sinister aspect of the nefariously devious underworld. The government allowed the free flow of every drug available, onto the streets of their towns and cities, to immunise the young men into a state of apathy, to be triggered at a time in the not too distant future. The thought hit him like a bullet.

"So they have been preparing for this war for some time?" Merlin was astonished. The gravitas of his newfound understanding sunk in.

"Not only have they been preparing, but they have already chosen their Space Force. That is why we can now recognise all the symptoms. You do realise this is no different to the wars we have fought in the past against Germany?" Simon reiterated.

"Yes, when I think about it now, both the German military industry used Christian prayer to challenge young men to fight on their side, whilst the English were attempting to get Christians to fight on their side!" Merlin admitted. Christianity had been their drug of choice.

"Yeah, but I need to remind you that Rice wrote 'I Vow To Thee My Country', long before war broke out. Almost six years in fact. It was then used by the powers who control public discourse, and who concocted that ridiculous war, and then even during the Second World War as a hymn inspired by the poem." Simon continued.

"Strangely, the hymn was made famous in the movie, 'Another Country' about the life of Guy Burgess." Merlin had watched the movie years ago.

"It was nothing like the first edition of Rice's poem. The story about the now infamous 'double-agent' Guy Burgess, who they said, had supplied Russia with Britain's military secrets, was played by the Gay actor Rupert Everett." Simon paused.

"But, what interests me is how a modern day Edward Snowdon, is celebrated by all those who believe he has helped to subvert the actions of the military-industrial complex! By supplying WikiLeaks with a vast amount of information on U.S. military activities, he has shown the Deep State up. Yet nearly one hundred years ago, Guy Burgess was vilified by a national pride that embroiled Britain and then America into a First World War, then later, into the Second."

"Yes," Merlin conceded, "it seems we have still learned nothing from history."

"The irony is that the words written by Cecil Rice were so far from the rousing hymn now sung at state funerals in Britain. He lamented death and destruction. He knew all too well what another war would do to the people of Britain!" Simon quaffed his pilsner.

"They even sung the hymn at Diana's funeral; she would have been incensed! The whole point of honouring the 'so-called' heroes of our society is to lament the loss of unnecessary life; not celebrate it!" The evening, so far, was turning out to be a roaring success.

"Another pilsner," Simon stood. "Let me get this one."

"Thank you," Merlin watched Simon turn on his heel and disappear down the stairs to the pub. Looking out onto that graveyard below, he wondered how many of those tombstones held the secrets of a society obliterated by the greed of a select few, who had orchestrated war from the ivory towers on Canary Wharf, and in the City of London all those years ago. He knew the Rothschild's banking family had funded the wars fought in Europe for centuries, sometimes funding both sides for profit. They had financed Cecil John Rhodes in his quest to consolidate the De Beers mine in Kimberley, they had financed the Boer War that dispossessed the people of Southern Africa of the wealth that lay below the ground. It was their interventions in Zimbabwe recently that had overturned a Two Thousand and Eight election in Zimbabwe and ensured the diamond fields of Marange and elsewhere had been controlled by Mugabe and his generals. That flood of diamonds out of Zimbabwe had never been allocated to the Zimbabwean economy, and the cartels had seen meteoric rises in their profits. This new war was to be fought over what commodities? There was always something!
"What you thinking about," Simon returned to find Merlin deep in thought.

"Just looking at those gravestones and thinking about who those people were." Merlin smiling, accepted another draft.

"You know, I often walk through here and think the same thing." Simon agreed. "It's almost as though we are on the same wavelength!"

"Yes, a bit spooky, hehe!" Merlin laughed, the sense of a freedom from the demons that had been chasing him was a blessing.

"Can I be brutally honest?" Simon was feeling at ease, to speak his mind; or perhaps is was the intoxicating effect of the beer, and a friendly conversation.

"Yes, or course. What do you wish to tell me?" Merlin felt their friendship blossoming.

"When you speak of feeling spooky! I have been witnessing angels all around you since we have been sitting here." Simon kept his intense eyes focused on Merlin.

"Okay… " Merlin was a little taken aback.

"They are images of your consciousness, projected into my psychic vision." Simon explained.

"You mean, that I am projecting my own thoughts into the etheric world, and you are picking up on the people from my past." Merlin needed to explain it scientifically for his own understanding.

"Yes! Exactly. You're thoughts manifest real images, through the power of your Consciousness. The idea of ghosts, or of spiritual beings, is a conscious assessment of our ability to slow down your brain waves, to a Gamma Energy Frequency, in which anyone who can pick up on your Consciousness, is able to visualise the thoughts of your mind." Simon expanded his discernment.
"You mean that I am able to project my thoughts telepathically into the ether, and you are capable of receiving them?" Merlin quizzed.

"That is precisely what I am able to do." The breeze from the churchyard wafted through the wooden panels on the deck, but Merlin was unperturbed by the chilly air.

"Yes, and when I see these images they are as real as watching a video. I know that the image is being projected onto my screen in my living room, using electronic wizardry, but I still recognise the characters on the screen. They appear as an electro-magnetic translation of a pre-defined signal, created from a real-life studio. But they are none-the-less real." Simon espoused.

"In exactly the same way, I am seeing your electronic signals, emitted from your brain, through a series of transmitters in your head, and I can receive them in an electronic format, and through my Consciousness, I am able to project them as a three-dimensional picture." The vastness of space and time just became imaginable, as Simon explained his interpretation of Spirituality.

"That is absolutely fascinating!" Merlin enthused. Simon knew what the next question would be.

"Just so that I am clear on this. What exactly can you see?"

"Ahh! Yes, I have been witnessing a lady, somewhat frail, with a beautiful face, and lovely smile; but she looks sad. She has been standing over your left shoulder for some time. I can see her eyes and they are aquamarine. Perhaps, she is your wife?" Merlin smiled. He had always sensed Mags around, but knew he had so much to say to her.

"What is she wearing?" Merlin asked.

"She is wearing a wedding dress! But it seems to keep changing from a white, veiled satin, to a green, rough cheese cloth, with ruffles around the neck!"

Merlin smiled. A sad but consenting smile! Mags had never been afforded the joy of a wedding day, and Merlin knew her favourite colour. They matched her eyes perfectly and were the predominant colour in her wardrobe. He had still not cleared out the closet where her clothes still hung.

"Thank you." Merlin needed no further affirmation.

"How do you suppose these projections are cable of being made, from a purely scientific perspective?" Merlin asked.

"It has a lot to do with Quantum Energy Frequency." Simon repeated his theory.

"I believe that the Buddhists had a head start on most of us, but their knowledge was passed on through a tradition in the East, which is also relevant to many ancient societies. You see, contrary to our Judeo-Christian background, the Hebrews did not have a monopoly on divine intervention, despite what they would want you to believe. Their traditions came from Utmoses, the leader of a breakaway group of Egyptian slaves, whose lives had been thrown into turmoil by a catastrophic natural event, some two thousand years before we even heard about Jesus." Simon expanded.

"Yes, I know about the Hebrew exodus from Egypt, but where did the Egyptians get their knowledge? I am one of those sceptics, who can see the evidence of the pyramids and that it was not the Egyptians who built them." Merlin agreed.

'My understanding is that the Egyptians believed in the Sun god Horus, and the legends of Horus were passed on to them through the ancient Sumerians. They may have received their knowledge from the Vedic tradition, and so it may go back a hundred thousand years, or more!" The conversation flowed.

"Yes, I once met a Christian, who believed that the world was only six thousand years old." Merlin laughed.

"Oh yeah. Give me a break! Those creationists love to ignore all the scientific evidence, but they have never truly understood the etheric evidence." Simon offered.

"Uhmm! What do you honestly believe?" Merlin was open to all ideas. He had never been trapped by the fear projected by the church on a society, largely superstitious because they had so many questions they could not answer at a time when the church controlled the flow of knowledge.

"I believe that the church destroyed the library of Alexandria, because it contained evidence of all these ancient mysteries, and have controlled the information from that library for over seventeen hundred years. If we could access that library today, we would have Zero Point Energy, levitation devices, and the ability to heal through Transcendental Healing Inspired Sound Therapy."

"But where do you think the ancient people got all that information about the technologies housed in the Alexandria library?" Merlin was channelling.

"If you are asking me, do I believe in ancient aliens, my only answer is I don't know for certain?" Simon conceded.

"My sense of where we come form is steeped in a Consciousness of evidentiary material, hidden from the world, so that a select few can continue to dominate the discourse and maintain control of power and money."

Merlin had an indication that Simon had elaborated his understanding from a position of knowledge, but was he channelling this knowledge from a position of spiritual knowledge?

"The truth is being revealed." Simon continued. "Little by little, as human beings evolve, as we are doing every generation, the next generation will uncover more of these ancient mysteries. The church no longer has a grip on the dissemination of knowledge, and so I believe this new generation of youngsters will be able to gain more insight. It is like the idea of enlightenment was to the early Gnostics, but now the modern equivalent to the library of Alexandria is the inter-net. We are all connected, electronically, but what the Zed-generation need to know, is that we are all connected transcendentally!"

"Is that where the idea of serendipity comes from?" Merlin was aware that their conversation was flowing towards an irrefutable science-fact.

"I understand the act of serendipity' which is described in the dictionary as an occurrence and development of events through chance in a happy or beneficial way, or coincidence!" Simon motioned with his fingers. "The Vedic tradition calls it a happy accident!"

"However, as all spiritually super-conscious people know, there is no such thing as a chance meeting, or occurrences that seem to happen fortuitously. The basis for serendipity is the alignment of our spirit, when two or more positive spirits are working together to formulate an outcome." Simon was a trove of information.

"In fact the origin of the word relates to a gift of prophecy or the ability to foresee events in the future. Christians know this to be the work of the Holy Spirit, or the gifts of prophesy. So, in my diaries, I suggest that the repeated incidences of the 'Word', in italics and the reoccurrence of the same themes that I refer to are in fact works of the spirit. These seemingly continuous references, and inexplicably related readings, and lessons are affirmations of the spirit, and how the spirit brings our attention to knowledge of these truths."

"So, what is the definition of 'Spirit'?" Merlin enquired.

"In scientific speak it would probably be called a Consciousness. Maybe even a Global Consciousness connecting all sentient beings. I don't know for certain, because nobody truly knows!" He paused thoughtfully.

"In English, the word to meditate means to ponder. But in Hebrew, it is the word 'hagah', which means to utter or mutter under your breath." Merlin knew this, he could not help but think how Jewish this sounded!

"In other words, when you meditate on God's 'Word', you speak forth or confess his 'Word' instead of just giving it mental consent."

"Imagine if we can visualise someone else's thoughts through a projection of their consciousness, just imagine how much more powerful would be the mental causation of some sentient being, who was our genetic fore-bearer?" Simon offered his synopsis.

"You mean, if we were in fact made in the image of that being?" Merlin was catching on.

"Yes, precisely! The Jews believe we were made in the image of God. But what if we were in fact made in the image of a much higher intelligence than ourselves?" Simon laughed self-consciously.
"Then that would make complete nonsense of little green men running around trying to abduct us!" Merlin conceded.

"This goes to the very heart of my argument. The governments of this world control the discourse through mainstream media and are attempting to sell us a story about extra-terrestrials. But, what if those ET's were in fact a highly evolved human being, who are our ancestors, and whom we can communicate with through our brain waves, as a consequence of being connected transcendentally?"

"That would explain why they keep everyone ignorant of the truth of these higher entities, so they can sell us a war against an unseen enemy, and keep everyone fearful for another two thousand years!" The penny dropped and Merlin knew why he had always been suspicious of their motives.

When we connect the synapses in our minds, connecting the pathways to our true potential with ultimate capacity, then in essence we are using our minds, to have the capacity to know, or gain knowledge, and to telepath messages through that unseen aspect of our world we call the vast unknown. This is a multi-dimensional universe and with our minds we have the abilities to form ideas, and to transmit that thought energy far beyond what would be considered the norm.

"Yes! That is why they are selling a fictional story about ET and training the youth to play war games on videos. The third world war won't be fought over nuclear bombs, or chemical weapons. They are so much less effective than a war that controls the minds of people through their Consciousness!" The conversation had now gone full circle, but there was nothing coincidental about it.

As Simon and Merlin made their way down to Merlin's car, there was a Monsoon outside, or so it seemed. But as they turned the corner towards the churchyard and access to the car park, Merlin bumped directly into a colleague from work. She looked somewhat sheepish, smiled and ducked back under the cover of the restaurant doorway.

Emerging from the restaurant, and caught like a herd of Deer in the headlights of an articulated lorry, a group of study supervisors stood, wide-eyed and somewhat shaken.

It was the bearded man and a gaggle of the female study supervisors from school. Each surveyed him, recognising their predicament, then huddled together.

The does in the group sought shelter under the eves, turning to their dominant buck, and then Merlin and Simon were past them and safely under the large golfing brolly Simon had brought, skipping through the puddles in search of Merlin's car.

"Who was that?" Simon asked as they made their way past the ancient tombstones, but Merlin just laughed.

"Education is the most powerful weapon which you can use to change the world."

- **Nelson Mandela**

The Tree of Life

On Monday morning, of all subjects, Merlin found himself in a Year Ten Geography classroom, conducting registration. The kids were still hyperactive, after a weekend that many spoke of as incredible.

"Sir, Sir, did you watch the rugby on Saturday," the bellow had come from none other than Lochlan.

Merlin liked this lad. He was outgoing, but had his feet firmly on the ground. "No, I'm not much of a rugby person," admitted Merlin.

"Sir, Sir, we beat the All Blacks!" His cry was almost as loud and as persuasive as a New Zealand Hakka.

"Yes, I heard," Merlin had spent Sunday in his favourite coffee shop reading the broadsheets.

"It was incredible," he broadcast to those in the class, interested. "We are going to win the world cup this Saturday."

His persuasiveness a chant that the lads took up, but which fell on deaf ears, as the girls in the class shunned his enthusiasm and rebuffed the lads by resorting to social media. Merlin could not help but feel the call of good old-fashioned schooling.

"That would be a wonderful boost for the country," Merlin conceded. The Brexit debate was front and centre after three and a half years of public vilification by the ruling class, and commoners being told what was good for them.

"What do you mean?" Lochlan was not a social butterfly. His world view was from the base of the scrum, where he mustered his troops and played Eighth Man.

"Well, I'm just thinking that the media is always keen to distract everyone into thinking about something other than the political troubles we are having. So, when the country does well at sport, it becomes a welcome distraction from the troubles of government." Merlin was not sure how much would sink in.

"Oh! You mean that the Illuminati keep us dumb, so we can't question what they are doing?" It was Brookland.

"The Illuminati?" Quizzed Carlos. He was the Spanish lad whose dark curly hair and sultry good looks, gave him an air of femininity, which clashed with the fair-skinned, brush-cuts of the bigger English lads.

"You're such a queer," Jason shouted him down. He was the outsider.

"Enough of that," Merlin chided him. "Jason, you know you can't use that form of discriminatory language!" Merlin was up and out of his chair.

The class had fallen silent. Jason shrunk back, not so much because of the looming presence of Merlin, but because he realised his mistake. Socialization had bred an independent understanding of decorum in classes throughout the English countryside, but clearly what was still being preached in some homes, spoke of an unhealthy obsession with bigotry.

"Sorry Sir," Jason looked suitably chastised. There was a consensus of overstepping the mark, and the class held their attention on Merlin. Even the girls looked up from their smart phones.

"Okay, I won't take this any further, but I want you to apologise to Carlos, now!" Merlin held court.

"Sorry, Carlo," Jason muttered.

"Okay, seeing as we are in a Geography class, who can name the flags on the ceiling?" Merlin diverted their attention to the flags draped lazily across the class ceiling.

"Oh, yes Sir," shouted Lochlan. His hand raised as if to redirect the attention back to him.

"Okay, let's start in the corner here." The flags were arrayed in a seemingly diverse manner, with continents, hemispheres and longitudes displayed somewhat erratically. It was a reminder to Merlin of the power of globalism, but still declared an allegiance to inclusivity. Perhaps it was a way teachers could speak to the influence of migration as a factor in world politics, because there was no structure to the layout.

"Greece, China, Australia, Norway, ummhm, United States…" Lochlan proceeded. The Year nines suitably distracted helped him with the less obvious, and some were completely foreign.

"That is the Gay flag," It was Silvina. In the opposite corner to the direction Merlin stood, was the LGBT+ flag. The Rainbow flag! Merlin turned just in time to see the boys turn on Carlos once more.

"That is interesting," Merlin conceded. "I would not have considered the LGBT+ flag as being representational of a country!" It seemed the Angels were redirecting the conversation once more.

"Carlos is Gay." It was Alfie again.

"No I'm not!" Remonstrated the young man once more. It seemed there was a deeper, more sinister plot seeping through the underbelly of the class substructure.

"Okay, Alfie. That's enough!" Merlin had tried to change the subject, but it was obvious that something, some deeper issue, was required to be dealt with.

"I want to remind you all," Merlin directed his attention to the lads in the East corner. "We are not here to be discriminatory, but seeing as the subject is a topical one, I need to make it very clear, that in a class of thirty students, it is inevitable that at least three of you, may eventually identify as Gay or Lesbian, or perhaps even Bi!"

"Yes, you're Gay," Alfie seemed vindicated. Merlin turned once more in disapproval.

"No! I don't want to be Gay." Carlos was mortified. His reaction told Merlin all he needed to know.

"Carlos," Merlin soothed him. "You may not be Gay, and by someone telling you, you are, does not make it so."

"Now, Alfie. I want to also remind you, that in English we have a wonderful expression, which is; 'He who shouts loudest, has the greatest to hide!' Remember, when you point a finger at someone else, there are usually three fingers pointing back at you." Merlin raised his eyebrows.

There was an uncomfortable awkwardness amongst the lads in the corner, and if looks could be deciphered, the language was one of silent brotherhood. Merlin understood that statistics played a significant role in determining outcomes, but socialization would never be consequential. If three of the lads, or girls, seated before him were to eventually identify as LGBT+, then the chances were, half the lads at least, would be experimenting to determine their eventual outcome.

Carlos seemed disquieted, and Merlin resolved to take him aside and ask him if he was being preyed upon by some of the bigger lads. In the interim, only education and a consistent resolution towards communicating the truth would help to move that discussion forward.

The bell sounded, and all was forgotten.

Back in the staffroom, the air of discomfort was so pronounced that not a single Study Supervisor could even bring them selves to greet Merlin; that is until Pauline walked in!

"Good morning Merlin," Pauline was her typical bubbly self.

"Ah, good morning Pauline." Merlin smiled, his warmth received. He hoped she would have some good news for him, about Josh.

"How was your weekend?" Pauline had been on a retreat, so Merlin knew the question would inevitably lead to that discussion.

"Extremely interesting," Merlin was alluding to the Friday evening incident, but would need Pauline to ask, such was the social etiquette.

"Oh! Lovely, what happened?" Pauline was eager to tell him her news.

"Well, it may need to wait until later," he smiled charmingly, no effort to not be overheard by the gaggle of ladies.

"How was your retreat?" Merlin asked.

"Yes, oh! Wow!" Pauline gushed, "I was meditating on Sunday morning, and I literally felt myself lift up, out of my body and before I knew it, I was looking down on myself."

"Wow, what a wonderful experience!" Merlin encouraged.

"It was so surreal that I felt guilty, some how; then immediately I returned back into my body!" Pauline was conflicted.

"Why?" Merlin coaxed.

"Well, I was there to help my brother with the retreat, so I felt I should not be experiencing an out-of-body trance." Pauline's eyes searched his for a rationale.

"Oh my goodness," he echoed her dismay. "You should allow yourself that blessing. There is no reason to limit your Spiritual expression. Remember, we are Spiritual beings, trapped in a physical shell." He repeated Simon's words, feeling like a convert.

"I know," Pauline lamented. "But I knew I had to get back to prepare the lunches for the paying guests!" Merlin felt her anguish. He knew this was how the church had trapped the faithful for two thousand years, and why now, so many were turning their backs on those limitations.

"My sense," he admitted, "is that in future, allow yourself that expression of true divinity, and release your soul to existential travel. This is the way our consciousness learns of our past lives."

"It felt weird," she agreed, "but exciting at the same time."

"Remember, the Bible is a group of books, some written during the Exodus, others written during the Exile, and then the later prophets written during the occupation of Palestine. In all these events, the Jewish people were recording their stories verbally, or putting their thoughts down in parchment, during times of struggle." Merlin changed track.

"Each of those stories, were either mythical, like the book of Genesis, or were related recordings of real people, in historical contexts. The reason I am telling you this is that the people who recorded the stories, were the people who controlled the narrative." Merlin encouraged.

"We must never feel guilty of having a Spiritual experience, because that is how God speaks to us."

"Yes, I know that all my childhood experiences were at church on a Sunday morning, and always about having to keep quiet and listen!" Pauline lamented. Merlin could feel her pain.

"Yes, but it is always the leadership who dictate the narrative. When you are able to express yourself freely as a child of God, you will find that the true heaven is actually an expression of your own consciousness. Our memories are an integral part of our subjective experiences as Spiritual beings. The part of your brain that allows you to recall your past experiences, is called the Limbic brain." Merlin explained.

"So, was I accessing this Limbic brain, when I was meditating?" Pauline grasped.

"Yes, this part of your brain allows chemicals to dictate your mood, and is the functioning part of the brain that is the seat of our conscience. This is where we have our creative centre. So, when we are learning, it is about connecting those new synapses in the brain. The Neo-cortex is our thinking brain. It is quite simple really, because when we are learning, we are forging new synaptic connections." Merlin was attempting to keep it simple.

"Wow! So was I really experiencing an out-of-body event; or do you believe it is more to do with my memory?"

"Both!" Merlin smiled. "I believe that the chemicals released into your brain when you are meditating, allow you to reconnect with past memories, but also allow your brain to imagine your Spiritual self. Remember, when you slow down your heart beat, channel your energy to the Limbic brain, and your vibrational frequency is at a minimum, you reach the status of gamma wave energy." Merlin inspired.

The Limbic brain is your emotional brain, and provides the chemicals in your brain that allow you to feel euphoria, or fear, or a sense of peace. The Limbic brain is now free to instruct the whole brain chemically, and this allows the body to form new genes to generate greater understanding of what the subconscious mind has already understood."

"So the subconscious mind, is our Spiritual brain?"

"Yes, precisely!" Merlin was preaching to the converted.

"When your actions begin to equal your thoughts through praying or meditating, the Limbic brain, which is also called the autonomic brain, allows you to control stress. So, by continually meditating, we learn to change our thoughts, chemically. It is quite remarkable, because we literally go from knowledge, to experience, to wisdom. Or as the ancient people believed, from mind, to body, to soul."

"It that why you said that we are Spiritual beings, disguised as human beings?" Pauline used an interesting turn of phrase. He had never thought of himself being in disguise, but now that he thought about it, if humans were Spiritual by origin, by changing our ability to resonate at higher frequencies, would make us visible to the human eye; then we would by default be disguising our true elements.

"When we change our chemical brain, everything changes around us. Our new thoughts, beget a new reality." Merlin reiterated. So, new thoughts, which turn to new choices, which induce new behaviours, which become new experiences, then lead to new emotions? He questioned himself. That would be a real subject, if possible for his Year eleven Science class!

"I get it," Pauline acknowledged. "It's what we refer to as the Kabbalah. The source of all knowledge."

"Uuhhmmm, indeed!" But Merlin knew that the tree of life is an example of a diagram used in various mystical traditions. It usually consisted of ten nodes symbolizing different archetypes and twenty-two lines connecting the nodes. The nodes were often arranged into three columns to represent that they belonged to a common category. However, Merlin rationalised that the complexity of these mystical beliefs were not as complex as first imagined. If his students would be able to quieten their minds from all the distractions of the modern world, he was convinced they would be capable of these insights. His question about Josh would wait.

The bell went, and Merlin would wend his way down to the Art Block, all the while musing over the likelihood that Pauline's experience, would ultimately serve as an example of how Spirituality would win the day!

"If you want to find the secrets of the universe, think in terms of energy, frequency and vibration."

- **Nikola Tesla**

Friday Evening Revisited

During the week, Simon contacted Merlin to say he would be watching the rugby on Saturday morning, and would Merlin like to join him. Merlin had declined, but agreed to meet Simon once more at the local pub.

Merlin arrived to find Simon ensconced in his comfortable seat, overlooking the graveyard.

"Good evening, how has your week been?" Simon asked.

"Very interesting," Merlin was keen to tell Simon about the events of the week.

"Ah, pray do tell!" Simon had a mischievous smile.

"Yes, it has been a roller-coaster, to be honest." Merlin sat, beer in hand.

"What do you know about the LGBT movement?" Merlin had left out the Q as a mark of respect. There was nothing queer about Simon.

"In what respect," Simon recognised the open-ended question.

"Well, its just that I had a young lad in class Monday, whom I suspect has been targeted by a group of lads, and I can't explain my sense of concern, other than I believe they are taking advantage of him." Merlin had that uneasy feeling again.

"Taking advantage, as in sexually?" Simon lowered his voice.

"Yes, I get the sense that they have some kind of hold over him, which is unwarranted."

"Well, if the Hite Report and all the subsequent surveys done regarding childhood sexuality have any relevance, it is likely the boys in question have discovered sex, and are likely manipulating this lad for their gratification." Simon admitted.

"Oh dear," Merlin's suspicions were affirmed. "I know that the group in question are loitering in the streets after school, but I had no inkling they were that way inclined." Merlin had recognised this gang was a rough crowd.

"No! They don't have to be Gay," Simon explained. Merlin knew this he had just never experienced it.

"The lads are testing their own sexuality issues, and often at this age, they will have identified a younger or weaker lad, whom they then coerce into providing sexual favours. It is not that they will identify as Gay, or that they necessarily have Gay inclinations during puberty; it is a supply and demand issue!"

Good God, Merlin had never heard this explained with such forthright simplicity.

"You need to understand, the unspoken rules of teenage sexuality." The words with Simon's voice, lowered but soothingly sunk in.

"So, you are saying they are demanding sexual favours from this lad?" Merlin would have to intercede.

"Demanding, or coercing, it may be that they are all simply inquisitive, and looking to experiment." Simon said.

"What if the lad in question does not want to play along?" Merlin had heard his plaintive cry. Carlos might be a victim here!

"Believe me, if he did not wish to play along, he would find simple ways of avoiding them." Simon offered. "That is, unless they may have some form of evidence they are using to coerce him with."

"Like what?" Merlin had only ever taught university students. They were another group entirely, but because of their age, they often had already determined their sexual classifications before embarking on a university education.

"Well, today, because of the proliferation of mobile phones with cameras, they often record these activities, and it may be that they are threatening him with disclosure, if he does not play along!" Simon conceded.

"Oh dear!" Merlin had visions of suicide and all kinds of self-harming going on.

"The key to solving this issue, is to confront the lads who have been bullying him, and demand that if they have any video material of these activities, they must destroy them immediately, or face the consequences." Simon had dealt with positive affirmations through youth leadership programs.

"Often when faced with being outed themselves, they will realise that the issue will soon escalate into an embarrassing situation for themselves."

"Yes, I have heard that these videos are used for cyber-bullying, but I was not aware how perverse this really is." Merlin now had genuine concerns for Carlo's safety.

"What you can do, is Pray into the issue, and ask that the lads in question, discover their true sexual identity, and if they are innately straight, they will move on and form relationships with the girls in their group. But often, some will prefer to remain sexually active within their peer group, until they gain the confidence to embark on a permanent relationship; girl or boy!" Simon understood this better than Merlin, with all his sociology knowledge.

"The problem is that schools prefer to bury their heads in the sand, when it comes to sexuality issues, because the protection mechanisms in place today in schools are so convoluted. To avoid any semblance of impropriety from being raised, these teachers simply walk around ignoring all the obvious clues. Remember, boys particularly, will always want to experiment, and if the school maintains repressive regulations in terms of allowing young men or women to come forward with their sexual identity, those schools are planning to fail."

"Yes, well, it is evident that there is an exceptional amount of homophobia within the teaching staff!" Merlin explained.

"Ahh! If there is blatant evidence of the teachers continuing a bias of bigotry, then they are setting themselves up for failure. Ofsted should be advised, and mechanisms installed to prevent further abuses." Simon was aware of these mechanisms, after having been with youth programs.

"Well, as it transpires, I became a whistle blower several weeks ago!" Merlin grimaced. The past few weeks had been purgatory for him.

"Oh! I wondered about that." Simon was concerned. "I noticed an edge in your manner, ever since you introduced me to James." Simon had thought it odd.

"Yes, I overheard a group of Study Supervisors discussing a transgender student and sharing the details from the computer system at school." Merlin had not wished to burden Simon with his own trails.

"Oh my goodness!" Simon sat forward. "I had an inkling something was wrong."

"Yes, and since then I have been targeted by these people, with snide and negative innuendo." Merlin tried to put a brave face on.

"Okay, I get it! They are using the classic tactic of offence is the best form of defence. Your best defence is Prayer." Simon was unequivocal.

"Yes, I have tried to spend some time in prayer, but often it does not feel the right thing to do. I want to take this to Ofsted, but my sense is they will ignore me, just as the school authorities have done." Merlin complained.

"No! Don't feel it is your fault. You did the right thing. But often we don't Pray long enough to ensure our concerns are heard by Father Spirit. In fact, we should pray together, and that way, when two people gather together in Prayer, the Prayers are heard far more readily." Simon was quoting from his Biblical references.

"Yes, but living alone, it is not so easy." Merlin smiled. Even Mags had been a non-believer.

"I know, it is particularly difficult when you are not a regular church goer. Sadly the church itself has to shoulder some of the blame. But when two believers get together and they Pray for a resolution to a specific problem, I am convinced those prayers are heard." Simon was a believer, but because of his own sexuality issues, he had been turned away from his church.

"Well, if you would be willing to Pray with me," Merlin's voice trailed off.

"Off course I will." Simon grinned. "There is nothing that Father Spirit does not hear. Even if you are a moderate believer, there is something uncanny about spending time in Prayer or meditation." Simon offered.

"When I was a young man, about fifteen years of age, I was a bit geeky, and had a set of buck teeth that aroused a great deal of spiteful remarks, even from my brother. But, I had also discovered through my isolation, that Prayer was a remarkably powerful antidote to hatred. I have never told anyone else, but as a young Gay lad, living in a particularly conservative environment like Rhodesia, during the war of liberation, I suffered atrocious attacks of vitriol from a number of lads in my peer group. One afternoon I was outed by these lads, and I was forced to recognise my sexuality. It was grim, but through Prayer and talking to God, or as I call him, GOD, which is an acronym for Good Orchestrated Divine power, I was able to work through my concerns. Before long, I was being invited to parties and being surrounded by friends who had now recognised that I was a kindred spirit." Simon took a swig of beer.

"It is remarkable, but through my Prayer life, I was introduced to other lads, who were also going through exactly what I was experiencing. No one was in the closet any longer, and even given the circumstances of pre-independence Zimbabwe, I was soon being accepted into certain social constructs." Simon quipped.

"It was hugely empowering, and before long I was playing first team rugby and surrounded by adoring lads, who wanted to be my friend." Simon looked back wistfully.

"Incredible," Merlin was aghast. The power of Prayer had not only allowed Simon to be honest with his peer group, but ultimately to be honest with him self.

"Remember, the Apostle Paul, or Saul as he once was, was homosexual!" Simon doubled-down. "The thorn that he had in his side was his sexuality, and any church goer who denies this, is not looking at the evidence. The letters he wrote, were often a cry for help. Anyone with any grasp of basic psychology can recognise that Paul was in the closet, and all his relationships with young men were fraught with conjecture." Simon was in his element.

"Yes, I have often wondered about that." Merlin agreed. "For example, why did Paul have a fallout with Barnabas on his first journey, and why did Paul not want Mark to join them on his second journey?"

"There you go!" Simon erupted. "Thank you, I always had my doubts."

"Yes, it seemed odd to me when I first read Acts, but I needed to put my sociology professor cap on to get into the meat of it!"

"I think we are underestimating the power and relevance of the New Testament Bible, as a story of Christian ideology." Simon presented his opinion with a level-headedness so often excluded from church dogma.

"The problem we have today is that the church has been hijacked by the Catholics, who continue to feed off fear and divisiveness, instead of Praying for solutions." Simon knew that in a world, which has been commandeered by the new world religion of consumerism, there were solutions for all the animosity still prevalent, two thousand years later.

"Can we Pray later for the young lad at school?" Merlin asked.

"Yes, I would love to pray with you." Simon rose. Can I get you another,'" he gestured, empty beer glass in hand.

As Simon went off to the bar, Merlin thought about the Bible, which have survived the test of time and reminded him of the truths of antiquity, borne out by sociological constructs of a civilization which, not only prospered during a time of great unrest; but became the dominant format for constructive thinking, despite the evil elements of Nero and many Roman emperors who followed. The wisdom displayed in The Gospel stories, were a stark reminder of how society had been led astray by a Global Elitist Agenda.

Given the sum total of the Parables, not to mention the plethora of healings documented in the Gospels, there was a vast library of knowledge that humans could learn from, despite the attempts of the liberal compassionates to destroy the historical accuracies of those texts. The truths contained in the Biblical texts had not only stood the test of time, but were now revealing the science behind so much of what the scientific world have been missing, in order to explain their Quantum Philosophies. The Quantum Enigma could only be explained by Biblical narratives, as Nikola Tesla had contested, when he had said: "The day science begins to study non-physical phenomena; it will make more progress in one decade than in all the previous centuries of its existence."

"Here we go, I don't want to get too intoxicated, because I want to up early to watch the rugby final." Simon returned with drafts in hand.

"Ah, yes, England up against South Africa!" Merlin thought how ironic!

"Yes, and tonight I am going to Pray for the Springboks to be filled with the Holy Spirit, and push the English pack off the ball, then turn their lineouts into a complete shambles." Simon grinned. "I hope you don't mind?"

"Not at all," Merlin laughed. "It's not one way or the other to me."

"But seriously, I think that we need to dominate up front, keep the possession from the English tight five; somehow isolate the front row, and weaken them, then spin the ball to our wings." Simon outlined the basic principles of tried and tested rugby success.

"Yes, I believe that is the way to win any rugby game!" Merlin enthused.

"Yes, but I am quite serious when I say, I am Praying for the English team to become disheartened, weakened and I believe that the Holy Spirit will suck all their energy out of them!"

"My thoughts at night are often on what I call 'Viewsion', or as I have termed this power, 'The ability of the mind, through Spirit, to view the vision of my desires and construct a hologram of what I have perceived, so as to conceive the manifest form as a visual experience." Simon admitted.

"You do know that the act of visualizing your goals is actually based on neuroscience principles?" Merlin offered. "In fact, the other day I was telling all my students about Intentional Technology."

"Yes, that is the scientific representation of how the global consciousness works. When we Meditate and Pray in 'The Spirit', there is an incredible energy that is created, through The Torus. What Spiritualists call the aura. But it is so much more. It has the ability to connect us with others, and with the Universal Forces.

"Yes, and I believe that is the essence of all Prayer. By creating a static image or even a mental movie in my mind, I can activate a group of cells in my brain that reinforce the image and the outcome you want to achieve." Simon reiterated.

"Interesting!" Merlin nodded. "But how do you project those thoughts into the world, so as to change the outcomes of other peoples' experiences?"

"I project my thoughts, through focused isolation of a definitive objective, and by honing in on that specific objective and the people involved, I can change the way they view their outcome. For example, I will focus on the big black second row forward, and Pray that he is rendered entirely obsolete. Unless he is able to counter my Prayer, through redirecting his fears and doubts about himself, he will absorb my energy field of thought, and constantly be feeling inadequate. I know it sounds quite unfair, but psychological warfare has been used for thousands of years, and often it is people like myself who have been targeted!" Simon offered his explanation.

Merlin was in complete agreement. He would be intrigued to see the results of the game in the morning.

"But how would a team counter this psychological warfare?" Merlin wanted a scientific answer.

"Simply reinforcing the positive outcomes we desire, instructs our non-conscious brain to develop what I call a powerful Habit Loop, which immediately works on helping us to achieve our goals." Simon conceded.

"But what if the person you are Praying for is also Praying for a different outcome?" Merlin was not convinced.
"It must have integrity. For example, I believe in Karmic Justice, and this is not isolated to Buddhist or Monotheistic religions. It is the work of a Spiritual Power that connects the Universe. Even non-sentient creatures, or what we believe to be non-sentient creatures, must have a connection to creation. So, if we consider that every Hydrogen and Oxygen molecule has an energy, formed by the proton in its nuclei, then it is conceivable that each molecule speaks to each other molecule through that latent energy." Simon waited for Merlin to acknowledge his theory.

"Yes, that makes sense." Merlin nodded.

"If each molecule forms a bond, through that energy, then the Universe must be connected by each molecule in synergy with each other. A proton, has a memory, which holds it in suspension with each nuclei. If our basic building blocks of Life are able to communicate with one another, then why not the collective?" Simon speculated.

"Okay, I get it." Merlin approved.

"The Universe is one seamless energy Torus, with each organism on Earth and in the Ether, capable of communication. So, when I Pray for Mario Itoje to loose heart, because his intentions have no integrity, then he will feel the Universal powers shift away from him, and they will be in opposition to him. My understanding of why the English Rugby Football Union offered each player in the squad £125,000.00 if they win the final against the Springboks, is an indication that there is no integrity in their pursuit; it has become a function of monetary reward, and not national pride."

"I believe that by Praying for integrity to be paramount, the English team will suffer karmic justice. I am simply the messenger, but the Holy Spirit, or global consciousness, is the mechanism." They both looked at each other, Merlin's discernment growing.

"So you are saying that we can manufacture the work of the Holy Spirit through us?" Merlin asked.

"Yes. Can we pray for an outcome, and should there be integrity, the outcome is manifest. Let us pray for your young lad, and I will show you how I achieve this outcome, through what I call my Christ Consciousness Healing Prayer. It's what Buddhists have been using for millennia; chanting."

"It's a part of what I refer to as the revealing the hidden structures of quantum entangled states." Simon paused; Merlin was listening.

"Quantum physics investigates matter and energy at its most fundamental level and so a particle may be, respectively a photon or electron. By using Quantum Optics, this effects light in the form of photons. To look at the properties inside these photons, or light particles what is required, is the manipulation of them for either information processing or for sending communication signals. This is key to understanding the Quantum Enigma. Light passing through a prescribed series of slits in a given board, will either behave as particles, or as waves. To determine which one, they will behave as, depends on our vantage point; so in reality, light is subjective, and requires our perception." Simon was on a roll.

"The reason why photons are used is because they are light. It's the fastest object in the universe. Light is also quite easy to control, so it can be observed in all these fundamental properties of quantum mechanics with just simple lasers. But, when we add mirrors to the equation, passing photons through a labyrinth of sequences, projected by laser light into a complex structure of refractors and mirrors, the result is astounding."

"Because these Photons do not have mass, or 'M', they are easily manipulated, and they behave in the manner predicted by Nikola Tesla, when he said; "If you only knew the magnificence of the 3, 6, and 9, then you would have a key to the universe." The key to understanding entangled states, is then a 3; 6; 9 code. What he was referring to is the combination of Quarks, Leptons and Bosons. Consistently, nature reflects matter, and anti-matter in the form of sequences. This is the God Principle, which dictates all interactions in our Universe."

Merlin smiled; this should be interesting, but at least they were alone on the deck, the late autumn weather, somewhat inclement.

Simon began; "Ka, Ra, Sa, Ta, Ah, La……"

"An investment in knowledge pays the best interest."

– Benjamin Franklin

Schooling

Merlin had walked into class on Monday morning, knowing there would be a few despondent faces. However, he was quite amazed by the sense of dispassionate despondency that filled the air, particularly in the Year Ten Beliefs and Values lesson. Lochlan was seated at the back of the class as Merlin entered, and nobody sat up as Merlin entered.

"Good afternoon class," Merlin attempted to inject some enthusiasm into the atmosphere.

"Hello Sir," several of the more keen students muttered.

"Oh dear, it looks like everyone would rather be somewhere else!" Merlin understood it was after two o'clock, but even he was surprised at the general lethargy.

"Yes, sir, we are all a little cheesed off." It was Lochlan, looking up from his smart phone.

"Why, who died?" Merlin made a vain effort to inject some humour.

"The English rugby team, that's who!" Hollered by Brookland, he had a somewhat more realistic opinion of the results.

"Okay, I understand why you would be a little despondent," Merlin responded, "but has anyone asked themselves why South Africa won, and not the English!"

"Because our team is crap!" It was a somewhat cynical Conan.

"No, they just got out-played," Lochlan injected.

"Uhmm, did they get out-played, or were they simply too confident?" Merlin had read the game summary from every angle of the broadsheet exponents of 'after-the-facts' wisdom. It was remarkable how concise opinion was, when the facts were laid bare for all to see.

"Well at least the ref didn't cheat," It was Conan. His Irish pedigree, no contestant for an unerring Welshman.

"Yes, they didn't even win the scrums," Lochlan lamented.

"Ahh, yes, they were supposed to do that, weren't they," Merlin expressed his understanding.

"We had the heavier pack," Brookland echoing some sure-footed ounce of paternal wisdom no doubt. At least he was willing to claim ownership of that failed incursion.

"The wonderful thing about sport, and particularly rugby," Merlin offered, "is that the opponents today, don't have to face each other down the barrel of a gun!"

"Oh! You mean they don't have to go to war to win the game?" Lochlan interacted.

"Yes, because if you think about it, just over one hundred years ago, those same forces, England and South Africa, were fighting the Boer War." Merlin expressed.

"Yes, and the English won that war." Conan piped in.

"They did indeed!" Merlin agreed. "And what do you imagine the English did, to win that war?"

"Ah! Yes, they had a better army." It was Lochlan once more.

"Yes, they had a superior armed force, better armaments, but they also had a better strategy." Merlin claimed.

"Oh, so you are saying that the English team did not have a better strategy?" Brookland announced.

"Yes, because they were outwitted by a better coach." The broadsheet experience was essential.

"Yes, well our coach is shit!" Conan could not contain his cynicism.

"But it is more that that." Merlin paused. "It is because the English had gone into the game at a serious disadvantage." Now he seemed to have an active audience, Merlin determined to make hay whilst the last of the autumn sun was shining.

"You have to look at the consequences of their preparation and what happened going into the game." Merlin stood now, holding court.

"The English had won their game against a previously unbeatable New Zealand, and they had won handsomely. The South Africans had lost to New Zealand in their opening game, and the English team were very confident going into the game." Merlin continued.

"They also had been told by their coach, and their management team, that they would be paid a two hundred thousand pound bonus, each, when they won the game." Merlin drove home his point.

"What? Two hundred thousand quid," Conan barked his contempt.

"Yes, two hundred and twenty-five thousand to be precise!" Merlin explained. "But the money was not their only failing!"

"What do you mean?" Lochlan was all eyes.

"Well, I believe that the English team did not have the right mental attitude, and more importantly, I don't believe they had the right psychic outlook." Merlin down-played what he truly believed.

"Oh, like they got psyched out?" Lochlan echoed.

"Yes, in a way," merlin agreed, "but they also seemed to lose spirit right at the beginning when they lost their front-row forward."

"Sinclair!" Lochlan crowed. "He got knocked senseless."

"Yes, and he was a key player in the scrums." Brookland offered.

"Indeed, and not only did they lose the advantage in the scrums, but any strategic thinking leader would have played to their strengths, and not given away so many penalties." Merlin was awash with ideas.

"How do you stop them from having penalties?" Lochlan was fully engaged.

"You don't concede scrums in your half of the field."

"But how do you not concede scums, if the team attacking you has a stronger pack?" Lochlan again.

"You change your strategy!" Merlin explained. "The British forces in South Africa had a superior fighting force, better guns and supply of resources, because the war was funded by the wealth of the London banking elite. When the Boers realised they could not beat the British army on the battlefield, they used other tactics. The British forces had to be supplied with food and ammunition, along the already identified tracks from the Cape, to the interior, where the Boers were stationed. So the Boers used guerrilla warfare to attack the supply chains, then weaken the advantage of the British." Merlin still had their attention.

"When the British realised they could not beat the Boers strategy, they turned to playing dirty." Merlin smiled. He hoped that at least Lochlan and Brookland would understand.

"Are you saying that the English should have played dirty on Saturday?" Lochlan.

"No, because that would have further distracted their original game plan. When the British forces realised they could not contain the Boer tactics, they embarked on a 'Scorched Earth' policy, where they burned all the Boer farms, which supplied them with much needed food, and then they placed the women and children in the concentration camps, which further weakened the Boer forces and destroyed their moral." Merlin knew his history. It was a pity that so many British youth today, did not know it too.

"When the hideous living conditions in those concentration camps began to result in the mass extermination of those women and children, with tens of thousands dying in a single one of those camps, the Boer soldiers conceded." Merlin had their undivided attention.

"Even though they won the war and took control of the government of South Africa, and their main intention, which was control of the gold fields on the Witwatersrand, and the diamond mines, which subsequently produced the Cullinan diamond, they ultimately lost the war of the hearts and minds of the South African people."

"What is the Cullinan diamond?" Conan asked a positive question.
"The Cullinan diamond is the largest diamond ever found, and the diamond was so big it was cut into several very valuable stones." Merlin answered. "Does anyone know which diamonds?"

There were some blank faces. "Perhaps if I mention the Tower of London."

"Oh! Yes Sir, is it the Crown jewels?" Conan again.

"Yes, well done Conan. It is the stones that sit on top of the Royal sceptre, and on the crown used during official ceremonies. The main stone is the 'Star of Africa'."

"Yes sir, I have seen them." It was Brookland. "My mom and dad took us up to London last summer."

"Okay, so you have seen the size of those diamonds," Merlin.

"Yes, they are huge! The tour guide told the German tourists next to us, that the diamond on the sceptre is worth over a hundred million pounds." Brookland confirmed.

"Yes, but think of this! The City of London earns two billion pounds annually from tourists who visit the Tower of London." Merlin knew it was the largest money-making-racket he had witnessed in his lifetime. Ironically, that diamond was sold to the Royals for a pittance in comparison, and South Africa was the poorer for it.

"Ultimately, the war cost many lives of innocent people, and the South African Afrikaners have not forgiven the English. Today, there are communities in South Africa who still do not speak English, and they have developed an uncanny ability to produce rugby players that can take on world teams, and beat them!"

"So the Springbok team won the world cup, because of the Boer War?" Lochlan seemed satisfied. He no longer needed to lament.

"Yes, and not only were the English defeated by a team that was bigger and stronger than them, but they were beaten by a team who were born in Southern Africa, and who are South African." Merlin allowed his point to sink in.

"England's coaches need to go back to the roots of rugby in the country, and build their core team form the strength of rugby at grass-roots level; and not import all their players." Merlin played his trump card.

"But because they have chosen money as a motivating factor, against the real purpose of why rugby developed as a game, they cannot win with such a strategy. If we look at where rugby started, the passion for the game, was based on the pride of its teams competing for the glory of the ultimate prize. To retain the winner's trophy!"

Merlin allowed the point to settle in their minds, and as it saturated through to their moral consciences, they all smiled for the first time that afternoon.

"But we have a lesson to complete," Merlin looked up to see that the clock above the white board showed that fifteen minutes had past and he had not begun the lesson.

"Nooo!" There was a universal lament. "Sir, can't you teach us more, the stuff we have to study for B and V is so boring." It was Conan.

"Yes, yes, please sir, can't we have a discussion about the rugby." Lochlan's passion was renewed.

"Well, we are supposed to be looking at moral values in society." He allowed his comment to settle the class.

"Why don't we make a list of ten issues, that you each feel should be addressed by society, to resolve the world's problems?" Merlin could see the correlation that might satisfy the B and V teacher.

"I will walk around and we can discuss each issue, as you think of them." Merlin gave them an escape from the tedium.

Walking from desk to desk, Merlin weaved his way through the class as they began to write down their ten points.

"Okay, Conan, your first point is interesting; 'the world needs to chill out?' Thank you for that, I can see we will make a philosopher of you yet!" Merlin moved on.

"Lochlan, your first point is the crux of our social dilemmas; 'Money is the problem, because people just want more and more'." Merlin paused. "Perhaps we need to expand on why there is such a demand for money?"

"Because people are greedy," Brookland, seated next to him sat up as Merlin hovered.

"Okay, that is a good point, but why do we place such reliance on money?" Merlin quipped.

"Because they have not been able to recognise their ability to get by without it? Lochlan replied. Merlin sensed his mother's dinnertime conversations brooding. It reminded him of Christopher Budd, a commentator on social issues, who had once lived a few miles from where these lads were now being schooled. Budd, like so many of his anthroposophical predecessors, had concluded, that 'the emptier a cup becomes Spiritually, the fuller it gets'.

"Uhhmm, that is intriguing. Let me read something that might get your creative juices flowing," Merlin returned to his leather satchel and retrieved a little yellow covered book. Flicking to a well-worn page, he returned to their desk.

"Capital, and the economic process it belongs to, is in no sense antithetical to social progress. On the contrary it balances the emancipation of the individual with implicit social responsibility. Taking this potential as a yardstick, one can sense the tragedy, the unfulfilment of our times. If capital is placed in society in accordance with its economic nature it can only beget social tendencies. One of the lies of our times is the idea that capital is antisocial. Where should capital go socially?" "That was from Christopher J Budd, a 'Prelude to Economics'" Merlin flipped the cover over to show them.

"Does that mean capital is money?" Lochlan queried.

"Yes, that is the inference in this context, but it is a bit deeper than that. I believe Budd is referring to the fact that capital need not be money in our physical world." Merlin elaborated. "It could mean that capital may have a form of transaction that does not require money in its purest sense."

"What other forms can capital have?" Brookland was first.

"Well, capital may take the form of a Spiritual capacity, which transcends the need for a wallet full of cash." Merlin offered.

"What? Like Jesus!" Lochlan came from a long line of Irish Catholicism.

"Yes, but remember, Jesus and the Disciples used money all the time. In fact, it was Judas, who was the money guy, who supposedly betrayed Jesus because of money!" Merlin pointed out.

"Yes, but Jesus did not need money, he could just walk into a home and eat their food." Lochlan.

"That is true, but Jesus used money as a form of bartering, even in a time when the Romans were occupying Palestine." Merlin was enjoying this discussion.

"Jesus said that they should give money to Ceasar!" Lochlan was drawing from a Sunday morning conversation.

"That is true, but he was referring to taxing, and when the Disciples were collecting money from the people who supported Jesus' ministry, they would have, in fact been subject to paying the Roman's tax on their collections." Merlin knew there was no mention of this in the Gospels.

"Why do we pay tax?" It was Conan, eavesdropping from his desk a few yards away.

"Interesting question Conan. Write that down as one of your points." Merlin praised the lad, despite there being an unwritten air of rebelliousness in his manner.

"Tax has been levied by governments and kings for thousands of years, because a social construct, such as a city, or state, required social services to ensure the place was maintained. As soon as we concentrate a large number of human beings into a social dynamic, we must keep order, otherwise the system fails."

"The problem with human nature, is that as soon as you give the power of collecting that tax to one individual, or individuals, there is always going to be a risk of human greed, and of one person, or persons attempting to profit from the system."
"Is that why my dad says we have to have Brexit?" Brookland was on point.

"Well, yes, that could be a good reason why a lot of people want Brexit. However, having bureaucrats in the European government collecting obscene amounts of money, to run the E.U. is a fundamental assault on our human sensibility. Think how the tax collectors during the time of Jesus were scorned by the people!" Merlin expanded the argument.

"The problem with having all that power centralized is that it leads to abuses, inevitable as it may sound, there are systems that have worked socially, even when people have pooled their resources." Merlin offered an escape from their Brexit concerns.

"Is that what Socialism is?" Lochlan ventured.

"No, in point of fact, Socialism relies on a State that collects tax from a working class, to ensure that a non-working class are catered for. One of the lies spread by mainstream media, is that socialism is good for uplifting people; it is not!" Merlin expounded.

"Why is it not good?" Lochlan had obviously been told it was.

"Two critical factors dictate Socialism; the first is that there must be an abundance of wealth, collected from a working class, and the second is that there needs to be a bureaucracy that is able to help distribute that wealth without the temptation to profit themselves!"

"The truth is that no system is ideal, and when we look back at the Biblical texts, even Jesus had to contend with a greedy administrator; Judas Iscariot." Merlin concluded.

"So what system is ideal?" It was Conan; Merlin sensed a warming attitude, despite their first, frosty encounter.

"Well, one of the most documented systems in history, is the Qumran community of Israel, which is famous for the 'Dead Sea Scrolls'." Merlin explained, as he turned to speak directly with the young lad.

"Ah, yes, they lived by the Dead Sea?" Conan had heard discussions of this community of people, who had defied Roman occupation, two thousand years ago, and had written many scrolls about their philosophies.

"Indeed Conan, well done. They were able to avoid the Roman occupation for many years, hiding in caves next to the Dead Sea. But the Roman's eventually flushed them out, forcing them to flee, because they were not paying taxes towards the Roman occupation; and now we have the Roman Catholic church." Merlin was as cryptic as he would allow himself to be.

"So the Catholic church replaced the Roman army?" Conan was as sharp as Merlin had suspected.

"In part, yes. It is important to understand that there were two main factions of the Christian church; one was based in Rome, with Paul, and the other was lead by James, who was the brother of Jesus."

"Each collected taxes, or bequests from wealthy members of the church, which were spent on helping the poor and the hungry, but one faction of the church became entrenched in the need to display grandiose aspects to its wealth, and that is how we ended up with the Vatican." Merlin edged.

"The Catholic church is the largest land owner in the world!" Conan added.

"Okay, I did not know that, but I imagine their land holdings must be substantial. It's the same as the Queen, who is the largest land owner in Britain." Merlin encouraged.

"Yes, and the Queen and the Pope are the head of the Illuminati!" Conan was leading the conversation once more.

"Okay, I would like us to focus on how we can make this world a better place; so think in terms of why the Queen owns so much land, and yet we have homelessness in evidence everywhere."

"Because she is greedy!" Conan observed.

"Perhaps this has more to do with institutionalised wealth accumulation, which when centralised in the hands of a select few creates an imbalance in society. I believe that money is like energy; it flows to those who are capable of offering solutions to the needs of others. It is like a magnet that attracts an opposite magnetised force-field." Merlin explained.

"The Queen is wealthy, but she does not control the land holdings, and the value they represent. The system requires her to appoint people to do so. However, if she truly wanted to solve the homelessness problem, she could elect to compel an edict, which would allow that land to be distributed fairly." Merlin was no royalist.

"The Travellers don't have any land!" Lochlan advanced an opinion. "Perhaps she could help them to have parks where they could stay, before moving on to the next one?"

Merlin turned; he looked into those green eyes, searching for the origins of such immense wisdom. Merlin recognised the origins of the socialistic gene, and could imagine a day when this generation would be in charge of government.

"My understanding is that we have reached a status in our society, where the values we wish for ourselves, have become the focus of a great awakening of the social classes, whose previous values depended on hard work. I believe we are moving towards a system of self-government, determined by our raised awareness of our own consciousness." Merlin returned to the front of the class. Every face had followed him.

"Several years ago, there were two economists called Strauss and Howe, who predicted that we could virtually map the progress of our societies, by looking back at the past four generations and recognising a pattern that repeats itself. Every twenty years, with an absolute certainty, appears to change its core values. They predicted your generation and said that you would be great reformists, forcing governments to change the way they did business." Merlin elaborated.

"Today, you are known as the Zed-Generation, the last of a series of letters that defined the past three generations. The world of marketing, talks about the Baby-boomers after the Second World War. That was eighty-years ago. Then came Generation X, who, were prepared to embrace new technology. This was the generation, which took humankind 10 steps forward on the evolutionary ladder. Then we had the Generation Y group. Why do we have Capitalism, versus Socialism? Why do so many people go hungry? What can we do, as individuals to change the way people behave? These are questions we as the Generation Y, have asked. They are also known as the Millennials."

"But soon, the next generation, which will be called the Zed-Generation, will emerge. You are the kids of tomorrow, who are predominantly born out of wedlock, out of loving, monogamous and conventional relationships. With fifty per cent of the population divorcing and a large percentage of you kids growing up in single-family units, you will be asking a different question entirely." Merlin smiled.

"What question will that be?" It was Sarah, she had sat quietly taking in everything that was being said.

"You choose!" Merlin offered.

"I want a world that does not treat people unfairly." Sarah's eyes lit up.

"Yes, and you are the same generation type, who went to war in nineteen-forty. It was your great-grand parents who suffered under he Nazi occupation of Europe; it was your grand parents who often had no fathers, having lost their fathers in the war. You are the reincarnation, if you will, of your great grand parents, and you are in a war, which will determine whether you live; or quite literally die!" Merlin let this point sink in.

"What war are you talking about sir?" It was Brookland.

"What do you think is the most pressing issue, affecting your generation today?" Merlin paused.

"He's talking about the drug war!" Conan exploded; don't you get it?"

"Indeed, Conan. Well done." Merlin coaxed. "I believe, your generation will determine the future of humans in a manner that has never been experienced before. Not even the Second World War had the mechanism to destroy as many lives as we are witnessing today."

"Drugs are everywhere," Sarah conceded.

"So, if you were to change the world, what would you do?" Merlin encouraged her.

"I would start a Youth Club, and educate the youth in West Scowlsdown about the dangers of recreational drugs!" Sarah had a pair of blue eyes that penetrated the soul and seared the conscience.

"Yes, that is what I am looking for!" Merlin enthused, "Let's get these points down on our lists, then we will have started the process of saving our world." He was aware of the transaction that occurred when thoughts were converted to a written pledge, and by cementing those thoughts in writing, the Limbic brain could begin the manifesting process.

"What will the next generation do; if we survive?" Lochlan was sensing the gravity of their cause.

"Well, they will be born predominantly through A.I. or Artificial Insemination. Mostly without fathers, or without mothers in some cases! Born to surrogate fertility wombs, and snatched away to be with their biological parents, or parent. These will be the Omega Generation of kids, and aptly, they will be the last generation of children, as we know them. They will be the Omega and the end generation. After the Alpha, and before the end of times as we have come to know our world. The beginning, and the end! Their generation will bring a closure to a world that has lost all sense of compassion and with which the dawning of the end time will beckon." The class sat in awe. Everywhere, they fidgeted; mobile phones abandoned.

The faces told him everything he needed to know; they did care, and below those sometimes sullen, switched off exteriors lay the beating hearts of lions.

"Education is the passport to the future, for tomorrow belongs to those who prepare for it today."

– Malcolm X

Saving the Youth

It was Saturday morning again before he knew it. Merlin awoke early as was his routine, ventured out into the garden to catch the early morning sunrise, as he pottered around the garden tending to the last dead flower pods, pruning and generally preparing the garden for the coming winter. The function was brutal, but brought new and sustained life in the spring.

The days were drawing in and soon daylight saving would change the evenings into dark, lost causes. It was remarkable how the switch of one hour saved by pushing the clocks forward by sixty minutes, would challenge the reality of time and space. The psyche of the youth changed appreciably, as the mornings dawned with a greater clarity, but the evenings drew in, stifling the daylight hours for a youthful population, whose only free time was cut off like the proverbial stems of those rose bushes.

Merlin would appreciate the rationale, but what those in authority had neglected in the process of attempting to gain more productivity from their workforce, was that nature still remained in tune to the circadian rhythms of mother earth. Gaia, had a remarkable ability to embrace changing seasons and it was these cycles of life that brought a balance to the world.

But, when man stepped into the fray, in an effort to place his hand upon the natural cycle, he invariably created chaos. The birds and the bees did not change their cycles of function simply because humans felt the necessity to. In that wonderful analogy, Merlin sensed a dichotomy, and realised that it was man who was alien to this planet.

Imposing his will on nature, forfeiting the benefits of the seasons as a purpose of revival, and negating the opportunity to spare Gaia any further challenges, humankind had improbably brought about a dysfunctional society!

Showering, then making his way around the front entrance, Merlin made his way to the driveway, intent on his regular morning coffee ritual. Merlin was making a mental note to ask Simon what his opinion was on daylight saving.

It was as he rounded the corner of his bungalow that he heard a metallic noise from behind the car, and then a head appeared from the left-hand side of the Korean sports-coupe, slightly flushed, as if he had been physically working.

"Good morning Josh," Merlin alerted to his unusual location on this side of the fence, watched as Josh leapt sideways, startled by the greeting.

"Oh shit! Oh…. I'm sorry Sir, it's just…. You made me jump!" Josh was clearly off-guard.

"My apologies, have you lost your ball," Merlin suspected that was not the true reason for him being there, but would allow the lad to gather his thoughts; intuitively projecting, was what he was actually doing, thereby giving the lad an opportunity to defend himself.

"Ohh, yes Sir, I thought I may have kicked it over the fence..... but I can't find it!" Josh gratefully accepted his reprieve.

"Is it not underneath the car then?" Merlin smiled.

"No, no, but I will have a look again later," Josh offered, rushing headlong down the drive, a somewhat ruddy glow to his naturally brown skinned face.

"Okay, I hope you find it," Merlin offered, all the while keeping up the ruse, for the sake of civility.

"Oh, yes, thank you Sir," Josh disappeared down Fairdawn Crescent in the opposite direction to where Merlin was headed.

Merlin unlocked the car, climbed in, and sat for a moment. The previous memory of Josh's night-time escapades returning to haunt him.

Merlin was convinced there was a nefarious intent to the lad's actions, but would not give him reason to venture suspicion from the lad. He needed evidence, and now he had some, but would need to ask Simon his opinion.

At the library, Merlin parked directly opposite the library, in the public car park, and crossed the road, having waited for the pedestrian lights to change. Inside, he found Simon in the coffee lounge, motioning to him to follow him to the large triangular shaped plate-glass windows.

"What's up?" Simon was intrigued.

"Good morning, I am just a little suspicious," Merlin pointed to the car facing the library below, explaining to Simon what had just transpired.

"What do you think he was up to?" Simon quizzed.

"I don't know for certain, but if we wait a minute, we might just find out." Merlin looked worried. He had no understanding of the workings of the clandestine world of drugs, but something has piqued his curiosity; and it was a sense of foreboding.

"Do you suspect he has done something to your car?" Simon was beginning to feel Merlin's anxiety, seeping through the air between them like an insidious gas.

"Not necessarily to the car, but perhaps what he is using my car for!" Merlin's imagination was provoked by a deepened sense of psychic fortitude. The experience earlier was beginning to dawn on him like the rising sun.

"There!" Merlin motioned to him. Simon looked to the left, as two young lads, perhaps as young as ten or eleven, but not any lads he recognised, appeared through the warren of cars parked below them.

They made their way to merlin's car, not hesitating, as the younger of the two, short-black hair, shaven to a number one, reached below the left-rear tyre fender, and withdrew a brown package, then dropped it into the older boys backpack, before zipping it and both lads headed nonchalantly back through the cars.

"I know those two lads!" Simon looked grave. "They are neighbours of mine down the hill."

"What school do they attend?" Merlin asked.

"I don't think they are at school presently." His eyes brows furrowed and he turned to Merlin. "I believe they have been using your car to ferry drugs from your place to here, and Josh is supplying.

Merlin stood motionless. His suspicions now aroused and vindicated, he shook his head.

"I can't believe that I've been duped for so long!" Merlin felt a conspiratorial guilt. "I should have said something to his mother weeks ago."

"It's not your fault," Simon consoled. "These lads have become increasingly creative in the mechanisms they use to supply drugs."

"Yes, but I knew about Josh using, and I should have said something." Merlin felt the pang of remorse, and his eyes began to well up.

"Merl, it's not your responsibility to keep tabs on these lads, it's their parents who should be doing so." Simon was no apologist for the parenting black hole that seemed intent on swallowing up these kids.

"Yes, I know, but I overheard Josh the other weekend, when you borrowed the car, and I was in the garage. I should have approached his mom!" Merlin felt like an accomplice.

"No! Your job is to mentor them at school; not to parent them at home. You don't have that responsibility." Simon reassured. "Look it's not too late, I can tackle those young lads when I next see them, and warn them about what we know."

"No! I don't want Josh to know I am on to him." Merlin began to backtrack. "His mother has a hard enough time with him already; I fear this may isolate him further." Merlin implored.

"Okay, I don't have to say that you know, I can simply say that I saw them in the car park, and noticed they were up to no good." Simon offered. "I not concerned about what they may think of me, as I have already had a run-in with the father."

"Oh goodness! I hope that you are not putting yourself in harms way?" Merlin coaxed, his worry founded on the stories he had heard about the drugs trade.

"No, you don't need to worry; I can handle myself. But the father is from Albania, and their mother is a lovely lass, but I think they are in over their heads." Simon mused.

"I know, most drug related crimes are purely financial, and most of the participants get drafted into working for the gangs out of pure necessity." Merlin was beginning to feel his heart beat, slow down.

"Let's go and get a coffee and I can explain what you need to do."

They turned, voyeurs no more, having witnessed a segment of reality they would both rather not have, and returned to the coffee lounge. Their drug of choice was the caffeine, extracted from the cocoa bean, grown by impoverished Africans and ferried to the coffee shops of West Scowlsdown. The only difference was the legality of a product taxed by a system intent on benefiting from slave labour, whereas the drug war was more than about tax. This was a war for the hearts and minds of the youth of the country, and one, which brought victims into the public domain, as sensationalized news reports, feed mass media hysteria for profit.

"You know that these lads are more than victims of a ruthless society?" Simon reiterated as they sat down in their usual spot.

"Yes, I know we have spoken about this before, but I was not involved previously!" Merlin lamented.

"You're not! Don't beat yourself up for something beyond your control." Simon was adamant. "Remember, you have given more than your fair share of service to the education of this country. If I had forty years of service, and could say I had mentored as many students as you have, I would be very proud."

"Yes, I know what you are saying, but I want to help the lad." Merlin knew his neighbour was not beyond redemption.

"You do know that he does not want your help?" Simon offered.

"Uuhhmm, I am not so sure! There are moments when I truly believe I have a connection with the lad. His father is never around, and I am certain he just lacks a positive male mentor." Merlin understood the issues of single-parented families, but having never had a family of his own, he knew he compensated too much by mentoring to every student who sought his help.

"Very likely, but the truth is he has to be weaned off the dope he is currently on." Simon may have had more experience with mentoring troubled kids, but Merlin knew it was not a dope dependency.

"I don't think it is drugs, as in recreational drugs!" Merlin raised his concern.

"What kind of drugs then?" Simon cocked his head.

"It is steroids." Merlin was matter-of-fact.

"You mean, like hypodermic syringe steroids?" Simon was shocked.

"Yes, I overheard him injecting himself." Merlin did not expound on what else he had become aware of. He knew this was the reason he had not pursued the issue with Josh's mother. He needed to be delicate about handling the knowledge he had.

"Wow, that's heavy stuff for a kid his age!" Simon gymed several times a week!

"I have a sense that his rugby coach is pushing him to perform at a level he cannot handle and this is forcing him to look for performance enhancing drugs." Merlin had obviously overheard the discussion in the garage.

"Well that is half the problem, when these lads feel they have to live up to someone else's expectations. It is unfortunate his father is not around to help." There was a pause as Merlin thought for a minute.

"Tell me, what gym do you go to?" Merlin was frank.

"I'm at the gym in the high street." Simon said.

"Oh, I think Josh trains at the health club." Merlin was scheming.

"Oh really, I know two of the personal trainers there. I know they have told me there is an issue with drugs being sold in the car park." Simon explained.

"Well, I wonder if they know Josh." Merlin looked hopefully. He really had no inkling how he would help Josh, other than the official route. This remedy required stealth.

"I could ask my friends if they know Josh?" Simon was smiling. He knew Merlin was looking for a way out.

"That would be helpful," Merlin agreed, "but there is one small issue!"

"What?" Simon sensed the build up had skirted some major issue.

"I overheard Josh tell his friend that the manager was peddling the steroids." Merlin let the truth simmer for a moment.

"Yes, I see now why you did not want to say anything." Simon was aware how little the manager of a gymnasium would earn, and especially one that was franchised.

"It's likely he is off-setting his monthly income with a supplementary income from the steroids. But if he is doing that, what else may he know about what is going on in the car park?"

"Oh my dear, yes! I had not thought about that." Merlin conceded.

"It may require some extreme caution," Simon admitted, he had hoped his friends might not have any involvement; if they did, he would be harming, not helping Josh.

"Okay, I can make some enquiries, in fact, my mate Brandon has been asking me to join the health club, so that we can train together. There might be an opportunity there?" Simon was about to say more, when there was a polite knock on the door.

Simon looked up in time to see a familiar face peering through the glass window. It was James.

Rising from his seat, Simon opened the door.

"Hello James, how are you?" Simon smiled.

"I am well thank you SI," James turned his attention to Merlin.

"Good morning Sir," he acknowledged.

"Good morning James. You are looking well." Merlin greeted the young lad. "How is school?" merlin had not seen him the past few weeks.

"Really good, thank you Sir," James gushed, "I just wanted to pop in and congratulate Simon on his team winning the world cup."

"Ah, yes, thank you. Didn't they surprise us all?" Simon grinned.

"Yes, well done Simon, I had forgotten all about the game!" Merlin thought about the conversation he had with the lads in class.

"I could not believe how well they played," James offered, a seemingly well offered 'peace-pipe', or was there more to this?

"It was an incredible performance, no doubt!" Merlin raved, "But I have to say, it went somewhat to script."

"Yes, it was exactly as you explained to me on Friday night before the game." Merlin had to concede the game plan had gone like clockwork.

"Yes, but we had some of our players injured." James protested.

"Indeed, that sadly was part of the game plan." Simon grinned sheepishly.

"What do you mean?" James asked, a conspiratorial look had passed between Merlin and Simon.

"No! Nothing sinister, it is just that when I spoke to Mr Drinkwater before the game, I mentioned we needed to isolate and minimise the effect of two strategic players, and it was remarkable how they had no influence over the game." Simon had used Merlin's surname so as to ensure James understood the hierarchy.
"Who did you say?" James and Simon were still standing, so he motioned for them to sit.
"Well, I thought we had to curtail Sinkler and Itoje. So when Sinkler went off early after colliding with his own player, I thought that quite random, but then I noticed the English did not play Itoje to his strengths, and he seemed completely subdued, whereas, the previous week against the All Blacks, he was dominant." Simon grinned.

"Why do you think that is?" James knew there was something Simon and Merlin were keeping to themselves.

"I can't say for absolute certainty, but a part of me believes it was prayers answered." There was a huge responsibility on him to offer a rationale that would not be misconstrued by the impressionable.

"Oh, what, like you mean Spiritually?" James was a church-goer.

Simon smiled and nodded.

"Then what about the prayers offered by the English fans?" James was no slouch when it came to understanding the Spiritual realm.

"I cannot answer definitively, but I do believe that the Spiritual powers work for the good, of those who seek answers to their greater calling. It's like when England and Germany went to war a hundred years ago, both claimed they had Jesus on their side, but only one was victorious." Simon waited for his comment to sink in.

"Oh, so the English won the war because they had a greater Spiritual power on their side?" There was an unspoken paradox.

"No, because they both believed in a Christian God, and they both prayed for victory. I believe it is because it was ordained, despite both having the same Spiritual beliefs."

"I'm confused!" James frowned. "How could God choose between them?"

"Because, in order to fulfil a destiny, sometimes the Spiritual world is required to side with one power over the other. Or, in this case, one team over the other!" Simon expounded. "Sometimes our prayers are heard, and sometimes not. It always depends on our sincerity."

"But I thought that our prayers are always heard?" James was reverting to his Christian doctrine of understanding.

"Yes, all prayers, like thoughts are Spiritual energy, and they are heard, because like energy, they have a departure point and a destination. When we pray, or meditate, those thoughts ascend into the Ionosphere, or into heaven, which ever you call the etheric realm of Spirit. For them to be returned, we must be open to receiving them. Sometimes we just don't open ourselves to receiving them. It depends on our Faith, not on our doctrine."

James smiled. It seemed he had understood the difference.

"It's like when my brother had cancer, I prayed for him and he was healed." The connection was indisputable.

"Yes, exactly!" Simon was elated. There was a real sense that this lad was smitten. Merlin would speak quietly to Simon and explain the potential for hero worship that may be misconstrued by the young man.

"It is remarkable that the more we seem to learn about science and all the progress we have made in recent centuries, that we ultimately have so many unanswered questions." Merlin added.

"Yes, but remember it was Albert Einstein who said, and I am paraphrasing; 'anyone who is involved in the study of science will soon realise that there is a Spiritual power manifest in the laws of our universe. One that is vastly superior to that of mankind'." The conversation flowed.

"But Si, the church tells us not to put our hope in science, but in Jesus!" James had slotted into a somewhat unusual, informal discussion.

"Yes, they do, but they have missed a huge opportunity to embrace science, because the very nature of Spirituality implies a deepened understanding of the unseen world. We know electricity exists, but we cannot see it!" Simon was in his element.

"So what should the church do to change?" James was forthright.

"I believe the church must recognise that the Gospels, as well as the Old Testament are full of stories that explain science. Ezekiel witnessed incredible machines in the sky, and Jesus was able to teleport himself over great distances. It is in the Bible, but the fundamental Christians only talk about sin, as though that is the only way to connect with Spiritual power. They will quote you all manner of texts that warn about false prophets and the like, but in the Bible it says we must seek the unknown." Simon elaborated.

"Yes, why did Jesus say that we can move mountains?" James was edging to the front of his seat; edging closer and closer.

"Because I believe that as we become more Spiritually aware, we as humans, will become more and more aware of these mysteries. It was Einstein who said that he used to receive the answers to his mathematical equations, in his dreams. Even Tesla was able to access a vast store of scientific knowledge by asking for answers to his understanding of electricity." The knowledge was available to anyone who asked the hard questions.

"Wow, does that mean I can get the answers to my physics papers by praying for them?" James grinned. It was ironic.

"Quite literally, yes!" Simon laughed. "But not in the way you might imagine. My suggestion is that when you go to sleep the night before you are writing an important exam, sit on the edge of your bed, in the dark, and ask Father Spirit to release all the knowledge you have learned into your cognitive brain, because it has been stored in your Limbic brain already. That is, if you were paying attention in class. The trick is to access this stored information, like a computer, your brain needs to access its memory files." Simon had a captive audience.

"Is that like why I can't remember things we have learned, but I find I know the answer, but just can't recall it?" The genie was out the bottle.

"Exactly!" Simon almost shouted, bringing the room to an abrupt silence. The ladies, hunkered over their tea cups and biscuits looked up and smiled.

"That is exactly the reason; you have to recall the information." Simon lowered his tone. "The problem most of us have, is to find a way of accessing that part of our brain that has stored all these memories. Like a computer that has exceeded its memory capability, we need to re-file the information, before we can reuse our memory function. The stuff is there, it simply needs to be reconfigured in a usable way."

"The more we use our Limbic brain, the easier it becomes to access our memory. This is true of Spirituality. The more we delve into the Limbic brain whilst meditating, or praying, the easier it becomes to access hidden information." The conversation was on a level few lads his age might comprehend, but Merlin could see that James got it.

"Yes, thank you, I know understand." James grinned; it was a look of great satisfaction. As though he had been released from a dark room, and seen the light for the first time in years.

Merlin sat listening to them for another half hour, then rising, made his apologies and left the two to continue unravelling the secrets of the world. The satisfaction was that in mentoring one lad, the chances were the ripple effect would create a tidal pool of action.

Words had power, and knowledge informed more than mortal man; it generated the very essence of existence, allowing humanity to escape the servitude of institutions that had held onto this knowledge for too long.

"The roots of education are bitter, but the fruit is sweet."

– Aristotle

Discovery

"Sir, sir, do you believe in extra-terrestrials?"

It was Oscar. The lad jumped up the moment Merlin walked into the registration class he was overseeing. The teachers had a habit of finding excuses to not make their commitments for registration, a process that was so arduous and regimented that Merlin had a sense of foreboding. If the students had to be monitored twice a day, then in every class, five times a day, making the role call necessary seven times a day, he felt it did not augur well for this society.

"That is a very interesting concept Oscar. My belief is that there is definitely evidence that a very advanced life-form, other than a Spiritual entity exists on this planet." Merlin gauged his response.

"Yeehh! You see, I told you Albert." Oscar was a precocious lad, five foot two, barely taller than some of the Year Sevens, but nonetheless self-assured.

"But, when I refer to these life-forms, I don't necessarily imply that they are extra-terrestrial, because the word, 'extra', and 'terrestrial' would mean they are not of this planet Earth!" Merlin explained.

"Are you saying they are from Earth and not from the Pleiades Constellation?" Oscar was insistent.

"No, my understanding is that we have co-existed with these higher life forms for hundreds of thousands of years, and that our ancestors were extremely advanced beings." Merlin had the rapt attention of the entire class.

"You mean that we were like the ancient Atlantis people?"

"Well, let's consider that! Atlantis is understood to be a mythological account, written by the philosopher and historian Plato, who lived two thousand-three hundred years ago. We are told he was writing purely to an audience of Greek academics, who would understand the symbolism written into the story of Atlantis."

"But, here is the interesting part. The Bible, which was written down as scrolls, in the ancient Judaic tradition of the Talmud, or the Torah, which is now known to us as the 'Old Testament', was written at roughly the same time. The scroll only became available during the Egyptian period, and the Hebrew people, who are now the Jewish population, are descended from that time." Merlin was attempting to keep it as concise as he could.

"But, the ancient people of that time were mostly uneducated, and it was only the ruling elite that had access to education." This was a moot point as far as he was concerned. Most Greek scholars embraced the mentorship academy for all its citizens, and early Jewish children were brought up to learn to read and write if they came from the Pharisee, or Sadducee clan, but most were not afforded an education. However history was always written by the victors and so on a balance of probabilities, the Bible was written by the Pharisees, who had used the oral tradition of passing down their history from one generation to the next. So the early Talmud, became the Torah, in writing." Merlin paused. The blank faces greeted him unsurprisingly.

"What I am saying Oscar, is that before scrolls and books, people sat around the camp fires, in ancient civilizations, and told their stories, so that the next generation would remember them!"

"Oh! Oh! I know what you mean," Oscar was jubilant. "When the stories were told, they sometimes forgot parts of the story, and made up parts they had forgotten?" He had posed it questioningly.

"Yes, to the extent that often, facts were super-imposed by fiction to allow the story to sound more interesting. Have you ever played 'broken telephone?"

"Yes, yes, that is when you sit around the camp fire and tell ghost stories then you have to pass it to the person next to you, and so on until it comes back to you." Merlin suspected Oscar was a Scout.

"Indeed! How often does the story get back to you completely fabricated?"

"Every time. It's a great game, and we always tell ghost stories."

Oscar feigned a sinister face and laughed from his stomach.

"Yes, exactly!" Merlin approved. The class now caught on.
"What I am saying class, is that sometimes a story starts off with good intentions, and when you receive it back from someone else who was not there when it was told, they have got the story completely wrong." Merlin was angling towards his point.

"Does that mean that the Bible is fiction?" Albert was a quite, thoughtful lad, with a lean, athletic build, and a remarkable intellect.

"What, I believe, is that the stories written down by Plato, are no less fictional than the Bible, and historical documents based on an oral tradition before concise documented scrolls were available are just that; uncorroborated." Merlin thought a while then added, "That means they cannot be officially believed, unless you could go back in time and witness those events."

"Yes, like you Sir! Like a Time Traveller." Oscar laughed again.

"Thank You Oscar." He loved the spontaneity of the lad's spirit.

"Sir, what about the evidence of ancient cities and stuff?" Albert was astute.

"Yes, let's consider that." Merlin turned his attention to the class.

"Who can tell me how we know that some parts of the Bible, and some parts of Greek history are true?"

"Is it because we have archaeological evidence of the cities that existed?" Albert was fully engaged.

"Yes, thank you Albert." Merlin was keenly aware of his deep-seated thirst for knowledge.

"The city of Atlantis was real." Oscar, not wanting to be side-lined, jumped in.

'How do we know that for definite?" Merlin dug deeper.

"Because there are lots of accounts of sunken cities in old traditions."

"Can you name some of those, apart from Plato's account?"
"Yes, Sir, there is a story I heard about when we visited the British Museum." Albert offered.

"Well done Albert. Can you remember the name of that story?" Merlin coaxed.

"Yes, it was about a guy called Gilga…something." Albert hesitated.

"Indeed! Yes, it is called the Epic of Gilgamesh, and the story was written on clay tablets, thousands of years before the Hebrew Bible." Merlin looked at his watch. He would want to get the registration done.

"Yes, I remember now! The story talks about a flood, like the one in Noah's Ark." Albert was exuberant. No longer would the girls just look at him as some jock, with a fit body.

"Yes, and why is that important Oscar?" Merlin deflected to the instigator for the finale.

"Because it shows that the stories were from the same oral tradition, and they were given from one generation to the next so that they would remember their history."

"Yes and that is important in the context of understanding where we come from, because along with all that evidence of archaeology and written clay tablets and scrolls, is the fact that somewhere, within all that information, is the truth."

"But, I want to finish by asking you one other fact." He paused again. The class listened intently.

"Who here, believes that we evolved from apes?" Half the class put up their hands, and then on realising that they may be wrong, several put them down.

"So, if we evolved from monkeys, and we have spent the past million years growing into human beings; what do you think a dinosaur, had it survived the supposed extinction event caused by an asteroid hitting Earth would look like, if it too had evolved?"

The class looked on with pained expressions.

"Don't you think that they might resemble some of the depictions we have been shown of Aliens?" He let that image simmer.

"Remember, if we evolved from apes, then why would it not be possible for dinosaurs to evolve into ET?" Merlin grinned.

"Oh, wow, they would be Reptilians!" Oscar had his prize.

The bell sounded for first period, and the class jumped up, buoyant and motivated. Merlin whizzed through the registration on the computer, recognising every intent face staring at him through the screen, as the class exited, to take on the week before exams would begin.

Back for tea in the staff room, the frostiness was still evident, but because Merlin and not given any indication to the Study Supervisors that he had been the whistle-blower, he nonchalantly went about his time, greeting one then the next, politely and without drama. It was their issue he consoled himself, and there was most certainly a sense of guilt in the air.

The day passed, until lunchtime with little fanfare, other than a very dramatic event that took him somewhat by surprise as Merlin had exited the staffroom on his way down the long passage, to visit the gent's room.

Standing outside the feisty one's office was a young lad, whom Merlin had seen there often at lunch break. But it was who was with him that surprised Merlin. The very young lass, whom it was evident, had been the butt of the vitriol levelled at the 'so-called Trans' student and whom Merlin had attempted to defend when turning whistle-blower.

"Good morning Gerald," Merlin knew the surname was Kennedy, but in the process of showing a sense of solidarity, Merlin felt he should loosen the protocol.

"Morning Sir," the lad skipped and averted his eyes, giving Merlin a demure smile, which drew the attention of his co-conspirator. She was a robust looking lass, but pretty in a tom-boyish way. Merlin smiled and nodded his head. She smiled warmly.

Continuing down the corridor, he noticed three larger lads heading towards him, and on the windowed side. The largest of the three was Archie. He was an overtly obnoxious lad in Year Ten, with an ego to match.

Merlin could see the lad sneering at him, a menacing condemnation of respectability, intended as some non-verbal social commentary on the fact that Merlin had greeted Gerald and his friend. Merlin smiled.

"Good afternoon lads," he would needlessly provoke any civility by addressing them by their names. These were the lost causes in the battle to save humanity, intent on self-destruction by any means necessary, as a default of an aggressive resistance to authority.

They ignored his greeting, all three now sneering, then turning to each other in a mock salute to their bravado.

Merlin held Archie's stare, then as the lad averted his eyes at the last minute as they passed, what followed disarmed Merlin, but for only a moment, as he recoiled from the brazenness of the attack.

"Ffuuuubbbbb – ffuuuuuubbebbb."

Archie had released a disgustingly wet sounding fart!

The two lads roared an approval of sorts, somewhat deflecting their potential embarrassment.

"Archie!" Merlin spun, just in time to catch the lad looking over his shoulder. "Come here you disgusting, loathsome creature!"

The two lads quickened their pace, leaving Archie in a quandary. The lad stopped. He turned and taking a visible stance that told Merlin he was in some discomfort; he braced himself for recrimination.

Taking a pen out of his pocket, and a notepad, Merlin wrote down a few words in black ink. Then as Archie shuffled towards where Merlin stood in the corridor, he defiantly asked; "Is that a note for detention?"

"No, I have told your class before, I neither hand out bad behaviour points, nor do I believe in detention!" This was true, as Merlin had proudly displayed during his tenure, he only awarded merit points for achievements in class.

"Oh! Then what is it?" Archie seemed disappointed. Behaviour deductions were clearly his badge of honour, to be displayed to his cohorts as some devilishly profound sense of accomplishment.

Merlin tore the page from his pad, then, handed it to Archie. "I suggest you speak to your mom about helping you to overcome your flatulence!"

Archie read the script, then looked up, clearly mystified by the diagnosis. "I don't understand!"

"It is the name of a brand of sanitary pants." Merlin explained, "Now off you go, and clean yourself up!"

Archie turned to find himself alone in the corridor, his cohorts having abandoned him, and Gerald and the young lass, having ducked into the feisty one's office, with grins from ear to ear.

Merlin, likewise turned, knowing that in his mind from that day forward, Archie would carry the nickname, 'Skiddy'!

"Knowledge is power. Information is liberating. Education is the premise of progress, in every society, in every family."

– Kofi Annan

An Inconvenient Truth

On the Saturday that followed, Merlin had been invited to meet a local pastor, who was keen to chat to him about his ministry, so Merlin asked if he would agree to Simon joining them; after all their regular coffee meeting was cast in stone; albeit with rugby an exception it seemed.

The coffee chat was going well, with the pastor attempting to explain to Merlin that he was in an extremely enviable position as a teacher and influencer, to provide a healthy alternative to his students, from the growing anti-social behaviour, evident in the town. Merlin's credentials as a Sociology Professor gave him an unmistakable advantage when dealing with these issues. Merlin was nodding politely, when suddenly, but unsurprisingly, Simon said:

"Humans will always aspire to be greater than they are already, through the Seven-Principles of The Godhead. It is embedded in our DNA." The pastor stopped speaking.

"However, when we access our Spiritual Capital, each one of us has the ability to transcend physical constraints, by providing a holistic alternative to pure physical requirements." Simon explained. He had been studying the Gospel story of Jesus, who had sympathised with the rich young man.

"I am not familiar with 'Spiritual Capital'." The pastor conceded with a haughty air of knowingness.

"Yes, I am sure you may not have an understanding of these issues and I am not surprised; but does your doctrine allow for an equitable sharing of resources, or has the church you represent become encumbered by indebtedness?" Simon was hinting of the Etheric Principle of The Lord's Prayer.

"We share everything that we receive, tithing our income with charitable institutions." The pastor showed no sign of being affronted.

"I am certain that is extremely generous of you on a micro-economic level." Simon smiled disarmingly.

"The point of my question is, what are you as an institution doing to help those youth in our streets, who have been disaffected by the drugs culture and the rise of criminality?" Simon waited.

"Well, we do what we can with the resources we have been given stewardship of." He grimaced.

"Yes, and I am sure your stewardship is unquestionable. My point is the church and the schools have abandoned those youth, because it has become too political, and no one is standing up for those left behind!" Simon was insistent.

"But that capital should gravitate towards schools, universities and hospitals, but it doesn't. It gravitates towards a lesser value of endeavour, because the effect of institutions is to dilute the benefits through consumerism. This is because as humans, we are naturally devourers, not sharers." Simon was adamant.

"Well, of course there are expenses that the church has to defray!" The pastor was defensive.

"I understand that, and the church has accumulated vast wealth, which is evident in the historically opulent churches, cathedrals and Vatican. What I am getting at, is that the early Christians, sold all their property to give to the orphans and widows. But, today, there is little evidence of this." The crux of his argument.

The pastor, whose name was still unknown to Simon, withdrew intuitively, sliding back in his chair.

"Yes, but I am sure Samuel has made every effort to share the resources the church has!" Merlin made a vain effort to retrieve the conversation and get back to a more harmonious discourse.

"No doubt," Simon added dismissively. "Why did your church ban the non-member youth from attending your Friday youth meetings?"

There was a silent expectation.

"Knowledge is also capital and should be shared, not hoarded. The state, the church and the powers and principalities have hoarded knowledge, in an effort to retain control of the resources of this world for too long. However, because they are losing their powers, knowledge is slowly moving into the global consciousness, and will ultimately prevail." He was impassioned.

"You know, we live in a society where money is hoarded. But money is not socially representative of society. Society by its very nature must strive for the ultimate capital in our DNA, which resides with Spirituality. When we become aware of our 'Spiritual Capital', like Jesus we can shrug off the manacles that money constrains us with, and embrace the divine Spiritual nature of each and every one of our true natures. We are Spiritual Beings, Living a physical reality." Simon made his point.

"The reality is that we are being coerced into buying something, every second of the day; there is not a second that passes, where we are not being tempted to part with our hard-earned cash." The advertisements on television and social media saturate our daily existence.

"We must destroy Consumerism as a religious cult." Samuel offered his perspective.

"That is an interesting perspective Samuel." Simon responded. "Are not all religions, man-made by default, a cult?"

"No, a cult is a fear-driven system of devising strict adherence to a policy of loyalty that can not be questioned." Samuel seemed at ease.

"Is that not also a legalistic interpretation of most Christian bodies?" Simon contested.

"No, because all Christian churches allow their congregation to stay, or to leave of their own free will." Samuel offered.

"Yes, I agree, but don't most churches play on the sinfulness of man, as a ploy to bind people into their ranks?" The insinuation hung like a Judas rope.

"Well, sinfulness is a weakness that we overcome with the love of Jesus Christ." Samuel was assured.

"That is comforting to someone looking for absolution from their sinful past; but what do you say about someone who has not lived a sinful past, by their own estimation, yet is condemned by the church?" There was a sense that Samuel might be walking into a trap.

"Well, we can not judge anyone, only God makes that judgement." Samuel returned, his eyes fixed on a potential incumbent.

"But the church does make those judgements by a legalistic interpretation of scripture." Simon countered.

"We only interpret what the Bible tells us, as God's word. The judgement is specific, and that only the righteous need not fear the Lord." Samuel preached.

"Anyone who is fearful of God, has already lost the war." Simon pounced. "Don't you believe that homosexuality is a sin?"

"Yes, because the Bible speaks specifically in Leviticus, and Paul preaches to the church about living a sinful life." He felt he was on solid ground.

"I note that you do not make reference to the most vital argument, used to condemn homosexuality. Genesis Nineteen! The premise of the story of Sodom and Gomorrah has become synonymous with homosexuality. However, the men of Sodom, were 'NOT' all exclusively homosexual," Simon had accentuated the word. Samuel eased his chair back.

"Because the Genesis reading refers to the 'married men of Sodom', and do not forget the two son-in-laws, betrothed to marry Lot's daughters! The son-in-laws did not believe Lot, and supposedly perished along with the other men of Sodom. Does this story, pertain to all men, who have had same sex relationships during their lifetime?" He let the question hang.

"If so, and we use the Hite Report on Sexuality, which some have unsuccessfully attempted to debunk, as our barometer!" Breathing in;

"It would appear that sixty-five per cent of all men, or boys, have at one time or another, had some sexual relations with another male. Regardless of how innocent those events may be, or how long ago they may have been, I suggest to you that you cannot, by definition exclude them." Samuel listened dutifully.

"Therefore, using Genesis nineteen as a starting point, and applying the nature of the Hite Report, by your reckoning, you have just condemned over half the world's population to death! Somehow, I seem to think, you are a little too eager! Is there possibly a skeleton in the closet you would like to admit to now, before you make assertions about morality based on Biblical references?" Samuel repelled in his seat. He was feeling the wrath of thirty-eight years of isolation being projected back at him.

"I note, also that you make no references to the Gospels, for good reason; and that is because there are no references to homosexuality by Jesus Christ. If you claim to be a Christian, then surely you should use His words as your guide?" Simon spat the words out.

Samuel was dumbfounded. No one had ever spoken to him with such authority. If the church had been his preserve, to sanction and vilify anyone who stepped out of line, it seemed that Simon was now making it evidently clear that a coffee shop on the High Street was not a place for Samuel to be proselytizing!

"You're interpretation of Genesis and Sodom and Gomorrah is not my understanding?" Samuel fought back.

"Yes! But that is precisely my point. It is your interpretation! Which ever way you view the idea of homosexuality, there is one fundamental concept the Christian church today has to admit." Simon laid out his argument.

"Okay! What is that," Samuel walked right into the lion's den.

"In today's world, where acceptance and transparency is the most important issue facing society, it is no longer acceptable to say that homosexuality is unchristian. It is far more relevant to ask the question, 'how can you claim to be Christian, and still be homophobic'!" The silence was stunning.

"But I am not homophobic!" Samuel attempted to defend himself.

"Ye; you say that, but your actions speak volumes. When someone Gay comes to your church, you either force them to recant their God-given sexuality, or you force them out!" The accusation was like a dagger to his heart; Samuel flinched.

"You see, my assessment of the chapters from the Gospels that deal with the Centurion's Servant, is categorical; the Centurion and his man servant, were lovers!"

This was way more than Samuel's sensibilities could endure. He looked on like a deer caught in the headlamps of a car.

"There is no evidence in the Gospels that is true!" He began a counterattack, trying to catch his breath.

"Yes there is!" Simon projected his voice, a symptom of never having been given the platform to speak back. "The very word used for a servant in Greek, which is how we have interpreted the gospel story, is a 'Pais', and that word was synonymous with a male lover!"

"You can't say that," Samuel attempted to rebut the claim.

"Oh yes I can!" Simon smiled for the first time since starting his conversation with the pastor, "It's in your own gospel stories that the truth can be disseminated. One account of this healing comes from Mark's gospel, and the other comes from Luke. Which one do you believe; because they both contradict each other?"

"Both have been quoted, so as to give contextual veracity to the rationale for the Gospel story." Samuel refuted.

"How convenient!" Simon was incensed. "When the leadership of churches can't explain something, they always revert to some mystic element that only the Holy Spirit is privy to." The admonishment was categorical.

"I understand you have to defend your doctrine, but if by that very token you propose, you were to attempt to defend yourself in a court of law, you would be found guilty of fabricating evidence. Which one is it Mr Simpson? Does the glove fit, or not?" Simon parodied his point.

"What does your church say about Jesus' advice about marriage to his Disciples?"

"That is very clear. They should not marry for the sake of the kingdom of God." Samuel felt on firmer ground.

"Yes, but don't forget the two glaring omissions you have made! Jesus says in Matthews Gospel, that he was aware of those who were born that way! Do you know that through contextual historical language analysis, ancient Hebrews did not have a specific name reference for homosexuality? Men who did not marry, were either considered Eunuchs, or they were pressed into service with the kings and emperors, to work within the royal harems. But, the word that interests me is that Jesus says: "There are those who are born that way.'"

Samuel was quieted.

"Any good philologist will tell you, that the term 'born that way' is a sure fire reference to homosexuality, in the context of Matthew nineteen, verses twelve." Simon launched a barrage.

"But your church is pretty persuasive about the Pauline Epistles, and that they were inspired by The Holy Spirit!" Simon reloaded.

"Yes, of course we follow the Epistleship of Paul flawlessly." The pastor was assured once more.

"But Paul himself was homosexual!" Simon stated this as a fact.

"How can you claim that?" Samuel smarted.

"Don't ask me; ask a sociologist like Merlin here." Simon entrapped Merlin, somewhat reluctantly.

"How do you mean?" Merlin smiled, somewhat apologetically.

"Merl, I know you have read the bible, and you may, or may not have an opinion, so tell me to shut up if you feel I am pressing you into this argument!" Simon grinned mercilessly. "When you read the Book of Acts, would you say that the Apostle Paul was extremely complicated a man?"

"I can't say for certain, but there are a number of issues, when read in context to any question of his sexuality, may be troublesome." Merlin was forthright.

"Okay, without leading you, what is the biggest issue?" Simon lay the trap for Samuel.

"I can't think of any verses, specifically, as I don't know the text verbatim. But there is the first and second missionary journeys to Asia, when Barnabas and Mark have a fall-out with Paul." Merlin gave a fleeting supposition.

"Okay, without any precise evidence of his sexuality; would you assume that the fall-out was somewhat petulant?" Samuel was by now an unwilling observer.

"I don't have a psychology degree, but from a sociology stand-point, it seems a little peevish." Merlin agreed.

"That's an interesting term of reference. In Gay parlance it would be a little bitchy!" Simon surmised.

"Yes, potentially, it is rather childish. But it may be explained that Paul was extremely passionate about his ministry?" Merlin was being accommodating; Samuel was shrunken back in his sofa chair.

"Yes, and my intention is not to be vitriolic, but the point I am making Samuel," he addressed the poor pastor; "is that I don't believe that the church itself has all the answers." Simon was conciliatory, having driven home his advantage.

"The church tries not to label individual behaviour, or judge anyone, but states our position as the Holy Spirit dictates." Samuel rose from his prostrate posture.

"I get that", Simon spoke to the man, a poor effigy of his former self.

"But you are quite categorical about the detail of a supposed five thousand year-old story, handed down in the Talmud, as oral history until there were scrolls to write on." The glaring inconsistency was epic.

"So what would you propose is the purpose of the Bible?" Samuel tried to deflect the argument. He was feeling distinctly uncomfortable.

"What would I suggest?" Simon smiled. "Well, Sam, I would say that when Biblical scholars finally see past the legality issues of church doctrine and the fact that these doctrines support a basic cult-type theocracy, I would say why don't we look at the facts."

"What facts are you asserting?" Samuel was keen to keep some semblance of decorum.

"You are aware of the Star Map, housed in the British Museum?"

"No. What is that?" Samuel looked genuinely interested.

"It is an Assyrian tablet, which has been carbon dated to around 700 BC, in the Royal Palace at Nineveh. The texts show it was one of the most important documents in the royal collection. Two and a half thousand years later it was found by Henry Layard in the remains of the palace library."

"An astronautic engineer called Mark Hempsell, at Bristol University and his colleague Mark Bond, dated the Star Map to approximately three thousand BC."

"The circular stone-cast tablet was recovered from the underground library of King Ashurbanipal in Nineveh." Simon added.

"The tablet is what is referred to as an astrolabe, and it is the earliest known astronomical instrument. The detail on the Star Map shows by modern computer analysis, that it is a match of the sky above Mesopotamia in the year three thousand one hundred and twenty-three BC. It is so precise, they can identify exactly which constellations and planets are pictured."

"Those astronomers of the day made very accurate notes of trajectory of the Köfels Asteroid, relative to the stars. What is interesting is that the observations suggest that the asteroid was over a kilometre in diameter and had a very close orbit to Earth." Simon explained.

"This trajectory shows why astrophysicists could not find a crater at Köfels, which is in Switzerland. The incoming asteroid clipped a mountain called Gamskogel above the town of Längenfeld. The geological and geographical evidence shows that, and then it collided with a mountain near Köfels." Simon could see he needed to explain the purpose of his lecture.

"When it hit Köfels it created a fireball five kilometres wide, that pulverized the rock and caused a landslide, which is still evident five thousand years later."

"They concluded that the trajectory caused a back plume from the explosion, similar to the impact of a stone skimming a surface of water, and forming a mushroom cloud that poured molten rock over the Mediterranean Sea re-entering the atmosphere over the Levant, Sinai, and Northern Egypt."

"It is so precise, they can pin-point the time to the early morning of the twenty-ninth of June three thousand, one hundred and twenty-three BC."

"Mark Hempsell was hinting at the possible fate of Sodom and Gomorrah!" Simon allowed his point to sink in. "So if we know that the island of Santorini was destroyed by a volcano, and we know that the city of Alexandria was destroyed by a tsunami, it is not too far-fetched to explain what happened to Sodom and Gommorah."

"You might interpret this in the Biblical sense as, 'Then the Lord rained down burning sulphur on Sodom and Gomorrah from the Lord out of the heavens'. You do understand that this is my interpretation based on science fact; not science fiction." Simon paused. Samuel was mute.

"What strikes me more about the evidence put forward by Hampsell and Bond, is the fact they never discuss of the one smoking gun made mention of in Genesis; the tar pits!"

"Because the debris from the asteroid would have fallen back to earth, in the wake of the asteroids trajectory, then the fall-out would have been made all the more catastrophic for the people living around the Dead Sea, because the land is below sea-level, with naturally occurring and highly flammable tar-pits." Simon alluded to the actual scripture from Genesis nineteen.
"To a group of largely illiterate and uneducated, superstitious people, this extinction event may well have appeared as though an omniscient god might have rained down this purgatory on the people. Just saying!"

The three sat in silence, absorbing what had just happened.

"I have a sense that the church has done a great injustice to the homosexual community. There is a moral to the story of Sodom and Gomorrah, but it is not about homosexuality! It is about excess as used by all people who flaunt their wealth. People like Grace Mugabe, also known as 'Gucci Grace' and others like her. These people will not inherit any 'Kingdom of Heaven', in a Spiritual sense, because karma will be their judge. Effectively, I believe in the universal power of karma, and it is the one principle Christians share with most other religions except Islam. They will consistently live with fear and anger, because they are selfish, not because they are deemed to be sinful!"

"The story of Sodom is allegorical. It explains the general consequences of behaviour if it is immoral. The raining down of sulphur never happened, but over time the story was exaggerated to show that there were people who were likely the victims of a cataclysmic event, which ignited the tar-pits in the Jordan Valley." Merlin had not said a word for twenty minutes.

"Those people who were living to a degree of excess, for which the event became a fable designed to warn against greed and unhealthy lifestyles of men and women whose aspirations were for so much more than what their society could tolerate."

"The 'tar-pits' are symbolic of the effect this event would have had on the psyche of the survivors of Sodom and the region."

"Remember, according to Genesis, Lot then resorts to living in a cave with his daughters and is so filled with remorse, that he takes to drink, and then commits the ultimate barbarity, having sex with his daughters! And they call us perverse!" Simon insinuated, but remained ambivalent of the accusation made.

He was willing, it seemed to accept that the church had made mistakes, but as Merlin now knew, he was no longer willing to remain silent.

What is tolerance? It is the consequence of humanity. We are all formed of frailty and error; let us pardon reciprocally each other's folly - that is the first law of nature.

- **Voltaire**

Purgatory Insinuated

"These conspiracies are so vast and interwoven, that the average person would never begin to understand the complexity of it all." Merlin explained to his class of Year Ten Business Economics students.

"The Eight families who form the plutocracy cabal are the Goldman Sachs, Rockefellers, Lehmans and Kuhn Loebs from New York. Then there is the Rothschilds of London, the Warburgs of Hamburg and the Lazards of Paris. Included are the Israel Moses Seifs of Rome. It is their ability to claim the resources of this world, as though it were their inalienable right, which sets them apart from every other wicked family. This is because they have no fear of a God, but the knowledge of the power of a directed, or what I believe is a channelled power of subconscious energy fields, made manifest by concentrated effort." Merlin was alluding to the Global Consciousness.

"Would it surprise any of you if I told you we are all connected on some level, to the Earth?" They all stared at him blankly.

"What do you mean connected?" It was Alfie.

"Well, imagine we all have psychic powers, and that my thoughts can be read by you! How powerful a form of communication would that be?" Alfie sat looking at Merlin. There was a glimmer of recognition.

"So, if I can project my thoughts into your mind, would you be able to understand the idea of Panpsychism?" Merlin proposed.

"What is 'Panpsychism'?" Alfie was intuitive enough to realise the significance of a psychic influence.

"Okay, so I must add a warning here; the ideas I am proposing may be considered pseudo-science by mainstream scientists, but to some people, like myself, who have studied human psychology for forty years, it is factual science."

"What is pseudo-science?" Lochlan asked.

"The study of anything the mainstream scientific community has not been able to quantify and assess with computational analysis."

"You see, Lochlan, scientists must have evidence of everything they research!" Merlin continued, "So it is understandable that they have to be able to document everything before it becomes accepted by the scientific community."

"What kind of evidence?" Lochlan.

"Analytical proof of its existence. Einstein had to develop complex equations that had to be backed up by mathematical equations of known calculations; Tesla had to prove that electricity flowed, and Niels Bohr had to explain the quantum mechanics of his complicated string theory, before they were recognised as science-fact." Merlin loved explaining stuff.

"Oh! I get it. There has to be physical proof?" Lochlan was getting it.

"Yes, exactly!" Merlin paused. "The irony though, is that sixty years later, scientists can not explain the string theory, and most have debunked it exists, because there exists what is called a Quantum Enigma; this is a mystery within the mystery. In other words," Merlin elaborated, as he drew blank expressions, "there is a hole in their so-called scientific evidence."

"They can't prove it exists?" Alfie was triumphant.

"Science, my lad, is made up of mistakes, but they are mistakes which, it is useful to make, because they lead little by little to the truth." Merlin quoted, smiling so as to enforce his parody of the quote from Verne.

"What do you mean by the truth?" The lad was flummoxed.

"What is the 'Truth', will only be known, once we have reached the end of our journey of discovery. I was quoting Jules Verne from his book, 'A Journey to the Centre of the Earth', but the truth is, we have never really been there, but who is to say we won't be able to go one day!"

"Yes, I understand. They said that about going to the moon before rockets were invented." Lochlan quipped.
"Don't be daft!" It was Alfie again. "We never went to the moon!"

"Ah, yes Alfie! Ever the optimist." Merlin laughed. "Try to remember one thing from this lesson if you will and that is; "Anything one man can imagine, other men can make real."

"Do you know what Nikola Tesla did, when he was told that alternating current would never catch on?" Merlin premised.

"He invented it?" Lochlan was on form.

"Yes, indeed. And he not only harnessed alternating current, but it is the most widely used form of electrical current used today. Even his rival, Thomas Edison had to admit defeat." Merlin was enjoying the repartee.

"What do you think happened to Tesla, Sir?" It was Sarah.

"In what regard?" Merlin swivelled to include the young lass.

"Well, why is he not as famous as Edison? No one knows who he was." She was correct.

"They didn't know who he was until Elon Musk came along and formed a company called Tesla." Merlin corrected.

"Tesla is a car?" Alfie piped up.

"Yes, but Tesla is an electric car!" Merlin cautioned. "The point of Elon Musk adopting the name Tesla was to show the irony of how little is known about the man, yet he was the greatest scientist of his time!"

"What else did he invent?" Lochlan was intrigued.

"Well, Lochlan, I suggest for home work, you look it up. He had over one hundred patents registered when he died. The reason that people did not know who he was is that he was so far ahead of his time, that he was considered to be a 'pseudo-scientist'."

"Perhaps that can be a project you can do for me, all of you." Merlin turned to the class. "Starting now, and seeing as we have no set work for cover today. You can use your smart phones and make a list of twenty things Tesla invented."

"Yeah, Yes Sir, you're the greatest," there was a chorus of approval, as students dived for their phones and brains were fully engaged.

"Sir, is it true that you told Oscar that you were a time traveller?" The rumour cycle was a great way of disseminating falsities, but in this instance, had proved a very effective way of inspiring creative thought.

"Yes, I told him that not only was I a 'Time Traveller', but that I am a time traveller." Merlin grinned.

"Oh! I get it!" Lochlan laughed at the vacant look on Alfie's face.

"No! I am just kidding Alfie. But I did tell him that, because I believe we are all time travellers." Merlin allowed the lad to gather his thoughts.

"What I believe, is not unlike what Albert Einstein believed." Merlin assured him. "You see, time and space are merely subjective components of what makes up our reality. You believe that you are in a science class because you were told to be here at this very moment in time, and space."

"But, imagine if you could perceive yourself being somewhere else right now; where would that be?" Merlin coaxed his answer.

"I would want to be at Wembley, watching the cup final." Alfie, true to form made his desire known.

"Exactly! You would wish to be somewhere you are passionate about." Merlin was angling for a simple explanation that would not confuse the lad entirely.

"So, reality is our perception of what we recognise through projected rationalisations of what our brain is telling us through our physical senses; sight, sound, touch, smell, taste. These are all sensory manifestations of what we can experience now, in this dimension. The dimension that we have been told is our truth!"

"Are you saying that we are only here, because we have been told that we are here?" Alfie was warming up, it seemed.

"Yes, that is exactly right. We know this dimension exists because we can sense it; but what if we could sense other dimensions? Would we be here, in this classroom, right now?"

"Other dimensions? Do you mean like being in a space warp?" Obviously the lad had been a follower of Doctor Who. But could he rationalise the concept, without having to reflect back to his fictional parameters; Merlin would have to gauge the depth of his understanding, otherwise it would be another rumour, falsely engaged.

"In a sense, yes." Merlin abbreviated. "The rationale for dimensions is not a space warp criteria. It is on a completely unseen level of science."

"You mean like pseudo-science?' Lochlan was listening.

"Yes, but purely because it has not been fully understood." Merlin wanted Alfie to catch on.

"Nikola Tesla was known for making comments about science having to begin to understand that there is an unseen force, which connects the entire universe together. But, it is not a universe based on what we have been told by astronomers and astrophysicists! The unseen aspects of science are the electro-magnetic forces that hold all atomic particles together, and not simply based on the gravitational power that we are told about." Merlin was now channelling some of the wisdom gained on his Saturday morning coffee meets.

"Not gravity?" Lochlan interjected.

"Not gravity, but an unseen force, that contains a dynamic of influence on our universe, that we currently have no control over. We believe in gravity because Isaac Newton sat under a tree, and supposedly, an apple fell and hit him on the head."

"This element, or dimensional force, is what Tesla was speaking about, and once we have accepted that it exists, despite our inability to quantify it mathematically; we will then be able to master our reality." There was a murmur from the back of the class. Merlin looked up to see several lads staring at him blankly.

"Sir, it says here, that Tesla blew up an entire forest the size of England, with a time machine!" There was concerned faces all round.

"Remarkable don't you think?" Merlin concurred.

"But Sir, that is like setting off one hundred atom bombs!" It was Alfie.

"No one knows for certain if it was a result of the tower he had built, or if it potentially was an asteroid; but one thing is for certain; he certainly got people to sit up and take notice!" Merlin elaborated.

"If you can get people to listen to you and to buy into your ideas, we can change the world for the better!"

"Yes, Sir, that is my mission." It was Sarah.

"But; if you are never willing to experience the challenge of stepping outside the boundaries of mainstream thinking, human society can never take those bold strides forward and create things like 'Zero-Point Energy', or for that matter; Time Travel!"

"What is a Zero-Point energy?" Lochlan asked.

"Yes, good question Lochlan. It is a quantum field of energy. Like a flux is a high-electrical charge when we experience an overload in the electrical supply system!" Merlin described.

"Sir, sir, it says here, that 'The advent of a Warp drive propulsion, taps into the energy in a pure raw vacuum. There is an extremely high charge in the vacuum, but we are immersed in that vacuum'." Alfie was reading from his smart phone.

"Yes, may I borrow your phone Lochlan?" Merlin turned to the one individual who he knew would relinquish his device.

"I want to refer you to a quote from Nikola Tesla; here we are:"

"Throughout space there is an energy. Is this energy static or kinetic? If static, our hopes are in vain. If kinetic, and we know for certain it is, then it is a mere question of time when men will succeed in attaching their machinery to the very wheelwork of nature." Merlin was reading from the smart phone.

"Wow, Sir! Does that mean that zero-point energy can be extracted out of the air?" Lochlan was now reading the quote, having been reunited with his device.

"It says that it is related to 'Dynamically Engineered Local Space-Time – Mercury vortex or mercury turbine engines with counter-rotating cylinders'. It is 'an anti-gravity propulsion system'." Alfie was ecstatic. Here was a subject he could finally get his mind around.

This guy Nikola Tesla must have been a boffin!" Lochlan was expounding.

"Well, that certainly gives us all a lot to think about!" Merlin was looking up at the clock. Sadly, time had not stood still, and the bell was about to sound.

"I would like you all to complete the list of twenty inventions from Tesla, and tell me what applications they are now being used for, one hundred years after he proposed them?" Merlin posed the challenge, but knew they would all relish the opportunity to do something different.

Packing his books after class, Merlin was alone in the room, when a voice called out to him from the doorway.

"Sir, sir, thank you!"

Merlin looked across to where a familiar face stood smiling at him. It was Josh.

"Thank you?" Merlin posed.

"Yes, Sir. Thank you for introducing me to Si." Josh was beaming.

"Oh! That is my pleasure. Has he been able to help?" Merlin was unsure where the conversation may lead.

"Oh yes, thank you Sir. I am now training at the health club." Josh seemed at peace with life.

"Oh, that is good news." Merlin had not been able to discuss the issue of his car being used for illicit courier services, since the last meeting at the library. With their usual coffee meeting interrupted by Merlin's insistence on asking Simon to join him for the social with pastor Samuel, Merlin had not had the chance to catch up on all the intrigues of West Scowlsdown.

"Yes, and Sir? Sorry!" The comment was posed as an apology; one that Merlin was eager to accept. Nothing more need be said, and Merlin's smile was all the evidence Josh required. He was forgiven, and thankfully that episode was forgotten. Merlin watched as Josh smiled, then turned as his classmates rounded on him.

"What's that 'bout." It was Jason.

"Na! Nothing!" Josh brushed off the question, his conspiracy safe with Merlin.

Merlin watched as the lads disappeared down the corridor, side-stepping the swathe of students arriving for their next class.

It was evident Simon must have secured a contract for the lad to train at a different gym, and that was a good outcome.

"Upon the subject of education … I can only say that I view it as the most important subject which we as a people may be engaged in."

- Abraham Lincoln

Beyond Reality

"Have you heard back from Samuel?" Simon asked, a somewhat sheepish look on his face.

"Hi Si!" Merlin was seated at their usual table, having gotten up early to wonder through the vegie market in Kings Walk, and chosen two large bags of succulent Sussex produce for the soup pot.

"No, I haven't, and in all likelihood I won't." Merlin replied. "I am sorry to have put you in such an obviously unnecessary position!"

"You shouldn't be apologising Merl." Simon grinned. "I just found myself reacting to forty years of Catholic lies and deceits."

"Yes, but I knew you had a difference of opinion to their stereotype doctrine, but I should have been more conscious of your situation."

"Don't give it another thought." Simon had vented his anger at the institutionalisation of that dogma, but he had no personal animosity to Samuel; he actually felt some pity for him.

"Okay, I don't think Samuel will have lost any sleep over it. After all, it was his invitation for coffee, I just didn't want to let you down." Merlin explained.

Yes, it is interesting that Christians who proclaim their righteousness, are usually the worst at delivering on their promise to God." Simon knew unequivocally that despite his sexuality, he was nonetheless a Chrisitian.

"How so?"

"Well, a so-called friend of mine in South Africa, whose response to an invitation to celebrate his birthday with him was treated with contempt, has left me cynical. I was disappointed at the time, because we had been friends for twenty years." Simon explained what had triggered his outburst.

"What is fascinating about that so-called Christian friend, is that he turned on me because of his own Etheric understanding of guilt. He had once invited me to a cocktail party at his home in Parkhurst, but when I arrived there, a group of his contemporaries with whom he had associated for some time, began engaging in a sexual orgy, right in front of me!" Simon blushed, more for the sake of those lustful ingrates, then because of his own embarrassment.

"Oh dear!" Merlin need not have asked further.

"Needless to say, I excused myself and made a hasty retreat. However, I must find it within my heart to forgive him, and put aside our differences." Simon elaborated.

"It is fascinating that instead of asking for my forgiveness, he proclaims to be such a devoted Anglican, and served as a Lay Minister and had a job at one of the most prestigious 'Think-Tanks' funded by the super-wealthy of South Africa, and shunned me." Simon needed to get this off his chest.

"What a hypocrite." Merlin sympathised.

"Yet God seems to favour him for some reason! His public life is all smiles and gratuitous greetings, but behind the scenes, he is leading a double-life. It is through a sense of self-loathing that he cannot bare to look me in the eyes?" The years since had mellowed him, but Simon believed that his faith was based on love and relationships, and the work of Rudolf Steiner seemed well placed to highlight the lack of Spiritual Justice.

"So my question has to be; why would God grant him so much privilege, and provision, yet I have been in a state of bondage and poverty for all these years?" The age old conundrum had left him perplexed and aggrieved.

"I am not a great Christian, but I am a great listener." Merlin offered.

"Thank you Merl." Simon paused. "The only conclusion I can draw, is that he must be fast heading to a place of eternal damnation, where his soul will writhe in agony, in a fiery pit of hell; or, the more probable answer, is that God does not care about the actions of our bodies, but on the state of our hearts!"

"Is he a good man?" Merlin prompted.

"Yes, he is not a wicked man, and he probably has never cheated or stolen from anyone, particularly not me; but it is quite strange that he has never apologised for turning his back on me!" There was a lilt to his voice, Merlin knew all too well.

"I don't think that your state of mind should be perplexed by such inconsistencies." Merlin offered.

"Yes, I know that anger is a poor substitute for justice. But there is an irrefutable law of Karmic Justice. Perhaps the Universe has its own ways of responding to grievances. But Steiner makes it very clear in his analysis of 'The Lord's Prayer', that the four lower principles of Spiritual Power are inter-connected." Simon had studied Anthroposophy.

Merlin listened; his soft features and pale blue eyes, were therapy.

"Because of the church, I have suffered from a sense of guilt for so long, it has been my own undoing. What exactly should I be guilty of?" The question was rhetorical.

"I was born in Africa, and as I grew up I began to realise that I was different to other kids. I could not put a name to this sense of 'difference-ness' until I reached puberty. As a loner growing up in an extremely conservative Salisbury, in Rhodesia, it was unheard of for men to be having relationships with other men, let alone orgies. But, what I realise now, is that it was happening all around me at school, but I was simply too shy and withdrawn to accept that it was a fact of life! Almost a 'Rights of Passage' to adulthood!"

Merlin remained focused intensely, as Simon let go of forty years of repression.

"So, when I eventually put a name to my condition, and determined later on at the age of twenty-one, to pursue my instinctive heart; it was to a clarion call of trumpets and an ascendency of my soul. I was finally able to determine that my love, could be returned by another soul. I don't believe that my misadventures of the past thirty-two years are, or could possibly be condemned by a loving Jesus, whose only desire, is for every human being on this planet to be happy." Simon contested.

"Well, I tend to agree with you Si." Merlin encouraged.

"It is so peculiar that the church has attempted to conceal the truth about Sodom and Gomorrah in the Genesis passage, and yet, they have all that archaeological evidence, let alone all the scientific evidence that boys going through puberty will have a same sex attraction, to some greater or lesser degree. Yet it is the chemistry of our bodies that will determine our sexuality and not some sinister dark-malevolent force, who turns perfectly wonderful young men into homosexuals!" The passion was there in his eyes.

"To me, it is not about who we Love; but that we Love!"

"Anyway, I just wanted to let you know that I was concerned that I may have embarrassed you in front of Samuel!"

"Goodness, No!" Merlin smiled. "I did not say anything at the time, because I am still learning all these things." Merlin conceded.

"Oh! Good. We didn't have a chance to speak after our meeting with Samuel, so I wanted to clear the air." The coffee room was abuzz with Christmas preparation activity, as elderly ladies broached topics like; where will we hang the stockings?

Merlin sipped his steaming mug and the two friends settled in for another topical discussion.

After an extensive chat, Merlin agreed to take a walk through the High Street with Simon. They were headed to the bookshop where an author was launching the sale of his new book. The early winter sky was peppered with high cirrus clouds, blown to smithereens by an Atlantic cold front. But the sun, briefly freed from the bondage of an intransigent weather cycle, blazed through warming their faces as they turned their collars to the blustery cold wind.

The dichotomy was breath taking. It was akin to the political atmosphere pervading British life; no one knew where Brexit would lead to, but everyone wanted some sunshine and a break from the persistent naysayers in the media.

"This reminds me of a monkey's wedding back home." Simon commented.

"A monkey's wedding?" Merlin jested. "What does the weather have to do with it?"

"We call it a monkey's wedding when the sun shines through a gap in the clouds, whilst it is raining above us." Simon explained.

"Oh, you mean, like a cloud burst?" Merlin contributed.

"Yes, but it is usually when the sun is setting, and we get these large cumulonimbus cloud formations that create huge thunder storms in the late afternoon when the humidity has built up for the day."

"How quaint, but you'd have to be careful using that terminology in this country, otherwise some woke warrior will want to accuse you of some racist slur!" Merlin quipped.

"Oh, don't worry about that, I am forever putting my foot in it." A smiling Simon winked.

"Working in the universities is a minefield of woke repression." Merlin conceded.

"Yes, I believe they have been overrun by liberal-minded apologists." Simon agreed.

"But it is so much worse than you can imagine!" Merlin was defiant.

"There is a wokeness about wanting to be politically correct, to such an extent, that most professors dare not speak up, and those who do get shouted down. It is an attack on freedom of speech and expression that has gone mad!" Merlin complained.

"May I interest you in my book?" The comment was directed at the pair as they stood outside the High Street bookstore.

"Yes, that is why we are here." Simon smiled in the direction of an elderly gent, whose loosely fitting military uniform embellished with ribbons of medals, looked somewhat out of place in the bustling heart of West Scowlsdown. Despite this modern day English town, in the heart of the Sussex countryside, it seemed a million miles from the trenches of France!

"Oh wonderful! Have you visited the battlefields?" His enthusiasm no less daunted by the hundred years since it all ended.

"No. No, I haven't." Simon sounded, almost apologetic.

"I have." Merlin joined the discussion. He sensed the irony of a conversation held meters from the town's Great War memorial.

"It is quite revealing." The elderly man enthused.

"I have no doubt!" Simon smiled. They still had not been introduced, so much was the camaraderie of battle hardened souls intent on sharing their memories, that Merlin realised the subject transcended generations and obviated the need for formal introductions.

"The 'Western Front' was the line of defence located in a long line four hundred and fifty miles from the Belgian coast, through the southern Belgian province of West Flanders and regions of northern and eastern France. Almost the length of the United Kingdom." Those translucent eyes of blue, glazed by cataracts and pitted by sun-scorched time, blazed as richly as they may have done all those years before. "Incredible to think how pervasive that war was." Merlin enjoined.

"Yes, the trenches stretched from the Swiss border, all the way to the Belgian coast." The conversation flowed.

"Well, if you would like to know more detail, my book is on sale today." The elderly gent redirected the conversation. Like a general coordinating an attack, he motioned to a table strategically positioned to catch the passing shoppers, but neatly appointed to take in the midday sunshine.

"Thomas?" Simon intoned. "Thomas Bennett."

"Yes, that is I." The old fellows jaw seemed to almost jut with pride, and the aged stupor, for a moment was lost.

"Wonderful to meet you. I am Simon, and this is Merlin." The introduction now formal.

"Merlin? What a wonderful name." Thomas was equally impressed.

"Yes, thanks to my mother's side of the family, we can date our family tree back to before the Norman conquests.

"I hope you don't put a spell on me!" Despite the years, it appeared Thomas had not lost any of the wit that at one time may have endeared him to another generation.

"No! I can only wish you well with your book. I believe this subject is such a powerful mechanism to draw people together, even in a time when we seem so divided." The inference to Brexit not lost on any of the three.

"Yes, it is sad to think that one hundred years after the Great War, we are still at loggerheads over who should be telling us what to do." There was a poignant irony in his tone, but Thomas nonetheless was resolute.

"You know," he lifted a well positioned copy of his hardcover offering, "we fought the Germans in the Second Battle of Ypres, then Vimy Ridge and the Battle of Somme! But the truth is, we were fighting to retain our right to determine our own laws."

"I think that is what Brexit is about!" Merlin agreed.

"Yes, it is remarkable that here we are one hundred years later and all we have to show for the war, are the trenches in Argonne, and the Verdun. All the other trenches have been covered over. It is almost as though we want to whitewash our history." Those steely-blue eyes, still had the fire of a bygone time projected into a new millennium.

"In truth, if the British army had not blocked the German advance at Nancy and Marne, you and I may well be speaking a different language today?" Thomas posed it as a question.

"It was that fierce defence of strategic landmarks by the Allied forces, that resulted in the deadlock, that ultimately ended with the German's entrenching themselves on favourable high ground." The military man within him, still eager to point out the strategic nuances of a past tragedy.

"The consolidation of the Front Lines consisted of trenches, wire defences, mined dugouts and deep bunkers, reinforced concrete emplacements and selected strongpoints." Thomas, having opened the book, pointed to a meticulously drafted map.

"What turned the war in the favour of Britain?" Simon interjected.

"The Battle of Flers-Courcelette, which was part of the Battle of the Somme on fifteenth September nineteen sixteen!" Thomas was certain.

"How interesting," Simon had travelled through the battlefields of Southern Africa and seen the trail of destruction the British army had wrecked upon the Boer forces and earlier the carnage of Rorkes Drift and Isandhalwana. Each of these battles had been strategic defeats and victories, but in each the British had learned invaluable lessons.

"What was it that gave them the advantage?" Simon knew enough about war to know every major battle was determined by some facet of superiority in either strategy, or technology.

"The Tank!" Thomas was adamant. "The Lincoln Machine, as it was known was designed by William Tritton, but was the result of a committee established in February nineteen fifteen by none other than Winston Churchill. The committee was made up of naval officers, politicians and engineers. This was the beginning in truth of the push for superior fighting machines, which would obviate the need for needless human sacrifices on the battlefield." Thomas was impassioned.

"So the committee was no less the fore-runner to the Military Industrial Complex?" Simon drew the connection.

"Yes, if you wish." Thomas conceded. "The first tanks were not very effective, but the committee continued to design them so that they would not get stuck in the trenches, or shell holes."

"This is so interesting, because the war against the Boers was also a stalemate, which is until the British used their scorched earth policy to force the Boer resistance into submission. The tank was the beginning of a move towards mechanised armaments designed to create a strategic advantage." Simon may not have known too much about the Great War, but it was difficult to see how battles could be won.

"Of course, yes. I agree that the British army employed devious means to defeat the Boers, and we also invented the concentration camp, long before Hitler and the Nazis." It was Thomas' turn to be apologetic.

"Fascinating!" Simon lifted a copy of the book from the table, and turned it over to read the introduction to the author on the dust cover.

"You know, we are fighting a war here in the streets of West Scowlsdown, in a way, not different to past wars?" Simon continued.

"We are?" Thomas seemed on the back foot for the first time during their short discussion.

"Yes. It is a war on drugs, and the combatants are no older than the kids who were sent to the trenches a hundred years ago!" He was sombre.

"Oh, I see!" Thomas recognised the obvious correlation to warfare.
"The interesting thing for me," Simon continued, "is the need for a strategic mechanism to defeat the obvious creep of this pervasive destruction within our society."

"I get it." Thomas seemed initially at odds with Simon's interpretation, but he soon recognised the similarities to a war, fought from trench to trench for two years, before a strategic advantage was invented.

"The point I am making, is that when those soldiers went to war in France, to defend Belgium, France and ultimately Britain from tyranny, those soldiers were drafted into a war, which was fought to contain German ambitions to dominate Europe. Given the EU is seated in Brussels today, it is a powerful symbol of how Britain has been stabbed in the back by the very people British soldiers went to war to defend." The sense of betrayal was agonisingly obvious.

"The kids on our streets today, are fighting a war of attrition, designed to destroy the very fabric of our society, yet the European Union have consistently fought to obtain open borders and drive the British economy to its knees. You only have to look at how they have allowed unrestricted migration into Europe, to understand that their ploy is no less nefarious than the Nazis, or for that matter, German conquest in the Great War." It was time for Simon to sound impassioned.

"Yes, I understand." Thomas nodded his head. There was a hint of defiance in his manner, but Merlin could see that this was a war he would have to leave for the younger generations.

"I believe we can learn so much from our history, and that is why I think the majority of Brits voted to leave the EU. Sadly, the suits in Brussels, despite our defence of them a hundred years ago, have no intention of defending us.

"That is intriguing." Merlin chipped in. He was the observer, using his wealth of sociology knowledge to pin point the strategic issues. "The very strategy to defend our youth may well have started with Brexit!"

"How so?" Thomas looked on.

"Well, if we are fighting a war for the hearts and minds of our youth, who have been attacked by a pernicious system of permissiveness, perhaps the strategy should be to appeal to the very reason why the young men went to war a hundred years ago?" The question raised but left open for opinion.

"Ah! Yes, that is a valid point." Thomas was back in the fray.

"The First World War was the very first war to conscript soldiers. Whereas all the wars before were soldiered by men who were either mercenaries, fighting because of a financial consideration, rather than because they had any philosophical reason to fight, or they were aligned with a specific faction. Either way they were paid to fight, or as was often the case, they recognised the opportunity to benefit themselves through warfare." Thomas was a historian.

"So, they went to war in France because they understood it was the right thing to do?" Simon injected his thoughts.

"Yes, and that was also the reason young men went to war against Hitler." Merlin contributed.

"So, if there was to be a Third World War, would the same psychology be required?" Simon was thinking laterally.

"Yes, because no one would want to go to war today, knowing what we know about the savagery of war, unless they had a deep-seated conviction of the consequence at risk!" Merlin offered.

"In other words, if China, which now has the largest paid national defence force in history, were to occupy the Philippines and Indonesia, to gain access to their oil and gas reserves, who would be required to stop them?" The question was subjective.

"They have already annexed vast portions of the South China Sea from the Philippines." Merlin had to remind him.

"Yes they have, and like the Japanese who did the same in nineteen thirty-three, there was no one to stop them." Thomas was sure the solution was a matter of elimination. That is of ideas!

"Well, if China were to expand their empire outside of the permitted territorial waters of the South China Sea, they would meet the full force of American technology." Simon had researched the latest in US military capability.

"But today's youth have access to so much more information on the internet. Smart phones and tablets allow them to download the latest info and even the mainstream media can't keep up."

"So what would you need if you were a military strategist today, to conscript a nation of young men and women to fight a war?" Simon directed his question at Thomas.

"Oh, I think that the next war will be fought by technologies we have not even seen yet! If tanks swung the war in favour of Britain during World War One, and the blitzkrieg of the Nazi army was responsible for the invasion of Poland and France, it would not be surprising that any future war will be fought with the latest secret weapon!"

"But it would not be nuclear?" Merlin interceded.

"No, definitely not!" Simon was adamant. "The next element of warfare will have consequences for our world and inevitably for the youth, which will resonate for the next thousand years."

"This insidious drugs war is being fought as a battle of attrition, as I said. These young men and women have so much to contend with, given the onslaught of fentanyl, cocaine, heroine and the amphetamines that are flowing across the channel into this country is so pervasive, there is not one person under the age of twenty who has not been affected in some way by this scourge." Simon sounded the warning.

"Is this not a family breakdown issue?" Merlin queried.

"Yes, to the extent that divorce is at an all time high and single family bread winners have created a disunity in the families. But this is not new, because throughout history when men went off to war, mothers were left to raise the children. This is not a consequence of war today, but a direct destruction of the nuclear family." Simon added.

"The rot set in with the EU and the PC brigade." Merlin laughed.

"That is so true! I was so aware of this wokeness when I got here."
"Yes, from a sociology point of view it is hugely troubling." Merlin agreed.

"That's why I like listening to Jordan Petersen. He lends a remarkably succinct commentary to an otherwise convoluted attempt to undermine the real issues of sociological traits among humanity. We are in the midst of a battle for the hearts and minds of our youth and they have had their minds poisoned by what I believe are malicious forces, who want to unravel societal constructs that speak to a natural order." Simon was unapologetic.

As noon arrived and the crowds gathered in the High Street, Merlin was about to take the book he had now purchased from Thomas and head home, when there was a tap on his shoulder. Turning he was greeted by a huge smile.

"Hello sir." It was Lochlan and a group of the lads from school.

"Hello Lochlan, Brookland, Tom, how are you lads doing?"

"Good sir, we've been down at the school fair." They were in high spirits.

"Oh, yes," he had forgotten the event was on. "Are you lads looking to set up your business in town?" Merlin jested.

Ah! Haha, yes sir. One day we will have the best shop in town." Lochlan was definitely the spokesman. The other lads hung back, giving Simon a somewhat circumspect look.
"Hello Sir," Lochlan finally acknowledged him.

"Hi, where do I know you from?" Simon turned to greet Lochlan having completed the purchase of his book.

"The gym." Lochlan was a confident lad. "You trained Josh the other day." It was more of an accusation, than a comment.

"You know Simon?" Merlin interceded.

"Yes, sir, he is at our gym." Lochlan spoke up, as the others hopped from one foot to the other.

"Oh good, because Simon here is my friend from South Africa. He has been helping Josh at my request." Merlin felt the necessity to level the playing field.

"Oh! I see." Lochlan may have not known this, but now he realised he had overstepped the mark. "It's just that Josh was training at the other gym, and now he is at ours."

"That's okay Lochlan. Simon has been very helpful." Merlin could see how the lads must have drawn an inference from the situation that was off track.

"Yes, hello. What is your name?" Simon jumped in.

"Lochlan sir." He seemed embarrassed.

"Hello Lochlan. Yes, I have seen you at the gym. Keep up the hard work." Simon let the acknowledgement hang.

"Oh, thank you sir." The lads seemed at ease now.

"Hi, Simon." Simon reached forward to shake Brooklands hand. Then in turn Tom, then finally back to Lochlan. Merlin appreciated the momentary lapse in civility had now been restored. It was remarkable how with human nature, we are so readily willing to jump to conclusions. This, he knew, was how the rumour mill started, and all the sociology in the world would not change that. Wars had been fought over less circumspect mistakes, yet the moment had been saved by forthright dialogue, and a willingness to address the imbalance.

Merlin knew Josh was now in a good place. But he would speak to Simon and suggest he mentor the older lads, perhaps a little discreetly, given their penchant for taking umbrage over the seemingly innocuous mistaken connection between Josh and his new training partner.

He smiled and rather sheepishly, the lads said their good byes.

"Learning is not attained by chance, it must be sought for with ardor and attended to with diligence."

- Abigail Adams

Forging Ahead

"Sir, Sir!" The cry for recognition was a plaintive one, amidst the cacophony of noise.

Merlin had only recently walked into the class. It was Monday morning and the students seemed on edge, more so than usual.

"Alright, settle down class." Merlin raised his voice marginally, but it was the tone that cut through the maelstrom of manic mischievous antics. Here, a cymbal clattered, and a drum boomed, but the overall effect was sheer disharmony.

Again, he raised an octave; "Class, settle down, put the instruments down and sit, please!"

"Sir, Sir, did you hear about the terrorists on London Bridge?" It was Oscar.

Merlin looked in his direction. The class followed Merlin's gaze, and their attention turned to Oscar.

"They weren't terrorists, they were muzzie Jihadists!" Jason with an inimitable bellow, belted out his opinion.

"Jason!" Merlin's patience snapped. Finally, the class was silent.

"Yes, I have heard about the attack." Merlin had allowed the silence to echo through the studio, for just long enough.

"Sir, they stabbed people with butcher knives!" Oscar was on his feet still, parodying the slashing and probing movements of those diabolical deviants.

"Alright, sit down Oscar. Enough about terrorism. Our purpose is to spread harmony, and peace, through our wonderful musical talents!" Merlin grinned.

"But sir, why do we have to do music?" Oscar bleated.

"Because it is in our curriculum, and hopefully one or two of you will go on to become the next famous musician or singer; but if none of us practice it is unlikely to happen!" Merlin clarified.
"But sir, I can't even play the piano!" Oscar lamented.

"I know, I heard." Merlin grinned further. The joke was now clear to all in the class, and they guffawed at Oscar's expense.

"But, the truth Oscar, is that your talents lay with your great intellect, and I have no doubt music is not an essential part of what you will become known for!" Merlin encouraged.

"Right! Now that I have your attention your task today is to complete your projects you started last week. You are to build a musical theme to a caption you have created. So, if you would get back into your groups, I am going to assist you are best I can, but I want you working together as a team." Merlin was reading from the cover sheet.

"Sir, can we record other instruments that are not on the computer?" Tammy spoke up.

"Yes, but keep in mind that if everyone is using external instruments, it will cause chaos, so if you need to record externally, put your hand up and the rest of the class is to remain silent." Merlin realised this may be an impossible task, but he was willing to give it a go.

"So, everyone, working in your groups, put your earphones on, and I will walk from table to table to assist if I am able to." The class finally became a cohesive orchestra of three or four students, gathered around one computer, and ideas began to flow.

As Merlin began his rounds, the obvious exception became apparent. Oscar, and Albert were not working together.

"Okay, Oscar, you are supposed to be working with Albert, and who else is in your team?" Merlin queried.

"No, it is just Albert and me." Oscar lifted his head.

"Well then, why aren't you working together?" Merlin had spotted the breakdown in communication.

"No, its fine sir," Albert injected. "I am doing my project, and Oscar has his." The lad seemed casually inhibited.

"Okay, but what is your project?" Merlin rounded on Oscar, who was browsing the web.

"I am still looking for stuff." Oscar was unapologetic.

"That is understandable Oscar, but you have had this past week to decide on a project. You need to choose now and then we can get some options going on your melody." Merlin was out of his comfort zone, but teaching was teaching; it required a deepened sense of understanding the desire every child had, to expand and inform the mind.

Just as Merlin said this, Oscar downloaded a picture of two ladybird beetles, mating. The child was obviously bored stiff.

"Oscar! I know you are more intelligent than this." Merlin recognised the cry for help.

"But, sir, this is my theme for my project!" Oscar grinned. He was beginning to exasperate Merlin, but all was not lost.

"Oscar, you know that is not true!" Merlin decided intervention was essential.

"No, I promise it is." Oscar pulled up several jpegs that he had created. All, sadly, it seemed had a common theme. The lad was frustrated and lashing out. This was an obvious ploy.

"Okay, Oscar, I can see you are trying to get my attention! What is the issue here?" The rest of the class were gamefully employed in their task, and Oscar had Merlin's ear.

"It is nothing sir, I mean not really!" Oscar smiled sheepishly, and Albert turned, a menacing frown on his face, earphones on, but obviously intent on side-tracking him.

"So you say! But if you need to speak out, I am here to help." Merlin let his offer stand. Then just as he was about to walk away, Oscar spun his chair around.

"Sir, if you like boys, does that make you gay?" The dam burst.

"Okay, so that's what this is all about?" Merlin focused on Oscar, allowing Albert to eavesdrop, but knowing intuitively this was akin to what would be required of a marriage counsellor.

"I wanted to write a theme song about being gay!" Oscar's intellect was his finest attribute, but also the potential catalyst for destructive discourse.

"Oscar, you are thirteen years old and your body is going through incredible changes that create all forms of imbalances in your emotions and in your thoughts. As a sociologist, I must say I have counselled thousands of young men through university, but never been asked to intervene with underage students!" Merlin was persuasive, but critically kept his distance, professionally.

"But Sir! I am completely aware of my emotions!" Oscar retaliated.

"Well, then I suggest that you may find that if you know who you are right now, and that your attraction is unequivocal, then express yourself in poetry, or some form of dialogue; but downloading those pictures is not helping." Merlin appeased.

"Do you think that is immature?" Oscar was forthright.

"Oscar, you are thirteen years old!" Merlin reiterated. "I don't believe in attempting to force a lad to be any more mature than they are able to accommodate within their own intellectual capacity. However, with you, I recognise that your ability to transcend ideas and thoughts is a powerful catalyst. Perhaps, if you feel you need to express your identity more earnestly, you might want to speak to one of the counsellors, or perhaps sit down with your mom or dad, and have this conversation with them."

"I have sir!" Oscar was clear. "My mom says I should live my life with my heart on my sleeve."

"Good! That is a wonderful affirmative attitude. If your mom is comfortable with your identity, notwithstanding you still have a substantial amount of growing to do; you're in good hands." To Merlin this was beginning to resolve itself well.

"What I would say, as a last caveat, Oscar!" The lad smiled warmly.

"Just be aware that others, particularly in your class, may not see your conviction in the same positive light you, or your mom does!" Merlin remained supportive, but in life, he knew all too well, there was always going to be opposition to changes in societal boundaries.

"The class system in Britain has been around for centuries and homophobia was introduced by Victorian laws as a means of repressing the hordes of land dwellers who migrated to the cities during the Industrial Revolution. As a result of this influx of mostly men from the farms, seeking work, when the demand for cheap labour exploded and farming became mechanised, the Victorians began a systematic repression of Gay men." Merlin's voice soothed.

"But why did they need to do that?" Oscar was passionate.

"Obviously in those days, they were not called Gay, but we now know that homosexuality has been around since the dawn of time. Those laws introduced by the Victorians created a class divide, and the elites have maintained this divisiveness ever since." Merlin did not expect Oscar to be privy to the demerits of those socio-economic politics.

"Sir? If they did it to maintain a class war, why was Oscar Wilde imprisoned? He was in the Upper-class and a well-known writer." Merlin looked upon this lad with a growing respect.

"Gay men were ostracised by the church, regardless of their class, but civic society and even the education system were largely the preserve of academic men, and educated men were often gifted in scholarly pursuits, rather than sporting prowess." Merlin explained.

"Oh! I get it. They were intellectuals because they spent more time studying, than playing sport?" Oscar interpreted.

"Yes, in a sense, as was the church filled with homosexual men, because it was often a convenient escape route from persecution."

"So they only persecuted Gay men who were obviously Gay? But why?" Oscar pressed.

"Because they did not understand them. Those laws were introduced as a means of controlling a sharp increase in the numbers of men seeking companionship in the cities. In my opinion it was purposely done, so as to keep people living in fear."

"Why do they want us to live in fear?" The lad immediately picked up on the crucial issue.

"You know you asked me at the beginning of the lesson, if I had heard about the London Bridge attacks?" Merlin asked.

"Yes, I know the terrorists hate Britain!" Oscar did not mince his words.

"Well, the reason they did so is so that the people of Britain continue to live in fear of terrorism. Their attacks with knives, stabbing innocent people, is not intended to change our system of government, because they know they can never hope to achieve that with random attacks by individuals; but they can hope to keep people fearful of potential attacks, by using the psychology of fear to maintain their advantage." Merlin explained.

"But!" And Merlin paused long enough to ensure Oscar was entirely focused. "I believe that these attacks are part of a far greater, and far more sinister and deceitful attack on our people."

"How?" Oscar listened intently.

""Because, the elite powers, who control, not only the media discourse, and who maintain control over the flow of money and resources in this country, and the world, can continue to make vast amounts of money, by selling that fear as a neatly packaged funeral plan, or an insurance policy against being attacked in the street, or an assurance policy for your life, so that if you die in a knife attack or an explosion, your family is covered by the payment of a lump sum of money." Merlin elaborated.

"Oh! Like the movie I watched, where this man gets to solve crimes by being able to time travel back from the moment of the crime, and then change the outcome?" Oscar was attentive.

"Yes, in a sense, that story plays on our fears too." Merlin acceded.

"Remember, that the Insurance companies can only turn a profit, if you have something you are scared of losing. That is what insurance is! The reason they have adverts straight after the news on television, is to force the viewer to form an association between the fear itself, and the opportunity to seemingly provide a solution!" Merlin may have been stretching his analogy, but there was no doubt the secular world required fear to perpetuate their profiteering.

"Oh, I get it. It's like they use the terrorism as a marketing video!" Oscar shouted triumphantly.

"Yes, in a somewhat insidious manner, I believe that is true. If you were to ask your mom if she remembers seeing advertisements for insurance companies on television when she was young, you may find they did not exist. Fear is a greater evil, than evil itself!" The jury was in.

"When a human being experiences fear, there is a chemical reaction in the brain that cause a hormone called cortisol to be released. This is what we call the 'fight or flight' syndrome in psychology. Cortisol is the most toxic of hormones because it renders a person incapable of making rational decisions. It usually results in people cowering in the corner; or rushing out the next day to buy insurance." There was no doubt in Merlin's mind.

"Yes, and that is why they constantly put these videos up on social media, and in the news, so they can get everyone anxious." Oscar recognised the dichotomy, where other youngsters would not.

"Indeed!" Merlin applauded. "I call this the Powers and Principalities. This is how they have maintained their control over society for thousands of years."

"I get it sir. They keep people scared of something they cannot control, and when it happens, that reinforces the fear." The lad was an uncanny learner.

"My sense is that when we buy into that fear, they have us over a barrel; but when we fight that fear, they lose." Merlin added.

"Like that man who ran after the terrorists and was going to distract them so that they would not stab anyone else?"

"Yes, precisely!" Merlin could not believe he was having this conversation with a teenager.
"The fight or flight syndrome is what creates this opportunity. If people are paralyzed with fear, they are lost. But if they are able to transcend their fear, and have the courage to confront their attackers, they will always win." Merlin enthused.

"Sir, is that not what we were talking about earlier?" Oscar made the connection. He was so far ahead of mainstream thinking, Merlin could only marvel at the intellect of this lad. Merlin smiled.

"Sir, I know I am gay, because I have always been attracted to other boys!" He was unequivocal.

"Then, Oscar, I am certain that is true. And you make your own destiny by affirming those truths that resonate with your soul." The conclusion was there for the reaping.

"Sir, I am so happy we had this conversation." Oscar grinned, a wide dimple-filled expression of satisfaction.

Merlin rose from where he had been kneeling on one knee, the other foot stretched behind. He smiled at the lad, and then turning, noticed Albert had been listening intently.

As the class came to a conclusion, Merlin had the students pack all the instruments away, and the last to leave was his indomitable disciple, Oscar. The lad walked out with Albert in tow. Then as they reached the doorway to the music hall, Merlin caught a glimpse of a knowing look between them.

Oscar reached out, touched Albert on the shoulder, and they disappeared out through the car park.

"Man can learn nothing except by going from the known to the unknown."

– Claude Bernard

Intentional Technology

"What are you reading?" Merlin arrived a little later than usual and found Simon sitting at a desk in the main library reading area.

"Today's newspaper carries a story about Gay Marriage being accepted by the Northern Ireland government." Simon was elated.

"That is wonderful news!" Merlin read the headline.

"Yes. What it shows is that God has determined that Gay people should also be happy. What if that law had been turned down by the Northern Irish Parliament? That would have meant that ten per cent of the population of Belfast and the whole region would have been disenfranchised!"

"That is remarkable given that the Irish republic has had a Gay Prime Minister for the past five years!" Merlin remarked, knowing that these inconsistencies were a part of the dichotomy of society.

"If it were not the purpose of society to embrace all communities, we would all be living as nomads. But we don't. Why therefore should Gay people not be embraced? In an ideal world, God would not have created people who would be marginalised. This is contrary to the laws of nature, but I am convinced that Gay people are born for a reason!" Simon was unrepentant.

"I know exactly what you mean!" Merlin added, "I just cannot believe in this age, when science has offered so many answers to humanity that the church still persists with its antiquated doctrine!"

"Imagine if you will," Simon painted an imaginary picture with his hands, "a herd of antelope stretched out as far and wide as was once seen in the Savannah grasslands of Africa. They numbered in the millions. Then imagine a draught, which would result in the decimation of those herds, whittling their numbers down to a manageable level. This is precisely what has occurred for millennia here and in other parts of the world. So the point is this. If nature determines to reduce populations where they are unmanageable, is it not conceivable that God may also determine to reduce our populations by switching on the Gay gene?"

"Yes, or course, that makes complete sense." Merlin agreed.
"Gays are born, they are not a product of their environment, and if this is unbelievable, simply look at large families like mine, where two of the four male siblings in our family were born Gay. My brother Jeremy was Gay from a very young age, and this is unfathomable, given the circumstances we were brought up in. No degree of nurturing would have changed those circumstances. I recall him bringing his boyfriend home when he was about fifteen. Now my father was a staunch conservative and had he had an inkling of this, he may well have lost his sense of

civility, as was often the case. However, these were unspoken issues, which the rest of my family seemed to gloss over, and move on." Simon remarked.

"With such an obvious Gay person in the family, it became evident that Jeremy was born that way. There are not any schools that one could attend, where he learned that behaviour! So unless God had ordained it, why does it occur? Gay people, rightly, have been victimized by a society which has no understanding of that ten per cent, yet there are societies in the Pacific Islands, and in South America, where indoctrinated Christian religion had not become institutionalized, and where villages embrace the 'Gay' men and women in their midst. The Catholic church in particular needs to chill a little and understand that God is testing us; and some may be found wanting, but ultimately we must 'Live and let Live'."

"There was a sports program on last evening about Israel Folau, the Australian rugby player." Merlin saw an interesting connection.

"Oh yes, he was banned from playing rugby because of his homophobic comments on social media." Simon knew the story.

"Yes, and now he has been selected to play rugby league for a French team." Merlin commented.

"Uuhhmmm! I know he has been unrepentant regarding his stand on his beliefs that Gay people should be forced to repent and give up their sexuality!" Simon pointed out the hypocrisy.

"Our World would be a more loving, kind and tolerant place if we could simply allow others to be who they want to be. It is the fear of punishment which forces Gay people to live unhappy and unfulfilled lives." Merlin was quick to add.

"Perhaps with these new laws being passed in England, Europe, and California, we may begin to become the society that God intended, and Jesus Christ aspired to?" There was hope in Simon's assessment.

"It is fascinating though," Simon put down the newspaper. "You know, the gospel of Matthew, in the nineteenth chapter and verse eleven, speaks about divorce, being Gay and the discipleship of those who followed Jesus!"

"Here is Jesus telling us through the New Testament that, and I am quoting:

"This teaching does not apply to everyone, but only to those to whom God has given it. For there are different reasons why men cannot marry: some, because they were born that way; others, because men made them that way; and others do not marry for the sake of the Kingdom of heaven. Let him who can accept this teaching do so."

"It sounds to me that Jesus was telling his disciples exactly what we are experiencing today!"

"Yes. That is my interpretation! You know, Matthew then goes on to relate the story that Jesus told about the 'Workers in the Vineyard'. The moral of the story is that Jesus welcomes all, who forsake their lives and come to find the Kingdom of God. It is never too late to do so, and God, like the owner of the vineyard, will welcome anyone in and pay them handsomely, because it is God's Will. He is a generous God, who is willing to accept all into the Kingdom of Heaven, regardless of their circumstances."

Simon allowed that thought to permeate, not just Merlin's, but also his own understanding of what Jesus actually taught his disciples.

"There are so many inconsistencies in the Bible!" Merlin exclaimed. "I just wish that people would look at the real Jesus in the story and realise there is no ways he would have been judgmental."

"My faith has never been daunted by the negativity of church doctrine, so it does not matter to me what they say! But, when I am challenged, like I was the other week, I will not allow them to bully me, or anyone else into believing that God would punish Gay people. I mean, look at how ridiculous this Folau guy sounds when he goes around preaching on social media! I don't believe that Jesus would agree with him if he were to return today." Simon was adamant.

"The thing is though, if Folau were to be preaching in a church, Jesus would likely walk in, throw him out the church and explain to the congregation that he only preaches love."

"I agree." Merlin was loving the feistiness in his friend's eyes. "He was a passionate advocate, yes; but he would not suffer fools!"

"One thing I find intriguing about the Gospel stories, is the evidence that Jesus was a Time Traveller." Merlin sat upright, as Simon spoke.

"Imagine that Jesus was able to defy the laws of space, time and gravity, by using electro-magnetic powers to move around! The theory is not that unbelievable and there are many examples of just how he did so. The references in the Gospels are not entirely unlike the descriptions of Daniel in the fiery furnace, or of the teleportation of the prophets, when they were required to move around; but the greatest of all these examples that we know has been proved by eyewitnesses in the Gospel stories, was the transfiguration of Moses and the Prophet Elijah, not to mention the ascending of Jesus into heaven." Simon spoke eloquently.

"Why do you think they are so important?" Merlin was having a déjà vu moment. His thoughts went to young Oscar and the affirmation that this lad was an old soul, really became evident.

"Because they prove that our belief in God, and our ability to imagine Jesus as the man who was sent to Earth as a saviour for humankind, is not entirely outside the scope of Quantum Mechanics. And here is why!" Simon launched his assault on the churches interpretation.

"If electro-magnetic forces are ten to the thirty-ninth power of gravity, and we can measure the forces of gravity; then imagine how powerful that force of electro-magnetism is! What would the power of that given energy be?" Simon expounded.

"Quantum mechanics and the relevant theories are all very well documented, but there is one fundamental law of power scientists just can't get their minds around!" Simon continued.

"There appears to be one energy field, projected by five different mirror images of itself and of highly energized sub-atomic particles. They can all be determined from the way a particle within a living cell behaves, and the nucleus of a cell contains highly energized matter." Simon had an avid audience of one.

"That is the Proton and the Electron." Merlin agreed.

"Yes, and now it is believed that these sub-atomic particles are able to move between the 'Seen' dimension and the 'Unseen'. The Biblical reference was uncanny.

"So that is how the power Jesus was given through the Holy Spirit, allowed Him to move around freely, often disappearing from a crowd, and re-appearing somewhere else." Simon elaborated.

"It is that power which is able to manifest through unexplainable healings. When the mind is projected through directed prayer to the object or subject of our thoughts, we are able to transform that matter, into alternative forms. So unhealthy cells can be made well." This made sense to Merlin.

"I agree, because the human body is capable of replacing every cell at least once every seven years." Merlin was aware of cellular reconstruction.

"Projecting negative energy can kill off healthy cells, and the process of decay becomes, the exact opposite of the healthy healing of cells……!" Simon paused.

"I have a powerful sense that this is intentionally aimed at affirming my thoughts about consciousness." There was a fire in his eyes.

"Would you believe I was having this exact conversation with a Year nine student the other day?" Merlin enthused.

"Really? No, I would not be at all surprised! These kids today are developing a consciousness of reality that we could only dream of!"

"Yes, I agree. This is a process of what I refer to as In.T. or, 'Intentional Technology.' It is the psychology of what determines the manifesting, or visions of truths we wish to affirm to reality." The conversation affirmed why Merlin was glad he had met Simon.

"It is the studying of visualisations!" Simon concurred.

"It is fascinating that Walter Benjamin studied this phenomena, yet we still only know a tiny element about the subject. He is quoted to have said; "Those who do not learn how to decipher photographs will be the illiterate of the future.""

"I am not familiar with his work." Simon conceded.

"Well, I believe he has an important role to play in deciphering the 'Seen' and the 'Unseen'." Merlin offered.

"Oh! Really." Now Simon was sitting up.

"Well, the quote that got my attention is; "Even the most perfect reproduction of a work of art is lacking in one element: that is its presence in time and space, and its unique existence at the place where it happens to be." Merlin para-phrased.

"Fascinating!" Simon listened.

"Yes. He also said; 'The camera introduces us to unconscious optics as does, psychoanalysis to unconscious impulses.'"

"Is he referring to the conscious mind's ability to take a static photo that is stored in a memory loop, for future use?" Simon asked.

"Yes, that would be a simplified assessment of the conscious functioning of memory." Merlin accepted.

"Well our bodies are the sum total of all our cells, some fifty-trillion of them, which resonate at a pre-determined vibration. Each cell has a memory, which is how the cell is able to recall its function. When we have a healthy vibrational resonance, our bodies are healthy – when that vibration is out of resonance with the rest of the body's cells, it becomes unhealthy. This is a very simple concept. Like a musical instrument, which is incorrectly tuned, the cell begins to vibrate at a rate, which is not in synchronicity with the rest of the cells around it. So, like that musical instrument, the body rejects that vibrational frequency, and the cell self-destructs; but not before it has infected the surrounding cells with its poor energy." Simon was effusive.

"That is the definition of cancer!" Merlin marvelled.

"Yes, and 'Constructive Interference' of those cell vibrations is what happens when the body resonates at a healthy vibration, and because the vibrations give off a sound wave, that wave, is picked up by the rest of the body as the body becomes aligned with itself." The effect of Cymatics on the human body was well researched." Simon extrapolated his assessment of the function of cancer cells.

"Ah! Yes, that is the study of vibrational phenomena." Merlin added.

"The phenomenon of Coordinative Resonance, versus Fractal Non-linear Resonance." Simon elaborated. "Electromagnetic waves can make things vibrate at their resonant frequency too. But they only affect things that are magnetic or electrically charged; like electrons, protons and molecules."

"So what you are saying, is that microwave and x-ray energy from electronic equipment causes disease?" Merlin concluded.

"Yes, and the reason people get sick, is because as Rudolf Steiner explained, even before electron-microscopes were available, is that viruses are caused by toxins in the liver; this is the production of exosomes which contain Viral-infected cells which have been shown to shed exosomes containing cellular and viral-specific components like messenger-based Ribonucleic Acid, which effects protein synthesis." Simon was in his element.

"This is true also, for other bodies around us, and why it is possible to communicate on a sub-conscious level with other people, or even animals. This is why you can be 'in-tune' with other members of your family, and often how we find our 'soul-mates'. Our energy field resonates with them, is recognized by them, and we intuitively 'like' them, and they 'like' us." This was the definition of love.

"This is no more than a symphony of 'Love'. This was the energy that Jesus, resonated." Simon concluded.

"Biological incubators/bioreactors are a vital piece of equipment required for the growth of many cell types. Incubators are ubiquitous in any cell biology or DIYBio lab and at their heart they are simply warm, humid boxes with temperature and atmosphere regulation." - Andrew Pelling

Defying Gravity

"Is levitation unrealistic? According to certain scientists, 'No'!" Merlin was addressing his Monday morning science class, covering for an errant teacher whom it seemed, had no passion for teaching.

"David Blane can levitate!" It was the inimitable Jason.

"Yes, Jason, that is magic in the literal sense of the word! But who knows where the idea of magicians comes from?" Merlin felt the need to accommodate the young man, without giving him his usual podium.

"Yessss, yesss, Sir. I know!" The voice squeaked in a familiar, but comforting tone.

"Yes, Oscar."

"My dad told me that the magicians in the Bible came from the east!"

"Don't be daft, the Bible is a load of nonsense!" Jason felt the need to impart his wisdom.

"Actually, No! Jason, you might be wrong on that" Merlin turned to him.

"Oscar is correct. The word 'Magi' comes from the Bible and is mentioned three times when Jesus was born. These were very wise men, or as we would say today, 'scholars' of the hidden mysteries of magic."

"Sir, Jesus was also a magician!" Oscar trumpeted as his voice broke, officially sending the class a message, that the lads knew all too well.

"Well done Oscar." Merlin was feeling a sense of pride, like a father eagle, as his fledgling leapt into the unknown.

"The reality is that there are many examples of what the ancient people knew, that our society is still coming to terms with. For example, the instances of magical events happening in the Bible, are numerous. But, our ancestors have forgotten so much, because these truths have been kept from us for thousands of years."
"That's the illuminati sir," Oscar barked.

"Well yes and no!" Merlin was ambiguous. "There are many texts of the ancient people that exist today, but for some reason we don't seem to be able to interpret them; or it is possible that our understanding has been suppressed."

"Jason. Your family are related to the ancient Celtics? What does your family say about the idea of ancient civilisations?" Merlin targeted the one person he knew would have heard these mysteries made mention of; but had he been listening?

"My granny told me she used to go to Stonehenge every year in March to perform some magical thingy and then the sun would come up early in the morning and then she would stay for the day!" The young man puffed out his chest.

"That is the witnessing of the Spring Equinox." Merlin smiled. "Why do you think they celebrated spring?"

"Ohh, I know!" Oscar chirped.

"Yes, Oscar."

"It is when the farmers planted their seeds for the summer season, and the sun always comes up at the same time every year."

"Well, yes, that was the theory, but why do we not celebrate this as a society anymore?" There was a sea of blank faces.

"Is it to do with religion?" Jason asked.

"Yes, well spotted Jason!" There was an easiness in the air that Merlin had not witnessed before.

"Religion was one reason that these practices were suppressed, but what else do you think has changed our understanding?"

"Is it to do with astronomy?" Oscar pointed out the obvious.

"Yes, indeed it was, Oscar, well done. The study of the planets and the cycle of nature, which was known to the ancient people, has become common knowledge today because we have telescopes and computers, and we can track the orbits of the solar system." The evidence concluded so much more than what ancient man had known; or had it?

Who knows what the 'Precession' is?" Merlin invited. Blank faces.

"Okay, I would not expect you will have heard of this yet!"

"This is the scientific study of the Earth's tilting action, as it rotates on the axis of north to south-pole." Merlin lifted the plastic globe that conveniently sat on the front cabinet.

Picking up the globe, he demonstrated. "As the Earth spins, it does not stay fixed in one plain, but wobbles back and forth in a series of cycles, and this has only become known with modern calculations." He let the globe wobble backwards and then forwards in a mimicking of the motion.

"But the interesting thing is, this movement was also known to the ancient people, and your descendants," Merlin accentuated his point, turning to Jason, "knew this thousands of years ago!"

"So the theme for today's lesson is about the Earth's cycle of orbit around the sun, and the reason we need the moon to create a gravitational force on our oceans. It is fitting that on the fiftieth anniversary of the lunar landings of Neil Armstrong and Buzz Aldrin, we should be studying these forces." Merlin paused to allow the class to settle.

"Okay, so I want you to open your work books and draw the orbit of the planets around the sun, from memory, and if you can remember, what the orbit of the moon around the Earth looks like." Merlin, content the class were now focused on the task at hand, sat down facing the one really inquisitive face in the room; Oscar it was who sat at the front desk facing Merlin.

"Sir, should we include the time it takes them." Oscar was on point.

"Yes, let's get as much detail in your diagram, and I would like to see if you can explain the reason for the different orbits." The class eagerly flipped open their books.

"Remember to include the gravitational pull of the different planets and how they affect each other."

"Sir, what causes the moon to orbit the earth, but it does not spin?"

The lad had such an enquiring mind Merlin knew he should be in a school for talented students.

"Well Oscar, the evidence of ancient astrological events shows they have had a huge influence on our past history. For instance, can you think of what palaeontologists use to explain the demise of the dinosaurs?" Merlin posed a question within his answer.

"Asteroids sir." He was drawing as he answered.

"Yes, indeed. The evidence of fossil archaeology gives scientists a blueprint for what causes extinction events." Merlin continued. "The real issue is that we have this evidence of past extinction events, yet the moon has a peculiar role to play in the Earth's past and undoubtedly will also do so in the future."

"So, sir, do you believe that the moon is not a natural lunar satellite?" The lad smiled.

"Ah! Yes, the famous conspiracy theory about how the moon always presents one face to the Earth, where all other lunar objects in our solar system rotate on their axis." The evidence was conjecture, however, as with all conspiracy theories, there was a plausible smoking gun!

"So, what do you believe?" Oscar pressed him.

"It is interesting that both the American and Russian astronaut programs stopped sending men to the moon after the successful Apollo missions." Merlin conceded.

"Sir, do you know that my mobile phone has more memory function than any of the Apollo space craft that were supposed to go to the moon?" Oscar pulled his phone out from his pocket.

"Yes, amazing to think how our technology has moved on in such a short period of time!" The enigma warranted speculation.

"Oscar, do you recall the lesson we had about Intentional Technology?" Merlin was weaving a skein together.

"Yes, and I still practice that image thing every night before bed." The lad enthused.

"Great, because if you can imagine the technology that the Apollo astronauts used to navigate their way to the moon and back, it had to be so precise that had they missed their mark on the entry into the lunar atmosphere by a millisecond, they would have either plunged to their deaths on the moon, or gone sailing off into deep space with no chance of ever returning; that's how difficult that was!" The calculations were evidence of how powerful the human mind was.

"If Nikola Tesla, or Albert Einstein were able to perceive their amazing formulas for electronics and quantum mechanics through what I refer to as 'Mindfulness', then imagine how powerful your mind will be, if you continue to focus your mind on your studies and all these mysteries?" Merlin laid it out.

"I have dreams sir!" Oscar admitted. "But not just ordinary dreams about life and, you know, stuff!" The lad blushed. Un-phased, he gathered his thoughts again.

"I see equations in my mind during my dreams."

"Fantastic Oscar. That is the beginning of something amazing!" Merlin cooed. "I want you to consider something new. Do you understand the concept of supernatural power?"

"Yes, but do you mean, like supernatural stuff in the bible." Oscar's dad was a Polish Catholic.

"In a sense, but I am referring to Spirituality more than pure Biblical texts." Merlin offered.

"Yes sir." The lad put his book down on the table consciously and listened.

"Well, science is the study of nature and how the natural world functions in cycles. So when science is able to replicate nature through processes of random events and experiments, nature reveals itself in Quantum Mechanics. So, scientists observing the natural order of the universe, are able to discern how nature is formulated; because all of nature operates from mathematical formulae, upon which they are able to determine answers to important questions!" Merlin waited to ensure Oscar was following him.

"If we consider nature to be created, then God would have placed those formulae there for the purposes of being calculated, otherwise he would not have given us a brain capable of discernment. A living, conscious brain, which is capable of millions of random calculations per second! Therefore, nature has been carefully prepared to reveal its' secrets over time. It is our function as discerning human beings, to attempt to formulate these equations. If nature is to function optimally, it must be in synchronicity. In other words, it must be capable of resonating within its sphere of influence. This presupposes there must be a 'oneness' in nature to allow a natural flow of energy, through particle and wave formations."

"Oh, you mean like Quantum Entanglement?" Oscar cut to the heart of the issue.

"Yes, exactly and I believe we are all connected by a force we have no control over other than to embrace it. If oneness with nature is the sole purpose of human existence, and we are intent on thriving through the process of creation, then there is a remarkable process under way, initiated by science, which is a direct result of the desire of man to understand his environment and the meaning of life." Merlin paused again.

"You once asked me if I was a time traveller." Merlin weaved his magic.

"Yes, because I thought you understood more about what I believed, but none of the other boys knew what I was asking!" Oscar poured out his understanding of consciousness.

"We are all connected and Time Travel is possible in our deepened state of 'Mindfulness'." Merlin had posed the rhetorical question, knowing he would draw young Oscar into a conversation.
"This is how Albert Einstein, Nikola Tesla and other great minds were able to communicate with these universal powers." The mention of these scientific deities sparked the lad's imagination.

"I know!" Oscar crowed. "Einstein saw images of his equations and Tesla saw blueprints of his designs."

"Indeed they did. So, if I am opening a portal to Extra-Sensory Perception, my thoughts are received by those whom I wish to communicate with, because some part of my DNA is projected through the Ethernet to connect with a particle that was once a part of my own Consciousness and is now linked to the person with whom I am attempting to make contact." Merlin spoke with an authority he would previously never dared to.

"Are you saying that we are all connected by particles?" The lad was enthusiastically imbedded.

"Yes! This is the process of Quantum Entanglement. Invariably, because I am attempting to get someone to respond in a particular way to achieve a specific goal, the entanglement theory proves that the opposite happens; one particle spins in one direction, and the other, connected to the person with whom I am mindfully requesting a response, spins in the opposite." Merlin explained the conundrum experienced by the scientific community.

Oscar listened intently.

"This is the explanation for the Quantum Enigma scientists have never been able to fathom." The theory had been the bane of scientists for half a century.

"How does the mind of one person connect with the mind of another?" Oscar could not grasp ESP.

"I know that the Global Consciousness works seamlessly in every organic and inorganic molecule in the Universe." Merlin was categorical. "This is the study of Panpsychism."

"Panpyschism?" Oscar had never heard of this research.

"Yes. Rudolf Steiner famously said we must, 'Think of a physical body, like ours, composed as it is of the same substances and forces that are in what seems a lifeless world around it. The physical body could not go on existing without the inflow into it of matter and force from the surrounding world.' Merlin para-phrased.

"Oh! I know who Rudolf Steiner is!" Oscar exclaimed. "He lived here in West Sussex."

"Yes, Oscar. He proposed that our physical bodies, were by definition a continual thoroughfare for all the molecules that are in them. Life flows into and out of our bodies continuously, with water the main element, consisting of hydrogen and oxygen. The hydrogen is the fuel, the oxygen the life-blood for cellular growth, and carbon elements the substance." Merlin elaborated.

"Yes, my dad says that we should treat our bodies like a car; we must have fuel to make it go, and water and air to keep us cool." Oscar grinned triumphantly. Merlin could not fault his summation, but there were two elements still required.

"Yes, the body is no different to an engine. In fact our bodies are like an organic engine. To provide energy we must have oxygen, fuel and water. So, if each of those elements at one time were of the outer-world and at another time within us, then at one point in time you and I shared those elements. In the course of seven years, the entire material composition of our human body is renewed, by osmosis." Merlin paused, a quizzical look emerging on Oscar's already impish face.

"What is 'osmoeses'? The lad repeated the word phonetically.

"Ah! Yes, this is the key." Merlin speculated. "When the body processes mineral elements through the combination of drinking water and eating, those minerals form concentrated elements that replace the nucleus of cells. But every one of those nuclei have a memory of its previous existence, just as a computer chip stores data for a smart phone." Merlin expressed himself in a language the lad could equate his own life experiences to.

"So, you are saying we store memories of other people?" Oscar frowned.

"Not exactly! Your DNA will record every element you were born with, because that is fundamental to you specifically. Like a magnet attracts an opposite charge, your DNA will attract those elements it requires to regenerate itself." Merlin explained.

"Does that mean I have a completely new body now that I am nearly fourteen?" Oscar proudly preened his muscular forearms. The lad was a very capable gymnast.

"In a word, yes." Merlin smiled, knowing Oscar may have been intonating at more than Merlin was privy to know; or wished to know.

"But more importantly, because your DNA is pre-conditioned to allow your body to grow in a specific way, it can only attract those elements to which it has an affiliation, intuitively." Merlin may have lost the lad.

"A computer program has to be fundamentally re-programmed to allow another code to work within its formatted essence." Merlin used computer lingo.

"Oh, I get it; I cannot play Nintendo games on a PlayStation."

"You are perpetually renewing the substances of our physical body, but there is pre-determined format." Merlin quoted.

"That makes sense sir." Oscar was deferential; but Merlin knew there was a gifted mind working overtime behind that smile.

"But how do we levitate?" The question was still begging to be answered.

"Okay, good!" Merlin knew the lad had not lost the focus of the real lesson.

"So the critical issue here, is to avoid using ESP to force my outcome on someone else, but rather leave the entire Quantum Formulae to the Spiritual world. The outcome will be determined by the 'Creator' or what I like to suggest is the Global Consciousness; what Christians call God; and in ITs own time, the answer to our Mindfulness will appear, because that is how the formula works." Oscar was avidly following the conversation.

"To para-phrase a well-known academic on esoteric issues; in order to know a subject, we must experience it and then the being is the model on which Spirituality is based. In other words; we make our own reality! We can literally become our own 'Reality Architects'."

"Wow, I like that! I want to be an architect." Oscar insisted.

Merlin continued; "Yes, but not the kind of architect you are thinking of Oscar. A Reality Architect has the power of creating his own destiny; the power to create the world he wants, through creative thinking. When we get rid of all the unnecessary clutter of life, the world becomes a simpler place; it is then we can re-create the world we would all wish to live in."

"This is why we all have be given the ability of free will. It is so that we can learn, and through that knowledge or Gnosis as it was named in the Bible, we are empowered to live in the power of the Spirit, or Global Consciousness. We are truly connected, Spiritually" But Oscar blinked twice.

"Do you understand what Spirit actually is? Not some 'airy-fairy' discussion about angels with wings!" Merlin asked.

"Oscar is a fairy." Jason, who had been eaves-dropping, could not help himself.

"And you would know that Jason!" Oscar shot back. The red-headed lad became flushed, and sank back into his seat, defeated.

Ordinarily, Merlin might have intervened, but Jason's ego was deflated; yet Merlin knew this lad was far more academically inclined, than he was willing to project to the class. In fact, Merlin was of the opinion that Jason was hiding his real intellect, for fear of being equated to Oscar!

"Once we recognise that we are all connected Spiritually, and no one person has a monopoly on righteousness, it is then that we can move forward out of slavery." Merlin offered an expression Oscar would relate to.

"Oh, I get it," The lad beamed. He turned and gave Jason a knowing look. Jason avoided him pitifully.

"That is central to being, and when we have experienced that 'knowing', then we become centred in our being; essentially we move from Spiritual beings to become human-beings!" Merlin breezed past the distraction.

"So, we are spiritually aware first; then we become human?" Oscar attempted to simply the process for his own minds sake.

"Yes, indeed! We carry the essence of our Spiritual Life from previous incarnations; or past lives, into our existing life." Merlin allowed that though to sink in.

"Therefore nature does not interfere with the processes, as the science becomes part of a revelation of the cosmic order. The Universe has given us science to determine our various processes; yet mankind insists on destroying nature. But nature would not have been revealed to us, should there have been no Cosmic Consciousness." Merlin recognised this was a revelation of significant magnitude.

"But what is the Cosmic Consciousness?" Oscar dug deeper.

"The natural order is dictated by a force field around the Earth, which we know to be created by electro-magnetic frequency fields." The Torus, as he knew it to be.

"You mean the polarity forces that determine the magnetic poles?"

"Yes. Birds use this field to migrate, and Cicadas are awakened every seven, or thirteen years as a consequence of the vibration of that energy, in the core of the Earth." Merlin responded.

"Oh! Is that like when the Earth has a natural vibrational energy?" Oscar probed.

"That is correct Oscar. It fluctuates from one year to the next and awakens creation accordingly." Merlin was enjoying this discussion.

"So that is the consequences of science on the natural order?" Oscar had not taken his eyes off Merlin for five minutes.

"Yes!" Merlin smiled. He loved the process of teaching.

"Sir, you started the lesson by asking us if we believed in levitation." Oscar enquired. "Yes, in just the same way we use Quantum Entanglement!" Merlin searched the lad's eyes for a glimmer of understanding. The theory of quanta, or Life Force, flowing throughout the Universe was his passion. The lad smiled; a knowing in essence.

"So, I believe that by reversing the Quantum Mechanical theory of the Casimir Force, we can change the behaviour of atoms and subatomic particles that are the glue, which bonds physical entities together. The Casimir Force does not owe its existence to electrical charges or gravity, but is the fluctuations in all-pervasive energy fields in the intervening empty space between objects, which allows atoms to stick together." Merlin explained.

Oscar was listening intently, when suddenly the bell rang. Pandemonium reigned as all the students rushed to get their set-work collected, before rushing off for their lunch break.

Merlin sat, reflecting on the diagrams turned in. The question was indeed, how? Merlin sat in thought, reflecting on how he may have answered the question posed in a university lecture hall.

One student had lagged behind; it was Oscar.

"Sir, how can I learn to levitate, Sir?" The question posed was as ancient as the great glyphs and Sumerian cuneiform writing; but what about the great stone megaliths of Göbeklitepe? How old were they really; and how did ancient people move them into the positions they now command on a hilltop ridge, seemingly hundreds of miles from where the rock was hewn from the ground!

"The key to levitation is in the art of focusing your mind on being lighter than air. Focusing on objects to appear lighter than air." Merlin pronounced.

"Keep in mind that the space between atoms in a seemingly, solid object is vast, and that space, when focused on, becomes even lighter as we expand the spaces to allow more oxygen and hydrogen, and nitrogen, into those spaces. It is the focusing of the fabric of this space, unravelling the physical construct that we visualise, through psychokinetic power." The class had emptied and the students all happily chatting amongst themselves had deserted them; Oscar thanked him.

"Oscar, do you know what a bio-luminescent cortical field is?" Merlin watched his face light up.

"Is that what we call our 'aura'?" Oscar shouted triumphantly.

"Yes, it is Oscar. What do you know about auras?" Merlin wished to gain his level of understanding before continuing.

"Well, I do know that our human body has a vast network of veins and arteries that carry our blood around oxygenating all the cells in our body." Oscar contributed.

"Indeed we do Oscar. Do you know the extent to which that network operates within our bodies?" Merlin probed.

"Only that it is very long and that the corpuscles in the blood are like, billions." The words tumbled out.

"Are you aware that our hearts pump the living plasma of the Bio-luminescent Cortical Energy Field along the 60,000 kilometre journey of our hUman form?" Merlin was fielding a critical question. If Oscar could not grasp the 'biolumin conundrum', then Merlin would not indulge his curiosity further.

"Only that hUmans," he intonated the same pronunciation of the word, as Merlin had, "have the ability to raise, or lower the level of energy within their bodies, through meditation, or when they have an adrenalin rush."

Merlin understood Oscar was an athlete, but he wondered whose knowledge he was channelling.

"Excellent Oscar!" Merlin smiled.

"That is called the Balmer Effect and Balmer's Formula dictates that the varying levels of energy emitted by a hydrogen molecule as its electron changes its orbit, is determined by the distance it will move from its previous orbit. But these distances may appear is infinitesimally small in the context of our overall physiology; but in relation to the nuclei of the hydrogen molecule, it is immensely significant." Merlin repeated his basic understanding of the nano-particle biology.
"Hydrogen Clusters create Energy fields when they are in Free-Radical motion."

But when a Hydrogen Molecule is in suspension with another Hydrogen Molecule, united by an Oxygen Molecule, (to form water) it is vastly more stable. Water molecules held in suspension in the Di-pole created by the Energy between the two Molecules of Hydrogen and one Oxygen Molecule, create a precise flow within the Bio-Luminescent Cortical Field. This is known as Plasma, and is 'literally' the Life-Blood of the creative organic form. With the Cortical Field capable of extreme levels of Energy combustion, a 60,000 Kilometre chain of Arteries, Veins and Capillaries are the pathway to a ±25 Billion strong flow of Corpuscles, containing the suspended Hydrogen Molecules. Those Hydrogen Molecules can thus be a stable flow of Life-Giving Energy, to hold the outward appearance of the 'hUman form' in virtual suspension; or they can be de-stabilised to create an extreme Energy Field which is visible in The Balmer Formula, when Hydrogen Molecules reach a 'Free-Radical' Energy Incubation level.

As we all know, a 'Free-Radical' is essential for 'hUman' tissue growth, but the Free-Radical must be determined by a very simple mathematical equation. This is the effect known as The Riemann Hypothesis. This hypothesis determines the flow of those Free-Radicals in a Primary Numerical Function of instability that dictates they will be disrupted from the Di-Polactic Energy flow of Hydrogen Molecules in suspension, and will be met by Hydrogen Molecules, introduced into the Bio-Luminescent Cortical Field, through the lungs, which feed Oxygen and Hydrogen into the blood, via the bronchial network. When the oxygen is paired with a binary pair of Hydrogen Molecules, they are held in suspension, and contribute to the Plasma; when there is not enough oxygen feeding the blood, the Hydrogen Molecules form Free-Radical chains of Bio-Luminescent Energy in which temperature variation controls the orbit of the Hydrogen's Electron.

Depending on that orbit, the Hydrogen Molecule will either be in Suspension, or a 'Free-Radical'.

"Well today I have awoken to an interesting new world!" Oscar intoned, then smiled.

"Indeed Oscar. That 'World' is within us and I have no doubt the world is not a world order, but is naturally ordered. There is a place here, where all mankind will thrive, because, there is a plentiful supply for everyone." Merlin coached.

"So how can we make our world a better place?" Oscar broached the age-old question.

"We could all start by becoming more conscious of the world around us. Being mindful of the place each of us occupies, and grateful we have that space. No greed is necessary; it is that greed which keeps us all subservient to the elite classes." Merlin stifled his true feelings; concerned he may impinge on the lad's exuberance.

"That is exactly what my dad says!" Oscar was triumphant.

"He says that there is so much wealth in this world, but greed keeps people from sharing." The communism of Eastern Europe still freshly evident in the minds of migrants to Britain. Merlin would likely assess his father was a manual labourer whose experiences of capitalism had soared on the promises of European unity; but floundered in a class-based society where Royalty enjoyed such opulence; an opulence that that afforded them the luxury to bemoan a green planet.

"Oscar, I would like you to take the idea of levitation home with you, and meditate over the process." Merlin knew he had initiated some powerful force that would not be contained.

"Yes Sir. I will! Thank you Sir," the lad picked up his workbook, tossed it into the plastic storage unit on the front desk, and skipped through the doorway.

Merlin was bursting with pride. This was the son he had never had. The lad was gifted, but in a manner unlike the savants one hears about in the media. This lad had a consciousness way beyond his years that could only have emanated from the quantum memory of a past, or past-life experiences.

Merlin would be required to nurture that gift, without creating any animosity within the classroom. Oscar, it was now obvious, had escaped The Light, which draws the living towards a permanent servitude to the worldly realm; and was somehow able to navigate between life experiences without a genesis or new beginning. If ever there was an example of re-incarnation; Oscar was proof!

Spiritually he knew that the energy generated from the Savants, who channel Spiritual Energy from the deceased, was the same Spiritual Energy that is received when Christians or other worshippers meet in church or religious venues. The Spiritual powers he knew, do not have any connection to any religion, or favour any cult. What transpired with Prayers and Meditations is no different to what Dale Carnegie proposed a hundred years before. The subject of focus-minded people has always driven society forward. But he knew that Spiritual Energy can be, both good and bad. The Yin and Yang, were complementary and interconnected, far more realistically than religions were willing to admit. That interdependence in the natural world was what the Jewish People believed was the Yetzer Ha Ra, and the Yetzer Ha Tov; that innate wickedness and inclination to do good deeds, was not the preserve of the righteous; or of the wicked.

His sense, was that the ionisation of mortal bodies, when passing from Life to Spirit, took the essence of the mortal body, the very material of our human being and sent those molecules, whether hydrogen, oxygen, nitrogen, or carbon-based, into the atmosphere, where they became a part of the Ionosphere. This in religious terms was what humans defined as Heaven, or Nirvana; Shangri-La.

It was the ionised particles of our selves that have a connection with the very protons and electrons of those molecules, or nano-particles swirling around in the ether-sphere, and which have a memory, linked to our own DNA. It is that memory that allows humans to maintain contact with our Loved Ones. As below, so above, and it is likely that there is good energy in those molecules; as well as bad.

As Rudolf Steiner had correctly assessed, the Etheric body, is part of our Spiritual selves, and has the ability to find the energy to forgive ourselves, so that we can begin to Heal and move forward in Life. It was the guilt or fear of the Etheric Self that kept humans captive to institutionalised religion.

Once humans were able to recognise that we are all connected Spiritually, and that no one person had a monopoly on righteousness, it was then that Merlin believed they could move forward out of slavery, and into the Astral dynamic of Spirituality, where humans begin to control temptation.

This was what took place when Spiritual people Astral Travel. The limitations of this Spiritual power, can only be overcome, once humans had removed the Ego, which was the Spirit of Ahriman, and the evil spoken of in a church context.

The Duality existed, because it was the divine essence of humans to progress, and the only way they could, was to balance that Duality.

The answer he believed, was to attempt to remove the Ego, then etherically forgive one's self. For humans to Astral Travel into the Truth of knowledge, they had to limit the temptations of the physical realm. To do so, humans had to look inside our selves, literally, and change the energy of their very essence.

Merlin had to think of his body as a fifty-trillion strong energy field, with each particle of his body, able to seamlessly communicate with each other. Once he had mastered that ability to recognise the power each of those molecules had, then he was able to begin to connect the healthy living molecules, and purge the unhealthy, negatively charged particles, replacing them with healthy ones. Each human was made up of a fifty-trillion piece jigsaw puzzle, with each piece connected. To complete the jigsaw, one had to master the bigger picture.

Merlin suddenly realised, he had just answered his own question posed earlier in class; can human beings levitate?

"Noisy, rude and boisterous, the natural exultation of a suddenly enfranchised class; but bent on no other mischief than glorying over the villainous and self-seeking souls who have ground the faces of the poor and turned the pitiless screw of social and political power into the hearts of the 'common people' until its last thread had been reached, and despair pressed its lupine visage hard against the door of the labouring man.

And yet, at this moment when the night air quivered with the mad vociferations of the "common people," that the Lord had been good to them; that the wicked money-changers had been driven from the temple, that the stony-hearted usurers were beaten at last."

'1900 Or the Last President' (Ingersoll Lockwood)
Revelation of Consciousness

"This morning I was frustrated as I watched a news program of an interview with Lord Sugar. This man is a moron!"

"Yes, I tend to agree with you; he is a self-serving egotist!" Merlin was in full agreement with Simon.

"He attempted to explain to the viewers that the knife-crime epidemic is a result of a break down in families. No! Knife crime is happening because of drugs and the insidious industry that it creates, because of the lure of money." Simon was once more animated.

"Turf wars are fought because of the very basic human nature of greed, and when young men are faced with potential threats to their lucrative, but illicit businesses, they fight back." Simon elaborated.

"Stop the drugs, get these young men into 'Safe Spaces' where they can focus their minds on positive issues, or get them into advanced focus groups with meditation, and you stop them from wanting to be on the streets." The idea of a Safe Space, was not new.

"But how do we get them into a safe place, where they can begin to create constructive results?" He felt so passionately about this need, Merlin recognized the spark of light in his eyes.

"But what can we do to prevent more young men from becoming victims of this war?" Merlin's lament was as passionate a cry for common sense to prevail. He could make, but a limited contribution in the classroom.

"I have an idea, which I believe will work." Simon smiled; there was a hint of something mystical in the way his eyes glazed over.

"What is that?" Merlin grasped; searching for answers to help his students.

"I always use prayer, or what Spiritualists call 'Mindfulness'." Simon had met Merlin for their weekly get together.

"Ah, yes, the wonderful mind, or 'beautiful mind', is a precious asset." Merlin concurred.

"I refer to this as 'panpsychism' and in my opinion it is that the mind or a mindfulness as a science is a fundamental and global feature of reality. Our reality is created from the power of our mind in overcoming obstacles, or limitations in the thought process!" Simon elaborated.

"Yes, the human brain is a powerful tool, and we have very little understanding of its true potential." Merlin agreed.

"So, if our minds are fundamental to the way we perceive our Universe, then by changing the way we think about a situation, or our circumstances, we can change our reality." Simon knew that every great motivator and thinker in history had used panpsychism to create the environment around them.

"I know, but didn't Spinoza regard the mind and matter as simply an attribute of the eternal, infinite and unique substance he identified with God?" Merlin had researched the seventeenth century philosophy.

"That was his limited take on the Universe and how extra-sensory perception worked. You see, I believe that without the luxury of electron microscopes and energy-field photography, he was capable of understanding the source of that energy. It is only now that we can equate the energy of our auras, to that of our own powerful water-dipolactic resonance field." Simon continued, but Merlin had to stop him.

"Water-dipolactic? What is that?"

Okay, so we know that our body is seventy percent water, right?"

"Yes." Merlin was intrigued where this was leading.

"And we know that the body has an energy field that circulates through blood which is a sixty-thousand mile long system of capillaries, veins and arteries?" The question rhetorical.

"Well, that labyrinth of blood vessels carries blood plasma which is made up of water. Water has hydrogen and oxygen molecules and they are inter-connected by what is called the 'Water-Dipole'." The answer was evident.

"So, if a positive and a negative pole is required for an uneven distribution of electrons within it, the dipole nature within a water molecule creates attractive forces known as hydrogen bonding, allowing them to stick together." Simon had made the connection.

"So what you are saying is that the water-dipole creates an energy field?" Merlin surmised.

"Yes. And that energy field, or aura, which is called the Electro-Magnetic Frequency Field or EMFF has a consciousness, because each molecule of water has a nuclei, with an electron and a proton and each water molecule binds with the human cell to oxygenate and energise the DNA of the cell to function." There was an urgency in his voice.

"Well, if Human cells depend on those electro-magnetic interactions involving water bonds, then water is the polar solvent able to participate in those solutions. The hydrogen and oxygen interacts with proteins creating the bonding for cellular activity."

"Yes, I understand. But what has that got to do with Spinoza?" Merlin waited.

"The power of our thoughts are energy, and our brains are over seventy percent water, so the energy that is released by our thoughts can be recognised by the energy field of another human being, or any living matter." Simon concluded.

"That is the extra-sensory perception people claim they have when communicating non-verbally. Have you ever been in a queue and stared at the back of the head of the person in front of you?"

"Yes, it's weird, they always turn around." Merlin recognised Simon's point.

"Exactly! They know you are communicating with them, because they can sense your aura and it interacts with theirs."

"But how does this equate to God?" Merlin interjected.

"Because the experience people believe they are having in a spiritual event, is merely their own powerful recognition of an unseen energy, which vibrates at a resonant frequency within their own thoughts." The idea was not foreign to Merlin.

"Tesla said, that the key to understanding the Universe, was based on frequency, vibrations and energy. I believe he was referring to our own ability to communicate with an Electro-Magnetic Frequency Field Consciousness."

Merlin gazed at his friend. There was a liberation from servitude deep within those amber-green eyes.

"Can I share something I use daily for my meditations?" Simon wanted to share this new world he had created for himself.

Merlin smiled and nodded.

"By meditating and asking that we will see this world as a harmonious place of abundance, I believe we manifest that outcome.

If we wish not to see one person dominating others in their attempts to govern other people and countries, or their own; nor dictate financial opportunities for others, nor enslave anyone into working for no just reward, we can pray for that outcome.

If we want to see a free world, where politics no longer determines what a human being can do, but assists them to become the person they deserve to be, then focus your mind on that outcome.

If we want a world free from the agonies of poverty, determined by the wealth of nations which have resources that belong to them; and not to people from other nations, who have not got those resources, but are willing to plunder, and deprive the owners of that land of those resources, without a fair and equitable return, then we must ask these important questions. Why?

If we desire a world which respects the integrity of life, and entrenches the dignity of someone, not blessed with the education of other more fortunate people in countries, which can use their higher learning to deprive others less gifted, then we have to dream of that outcome." Simon had memorised his mantra.
"You mean that we can change the world by simply asking?" Merlin was beginning to realise the potential of this power.

"Yes, having researched the 'Quanta' and its effect on consciousness, everything and everyone is connected on the energetic level of a Global Consciousness; what I call The Torus."

"Oh! I know, it is a little bit like 'The Force' in the Star Wars movies!" Merlin saw the connection.

"Can I put this in perspective?" Simon was effusive.

"Sure. This really interests me." Merlin listened.

"A South African friend of mine once told me that the reality is studying for university will empower you with less than ten percent of what you will ever need to apply in Life. The other ninety percent will be 'Of God' knowledge. He claimed that the 'word' of God lacks nothing in everything we will ever require during our lifetime. The truth is we spend an inordinate amount of time studying superfluous knowledge of worldly pursuits that will never have any lasting significance. The wisdom contained simply by just reading Proverbs is beyond any measure of that which we will gain insight on through secular learning." Simon had appreciated this advice at the time.

"Now, I get what he meant," Merlin conceded. "Winston Churchill once famously said that if nothing else, we should all learn the Proverbs by heart."

"Yes, but I believe he missed the crucial essence of the phenomenon! We have to learn to understand ourselves first, and to spend valuable time in meditating and observing our most intimate thoughts. I believe that when we are capable of listening to ourselves, we can finally begin to receive the messages from The Global Consciousness; as Yoda would say, 'Luke, you must feel The Force.' That's the key!" Simon grinned.

"This friend shared his testimony with me once, about how his brother-in-law and he were on a weekend break away to Durban, on the beachfront, and bumped into one of his previous girlfriends.

As he got chatting he realised he had no cash to buy drinks so he made a decision to walk to Durban central to draw some money at an auto-teller. Walking to the ATM, he knew intuitively that he was putting himself in harm's way, as Durban then was not the safest place to be." Merlin listened intently.

"He was trained in martial arts, I had the utmost confidence in himself, and his ability to defend himself, if necessary."

"As he approached the ATM, three criminals with knives approached him from three different corners of the intersection. What he recalled was that he instinctively formed the 'Triangle of Defence', where upon only one attacker was afforded the opportunity to attack him at a time. However, the next cognitive thought he had, was when he woke up in his hotel room fully clothed, without any physical evidence of the attack, and he remembered thinking to himself, that he must have had a bad dream. But next to his hand on the bed, were multiple bank cards, and the only thing he could assert, was that when they attempted to mug him, he must have pacified all three and taken all of their bank cards!"

"He put the entire episode down to his faith and abilities, but he somehow knew that there had been a supernatural event. He says he felt surrounded by Angels." Simon added.

"What do you think happened?" Merlin was intrigued.

"Uhhmm yes! I would imagine from my own experiences; and I have had similar experiences in West Croydon, when I was attacked by two black lads after getting off the train." Simon interjected.

"I believe he evoked a supernatural energy, which some equate to Angels, but which is a pan-psychic summoning of The Force, or a supernatural 'unseen' resonant energy linked to our Electro-magnetic Frequency Field Consciousness." The truth was greater than fiction.

"What is that?" Merlin prompted.

"I believe that when we pray in the 'Spirit' of The Force, or The Toroidal Energy Field, by invoking a spiritual mantra, an energy shield goes up all around us. Similar in ways to a watery-shield. It is a force-field, similar to what we see in science-fiction movies!"
"Humans are evolving Spiritually!" Simon contested.

"Really! Why do you think this is happening now?" Merlin could equate the rise of intellectuals in the present era with the access to information and better living conditions, but there was an enigma even modern medicine and science could not ascertain.

"I believe that The Force is generating higher levels of energy, and humans are beginning to recognise that power. Why do you think we have seen incredible increases in our technological world?"

"Well, okay, but I get the sense that the exponential increases in technology we are witnessing have something to do with higher levels of learning, but what about men like Tesla and Einstein?" Merlin had seen their rise to prominence as an aspect of the technological era; but they were not just geniuses. There was more to it.

"Do you believe in re-incarnation?" Simon was forthright.

Merlin looked him in the eyes and responded after some thought.

"I would like to believe it is true."

"What would you like to think happens when our physical body energy is expended?" Simon quizzed.

"That is the age old conundrum. Because our Consciousness requires us to be in the present, it is difficult to equate the sub-conscious with a disparate reality of other dimensions. Our present minds cannot see through the veil of inter-dimensional energies; it is why the scientific community refer to it as esoteric." Merlin reflected thoughtfully.

"I agree, but we are now researching the inter-play of nano-technology identified by the Large Hadron Collider, and other experimental sciences, that cannot explain the behaviour of Leptons and Quarks."

"Not to mention how these known elements react to our consciousness!" Simon elaborated.

"I know that scientists have been flummoxed by the vast plethora of nano-technology particles." Merlin avidly researched all subjects that intrigued him.

"Yes, but why can they not explain the Quantum Enigma?" Simon contested.

"Well, that's it exactly!" Merlin reasoned. "I have a student who is remarkably gifted; you know, what people refer to as 'old-souls'." Merlin continued.

Simon had heard mention of those who were able to traverse the universal forces and reincarnate with a perfect consciousness of past-life experiences. As those eligible to continue their trans-dimensional existences proliferated, the world would become a more peaceful and humane place. Without the forces of Ahriman and spiritual entities attempting to mask the power of the Spiritual realm, those so favoured by their birth-rite would prosper and become the prominent leaders of society.

"I would say that Michelangelo, Da Vinci, Tchaikovsky, Chopin, Leonard Bernstein, Oscar Wilde, E.M. Forster, Walt Whitman, and not forgetting the most influential mind in the past century, Alan Turing, all had this capacity." Merlin offered.

"Yes, and Alan Turing suggested that Spirituality was so much more pertinent than the potential for artificial intelligence. He believed that A.I. cannot work because machines do not have the capacity of a human brain, to connect with spiritual entities, which is what makes us 'human' and a machine 'a machine." Simon added.

"Mindfulness, is the one common denominator of all those chosen to reach levels of outstanding acumen. Those who chose to use human powers, were destined to lose their powers." Merlin agreed.

"Yesterday evening, I went to see a movie called Prometheus. What is amazing is that the movie explores the idea of where we as humans come from, based on the Greek legend of the god Prometheus." Simon continued.

"Prometheus was the Titan god of forethought, and he like Alan Turing, attempted to better the lives of mankind." Merlin smiled.

"Yes, Prometheus was tasked with moulding man out of clay and making our lives more effective and efficient, but when the god Zeus, finds out that Prometheus has tricked the gods out of the sacrificial feast, in order to feed man, Zeus imprisons Prometheus." Simon realised that there was an analogy with Alan Turing, which was remarkable!

"Okay, but firstly, the assumption is that mankind will strive to achieve 'Knowledge' of our origin, until we have established the answers we require. Yet, in doing so, we will have acquired the one thing that differentiates us from the gods. So by becoming a god, we are no longer mortal." Merlin was on a roll.

"But that is the fundamental premise of artificial intelligence, which is the 'Holy Grail' of computing. Should mankind ever achieve this computing power, we will have recreated ourselves in the guise of a man-made machine, and this will make mankind obsolete." Simon conceded.

"Ah! Yes, but I would add, secondly; the fact that Prometheus desired to better the lives of 'man' goes to the heart of what differentiates us from a machine. It is the ability to have a conscience, and that is what ultimately forced Alan Turing to commit chemically induced suicide. He was troubled by the persecution of the British authorities whom it seems, had found his homosexuality troubling." Merlin explained to the effusive nodding of Simon.

"Yet God does not judge, as mankind judges. So why would Prometheus, want to make our lives better? Not because he felt sorry for us, but because he wanted to make us in the image of God or the 'gods', as the mythology goes." Simon added.

"I agree, but my third point is, if Artificial Intelligence were to become commonplace in our lives, God would no longer have a function." "The brain, and therefore by definition, 'the Spirit' of mankind is imperfect, because we have a conscience. This is the part of the brain that makes us question a decision, or second-guess an answer. So therefore, if mankind were to successfully create artificial intelligence, would that machine have a conscience?"

"The answer is no! Simply by creating AI, the machine, would be perfect, because machines that work on a binary coding, or an exact computation, are again by definition, incapable of making a mistake! Unless, that is, we were to program a glitch into its software." Simon answered.

"But, that does not exclude humans from attempting to create a 'Conscious-thinking' computer. Google are hell-bent on doing so, and there algorithms already control our on-line lives." Simon continued.

"Yes, but you'll like my fourth point! When Prometheus had been condemned to purgatory, Heracles saved him after succeeding in attaining his freedom. Zeus then created woman and opened Pandora's Box, thereby unleashing the power of deceit, which Prometheus had previously managed to contain." Merlin grinned.

"By doing so Zeus successfully created the potential reason we can be differentiated from the artificial intelligence of a machine. Mankind's ability to conceive diseases and suffering! A perfect machine would be incapable of self-destruction. It is only through our own fears and mortal conscience, that mankind can 'will' itself to death." Merlin enthused.

"That is true, and the very term dis-ease, is the fundamental factor that allows our Spirit to waste away. Would a machine, made of immortal code, be able to similarly self-destruct? Alan Turing was the one person immune to the wiles of women, who would have been able to answer that question, yet he was forced to an early grave, by the machinations of his mind, and the desire to be accepted for who he was." Simon was in his element.

"Alan Turing was driven to a terrible despair and early death by the nation he'd done so much to save. This remains a stain on the government of the United Kingdom and history. A pardon can go some way, to healing this damage, but it does not change the essential truth of what he strived for." He seemed perplexed.

"Then, lastly, the ideals of Prometheus are legendary because he desired to help mankind, but when Zeus attempted to eradicate Mankind, Prometheus prevented the execution of the scheme, and saved the human race from destruction. He deprived them of their knowledge of the future, and gave them hope instead." Merlin concluded.

"Yes, but Prometheus further taught mankind the use of fire, made them acquainted with architecture, astronomy, mathematics, the art of writing, the treatment of domestic animals, navigation, medicine, the art of prophecy, working in metal, and all the other arts." Simon added.

"Ironically, it is the very people who attempt to attain A.I. for their own benefit, who have lost their humanity!" Merlin's insight was astounding.

"But it is this very hope that will always differentiate us from a machine. Should we have the answers to our origins, as the protagonists in the movie Prometheus desire, we will ultimately have achieved that Holy Grail, and successfully managed to secure our immortality and ultimate usefulness? Why are we in such a rush to learn all the secrets of the Universe? It is mankind's Achilles heel, and yet it is what motivates us to continue. Striving to have the answers of our source-code, makes us subject to the whims of an artificial intelligence that might just replace us in the future. We need to act with restraint when seeking the mysteries of our origin, but dutifully continue to strive towards making our World, a more humane and hospitable place."

"This was possibly a thought of Alan Turing, and the motivation behind his desire to create the mathematical logarithms that now form a part of Computer Intelligence. Perhaps we should be striving for a more effective intelligent computer, and leave the ultimate answer to our existence, to God!" Simon reflected.

Merlin knew that the boy soldiers of the future, would be those chosen to make contributions to the world, previously only imagined! The power of those capable of putting their minds to the pressing issues of society, would become recognised more and more, as the gifted amongst us were understood and empowered to effect the changes required.

But without these great past contributions to society, this world would be the poorer, and a common denominator was that the Catholic church had hounded each and every one of them mercilessly. Without the savants of the world, progress would have been sketchy at the least; but Merlin could not help his realisation that these were 'the Peculiar People', the Apostle Peter spoke of in the Bible!
"The reality is that we can change the circumstances we live with, and we can project positive thoughts into the Spiritual Realm."

"Remote viewing is the practice of seeking impressions about a distant or unseen target, purportedly using extrasensory perception or "sensing" with the mind. Remote viewing experiments have historically been criticized because they lacked proper controls and repeatability." Simon explained.

"This is a fundamental aspect of my experiences. Before now, I have simply considered them dreams, in which, I have recalled past events, or subconsciously interpreted my desires for the manifesting of future events. Now I understand this to be precisely what I have been training my mind for, throughout the past six and a half years." The evidence he had gathered was convincing.

"In the past, I was always concerned from a Christian perspective, that I was opening myself to unwanted Spiritual energies." He grinned.

"But, now I am conducting my 'Remote Viewing' experimentation, free from any fear of being attacked by malevolent forces. In effect, I am powerful enough to counter any external, negative influences."

The question had arisen, because Merlin had shared a dream he had that morning, awaking in the early hours, with a vision of Josh, free from the anxiety of drug related issues, but in his place, he had seen in his mind's eye, a vision of Jamie. Why?

"It is easier than we think." Simon smiled. This flummoxed Merlin.

"What do you mean?"

"We pray for intercession!" The simplicity was in the brevity of words.

"What? You're honestly suggesting we pray for the drug epidemic to stop; and somehow miraculously it will!" Exasperated tones belied his exhaustion.

"Yes!" Simon cocked his head; it was a challenge.

Merlin gazed into his eyes and recognised those emerald green irises had been secretly hiding a messianic intellect. Yes, he had grown to respect Simon's intelligence, but this was in a completely stratospheric realm.

"Just pray?" Simon repeated.

"Yes, and we do so with positive affirmations of our expectant outcome." The silence of the basement walls became eerily resonant. The words echoed.

"You see, I believe what Nickola Tesla stated as fact, almost one hundred years ago; 'When science begins to study the unseen, it will make more progress in one decade, than in all the centuries before.'"

Merlin was familiar with the quote but had never given credence to the spiritual meaning. Tesla had believed that scientists were looking in the wrong places for answers, but he had never thought about the issue of Spirituality.

"When Tesla was alive, he had been suppressed by the elite banking fraternity, who saw his ideas as a threat to their financial cartels. He wanted to develop 'free energy' which he planned to roll out to the world, using towers like his Wardenclyffe Tower. But, what he was proposing was that the energy required to uplift every human being from poverty and servitude, was abundantly available, within our own psyche." Simon let the thought sink in.

"But I thought Tesla had failed catastrophically with the tower?"

"No, he had proved it was capable of directing vast amounts of energy in a focused direction, but had he been given the funding by Westinghouse and the banking clique, he could have provided abundant energy for all humanity, and think how effective a force for good that would be, if every human on this earth was capable of creative thinking, without having to fear where their next meal was to come from!"

"But what does this idealism have to do with praying?" Simon had diverged, or so he thought.
"What Tesla was alluding to, was the power of the human intellect, to direct powerful thoughts to manifest reality." Simon smiled disarmingly.

"What do you mean by that? Are you saying that we pray like a Dale Carnegie symposium, and expect the drug trade to simply cease!" Merlin, as tired as he was, began to perk up.

"Yes, and we can do this together." Simon's energy was infectious.

"You mean, we pray for the drug factories in China to cease producing fentanyl and they simply shut down?" Merlin's curiosity piqued.

"Yes, but the process is not a simple prayer, but a coordinated, projected intercession. When we pray, in groups of two or more, our thoughts are propelled into the unseen dimension, of which there are many. Past, present and future dimensions are simply determined by our perception of where we wish to direct them, then the Spirit does the rest."

"With our thoughts focused on the desired outcome, provided we have the exact same intentions, we will begin to see the manifesting of our prayers. Some use meditation, and others simply chant their intentions, but when we have a concerted belief of the greater benefit of our good intentions, then we will see our ordained thoughts created in the divine space of the Time Continuum." Simon paused to let this sink in.

"Realistically, Tesla was spot on. Our 'Good, Ordained, Divinity' is projected into the unseen realms, when we focus our intentions with integrity. The 'Quantum Enigma' that has stymied scientists and Quantum Physicists for a hundred years, is simply because the observers do not hold the same concerted desires. Science is only limited by ego. When scientists let go of their preferred knowledge, and allow spiritual wisdom to manifest, they will make gigantic strides towards solving time travel and much more."

Merlin sat back. The room seemed smaller. His mind was racing.

"You know what?" He blurted; "This is eerily similar to what I advocate to my students!"

"What's that?" Simon raised an eyebrow.

"I call it Intentional Technology, or In.T." Merlin agreed. "It is projected thoughts, channelled through the inter-dimensional world." All of a sudden, he realised he was speaking the same language as Simon; just in a different dialect.

"Ah, yes. I know what you mean." Simon had learned to accept that the brain was a conduit to the universe.

"Here's a thought. If humans can control the emotions of animals and our minds are so powerful we are capable of ESP, then, why not take this one step further and control humans, who can't equate to Spirituality?" He continued.

"Imagine a Quantum Computer that uses Qubits instead of binary systems. Qubits rely on a super-position between a One and a Zero, ensuring the computer is always in a state of 'Entanglement'." His forefingers held aloft in parenthesis.

"This relies on the spin of an electron within the micro-processor. But that electron works in exactly the same way a Neuron in the brain works! That on/off switch of neuronal activity is no different to a microchip. So, by controlling the outcome of a quantum computer we control the user using it. We must not fear AI we must use it against the very people who have tried to weaponise it against us."

"I think this is similar to what I have been reading up on; something called 'Remote Viewing'?" Merlin realised that the serendipity of his study and what they now were discussing were pertinent to this journey.

"Tesla once told a reporter that, 'his brain was only a receiver, in the Universe where there is a core from which we obtain knowledge, strength and inspiration.'" Simon paused; Tesla had a powerful influence on many, including the Spiritual.

"My sense of what he is talking about is The Torus. This is a powerful toroidal energy field which surrounds our planet Earth, and likely the Universe."

"He went on to say that he had not penetrated into the secrets of this core, but he knew that it existed. He said this, but could not fully appreciate the spiritual aspects of his discovery. I believe he had discerned the rationale, but had failed to grasp the intricacy of its origins." Simon elaborated.

"Of all Tesla's discoveries, his most powerful was the understanding that the entire Universe is energy and that this energy, is available to our minds and subject to the positive thoughts produced in our minds. For example, I know that by positive thoughts, we can maintain a youthful appearance, our positive thoughts can build healthy relationships, and ensure that we are loved and that this Loving relationship remains powerful and inspires us to have even more abundant Love."

"Ahh yes," Merlin knew what sociology had to say about this.

"Firstly we must feel loved. This is the conscious thought projected into the Universe that allows our consciousness to be received by other sentient, loving human beings. Those we project our thoughts to, so that they will receive those loving thoughts in a positive and productive wave of energy."

"This is not just wishful thinking, but concerted, co-ordinated and conscious thoughts of love. This is an example of how our desire for a 'soul-mate' actually manifests. To keep their memory, firmly etched in your mind, even if this is at a vast distance, allows for the positive reception of your thoughts." Simon was onto something.

"That is why relationships that are borne out of a shared common humanity work so well." Merlin had learned all too late, that Marge had not held the same passion for life as he.

"It also explains why, after the death of a husband or wife, so many widowers die shortly afterwards. It is almost as though their souls are linked over time."

"But that is not true of couples whose relationships were forced!" Merlin interjected.

"Yes, of course." Simon realised his gaff. "Yes, that makes complete sense.

"But the idea of Remote Viewing is a powerful force for good." He moved on swiftly.

"Imagine in your mind's eye, the object of your thoughts, and focus on how it will have beneficial value to society. Like, if we prayed for those Fentanyl factories to close down, or if we prayed for a revelation of the truth behind government cover-ups. The Universe will receive our prayers, or thoughts, as we project them in a concerted effort. The only obstacle to society solving the issues of social injustice is selfishness." There was a harsh reality evident.

"Indeed! That's why so many people still live in poverty and hardship, because no one else is prepared to pray for them. The worst thing that social justice pioneers could have done, was to farm out the fund raising of organisations to non-governmental groups, who claim to wish to alleviate hunger and suffering!"

"How so?" Merlin was intrigued.

"Well, the purpose of providing food and social equity to people in third world countries, is to help starving or destitute people, right!"

"Yes, I would like to think so." Merlin nodded.

"No! You see that's where they have gone wrong. The purpose does not meet the expectation, because two things happen; firstly, the general public give this money by donating a small amount individually to a group. But the recipients likely will receive pennies in the pound. That's their first error. The second is that once the donation has been made, the person who has made their contribution then forgets about the recipient, as their conscience is now clear; they can sleep better knowing they have made an effort to help some starving child in Somalia." Merlin gasped.

"But by clearing their conscience, they have discharged their responsibility further, and then completely forget about that child. They would do better to donate their three-pound to an organisation that meets to pray for that child in Somalia." The concept was not entirely new, Merlin thought.

"But, there is a subtle difference," Simon could see Merlin's confusion.

"Those that would get together to pray for the children of Somalia, would come from diverse backgrounds, they would have no specific religious affiliations, and their purpose would be to raise the consciousness of those in Somalia, not feed them!" Simon was triumphant, gesturing with both hands.

"Then, how could their hunger be satiated?" Merlin was confused.

"The reason for praying for them, would be to project powerful, self-sustaining, thoughts into their minds, from here, to Somalia." Simon continued.

"You see it requires a higher consciousness to alleviate poverty. Hunger is endemic; Jesus even confirmed this in the Gospels, when he said; "the poor will always be with us." He was making reference to the mind–set of people, not their economic status."

"So you are saying we should not feed them, but pray for them?"

"Exactly, but this is a co-ordinated, resonant, series of prayers, projected through our higher consciousness to theirs. All people have souls, and we are all sentient beings. Therefore, as we commune in the Spiritual, we can communicate greater powers of knowledge to those less fortunate; this is what I call a focus group. It is no different in many ways to what Scientologists call 'Postulating'; but it is so much more powerful because it is projected with Love!"

"There are similarities in motivational seminars, when the recipient is able to focus on the means of achieving his goals." Merlin understood sociological references in motivating his scholars.

"Yes, Dale Carnegie had a grounding in sociology and human behaviour, but to project those thoughts with powerful manifesting resonance, is subject to the laws of energy and motion; if the subject of those thoughts is not on the same wavelength, and receptive to the prayers and focused thoughts, then they are wasted."

Simon knew that thought energy field as a scientific fact, was viewed as a collection of energies or powers that are inter-related by their common theme or experience, and these thoughts were bound together as a functional unit.

"So, how would you propose those thoughts be equated to assisting a starving Somali child?" Merlin was intrigued.

"Just as Niels Bohr was unable to solve the Quantum Enigma, it occurs to me that a light emitted as a wave, may appear as particles in the experiment conducted to prove that quanta exist; but this is because the enigma requires an observation of the flow of the quanta, by an observer on the receiving side of the light emissions?"

Merlin was attempting to follow his logic.

"Well, if what is required is to prove the skeleton in the closet of the Quantum Enigma, is Consciousness, then light emissions in this experiment have a universal truth, shared with thought energy; they require someone to receive them as a conscious thought, which Bohr's described as the concept of complementarity!" Merlin simply focused his mind on the words.

"So, if thought energy fires thousands of neurons simultaneously at the same frequency generating a wave, they are no different to light energy, or photons, as both are electrical stimuli created by an electro-magnetic, ionised energy source. This is plasma, or akin to Spirit. If the special theory of relativity predicts that photons do not have mass simply because they travel at the speed of light; then thoughts, likewise travel even faster than the speed of light because they have are not impacted by gravitational forces. They exceed light speed and are instantaneously received by the recipient." Simon watched Merlin for a moment. Had he recognised the pattern of thought?

"I see," Merlin plucked the image from his right frontal lobe. "The person receiving the Prayers must receive then as wave energy, and not as particles!" He was triumphant.
"This is how the Spirit, or Torus is able to flow with unlimited abundance. As we give, the energy is unleashed and the flow of provision begins, with first, one great blessing then another and so on, until our Lives are blessed with unimaginable provision in every way. Jesus never had anything, other than his tunic and sandals." Simon explored his faith.

"Indeed; but why did Jesus also say: "The poor will always be with us"? Merlin expounded. There was a contradiction.

"I don't have an answer for that, Merlin." Simon conceded.

"Jesus taught us to love our neighbours as ourselves. This great edict from the Gospels is the fundamental law of the world. All man-made religions espouse this great law, but few actually live up to it." He admitted.

"I have read an interesting article about our DNA structure, and the double helix. The essence of the proposition is that human DNA is changing. We are being re-born into our new bodies, with a third helix, which will ultimately result, some say, in humans having twelve DNA strands." Simon offered.

"This is fascinating and explains to me, how it is possible that we survive deadly diseases." There was an edge to his voice.

"We are vibrating into higher-life forms, like the movie X-Men! We are mutating to gain incredible talents and psychokinetic powers. As our bodies transform, we are having struggles in the physical, but we must not be concerned, as we adapt to the cosmic influences around us. A fast track metamorphosis! This is not an evolutionary function, because these transformations are taking place in our generation. These changes are taking place in our 'living' bodies." Simon equated his understanding to the events unfolding around them.

"I know what the Savants are capable of, but how do we explain the rise of people who can literally create their own realities?" Merlin may have had the knowledge, but this was more akin to wisdom.

"Those who have researched this phenomena go on to say that our souls contain a 'God-essence' or 'Divine light', which can never be extinguished, ruined or taken away from us. Humans have a divine heritage, and follow our Earthly destiny." Simon knew it was more than simply about transformative medical interventions.

"Humans are nearing the end of an era where spiritual awareness is at its least influential of all times, and the influence of religion has waned! Yet there is an opportunity to rectify this with the work we do with those Savants."

"Natural gifts of healing and intuition are returning, but through our understanding of Panpsychism, and an awareness of The Global Consciousness, and it is up to each one of us to ensure we bring back the sense of awareness we have." Simon knew this because he was able to communicate telepathically.

"The idea of Panpsychism is to elevate our consciousness to the level of people like Tesla. We all have that capacity to perform amazing feats of supernatural power; whether physically, or intellectually. In the context of our past, we will keep us enslaved to that past, if we are unable to live in the present." The world in Simon's opinion was being held hostage by antiquated thinking.

"This is how the Spirit, or Torus is able to flow with unlimited abundance. As we give, the energy is unleashed and the flow of provision begins, with first, one great blessing then another and so on, until our Lives are blessed with unimaginable provision in every way. Jesus never had anything, other than his tunic and sandals." Simon explored his faith.

"This is the fundamental principle of manifesting." Replied Merlin.

"Yes, I know, but the real question is; why does mainstream education not provide a presentable understanding of manifesting in schools run by the state?" Simon knew the answer.

"Well, it does not form any part of the mainstream education curriculum, because it is considered to be 'esoteric'." Merlin advanced.

"That is the basic premise for their avoidance of the subject, but the truth is that mainstream education avoid any subject that cannot be quantified. But the greatest mind of the twentieth century told us that for science to progress beyond its understanding of the known world, it had to get to grasp with the unknown world!" Simon was quoting from Nikola Tesla.

"Yes, indeed. But mainstream teaching won't touch any subject that does not have a presentable script and answer. It has to do more with their denial of the metaphysics and an unwillingness to embrace the study of what is outside our objective experience." Merlin was truly gaining a grasp of the unseen world.

"If one advances confidently in the direction of his Dreams, and endeavours to Live the Life which he has imagined, he will meet with a success unexpected in common hours."

Henry David Thoreau - 1854

An Assault on our senses

Merlin, having been busy all weekend researching an incredible scientific breakthrough being touted by those responsible for the Large Hadron Collider and the vast source of evidence unravelling in the field of physics, was concerned.

Evidence was leaking out, that the source of all life, was even more complex than originally contemplated. The mystery of the positrons and muons that were discovered by Carl Anders in 1932 and then later upon more research in 1936, allowed scientists and Quantum Physicists to determine the mass of the muon. Where it was initially mistaken for a meson, due to the behaviour it displayed, which originally gave rise to the possibility it was an electron. However the fact that it did not undergo strong interaction, with other electrons gave pause to the fact that muons be reclassified. Along with the electron and the electron neutrino, it became part of a new group of particles known as 'leptons'.

But Merlin, striving to understand the wizardry of these nano-particles, began to suspect there was more afoot. Further research established there was a direct correlation between the God Particle, famously touted by Higgs, and authenticated in 2012, when the L.H.C. isolated the Higgs-Boson Particle made famous in the book by Dan Brown, and over-dramatized in the movie with Tom Hanks. However, the reality was starkly different to the fictional; and the film that grossed over half a billion dollars in revenue catering to the Hollywood alarmists, turned out to be a fallacy of the imagination.

It transpired through further research to be debunked by physicists and that no such anti-matter particle would likely be threatening humanity from quantum particle matter. As Merlin ascertained, it was humanity itself that required to be saved from themselves.

But out of the haze of disinformation came a rational answer to many questions being asked, concerning the C.E.R.N. L.H.C. It was the knowledge that a team of American physicists consisting of Lederman, Schwartz, and Steinberger had been able to detect of interactions with the muon neutrino as far back as 1962, and thus showing that more than one type of neutrino existed.

It was these neutrinos that required validation, and when finally, the L.H.C. was able to run the experiment, the true nature of the Unseen World, postulated by Tesla, was tantalisingly close.

The tau particle discovered in the 1970s, thanks to experiments conducted by Nobel-Prize winning physicist Martin Lewis Perl and his colleagues at the National Accelerator Laboratory at Stanford in California, gave a clue to the complexity of matter within the quantum field. The idea of particles so small that the most elementary science was still out of reach of these sophisticated machines, flummoxed the wise, but a simple thought evaded them. It was the evidence of an associated tau neutrino with a molecular footprint so small, yet measurable in millionths of a Gigaelectronvolt. It was this assertion that lead scientists to recognise how to study tau decay in nanovolts, or measurements of 10^9 and which showed the missing energy and momentum analogous to the missing energy and momentum caused by the beta decay of electrons.

Scientists now had their 'smoking-gun' and combined with the understanding that these tau neutrinos could be measured they set out to determine its specific mass. It was this 'mass' that surprised many, not only Merlin. If an Electron was the lightest, with a mass of 0.000511 gigaelectronvolts, or GeV's, while Muons had a mass of 0.1066 Gev, then it became evident that Tau particles were the heaviest and had a mass of 1.777 Gev.

This evidence initially had no serious impact on Merlin, until he had a conversation with Oscar.

"Sir, can you explain why I keep seeing these incredibly suspicious number sequences all the time?" Oscar was seated in the front row of Merlin's science class, as the work prepared by the missing Year 8 science teacher was being handed out.

"Oh, shut up Oscar," it was his self-appointed nemesis, Jason.

"Jason, let's be respectful of the questions other students ask." Merlin frowned. He understood why, but Merlin, despite his greatest efforts, could not reach through to the consciousness, he knew resided somewhere deep within Jason's psyche. Akin to Apollonius' Jason and the Argonauts, Jason was courageous and outgoing, but lacked the mental sophistication of his smaller companion.

"Sir! It is so peculiar." Oscar presented his query unassailed.

"You are pe...." One look by Merlin cut the word in mid-utterance, and Jason returned to his work page, cowering under Merlin's glare.

"What is that?" Merlin encouraged his Padawan.

"Well, Sir, I keep seeing the number 777, everywhere I look!" Oscar contested. "Even if I am walking down the street, I will look up and there will be a car with the registration 777!"

"Ah, yes, Synchronicity Oscar." Merlin spoke with a warmth that invited further exploration.

"What is that Sir?" Oscar pleaded. If the lad had once thought he may be slightly unhinged because of these visualisations repeatedly shocking his mind into consciousness, now he was feeling somewhat relieved it had a name.

"Synchronicity is electrical energy emitted in the brain Oscar. When vibrational energy is focused on the pictures we form in our brains, somehow those visualizations become our truths. We manifest them!" Merlin knew this was because the synapses in the brain were learning to connect the Higher Brain, in the frontal lobes of the brain, with the primitive Limbic Brain.

"Manifest them?" Oscar parroted.

"Yes Oscar. We can quite literally paint a picture in our minds of what we want, and then by focusing on what we want, unconditionally, without the fear-mongering of Church and State watering down what we desire; we create the physical attribute of our thoughts." Merlin was unequivocal.

"Oh, I get it. It is like 3D Printing! We frame the blueprint of our vision in our mind and by repeating what we see, eventually that vision materialises." Oscar's true apprenticeship had begun.

"Yes, you've got it!" It was a 'eureka' moment in their relationship.

"Sir, I often think of things I want, and then draw a picture of them in my notebook, and write the name of it next to it." Oscar could scarcely contain his excitement.
"Yes, Oscar, and with one great proviso, I will say that you can expect to achieve every one of those desires." Merlin added the caveat.

"What is a proviso?" Oscar asked.

"Oscar, it is the fundamental Law of Manifesting. What you ask for must have integrity." Merlin was concise.

"Integrity?" Oscar was aware of the concept. "How does that make a difference?"

"Oscar, if something, or someone has integrity, it means that your envisioning of that thing must have a value which is sincere and beneficial for all concerned. For example, if you focus on having a beautiful home to live in for your family, ultimately by working towards that eventuality, you will achieve your vision; but if you focus on having a fast car, just for the sake of showing off to others, that will not necessarily manifest!" Merlin paused.

"Unless, perhaps, you find yourself in a compromised form of employment or you win the lottery and where you feel dis-satisfied. In that event, invariably you will lose what you set out to manifest. That is why so many people who win the lotto, invariably end up losing everything they purchase."

"Oh, yes, Sir, I know what you mean!" Oscar excitedly responded. "I watched a program on television where the woman who won the lottery became a drug addict and ended up in jail."

"Did you know there is a reason for why that happens Oscar?" Merlin had an avid audience in the classroom, although there was an unspoken agreement that they not interrupt his mentoring; even Jason was quietly listening.

"It has to do with the positive energy that attracts good things to you." Merlin offered.

"Is that how we create wealth?" Oscar was on his game.

"Yes, but it depends upon an understanding of the creative nature of thought." Merlin added. "You see," added Merlin, when there was a momentary blank look on the boy's face. "Positive energy is creative energy."

"But what does this energy depend on?" Oscar was still unsure.

"It is dependent on use; in other words, use will determine if its existence is permanent." Merlin suggested. He knew too well that manifesting sometimes took years to put into effect.

"Oscar, we have to consciously realise the conditions which we desire to see manifested in our lives." Merlin eased himself off the desk he was seated upon. The boy simply watched him.

"Thinking is the key to creative energy, and steadfastly focusing on what we want from life, will attract all the elementals that generate the conditions for what we manifest." He circled the boy.

"But why is thinking key?" Oscar followed him, his eyes more attentive than usual.

"Because thought is Spiritual and the very essence of thought is therefore creative. For us to consciously control thought is therefore the basis for controlling our circumstances. When we control those elements we can control the conditions of our environment and, ultimately our destiny."

"But Sir! What is the origins of thought energy?" Oscar pleaded.

"Oscar? Do you understand the Theory of Relativity?" Merlin asked.

"Yes Sir, it is e equal to mc^2."

"Yes". Merlin smiled encouragingly.

"So, if: E equals MC^2 it stands to reason that mathematically, C^2 must equal E divided by M or;

Mass equals E divided by C^2

"We believe that all that we 'see' around us is created by 'Mass', and Mass is created by taking energy and dividing it by Light at the speed of itself - C^2 or c-squared. This is what we call 'Warp Speed'."

"Sir," Oscar continued. "My parents are Catholic." Merlin knew better than to ask why this was important.

"Well, I have always wondered why the miracles of Jesus seem so out of touch with our thinking today. But if C^2 equals Warp Speed, then the speed of light, multiplied by the speed of light, reminds me of the Catholic Nicene Creed," Oscar explained; "I believe in One God, the Father the Almighty, maker of Heaven and Earth; or the 'Seen' and the 'Unseen'. I believe in Jesus Christ, the Only Son of God; God from

God, Light from Light, True God from True God; Begotten not made, of One Being with the Father. Through Him ALL things were made." Oscar recited the creed.

"You see," Oscar advocated that familiar Sunday morning chant. "If what God creates through sending Warp Speed into an energy field, is what we 'see' as a 'Mass'; it's a physical object."

"But then the reverse must be true," he wrote in his work book for Merlin to follow.

If $E/C^2 = Mass$; then $\dfrac{Mass}{Mass} = \dfrac{E/C^2}{Mass} = 0$ 'The Unseen'.

"When we inject Mass into a highly energised field, through which we have projected Warp Speed Light, the object of Mass will have its atomic structure agitated by a Frequency that will render the object invisible." Oscar enthused.

"And, did you know the reason this is possible, is that the space between a neutron and the electron and protons of an element, are so far apart, it is equivalent to a football in the middle of a stadium, and the spaces between each molecule is what we visualise, and not the Mass."

"Yes, I understand that!" Merlin was now following his train of thought.

"The speed of light, is 186,282 miles per second, or about 300,000 kilometres per second; in a vacuum." The boy added.

"Sir, did you know that light emissions from the Sun, are not recognised as 'photons' in deep space, but as radiation. That's the reason why astronauts have to have heat shields. It's only when those photons reach the upper-earth atmosphere, that they are agitated by the electrons in air particles, such as oxygen, hydrogen, nitrogen and other gaseous particles, that the radiant heat of the photons are excited enough to reach 'warp speeds'. That's why photons allow us to 'see' the previously 'unseen'." Furrowed brows had relaxed and the boy smiled knowingly.

"Sir, life, as we see it is an illusion or fictional picture of what our minds think we see. When we change our view, we are capable of changing our reality." The Padawan was becoming the master.

"I get it," Merlin smiled back.

"The illusion of physical reality is created by the patterns of the 'Fibonacci Sequence', which is the Golden Spiral of Consciousness." Merlin interjected. He knew the sequence from 1, as to 2, and 2, as to 3, then 3, as to 5, and so forth, adding 8, 13, 21, 34, 55, 89, 144, 233, 377, 610, 987, 1597, ad infinitum, as the ultimate balance of creativity...and the closer to 1.61803 the ratio becomes, the greater the numbers were until it was infinitely big.

"This," Oscar explained, "is the evidence of 'the feeding of the five thousand'; two fish and five small barley loaves, multiplied into thousands. Our reality is merely an illusion of what we have allowed our minds to believe."

"Ah! That is why abundance is a function of the demands, our minds place on materialism." Merlin contributed.

"Yes, but when we change that view, we become abundantly rewarded with 'non-materiality', manifested to materiality." Oscar was elated.

"Reality is a consciousness program, or hologram simulation, created by digital codes in our DNA. Numbers, numeric codes, define our existence and experiences. Human DNA, our genetic memory, triggers, and remembers the digital codes at specific times and frequencies as we experience recall. We recall zeros and ones, just as a computer does. These codes awaken the mind to the change and evolution of consciousness." Oscar completed his thoughts. What he was alluding to was what Merlin had always recognised; the activation of twin spiralling human DNA was expanding and human consciousness was growing exponentially.

The brain is an electrochemical machine, or computer, that processes through binary code zeroes and ones that create patterns of experiences and realities.

"Be kind, resourceful, beautiful, friendly, have initiative, have a sense of humour, tell right from wrong, make mistakes, fall in love, enjoy strawberries and cream, make someone fall in love with it, learn from experience, use words properly, be the subject of its own thought, have as much diversity of behaviour as a man, do something really new." – Alan Turing

World War III

Merlin sat in the lounge chair, looking out over the car park and mused. He needed to understand the dichotomy of a system that placed young men, merely still boys, on the front line of this war.

What had started off as an adventure for many young men during the past wars, soon turned into a struggle for their lives! Boy soldiers conscripted into those wars soon realised this was no game. Standing on the square, watching the newly trained regiments marching past, they had looked so glamorous and exciting; and that was what the establishment depended on.

Thoughts echoed to the documentary he had watched on television the night before. It was an expose of the recollections of boy soldiers during the last world war. Comments that could equally apply to today!

"You don't think about the death of your comrades as a downer; you just think thank goodness it's not me. It's like that; its nature."

"Every man for himself. That was the order; make your own way back."

"The truth is, a child cannot find comfort from fighting adults; and I was still a child."

Merlin recognised that when seventy-one boys, under the age of eighteen went down with the HMS Hood, when it was attacked by the German battleship Bismarck, not one member of the global elite batted an eyelid. War required canon-fodder, and the coming World War III required a return to the dis-information campaign made famous by prior wars. Thousands of underage boys signed up for a war they had no understanding of in nineteen-thirty-nine. This war for the minds and souls of our youth will provide the final chapter in the story of a nation, held captive by a pernicious system designed to profit the few.

In all the wars of the twentieth century, this current war had begun as the Millennium had turned, and the drugs began to flow with open borders and global elites perpetuating the disorder required for the degradation of the values of a society already battle-hardened. But as the memories told of those fallen in past wars faded, and there were no gravestones as evidence of their passing, due to the preference for crematoriums and a lack of green fields to bury them; the boy soldiers once more raised their heads above the parapets, viewed the battlefields made clear by a rising demand for consumerism, and the glamour of a life on the wing, with fast cars and slutty girls, giving them encouragement to once more lie about their age.

These boys were evident in the car parks, on the sidewalks and in the green spaces of West Scowlsdown. Drawn to this recent battlefield, those too young to leave home, too old to be admonished by single-parent mothers, and brain-washed by social-media paparazzi glitz, were no longer willing to stand on the side-walk and watch the boy-racers with their loud exhaust notes, drive-by without clamouring for a piece of the action.

Like their predecessors in nineteen-fourteen and nineteen-thirty-nine, the soldier boys of West Scowlsdown wanted to be a part of that action. They saw the Arifs laying waste to a ten billion pound industry after their leader Abdullah Baybasin, had been jailed for organising a heroin empire and most of the heroin smuggled into Britain with ruthless efficiency. But the young Turks had inherited a much more chaotic empire, and County Lines were now, no longer the preserve of the Turks. The Albanian Mafia had moved in, taking all the good-looking girls, opening their plethora of shops as fronts for the trade, and the money-laundering racket, which had local law enforcement turning a blind-eye to!

As Merlin waited for Simon to arrive, he absent-mindedly looked out through the bay windows overlooking the car park, fully expecting to see those young lads again. But having had their ruse uncovered and their source of supply cut-off, they would likely have simply found another venue, and another initiative.

Merlin was thankful for Simon's intervention with Josh, and from all accounts the lad was now on the up-and-up; but there still lurked an element of boy soldiers, only too willing to become the next line of canon-fodder. It was remarkable in of itself, that given the level of safe-guarding imposed by the now defunct European Union, their subterfuge would be uncovered. The good news was that the good people of these United Kingdoms had recognised that deception and voted to out their insidious attempts to destroy Britain's society. But now was not the time to let their guard down; now was the time to remain vigilant and to uncover the perniciousness of the system that favoured those elite.

The streets had become their battleground, and the parks and recreation facilities a glory-hole for expedient gratification. Merlin knew this all-too-well, but he was ill-equipped to deal with the physicality of the challenge. He was better suited to mentoring and educating, but with Simon by his side, he would have an ally and could certainly make a difference. The challenge was; did the Youth desire his help?

But, as Simon arrived, a frown on his usually happy-go-lucky face, gave Merlin pause for thought.

"Hello Simon," Merlin offered a cautious greeting, unsure of what was fermenting beneath that scowl.

"Hello Merlin. How are you?" Simon offered up his usual polite greeting, but below that courteousness, he knew there lay an erupting volcano.

"Anything I can help with?" Merlin knew him too well.

"Ah, yes!" Simon changed his countenance with the brevity of a shape-shifter.

"Just had an unfortunate discussion in London Road, with a self-righteous woman, dangling her faith around her neck, like a scorecard." Simon offered up a grimace, the memory still too fresh in his mind.

"Oh, don't tell me it was one of those do-gooders with a crucifix again?" Merlin lamented.

"Yes, and the irony is, I was busy chatting with my mate Derek from the Spiritual church at the time. Isn't it interesting how some people just cannot help themselves?" Alluding to what must have been an interesting conversation.

"I was telling him how the 'sign-of-the-cross' has been used for thousands of years, even before Christianity, as a way of protecting oneself from evil forces, as the superstitious pagans had once done." Simon elaborated.
"Ah! Yes, the superstitions of the pagan tribes was a consequence of thousands of years of socialisation from the dangers that provoked many hunter-gatherers to form communities and live behind walls." Merlin knew that the advent of pastoral communities had led to once nomadic tribes, seeking shelter from marauding bandits, and other criminal elements.

"Yes, but their superstition was based on something, and I believe it was a consequence of stored Knowledge within The Global Consciousness." He paused.

"Somewhere, deep in their psyche, they knew of the dangers, and that they could provide a sense of Karmic protection through the power of rituals." Simon sensed the manner in which superstition played its hand was deeply-rooted in Panpsychism.

"Yes, that makes complete sense. But many archaeologists and ancient studies pundits, will still claim to this day, that the history of socially-adept mankind has only five-thousand years of history in the recorded record!" Merlin added.

"Exactly, but the research into Gobekli Tepe in South-Eastern Turkey reveals a historical record dating back twelve-thousand years, or potentially more!" Simon knew this to be the smoking-gun in the real truth of Mankind.

"Yes, what a pity the Turks have lost all that ancient wisdom," Merlin angled the conversation back to his pressing thoughts.

"Ahh! Yes, I get the social dig." Simon grinned. "But the reason I mentioned that, is that this dumb woman, filled with her pre-conceived diatribe about Satan and how anyone who is not a born-again Christian, will rot in hell, interrupts my conversation with Derek, and begins to shout her mouth off about homosexuals and how they must all be murderers!" Simon guffawed.

"She did what?" Merlin was incredulous.

"Yes," nodding his head in disbelief, Simon continued; "then she launched into the usual thing about loving homosexuals, because she was a Christian, when I asked her if she was a homophobe."

"She actually told she loved homosexuals?" Merlin joined his friend with a guffaw of note.

"Yes." Simon winked mercilessly. "Derek was so taken aback, he kept quiet throughout this moral crusade." Simon added.

"Why would she launch into an attack on homosexuals?" Merlin asked, the incredulity still an enigma.

"I think it was because Derek was wearing a pink shirt, but I cannot be certain. Perhaps it was because when she started on about Satan, I asked, is that Satan with a capital 'S', or a small 's'." He winked once more.

"Uuhhmm, I can see that may have provoked her self-righteousness, but even so; did you know her?" Merlin quizzed.

"Never seen her before, but I have to admit, I have a sense she was probably on a crusade before she saw me speaking to Derek."

"Perhaps it was the fact that I made the sign of the cross, whilst speaking with him! Who knows, but she is probably off to meet her chums for a good round of gossip." Simon's dig, a wonderful analogy of the hypocrisy on display.

"Be careful," Merlin was sober once more; "There is a tremendous amount of mental illness in our society."

"Anyway, it was somewhat entertaining, and I packed her off with something to gossip about;" he grinned. "I told her that perhaps the reason she was not wearing a wedding band on her marriage finger, was because she had talked her previous husband to death!"

Merlin could not help his mirth, but even so, it was remarkable how social convention was swept aside by religious fundamentalism. But he did want to discuss the episode about his students, and now was a good opportunity.

"Si," Merlin changed track. "Can I ask you for some help with several of my students?" Merlin knew he had asked Simon to intervene before, but this was now critical.

"Of course you can!" There was no hesitation. "What's up?" Simon knew from the intonation of Merlin's voice, that something big was afoot.

"My year nines have gone M.I.A. and I am concerned that they may well be in harm's way.

"What do you mean M.I.A?" Simon knew the military jargon, but not in the context of a group of errant teenagers.

"I mean, literally, missing-in-action!" Merlin looked haggard for the first time Simon had known him.

"There are three lads, Jason, Tyler and Jack. Now, Jack is a wonderful lad, don't get me wrong, but this Jason lad, is the son of Jay, a local businessman, and he has fallen under the influence of those two Albanian lads." Merlin explained.

"What does this Jason lad look like?" Simon knew most of the culprits in London Road, and had witnessed a lad fighting with one of the Albanian kids on the pavement outside the fried chicken joint.

"Big, red-headed lad, with a serious attitude." Merlin summed him up.

"Yes, yes, I know that lad. He is the ring-leader unfortunately." Simon concurred.

"Yes, but I know that he has so much potential to do so much more with his life!" An age-old lament that had been echoed millions of times over the centuries.

"There is a tremendous amount of cyber-bullying on social media, and I think that the big social media culprits need to do some serious soul-searching!" Simon rationalised his understanding of why these lads felt compelled to play hooky, but the real reason is truancy had been around since the dawn of time.

"I don't think this is simply truancy though! There was an air of conspiracy amongst their class-mates yesterday. I know it was Friday, but for the three of them to be away on the same day?" Merlin's appeal was rhetorical.

"I know how you feel Merl, but sometimes lads just want to buck the system; especially lads like Jason." Simon conceded.

"I understand that, although I was never one to miss a day of school. However, the conspiracy was all too evident, and you know what these lads are like; camaraderie and loyalty would not be out of place on a battle field!" Merlin understood these codes of honour.

"I can put some feelers out and get some feedback for you. Most of the lads who frequent the park have their 'comms' locked and loaded. They all know what's going on!" The valour of some of these lads was questionable, but Simon understood the principle.

"Thank you, I knew I could rely on you to get the info!" Merlin was grateful he had an ally with an inside knowing of what motivated these lads. In fact, Merlin was aware of the awe some lads had for this foreigner; because he had no skin in this race. His loyalty was to the greater cause, and Merlin knew there was a Spiritual angle to his motivation.

"Social media's effect on children and teens is one of my bug-bears," Simon was adamant these big tech companies were immoral from top to bottom; "but the truth is they have avoided all questions relating to research on teenage suicide, caused as a result of interactions on these social platforms and have attempted to claim that there was no 'bombshell' evidence that there was causal links to any of these teenage suicides."

"In fact, research done shows that thirteen per cent of British teenagers who became suicidal, or took their own lives, have done so, because of Cyber-bullying on social media platforms."

"But what can we do to stop this hatred and division." Merlin recognised that the schoolyard bully was now eavesdropping on every conversation worldwide.

"Well, why don't we start a Youth Club for these lads?" Simon offered a solution.

"That would be splendid. I know that the local Community church had a Friday evening youth club, but they mysteriously closed their doors to non-congregational children; not what I would term very Christian!" Merlin had heard staff talking about the need for a Youth Club in West Scowlsdown.

"I think that by getting these kids off the street and into a place of safety, we can achieve a great amount of good." Simon knew that there must have been a good reason for the church to be so brutal, but he was no fan of their leadership.

"Think of the benefits of getting lads like Jason off the street and into a safe space; in fact I have even thought of a great name for the club!" Merlin offered his assessment.

"Oh awesome. What would you call it?" The marketing of a Youth Club was key to its success. Simon knew all too well that branding was essential for success; it required a name that the lads could relate to.

"What do you think about calling it 'S-Squared' or S^2? Short for Safe Space." Merlin angled his pitch at the marketing genius.

"Very catchy indeed!" Simon closed his eyes, imagining the symbol as a logo, it would be very simple, but effective.

"Yes, I like that!" Simon painted the symbol in the air, manifesting the idea as he thought the idea through.

"The key is to provide a place where the lads would feel at home, but not under pressure from disciplinarian forces. The reason they are not at home is that they invariably have outgrown being bossed around by over-protective parents." Merlin assessed the sociological aspect of providing a Youth Club.

"Yes, but most of these lads have grown up in single-parent families, with an errant father, who could care less about them." Simon made his thoughts succinct.

"Yes, but we are not here to provide a fatherly influence; that's the last thing they need!" Merlin was quick to point out.

"No! You are quite right. The idea is to offer mentorship, in the form of a non-confrontational support group, and to focus on their strengths and not drum the negatives of discipline into their lives. I use the example of Christianity and why it has failed world-wide, and particularly in Western countries." He paused.

"There is a consciousness that I believe has superseded Christianity and is very relevant today, and that 'Consciousness' does not perpetuate fear-driven thoughts." Simon explained.

"The key to providing a welcoming environment for these lads, is to accentuate the positive, and where the lads feel they have fucked-up, we show them that they don't have to carry that baggage with them forever." Simon continued.

"Perhaps that is why the previous Youth Club failed; too much self-righteous piffle and not enough substance." Merlin alluded to the failure of self-serving conformists. He knew that progress in this world was made by non-conformists, who chose to pave their own way.

"That is interesting, because this morning I was reading about John Steinbeck's book 'Cannery row', where he alludes to the ideal of social stigmas."

"You know, the social ostracism that these lads suffer from society, is no different to the way American society shunned those early immigrants." Simon knew too well that Britain consisted of social classes, who would never be willing to recognise the struggles of the poor.

"Yes, I am familiar with his writing; didn't he say that the only way social ostracism could be overcome was by either, a man deciding to do better, and be kinder, or by being bad and challenging the world to end up doing worse things? My sense is that the lads of West Scowlsdown are caught between the head-lights of social media conformity, and a desire to break out from the social absorption of an elitism that has a stranglehold on our youth." Merlin voiced a long-held opinion on the class war.

"But remember who controls the mainstream media, and by default public opinion; it is the elites." Simon reminded him.

"Yes, but that is not to say we have to listen to them. The only reason lads today allow themselves to become victims to this class war, is because the elites have set them up to fail." Merlin was inclined to disparage the social elite classes because he had seen far too much evidence of their manipulation of the system in education.

"I can't argue that Merl, but I may add that we only become victims when we allow them to manipulate us." Simon was inclusive.

"But this goes to the very nature of fear-based politics as we mentioned earlier." He continued, his eyes searching for snippets of wisdom in the ethersphere.

"Drugs are a way of controlling the poorer classes." Simon added.

"Remember, it is the elites who control the flow of drugs into this country, through their grip on consumerism and the flow of trade. Marijuana is no different a commodity to those in positions of power, than is a can of pilchards from Spain. They control the ports and they allow contraband into the country, where they are able to maintain a class-divide. And, if you think I am exaggerating, just think about what is going on with the flood of illegal immigrants on the South Coast!" Simon argued.

"Those boats could be turned around and sent back, but the authorities take advantage of public opinion and so-called humanitarianism."

"But the truth is they could give a rat's ass for the immigrants; what they want is more smuggled people, working within the drugs trade, prostitution and the inevitable social dissent it creates. You watch; there will come a time when the government attempts to take away our personal liberties!" Simon was certain of this.

"But why would the elites allow more immigrants, when it is costing the country dearly to house all these people?" Merlin could not see the logic.

"Uuhhhmm! Let me paint a scenario if I may, from my past experience?" Simon asked; Merlin nodded.

"Many years ago, I was high-jacked by thugs at my brother's house entrance in Johannesburg. When the thugs had held me at gunpoint and scarpered with my car, my brother Tim and I, gave chase along the freeway. We were giving chase at high speed, and were completely in a zone. I am certain that the event was a re-enactment of something we had done before in a previous lifetime, because the events were so instinctive; so organised. Anyway, the culprits got away this time, but we eventually found the car, in Maputo, Mozambique. It had been bought by an unscrupulous Indian businessman. Go figure! Those crimes committed in Africa go unpunished, when there are cross-border occurrences, and insurance companies don't want to get involved! Why is that?" His question rhetorical, he proceeded.

"The answer to this question is steeped in the perverse attribution of globalism. The consumerism of the powers and principalities see this as a way of achieving distribution of wealth and assets, and the insurance companies have already factored into their premiums the losses, so they don't care. This results in a proliferation of crime and the unhealthy emergence of fear among the populace." Simon was reflecting.

"I believe that the crimes, and often the legal processes that follow, are not given adequate significance, because the world of corporate involvement in crime, is a benign tumour on the face of Africa. Corporate inaction is how they sell their product. Let me explain."

"Imagine you own an insurance company, and you need to sell car insurance! What you need is a motive for people to want to carry on paying their premiums. So, by helping customers to recover their possessions would work counter-intuitively. The customer needs to feel threatened, or dispossessed, in order to want to buy more insurance. So what we create is a vicious cycle of demand, driven by 'fear'." The scenario was painting itself out onto a vast canvass.

"So the answer I have discovered, is not to buy insurance. For twelve years, I have not carried any insurance on my cars, household insurance for possessions, or jewellery. The premiums I have saved have bought me more than what I lost on that car, all those years ago. This was a turning point in my Life, when I literally said, "Hey stop this carousel, and let me off." The irony is that I have saved on all my premiums."

"Enough that I can now replace all the household furniture stolen by my greedy business partner. However, the reality is, that if every one of us were to stop our premiums tomorrow, we would save on average enough to replace all our possessions over and over again. But because that 'fear' is so innately drummed into people, the reality is there is no way you are going to do so. Your own greed prohibits you from doing so!" Simon had hit upon the critical rationale for insurance.

"But imagine, if you will, a Utopian society, where you do not need insurance for your household goods, or for cars that are depreciating every day! The reality is that statistically, you may have to replace one of these items, at least once in your lifetime. But truthfully, would that have made such a significant difference to your world? The answer is no! Emphatically, your losses, if they were to be cumulatively amortised over your lifetime, are far less than what you pay out in premiums over the lifetime of those assets, or over the period you have been insured. That is why corporates are able to sustain themselves, because they can afford to pre-fund the risk, through corporate indemnity. The rich have the money to invest into insurance companies, and they watch happily as you get screwed by a system that could 'care less' about whether you lose your home, your car, or your television." Simon concluded.

"So, you are saying that these immigrants are allowed into this country so that the elites can profit from insurances?" Merlin summed up Simon's story.

"Yes, and if you have recently been watching any mainstream television propaganda, you will have noticed the vast abundance of commercials for household alarm systems, and not to mention car insurance. Theft is on the rise, and instead of tackling the root cause of the crime, the elite would rather you live in fear and buy their insurances!"

"The steady stream of migrants across the Channel is worrisome, but it indicates an even greater risk to the country." Merlin added.

"What is that?" Simon applauded Merlin's insights at times, and this was no exception.

"It is the reality of the negative population growth among the steadily growing affluent classes of the West, and a desire by the elites to maintain their grasp on taxes and pensions!" Merlin interlaced his objective view of the criminal melee currently dividing Britain's social classes, with a subjective view of this reality.

"The age-old story of 'fear-sells; and division quells!'" Simon gave poetic licence to the intentional assault of the elite classes on a society that was attempting to pull itself upwards by its collective bootstraps.

"Yes, but the petty-crime that ensues, funds the proliferation of drugs, and it is always the poor and the social outcastes that lose. Don't think for one moment that this class system is any different to the feudal systems of the past!" Simon grinned.

"No, you are quite right; but now they are just more subtle about how they screw you!" Merlin had a twinkle in his eye; what did he know that Simon was about to learn?

"You do know that the origins of the word F.U.C.K. did not come from the widely touted myth, that it was a feudal law that precipitated the use of the word." He had heard the story.

"Rumour had it, that the word originated when Feudal laws stated that the king or lord of the county would have first dibs on any of the wenches!" Fornication Under Consent of the King was the much parodied origins; but Merlin knew better. He was just having some fun.

"Yes, I know, but I would not put it past those in power to attempt something of the sort! Good God, just look at the philanderer in Number Ten!" Merlin mocked.

"Yes, and I would imagine it was not too much fun for those being arrested for such antiquated laws on homosexuality, until our generation overturned that prescription."

"Is it not surprising then, that the LGBTQ+ community takes such a dim view of the laws of this country, and particularly those in the House of Lords. They are a particularly awful bunch of inbreeds, starting with Sugar." The audacity of the lord in question still fresh in his mind.

"Those laws were maintained by the church right up until the sixties and I guess they owe many who were lost to the AIDS crisis an apology!" Merlin was in agreement.

"I think they are suffering from Karmic justice now, though." Simon assessed the declining numbers in churches as precipitating the demise of the establishment church.

"But that does not stop them trying to continue advancing shock-therapy for children who identify as homosexual!" Merlin knew that this electro-shock therapy still formed a major part of the fundamental Christian doctrine.

"The history of electro-shock therapy has a very sinister origin." Simon advanced. "Religious objections to same sex attraction between men have existed since at least the time of Henry VIII, back in 1533. But what is so ironical, is that particular philanderer was going around chopping the heads of his ex-wives to boot!" The hypocrisy could not be more obtuse Merlin assessed.

"Yes I know that Criminal Assessment Act extended the law to sanction any sexual contact between males around 1885. But they included any form of sex, and had homosexuality labelled a pathological medical or psychological condition!"

"Uuhhmm, I suppose that was more of, do as I say, and not as I do?" Merlin agreed.

"My understanding of those laws and what transpired is that the LGBTQ+ community should posthumously sue the British government for all the pain and anguish caused. Hell, they are happy to provide compensation to every coloured immigrant who was discriminated against; why have we not taken them on before now?" Simon lamented.

He knew the death of his brother Jeremy would have been completely avoidable, had Jeremy not been in major dispute with the Catholic church, who still advocated non-compliance with contraception; but that doctrine, he knew was more about keeping the poor in Third World countries, beholden to the church.

"It's funny," Merlin announced, conscious that it was not at all fun for those who had been marginalised by those antiquated laws.

"What's that?" Simon smiled; he took no offence.

"It's just that when I speak with students like Oscar, I realise that these lads, have an incredible contribution to make to society; if they are given half-a-chance." Merlin acceded to what he knew to be true.

"Yes, I call them my 'Peculiar People'." Simon acknowledged.

"What do you mean by that?" Merlin assumed he may have been intonating that they were simply different to everyone else.

"I mean, there is a Biblical precedent that Jesus speaks of, in which he calls on his Disciples and followers to be beyond the thinking of ordinary men. What, I believe he is alluding to, is that Gay men are invariably so talented, beyond what normal people can image, like the Savants we spoke of; but more so. The Gospel story tells us that the dead will rise again, and will live with the Angels in the Heavens."

He gave Merlin a wink.

"I believe that Jesus is referring to us! The Peculiar People!"

"But first we have to gain the knowledge of the ancients; we must be capable of truly grasping The Global Consciousness. The Torus is the power that we all pray into; it is the Torus that will guide young men to become more powerful and finally take our places amongst the leadership of the future." Simon was assured of his purpose.

"Yes, but how can these young men achieve this?" Merlin queried.

"I have a way of being centred in the Love of God, so that the energy that flows to God is positive; and in return He sends His Angels to fill that energy field with the Abundance of His Love. The Angels fill that energy field, because they are Spirits, attracted to Positive Energy. When we create a negative energy, with anger, or greed, or lust, we distance ourselves from the Angels. They cannot enter that energy field because they are repulsed by the negativity." Simon continued.

"We need to shine our energy out into the world, and this in turn attracts the Angels. With their presence in our Lives, we in return receive their energy and healing power."

"When we are alone and feeling abandoned, it is because we have created that sense of isolation. We have built that force field of negativity around us. That is why lonely people feel less loved." Simon paused in thought for a moment.

"But when we open our hearts to the prospect that the Angels are waiting for a sign from us, that we are willing to let them in, they sing with the company of Heaven, and return into our lives immediately. They are like our dogs; we rebuke them for bad behaviour, but the moment we return home, they are at the door, wagging their tails. They have unconditional Love, but we have to let them back. It is only in our own minds that we create a sense of the lack of Heaven's help. If we are truthful with ourselves, the flow of positive energy permeates outwardly, and the Angels are back in an instant. Don't think that they have left you for a moment; it is us that have chased them out!"

Merlin gazed in wonderment. His friend surely had a great contribution to make himself; Merlin only hoped he would live to see it. But for now, there was a cloud on the horizon, and the library officials were beginning to get edgy, as talk of a pandemic raised its ugly sceptre. Surely the Chinese would not have deliberately created a virus to spread around the world?

The future was now to be placed on hold and Merlin had already been advised that the teaching position he held may well be tentatively balanced for the coming year.

Either way, if it was as bad as the media were selling it, he knew that the very freedoms they were fighting for were meaningless.

But, Simon seemed buoyant and un-phased for now. The next chapter in the story of West Scowlsdown was about to get very interesting, indeed!

"I believe that the most ancient of philosophies, that of the ancient seers of India as presented in Spiritual Foundations provides the key not only for understanding consciousness, and our existence, but also for understanding that modern science can go no further until it realises the nature of reality as presented in the Vedas." – Toby Grotz 'Spiritual Foundations'

Notes to conclude: Down the Rabbit Hole

Stanford University wrote a paper, published in 2001, and substantively re-edited in 2022. This is an excerpt from that article:

The Study of Panpyschism: "Panpsychism offers an attractive middle way between physicalism on the one hand and dualism on the other. The worry with dualism—the view that mind and matter are fundamentally different kinds of thing—is that it leaves us with a radically dis-unified picture of nature, and the deep difficulty of understanding how mind and brain interact. And whilst physicalism offers a simple and unified vision of the world, this is arguably at the cost of being unable to give a satisfactory account of the emergence of human and animal consciousness. Panpsychism, strange as it may sound on first hearing, promises a satisfying account of the human mind within a unified conception of nature." (plato.stanford.edu/)

But what is Dualism in the Spiritual sense of the word? If the definition of Panpsychism is literally that everything has a mind, then the concept of Dualism is that human beings, along with other more evolved Mammalian species, have the ability to commune with one another 'Spiritually', but have an innate ability to contrast aspects of the cognitive mind, and Dualism is the state of having two main parts or aspects, (or the belief that we have two main parts or aspects).

The Chinese have the 'Yin' and the 'Yang', the Hebrews believed in the 'Yetzer Ha-Ra' and the 'Yetzer Ha-Tov', and the fundamental belief speaks to our nature, to do both good and bad! So human beings intuitively know when they are using their bad inclination, and this leads to a moral conscience, and invariably 'Karma'. Some individuals, however, have been very successful at suppressing that morality aspect, and thus the world is filled with evil people, who continue to do bad things!

Do you know that in the centre of your brain, you have what is called a pineal gland? This tiny gland, the size of a pinhead and shaped like a pine cone, secretes a chemical which is a neurological transmitter within our synaptic pathways called dimethyltryptamine (DMT). This chemical is released into your body when you suffer stress or trauma, and was originally considered to be the gland which was considered to be 'the spirit molecule'.

The Ancient Peruvian culture of infusing their drinks with DMT is a concoction called Ayahuasca. But my understanding is that these mind-altering substances need not be ingested to the body as the Shaman practise has alluded to; by recalling past hurts and trauma we have suffered as a human, we are capable of reproducing those emotions in our minds, when we concentrate on the pineal gland in our meditations, and thereby produce DMT naturally from within our own bodies. In other words, one can have a 'trip' by simply meditating.

If the idea of the ancient mystics, who had Spiritual experiences, and Buddhist monks who claim to have connected with 'The Source' have any correlation to DMT, then it is because the neural pathways of the brain are connected in ways that our conscious-thinking brain cannot achieve.

When those neural pathways are connected by the billions of synapses that are turbo charged into action, we experience a consciousness way beyond our own normal ability. This is exactly what Einstein and Tesla were able to achieve, and subsequently they were connecting to what I call the Global Consciousness.

What is The Global Consciousness? Well, simply put, it is our minds when we are connected as a species; animals have it in natural abundance. They communicate on a sub-conscious level. Plants have it as they are capable of communicating through chemically-induced scents.

Like the Acacia Tree that protects itself and other of its species, by transmitting a pheromone into the air, when large herds of antelope begin grazing in the vicinity of the tree and eating its leaves. This pheromone, when wind driven and sensed by another Acacia Tree, stimulates the release of a toxin that poisons the antelope, and may kill them when ingested in large quantities. This is the trees natural defence mechanism.

Humans are no different. We secrete pheromones and are capable of sensing the chemical pheromones of others in our species. But as we have evolved, those neural transmitters in our brains that recognise the naturally occurring pheromones, are dumbed-down by the external clutter of electro-smog.

Humans are unable to communicate to the extent we did once as a species, when we were hunter-gatherers and lived in caves, and had to protect ourselves from predatory animals. The Pineal Gland used to save our lives; now it has become obsolete because we have moved into cities, surrounded ourselves with security devices and created a false-sense of security.

The truth is, we have to consider that this is evolution. However, there are some, including myself, who believe that we can continue to invoke our naturally occurring DMT, so as to ensure we can connect with The Global Consciousness.

When there is positive energy between the two particles, unlike an electrical force, which needs a positive and a negative polarity for the flow of energy, there are two elements required to attract positive flows from the Holy Spirit. This power is released when the correct levels of CHeBE are evident. Coherent, Heart-based Emotion. We attract this energy to ourselves, and call this the Holy Spirit, because the ancient people recognised that there was a positive reaction when they had positive thoughts. When there are negative thoughts, however, those negative thoughts beget unwanted reactions. Keeping a positive attitude towards your emotions, and maintaining a coherent and concerted effort towards your heart, will always bring about positive powers of attraction. This is how the Holy Spirit is manifest. Jesus knew how to access that power through the Spirit.

Why then the elaborate fixation on a God, which created the heavens and the earth? (Mankind has always sought answers by looking to some external factors, when the power is within each of us to communicate through Gaia. 2017)

Simply, when mankind was in the infancy of understanding, it was vital for the cohesion of societies, to use metaphorical imagery when explaining these processes of attraction. So God becomes a metaphor, for the understanding of the God-force, which creates everything. God becomes Father, and we are created in his image, so God becomes a literal father.

As it would have been impossible to explain to a society for whom electron microscopes would have been unavailable, that the very existence of God is within themselves, and hence, we are created in the 'image of God'; then this concept would have required explanation on a humanistic level. The idea of a Holy Spirit stems from the need to explain that there is an energy field around people, like a Torus, which is able to repel and attract. The Holy Spirit exists, but on a sub-atomic level.

When mankind attempts to discover that God-force, or Holy Spirit, we are setting ourselves up to be God! Or are we? We are an integral part of that force. No other explanation goes anywhere near authenticating the truth. We are an energy field, like the 'Force', which connects each living creature.

The energy of the God particle or quarks comes from outside of our earthly realm. But where from? This is when Quantum Physics, and the study of particle-theory require a very broad-minded understanding of reality.

My affirmation of Spiritual Understanding is that 'I AM Spirit', and the energy of Spirit flows through me, as it does with every living organism. As I drink my energy Water (Mineral Water) in the morning before meditation, the individual particles of Hydrogen, Oxygen and Carbon 12 flow through my Spiritual Core, as The Torus, connecting Spiritually with every other living thing. This is The Bio-Luminescent Cortical Energy Field. When I AM Praying and thinking about those for whom I AM asking for healing, intercession, and justice, the energy of my H_2O Dipole, resonates with those living entities, and I AM able to change the very structure of their Spiritual being. I AM altering their Electro-Magnetic Frequency Field Energy.

The very electrons in my Spiritual Energy, My Torus, transmits messages through the universe to those to whom I direct this communication. This is extra-sensory perception, or Karmic Energy, and when my positive thought energy reaches the subject, or object of my Prayers, that energy field is altered accordingly. I AM communing Spiritually, or Telepathically.

The electrons surrounding every nuclei in my Spiritual Being, are transformed with the orbit of each electron enhanced to create an immense energy source, The Torus. I AM a giant Nuclear Reactor, pulsating with energy and transmitting this energy to all whom I direct it.

In our minds we have capacities, you know, to telepath messages through the vast unknown. Please close your eyes and concentrate, with every thought you think, upon the recitation you're about to sing. And please come in peace, we beseech you, only our love we will teach them, our Earth may never survive. So do come, we beg you. With our minds we have ability to form, and transmit thought energy far beyond the norm. You close your eyes, you concentrate, together, that's the way, to send the message we declare 'World Contact Day'.

But this is not the focus of what Karen Carpenter erroneously thought might be alien species from other galaxies. It was, and is specifically, the Spiritual power of what Tesla referred to as the Non-Visible' world. That which exists within a further dimension, that that which we are consciously aware.

Remote Viewing is a mind-body discipline. After exploring the in-depth research behind remote viewing, you may be interested in trying a session yourself. Learn how to hold a viewing session and interpret the results, as well as consider the consequences of accessing non-local information.

Remote Viewing is probably going to feel very different from anything you've ever done before. That's because it's all about learning to unblock your feelings, hunches and intuitive glimpses. People like musicians and artists, those who are trained to go with the flow, are more familiar with the creative process and tend to feel more comfortable with it. RV involves letting go of your preconceived ideas about what you are perceiving and instead, just going with the flow of things.

BE A PSYCHIC DETECTIVE

"Remote viewing involves a paradox: the more confident you feel during a session, the less likely you are to be accurate. What this means is that during an RV session, you're acting like a psychic detective, looking for clues within your own awareness for something you can't physically see or touch. Your conscious mind will probably tell you that it won't work. But it's wrong: It does work.

During an RV session, our conscious minds, which usually act like they know what's going on at every moment, have to surrender to the unknown. Our conscious minds like hard, concrete information: RV signals tend to be soft. Our conscious minds like certainty: RV sessions are the embodiment of uncertainty. Our conscious minds like to be right, as much as possible: while doing RV, we have no idea if we are right or not. And often after getting to see our feedback picture, we'll see a lot that we missed. And things we made up that aren't there.

RV is really a big ego buster. It's humbling for your conscious mind to accept that it's not as good as your subtle mind at this task, but it will get used to it. You just have to accept the idea that there are no bad RV sessions, if you learn something about yourself every time you do one.

And your conscious mind also has to learn to get together with your unconscious mind: the one who has access to non-local information. Believe me, it's a really profound learning experience to find out that your conscious mind, who feels like it's in control of your waking life, can only go so far before it has to hand off its job to another part of your awareness, your non-local self.

This is a big deal for many of us but it's good for you: you learn more when you're wrong about something than when you're right, and RV is no different.

Just so you know, there are many different styles of remote viewing, the main branches being Controlled Remote Viewing (CRV) and Extended Remote Viewing (ERV). The difference between these two styles is that CRV originates from psychic Ingo Swann and is a written protocol with defined stages. ERV on the other hand is an earlier system that is more like stream of thought and doesn't necessarily require pen and paper: you can use a digital or tape recorder to record your impressions. I'm not aware of any evidence that suggests that one system is more accurate than another. However, I learned the CRV system so my ideas stem from that line of thinking.

Now it's quite possible that you are a natural psychic and already have your own system for viewing. Just stick with what works for you. There's no right or wrong here. But if you've never done anything like this before, you can follow the steps below.

The first thing that you want to do is find a quiet place where you won't be distracted. RV is not so much a mental process as a sensing protocol. You use your awareness to become aware of your entire body and what its feeling. It's not just about mental concentration.

But the first step is to quiet your mind any way that suits you. It's called a cool down period. During an RV session, you want as little mental noise as possible.

Studies show that we have over 20 million bits of information from our physical senses each second. (And that's not counting non-local RV-type information). But we are consciously aware of only 16 bits. That's a loss of more than 99.999 percent of the information that we could have access too. The information is still there, but it's buried in our unconscious mind. Your job is to make sense of it and write it down before your conscious mind interferes in some way.

The goal of RV or any type of psychic activity is to become more sensitive to the really subtle information: to access it without distorting it. You're accessing a hidden channel of non-local information that is normally not available to you consciously.

One way to practice this during the day is to see how much sensory information you can describe in your immediate environment, as accurately as possible. You may think you know what's in your surroundings, but it if really take a look, you'll see it's more varied than you imagined. There are more shades of colours, more patterns, more contrasts than your conscious mental image contains.

A saccade is a quick, simultaneous movement of both eyes between two or more phases of fixation in the same direction. In contrast, in smooth pursuit movements, the eyes move smoothly instead of in jumps.

So, when you're practicing viewing, you're attempting to describe very subtle information that is much weaker than your conscious perceptions. If you're describing a photo target, and the image in your mind is 3D and very colourful, you're probably making it up! True RV impressions are very subtle, fleeting, and transient. Many people don't ever "see" anything while they're viewing. They may just get sensory impressions without knowing how they got them. The main thing is to write it down before the information disappears into your mind's deletion trash bin." Gaia

Printed in Poland
by Amazon Fulfillment
Poland Sp. z o.o., Wrocław

20470447R00134